The Book of the Watchers

Volume I

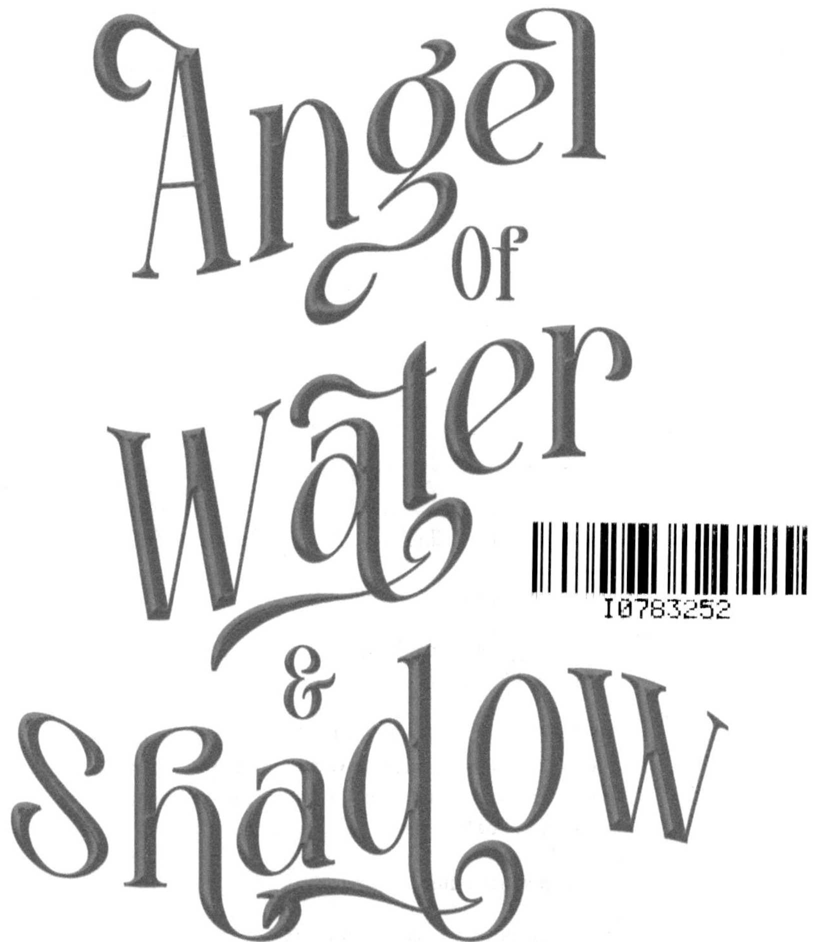

TORY GUYON

Angel of Water & Shadow

Copyright © 2023 by Tory Guyon

Cover design by Seventhstar Art
Title page by Miblart

First paperback edition May 2023

Paperback ISBN 979-8-9872391-0-0
eBook ISBN 979-8-9872391-1-7
Hardback ISBN 979-8-9872391-2-4

Published by Salt + Stars Press, a small, coastal imprint by Tory Guyon
www.saltandstarspress.com

For Kaia: my sun, moon, and stars.

THE BOOK OF THE WATCHERS

VOLUME I

ANGEL OF WATER & SHADOW

CHAPTER 1

Part of me wanted to stay submerged beneath the ocean's rippling surface forever. Under the melodic roll of the waves, it was easy to forget the worst parts of life. Why I had run here.

The water pressed into my eardrums, a weighted, whirring silence that thrummed with the beat of my heart. It flooded my mouth the second I parted my lips, rushing out with the air bubbles as I screamed. Something I'd wanted to do since noon that day—when my toes had caught on the unaltered hem of my gown as I walked across the stage at graduation.

With my surfboard pressed beneath me, it was impossible to feel the pangs of humiliation through the sparks of adrenaline. I was in my element, and I trusted myself, trusted that my knees would press into the buoyancy just enough to catapult me into a seamless carve.

Which they eventually did.

I burst through the water's glossy surface, sucking down an inhale, shaking bits of algae from my hair like it could also get rid of the image of the hundreds of people staring at me when I'd fallen.

Well, here people still gawked—but that's because I dove into monster waves and surfed the biggest sets. Not because I full-on face-planted during my high school's biggest ceremony.

I unpinned the saggy bun at the nape of my neck, the drenched, golden-brown tresses falling past my shoulders. Releasing a drawn-out exhale, I headed for the horizon, revived by every stroke of cold water as if I were being reborn.

Salt caked my cheeks, stinging the raw skin under my eyes. Wiping them was pointless. The tears burned but not as badly as my arms—those had the pleasure of paddling me two hundred yards *and* fighting off the slimy strings of kelp. When I reached the lineup, the moisture enveloping me like a thick blanket, a ghost of a smile touched my lips.

I was home.

And on days like today, when the parents, teachers, and fellow graduates' gasps merged with the voices woven together by my mind—the invisible ones, the ones that no one else but me heard—I gasped for breath and fought against the current because *I needed this*. I needed to fly without wings, needed the silence to speak louder than my thoughts, needed my instincts to beat faster than my heart.

So…I may have paddled out farther than necessary.

Popped up on my board one too many times.

Surfed longer than I meant to, preferring the sounds of the sea far more than the voices waiting to strike once my pruny feet met dry land.

When I finally staggered up the staircase carved into the bluff, my muscles melting into that addictive post-surf soreness, everything hit me all at once. My shitty morning, the weakness in my legs, the voices I'd been avoiding. As if their unbodied presence leaned against the iron railing with the other onlookers taking in the Pacific Ocean's force, and those that rode it—but they didn't.

Unlike human speech, theirs didn't have an obvious source. Or at least one I could locate.

At first all I heard was the wind whipping my ears, the faint drags against sand from my waterlogged leash. That's the thing about telepathic voices—mine, at least. They're nowhere and then, they're everywhere.

It started with one, weaving indistinct whispers into the crush of the grit beneath my bare feet, so sharp I had to walk on my toes. Then another, slipping wordless screams into the strained breaths of eager surfers rushing past me, so loud I had to shut my eyes. And the last, dropping a truly impressive array of inflections into the sighs of the tide, so intense I would've covered my ears if my surfboard wasn't already in my hands.

Ugh. Barging into someone's life wasn't the politest thing to do, but if they were going to commit, how about doing it on bus rides, during English homework, or awkward first dates, and *not* during my favorite activity!? I may have gotten out of the water, but I hadn't even had a chance to change out of my wetsuit! This was still considered my time—they knew that.

But I also knew my particular telepathic voices had a rebellious streak. Blowing out my mind and my senses and making me trip in front of everyone during the single most important moment of my high school career, had been proof enough of that.

So perhaps it was on brand for them to interject so soon, I figured, as I flipped my damp hair, held my surfboard high and my chin even higher. As I forged up the steep eroded steps, I tried my best to ignore the sudden tightness of my neoprene, the sudden chafing from the salt I hadn't yet rinsed from my skin.

My nails were inaccessible, with my arms still being wrapped around my surfboard, so I bit my lip as I trudged up the incline.

At the top of the stairs, I paused, teetering somewhat—pressing the heel of my palm into my forehead, trying to subdue the pounding in my head and the escalating pitch of the Voices—paces away from the footpath that led to the plushy lawn of the lighthouse. The natural spot to post up after a surf sesh, and a much better place to have an episode, where I wasn't on display to every jogger, surfer, and sightseer. If I could just make it a few more yards…

A swift prickle of my senses had them standing on edge like the hairs on the back of my neck. My brain was spinning like someone had put it in a blender. I couldn't make it any farther. So, I shimmied off to the side, and I anchored myself there, digging my toes into the dirt, all too aware of the harsh indent of my toe rings, while the Voices morphed into the sounds of the world around me.

The first voice tippy tapped across my skull in tune with the hermit crabs that scuttled over the reef. With what could've been a clack of their claws or a click of her tongue, she made her opinion known—as she always did. "What a silly way to spend one's time. Do you actually enjoy partaking in these mortal pleasures, Watcher?"

Um, yes. Yes, I did. Nothing beat riding a wave. But I wasn't going to answer that, not when everyone could see me and think I was talking to the air.

I gripped the ground tighter. Dried mudstone crumbled near my clenched feet.

It set off a slide, so small it should have gone unnoticed, but a second voice cleared her throat, rumbling with the moving debris. "Watcher, there are matters that need your attention. This is not one of them."

Quite the contrary. Surfing was of the utmost importance. Ignoring them, I glanced back at the lineup just to prove my point.

The break barreled towards the beach, and a third voice caught its momentum, her words crashing into my head harder than the waves pounding the shore. "She's spent the last few hours balancing on a piece of foam; what else do you expect of her?"

Please, nothing more than chillin' on the grass at the Santa Cruz lighthouse, listening to music, and waxing my board in peace.

I took a shaky step forward. A challenge. For the briefest of moments, I swore normal life returned and I broke their spell—at least to give myself enough time to bolt down the path, slip on my headphones, and situate myself beneath the tower's shade, I hoped.

Nope. The harder I fought against them, the more difficult they became, and if anything, they came back tenfold.

One, two, three voices became four. Four became five, and then came more. This many, this loud, they couldn't be deciphered; they couldn't even be considered voices. They were like tiny fireworks, exploding in my head. Like a meteor swarm, wiping out my thoughts.

My surfboard smacked the dirt. I tumbled to the ground after it. I was losing it—my grip on reality. I wanted to scream. I think I did. There just wasn't enough room in my head for this.

The *noises*. So many overlapping noises. Yet I could pinpoint every sound.

The *space*. So much empty space. Yet it still felt crowded around me.

The *colors*. So many vibrant colors. Yet they all melded into one.

Up, down, left, right, land, sea…it was all the same.

My blood turned to lead, heavy enough to drag me down. I lacked the strength to fight it, so I let it. Dipping my neck, I wrapped my arms around my legs and cocooned my head between my knees—the closest thing to a surrender as the Voices captured my mind, my will, my body, and finally my consciousness, as the spinning world curtained to black.

"HEY, YOU OKAY?"

A raspy familiarity cut through the dark like a searchlight through the fog. "River? River Harlowwww? You in there?"

The gentle wave of his hands had my eyelids fluttering. Bruised concrete finishes and frosted basalt rocks shifted in and out of focus. I imagined I resembled a castaway washed up from sea, limp and choking on the air like it was a mouthful of salt water.

The screams hadn't left, but at least in this world they came from the overhead gulls, not a group of omniscient voices.

"I—yeah, um…" Words never came easy after these episodes, but especially when the Grateful Dead Bears were walking off my best friend's t-shirt. With a few lengthy blinks they stopped mid-stride against the tie-dye.

"I thought I'd find you here."

I squinted towards his melodic voice, at his face haloed by the midday rays. "When'd you…" My clammy fingers slipped to catch hold of his.

"Just in time, apparently."

My stomach turned as the horizon shifted upright. "Thanks," I said into the fish-eye lens dangling in front of his chest, not ready to meet his panicked eyes.

He swung his woven camera strap behind his shoulder. "That was a rough one. Rougher than earlier. You good?"

I gulped, attempting to reassure him with frantic head nodding, huffing away the strands of layered hair that fell around my jawline, even though the movement made my head pound.

The Voices had fizzled to nothing but seafoam, but my body tingled from the surge in activity. At least at graduation, to the untrained eye, it looked like I'd just been clumsy as shit. But right now, at the top of this bluff, I was sprawled out like a starfish barely able to speak a coherent sentence—it was super obvious to anyone around that I'd suffered more than a trip and fall. Just thinking about it made my upper lip break into a sweat.

"I'm all good, just need a sec." I fixed my attention on a super-interesting barnacle at the end of the point—not really, but anything was better than Javi's crinkled brown eyes. Best friend or not, there was never anything fun about having someone pull you off the ground because voices-that-no-one-else-heard broke your mind harder than the explosives at a demolition site.

Not that he knew about that last part.

I'd share with him my wildest hopes and dreams, my hidden surf breaks, the last slice, anything. Anything…except the Voices. Because the risk of losing him hurt even more than suppressing my juiciest secret: that three other beings occupied my headspace.

Nobody knew about the Voices.

A light pressure to the web between my thumb and palm cut off my spiraling thoughts. I answered the soft pinch with one of my own—a sort of morse code Javi and I had developed to make sure I was still there. It'd become so second nature I probably had his fingerprints imprinted on my skin.

For whatever reason, Javier Ramirez loved my aura of weirdness. I couldn't understand the draw. When I was eight, dealing with the aftermath of my mom's death, most of my friends were too freaked out by my trauma and never talked to me again.

But Javi…It'd been almost ten years of that hand squeezing mine, of picking me up off the floor, of wiping tears from my cheeks…He was a keeper.

"Don't worry, we've got all day for you to recover." He looped his arm through mine, his skin a deep-rooted tan unlike my warm beige complexion that would never achieve that level of glow no matter how often I lay in the sun. Taking my thin smile as permission, he gently guided me away from the cliffs, while so *lovingly* telling me, "Well, all day until Grad Night. Which is in six hours. So you've got six hours."

"Appreciate the sympathy, bud." More like the lack of it. He deserved the playful pinch I gave his arm.

"Ow! There's the River I know. I was worried I'd lost you again for a sec."

"Still here." I shot him a teasing side-eye as he darted across the pathway, towing me behind him. "After my earlier snafu though…" I said as I caught up. "I don't think I'm going to go." Heat seared my cheeks, and it wasn't due to a sunburn. To be honest, I'd be perfectly fine never seeing my classmates again.

"Who cares what those people think? We've been prepping our outfits for-e-ver. I'm even willing to wear that crown of leaves you made me." Batting his eyes for good measure, he brushed his tight waves of jet-black hair behind his ears, fingers smoothing the slightly grown-out locks until they traced his neck. Our laughter scattered the roosting pelicans.

He had a point—the countless trips to the thrift store and dozens of hot glue burns we'd endured would be for nothing if I bailed. As of yesterday, we'd finally gotten our costumes in order, ready to embrace the theme: Shakespeare's Summer Solstice.

When we finally reached the lighthouse, what felt like one million years later, I folded against its brick wall, a thread of energy sweeping across my shoulders and tickling my spine. My toes wiggled reflexively over the grass, pliant and dewy from the ocean's spray. Multicolored specks swarmed in the distance like sand flies—tourists enveloping our seaside town to escape the inland heat. The tangled structures of the Santa Cruz Beach Boardwalk were visible through the lingering strips of coastal haze, high-spirited shrieks signaling the latest batch condemned to the Big Dipper's drop, one of my favorite rides—roller coasters provided me a sacred moment, when my screams superseded the others inside me.

I blew out a sigh, my body becoming as boneless as a sea sponge. The rhythmic pulse of humanity was intoxicating.

It probably had something to do with—okay, a lot to do with—my waning adrenaline, but from this vantage point in particular, with the corroded frame of the lighthouse humming with its peculiar life force at my back, and the seemingly endless sky and coastline that surrounded me…it soothed me like a maritime lullaby.

My eyes grew heavy, and I would have let them slip, if not for—

"We should probably grab your surfboard before someone else does," Javi said, breaking my Zen.

Crap. I'd left it on the bluff. I glanced over in that direction, a tiny bolt of panic zinging through me. "Oh please, no one's going to run off with my worn out shortboard in the middle of the day." The tension left my shoulders as the crowd parted, and my gaze settled on its familiar off-white gleam. "See? You're just anxious to get to Grad Night because Summer Solstice seems to be every girl's excuse to wear a crop top."

He shrugged, fighting a smile. "A gorgeous fairy queen waiting for me with flowers in her hair sounds like a pretty good reason to split, with your surfboard or not."

I rolled my eyes playfully. "I hate to ruin your Shakespearian fantasy, but I'm going to be late for therapy."

We strode to the overlook, my prized possession laying exactly where I had dropped it.

As I planted my surfboard atop my head, I felt his lens on me immediately and heard the faint click of the shutter. The silhouette of my bracketed arms arched out of my back, the low sun unfolding their shadows like wispy forelimbs. I extended my left hand just far enough from my board to flash a playful finger at my friend. Along with a *seriously?* look.

Javi claimed he'd always been "super into" photography, but really it was ever since we spotted the scratched piece of equipment at an estate sale two summers ago. He'd been playing around with FPS and aspect ratio and exposure composition since then—terms he liked to drop but were very much over my head. How quickly he'd gone from random snapshots and blurry nature photos to winning first place in exhibits and staying in the dark room till I dragged him out.

"I know sometimes your memory gets a little shaky after

an episode, Riv," he said with one of his *yes, now act natural, it's golden hour* looks back, "but did you forget that corn dogs plus costumes plus carnival rides make us, like, really, really happy?"

"Wow, does your sensitivity come and go that easily?" My mouth dropped open in a mock act of shock.

He motioned me over. "I love this one; your eyes look like little *azul* jewels."

I peered at the digital version of myself, eyes indeed sparkling, cheeks peppered with sun freckles, a carefreeness in my jaw, loose strands of golden-tipped brown hair blown across my face…Javi *did* have an eye. I wasn't a super-smiley, overly happy person by any means, but he managed to capture those glimpses of me, no matter how far they were from what I was feeling inside.

"Anyway, I'm a teensy bit sympathetic after finding my best friend starfished on West Cliff." He rotated the screen's mode to off. "But this is important; Titania needs me. Why do you have a therapy session *today*?" Pumping his fist in the air like a gawky version of *Braveheart*, he bellowed, "This is supposed to be the greatest night of our lives, the gateway to freedom, the rite of passage to our adulthood!"

I snorted, knowing full well the active role we'd *both* played in avoiding these rituals the last four years. Although, he had convinced me to go to a house party after the home-coming game that one time, and he did drag me to prom… but we spent most of the night avoiding the belligerently drunk lacrosse team, eating stale popcorn on the bleachers. Until the last song, when he extended that hand—the one always there for me. A twirl of my layered tulle skirts and I came to rest under his chin, tucked and swaying against his matching baby blue dress shirt. That part, at least, felt memorable.

Okay, so maybe I avoided these hormone-fueled gatherings more than he did.

We stopped at a salt-crusted bike rack, packed with colorful beach cruisers tossed against the frame by impatient surfers. After loading up my board, I turned my back to Javi and gathered up my hair, uncovering my wetsuit's zipper. He moved close, his fingers fumbling with the metal for a moment before it slid down. He pulled his hand away before he could accidentally brush the pair of linear scars on my shoulder blades.

My skin tingled against the cool ocean air.

"You're right. What good would a midsummer night be without its ass?" I pulled the damp sleeves off my arms and slid the rest to my waist, revealing the floral one-piece I wore underneath. "Look, therapy's the *last* place I want to be—other than Grad Night," I corrected myself, lips curving into a mischievous grin. "But I forgot to cancel, and if I no-show, I'll get charged and my dad will kill me."

I spun around to find him wielding his greatest weapons: that dramatic bottom lip and those big puppy dog eyes. He overemphasized his pout until he won and got a laugh out of me.

"Fine," I relented. "I'll go. Corn dogs on me?"

"More like corn dogs on our school, but I do appreciate the offer." He grinned before his focus moved from my stuck-out tongue to the worn-out strap that slid off my shoulder. "I'm assuming you might need to make a pit stop first?"

I pretended not to notice the flush in his tawny cheeks, but my body betrayed me, heat creeping over my face and neck. I quickly tried to fill the silence, forcing my voice light. "Yeah, the whole no shoes, no shirt, no service thing actually applies in a therapist's office."

"You'd think they'd make an exception. This *is* Santa Cruz. Even the library lets you in barefoot." He caught himself. "Not that I know from experience."

"Surrrre you don't." I swung my leg around my cruiser, about to push off with the other.

"Hey, River," he cooed. Full of mischief, those eyes, and I already knew the words that dared to be spoken, dancing in their carob twinkle. "Don't think I forgot it's your birthday."

I groaned. "Tomorrow."

"What better way to celebrate your eighteenth lap around the sun when we're already out celebrating freedom?" That arm rose again in a full-blown flex.

I could think of a million other ways to spend my birthday that didn't involve rubbing elbows with every single teacher and student who got a front row seat to my graduation tumble.

"Guess we'll just have to put a candle on top of the funnel cake. But that's as far as I'm going, Jav." I squinched my brows together, trying to be stern while he held in a smile, no doubt already plotting.

"Alright, alright. Meet you at the main entrance at six?"

The corners of his mouth stretched up and out, unable to resist a grin.

"As if I have any say in the matter," I teased as I pushed forward, swerving between the dried-out eucalyptus bark and crumbling potholes. Steadying myself on the wheels, I picked up speed as I biked across West Cliff Drive.

The breeze's subtle howls wove through my hair like natural whispers, stirring the first voice from wherever she burrowed. "I've never understood these earthborn rituals." I could've sworn I heard a yawn, as if she was…bored?

"That's because they're utterly pointless." The third voice nipped with the wind stinging my ears.

"Oh, loosen up, it's just a bit of fun," I murmured, trusting no one could overhear me as I wove through the groups of joggers, surfers, and bikers. "You might find it entertaining. I mean, who doesn't love a good Shakespeare festivity?"

Who was I kidding? Me, for starters. My fingers curled into the rubber handlebars.

"They've done these things since the beginning of time," the second voice said, tsking with the clink of the pedals. Not an approval, but at least she didn't pick apart my life choices in the aimless way I picked at my cuticles—like the other two did. "Nothing new here."

"Hapless mortals," the first sliced in as I faltered over a natural speedbump.

I clenched my teeth. "Despite what you all think, this *hapless mortal* might actually enjoy getting out and experiencing the world." It came out a touch too loud, earning very confused glances from a walking group I passed. Their raised brows did one thing for me at least—they caused me to take a long, purposeful breath. Getting riled up on a cruiser on a busy cliff path was not in my best interest.

"Keep telling yourself that." Laughter rang through the disturbed bits of gravel, the first voice's cackle catching on my tires. "We're a part of you, Watcher. You think we can't tell how you really feel?"

That was probably the most annoying part.

"But maybe I'm biased—I've never been a fan of William's." She dropped his first name like it was no big deal.

"Same." The third groaned with the rough brake of the car at the stop sign on my left. "That's beside the point though—the end is nigh."

I huffed out a sigh. Before, it might have made my chest grow tight, but after years of it, this "end of the world" talk was getting really old.

"Ah, so you want her to put her big girl pants on?" the first voice chimed with the bell of a passing bicycle.

"Don't we all," the third muttered, voice growing with power as it latched on to the siren of a speeding fire truck. "If she ignores her past any longer there will be no more gatherings. No more ceremonies. No more Earth."

"Really—"

"Okay." I spoke soft but swiftly, cutting the second voice off. "I get it. Bad River for going to school, for hanging out with friends, for doing everything a teenager is *supposed* to do. Can you stop being a buzzkill? You don't get to tell me what to do." And why should they be? They were nothing but air! Nothing but a delusion.

Then the red flash of the fire truck flashed across my

vision, and its rumble swept through my veins. The siren devoured all other sounds, wailing:

NO MORE EARTH.
NO MORE EARTH.
NO MORE EARTH.

The words punctured my mind like tiny corkscrews, pinning reality beneath. I pedaled backwards to brake and leaned to the side, careful not to plow through the fence lining the cliffs.

I stumbled for the kickstand, slunk into the seat, and blindly reached into my cruiser's front basket. As my consciousness began failing, my fingers locked around an item, its padded ends bent in my grasp. I thrust the headphones onto my head and hit play on the current track.

Outside of surfing, the noise-cancelling headphones were the greatest trick in my stash. They blocked out the world's rising chaos until nothing existed but me, and only me, along with the music, and I actually stood a chance at making it through the day. I kicked my heels into the pedals and recalibrated my senses while the Voices faded out and my playlist faded in.

CHAPTER 2

I DROPPED INTO THE PATCHED LEATHER CHAIR BEside the prison-style barred windows, the olive peasant dress I'd changed into during a quick pitstop at home catching on my beige high tops as I crossed my feet. As I bent down to adjust the fabric, a chill plucked a shiver from me. Even with the leafy greenery and lavender scent sticks and crocheted pillow behind me, the room still felt as cold and unhospitable as a jail cell.

My fingers tapped the armrests as the rhythmic splash of water striking tin rooftops filled my ears, despite the cloudless sky. I'd swapped out my indie rock playlist for a nature soundtrack after the Voices succumbed to the catchy soprano. My world and their words muted by the husky vocals, the riffing harmonica, and some of my own scream singing. Which I definitely belted out in public more than a few times on my way here.

Whatevs. I'd been heard shouting much worse.

My throat seemed to prickle at the thought. I brought my fingers to the tender nodes below my jaw, applying a light, circular, pressure. Swollen. From stress, or too much fighting with things that weren't even really there.

I clipped out a sigh. I didn't hate the Voices. But the Voices weren't *real*. It was just my mind using the world against me, bending the sounds and shapes and tastes and smells so I was forced to hear nothing but the sarcastic outbursts of the first, the silky views of the second, the harsh truths of the third… and their appeals to revisit a decade-old memory—something I was expected to do by everyone, it seemed. But I wouldn't touch with a hundred-foot pole.

At the brusque *click-clack* of heels, I pulled the headphones from my ears, resting them around my neck.

A woman observed me through thin, round tortoise-shell frames as she took a seat in the chair opposite me. Her big brown eyes glittered with curiosity like a California sea lion, behind bangs of raven ringlets. As she rolled her shoulders a shadow vaulted behind her, its tip grazing the ceiling before folding in on itself.

Ah, another new one.

Despite my surprise, I wouldn't let myself so much as shift a toe and accidentally reveal my frustration. I also wouldn't let myself linger on how much younger and prettier she was than anyone else I'd met with—she couldn't have been more than ten years older than me—or how she had one of those outwardly kind faces that looked warm, familiar, even though I'd never met her before.

I returned the look, waiting for her to make the first move. I didn't just give it up for free. That I'd learned the hard way, thanks to her *lovely* colleagues, who'd made me feel like my truths were part of a well-crafted sob story. The ones I felt like telling them, anyway.

If it were up to me, we'd spend the whole hour in an epic stare down.

Maybe then I'd be taken seriously.

My opponent broke first, in unknown defeat. "It's nice to meet you, River. I'm Doctor Fairmore."

I couldn't mask my satisfied smirk.

She fiddled with the silver medallion she wore around her neck, embossed with an angel blowing a trumpet. "I'm going to be taking over for Doctor Churchill, as you two discussed on Tuesday."

Right…I must've glazed over that part. As I now did with Fairmore's background, her accolades, and whatever personal details she'd shared—something about her god-daughter?—zoning out until I heard, "But enough about me. Do you have any questions, or is there a specific topic you'd like to start with?"

Her patience seemed authentic enough. Still, I clipped out, "No."

A pen clicked. "Let's talk about what's on your mind right now. What are you thinking about, River?"

My fingers twirled in my lap as the tip of the pen scratched against a fresh sheet of paper. I blew out an uneven breath as my ankle started shaking, and the nervous energy overtook me.

I turned towards the window and met my own bitter stare, the curl of my lip and the deep line between my brows giving away what I wouldn't say.

From somewhere in the room, I heard the faint hint of a murmur, even though the walls were thick and practically soundproof. It caught on the passing summer breeze and rattled my nerves like the gentle wind did the glass in the windowpane.

"I'm thinking about the surf." Not a complete lie—five seconds ago my tidal watch had started flashing over the epic wave height along the Santa Cruz coastline. Plus, I needed to say *something* before the murmur turned into a voice and the voice turned into the entire room shouting at me.

My new doctor clasped her hands over her camel-colored pencil skirt. "Why are you thinking about that?"

"'Cause I like surfing." *Duh*. "And I'd way rather be doing that…" I added under my breath.

She pursed her lips, the muscles in her face tightening as she narrowed her eyes.

I met her glare dead on, waiting for her wrath—there had to be a punishment for being so cavalier about everything. A monster had to be behind the mask of that round, rose-tinged ebony face. One capable of complete cognitive destruction.

After an insufferable moment of scrutiny, her expression shed some of its firmness. "How long have you been surfing?"

Not the fiery reign of judgement I expected. But maybe that was her plan, to look at me and stoke more hope than stars in a twilit sky. Then snuff it out and treat me like the problem, not the person I was.

My nails flew between my teeth. "Are you really asking me about this right now?"

Her attention flickered briefly. "Yes."

"Why?" I tore at a cuticle.

Her gaze was dark as midnight yet sparkling with possibility. "Because I want to get to know you."

Shock jolted me still. After years of enduring the churn and burn with others who deemed themselves worthy of the teenage psychological persuasion, Dr. Fairmore totally caught me off guard. She was so…nice. Genuinely. None of it made sense, especially the thawing hatred in my gut.

"Why do you want to get to know me?" An arch-shaped brow rose in question as I asked, "Don't you just want to punish me, diagnose me, and move on?"

"It's not my job to discipline you. It's my job to understand you and help you figure out the best way to manage your sensory episodes, so you can live your life." Her words were sharp, no bullshit, lined with promise, no matter how hard my mind raced to distort them.

"I want to start with you feeling comfortable." She sounded so sure of herself. Maybe she was sure of me, too. "I know it will take time. You've been through a lot—for a while now."

A while didn't even begin to cover it.

"Since I was eight." Word vomit. It came out so fast I couldn't stop it.

Dr. Fairmore leaned in. "Who taught you how to surf?"

"My dad."

One side of her mouth kicked up in a smile. "What is it about surfing you like so much?"

I was already softening, but now I melted. No therapist had ever asked me that before—well, no one had ever asked me that with such *interest*. As if she...I swallowed a lump forming in my throat. As if she actually cared.

I closed my eyes and let the drab doctor's office fall away, trading the springy cushions and hardwood floor for the infinite depth of the ocean and the rhythmic movement of the tide.

Even just imagining it, the sounds of everyday life seemed to dull, like a radio with the volume turned all the way down. I should probably be scared of the force that took my mother that clear June morning, but it only made me feel closer to her.

"When you're out there, it's you and the water." I inhaled deeply, imagining the crisp, salted air filling my lungs. "You don't hear anything but the pounding of waves. You don't think about anything except paddling as hard as you can. And when you're standing on your board, with the momentum behind you and the wind in your hair...the rest of the world seems to fall away. It's the closest to flying you'll ever be."

"It must be nice to feel that kind of invincibility."

"That's just it—you're anything but invincible." My words tumbled out faster as I met her incisive stare. "Mother Nature can screw you over at any time. But regardless, you put your faith in the water, let her wash away your vulnerabilities, and go."

Dr. Fairmore slightly tilted her head. "How does that make you feel?"

"Alone." Powerful. Blissful. Quiet.

"Why do you like feeling alone, River?" She stared back at me evenly.

The question rippled off the silence, gaining momentum with every pounding heartbeat. And soon it echoed in the room, all around me. It hummed in the floor lamp's flickering bulb, so blinding it dotted my vision even when I looked away. It rang in the water dispenser's leaky tap, so loud that every *drip drip* made me cringe. It screeched in the chair as I burrowed further into it, a sound so similar to nails on a chalkboard—oh, those were mine clawing at the leather.

When my lips remained sealed, Dr. Fairmore bent forward and closed the space between us. "Do you feel safer alone? Because then no one can leave you?"

Sweat beaded my hairline, my palms, the back of my neck as I fought to get ahold of my senses. Then the first voice tunneled into my eardrums with the *tick tock* of the wall clock, surer of the situation than I'd ever been: "She knows, Watcher."

Of course she knew I saw my mom die. It was all in my file. *Thank you, Captain Obvious.*

A strained sigh made it past my clenched jaw as the second voice carved her rebuttal into the grind of my teeth—an attempt to try and pad the brutal truth, but really it just stressed me the F out. "You say that like it's a bad thing? Watcher, there is something buried under all that pain—face it and release your power."

Right now, the only thing that needed release was the endless string of swear words I had for them. I bit my tongue, knowing how well that would go over with my therapist, watching her new patient curse the air.

Dr. Fairmore raised a speckled mug to her lips. The third voice billowed in the steam she blew off the liquid, seething with the heat. "How many times do we have to ask her to revisit the day Mira died?" My thoughts exactly. "Nothing ever changes, she sees what she wants—and she *wants* to live a lie."

I blinked, slow and controlled, zeroing in on the pressure, fighting the urge not to roll my eyes. No shit I didn't want to revisit the day that she left—the day the Voices entered. "Please stop," I whispered, only adding in the pleasantry for my therapist's sake.

Dr. Fairmore reclined, obviously thinking this response was meant for her. I wanted to explain, but my mouth went dry. I made the best first impressions.

"Are you trying to cause a divide?" the second voice countered evenly with the *clink* of the doctor's oval pink nails against the ceramic—a fidget so innocuous she didn't even realize she was doing it, so she couldn't know that it bored into my skull.

"Can't you see?" the third voice snarled, pulling inflections from the screaming patient next door. "There already is a divide! *Us* against her. By all means, try it with the mental replay. I'm just done believing anything will come from it. She never actually lets herself *feel*."

Oh, I felt it. All the way to my bones. I wore the guilt like a second skin.

A memory appeared in the forefront of my mind—for a fleeting moment, I thought it was an image of myself. I studied the woman it showed me a little closer: her butterfly sleeves flaring with the brisk curl of her arms as she collected shells on the beach. Beauty marks dotted an oval-shaped face, her skin glowing as if it caught the light of a permanent sunset. There was a soft bounce to her hair, and wispy bangs framed a stare bluer and more untold than the deepest part of the ocean.

I grazed my jaw, tracing a resemblance that didn't exist beyond photos and dreams. The woman wasn't me, but a person that would always be a part of me, locked in a moment I'd never escape from.

It's funny how much life can change in the calm stillness between heartbeats—one flutter we were chasing dragonflies and splashing in the shallows, the next it was storming and we were caught in a rip current.

I could only imagine what Dr. Fairmore might be thinking as she watched me struggle to say the words, so lost in my head, her brows creased with sympathy. "This seems to be a painful topic for you. We can change direction, for now, if you want—"

"I didn't mean for it to happen," I choked out, unsure who I was talking to. The Voices. My therapist. "I didn't want her to go." *I didn't want her to swim out after me.* Nearly ten years to the very day later, my head still shook, like I couldn't believe it.

She'd swum around the wharf. She'd trained in an Olympian pool. She'd surfed next to all the local legends. It didn't make sense that she'd drowned, it didn't—

The next words from my therapist came out so hushed I almost took it as ambient noise. "Who did you not want to go, River?"

I'd never say it. I struggled to even *think* it.

But after that memory…her face was all around me. "My mom."

Mom. The word sounded foreign, off-limits, like I didn't hold the privilege of speaking it.

I recoiled further into my chair, half expecting the memory to be swept away, just as she had. But it did something much more sinister—it changed.

My mom's jubilant gaze dimmed. Her lips curled, her teeth bared, not into a smile, but into a cry of pain. The blood left her face, leaving her translucent, like she'd just seen a ghost. Or maybe that was what she was becoming.

A tidal wave of grief crashed upon me at the thought, breaking me into a million pieces. My butt molded the seat, but it felt like I was falling through it.

My ears rang, bitten by the shrill winds of a fake descent. I lightly tugged on a lobe, using the opportunity to look anywhere but in front of me, and feverishly blink away the icy cold of an invisible wind. Nothing was working. Fairmore was waiting. I was stuck. I gripped my stomach as it dropped, as if stuck in a free fall, despite being on solid ground.

A question, from what felt like a lifetime ago, reverberated across my mind.

BECAUSE THEN NO ONE CAN LEAVE YOU?
LEAVE YOU?
LEAVE YOU?

"Yes!" With the word, my body unclenched, and the air became still and tepid around me. I stole a glance at my therapist. She remained staring, unmoving.

Then she reached forward. Not for my hand, thank

God—she must have known I'd be sensory'd out. But to offer me something. A tissue.

Tears dotted my skin like dew. When had I started crying?

I took the offering and gave one in return. "Yes. Being alone means I don't have to feel the pain of anyone leaving."

CHAPTER 3

Want to know the cure for a total mind warp? Costumes, corn dogs, and carnival rides.

Coming from a major low, I needed a major high. I pulled out my phone and feverishly pecked with my thumbs, letting Javi know I was out: Feed me some cotton candy take me to the top of the Giant Dipper and let my screams purge my thoughts from the last hour. Please.

Even if it meant sharing that moment with hundreds of my "closest peers."

After an embarrassing amount of sniffling and blotting my eyes, I finally got it together, and didn't need to be told twice that our session was over. I practically jumped out of my seat.

I busted out the front door of the office building, the blast of humidity not enough to stifle my goosebumps. My navy-blue cruiser waited at the bike rack, sparkling in the setting sun, the handles' rubber grips hot on my fingers from baking in the heat.

Playlist at the ready, I pressed my feet into the pedals, but slowed my roll, listening to the sounds of the world a little closer.

A cackle from the first voice carried on the breeze—no, wait, that was someone cracking up over a video they were watching on their phone. Spirited whispers from the second voice rose from the street—actually, those were from a group of kids walking by. Lively commentary from the third voice wafted through an open window—again, wrong, that was genuine excitement from the receptionists getting ready to go.

I was doing it again. Expecting the worst. *Trying* to distort the sounds. Unbelieving or undeserving of moments like this: Pure. Unambiguous. Quiet.

The Voices were bound to make a comeback, so maybe I should've been enjoying their absence instead? My headphones stayed put, looped around my neck as I listened— and actually enjoyed—the uninterrupted melody of summer as I biked to the Boardwalk for Grad Night.

The wind was easy on my ears as I barreled down a hill, zigzagging through the endless line of cars stopped in beach traffic, a pair of feet hanging out almost every passenger window.

As I careened around surfers balancing their boards on their heads and whizzed next to classmates shouting dibs for the best seat on the log ride, an unusual reflex tugged at the corners of my mouth. On an average day, I tried to drown it all out. But right now…I was one of them, simply enjoying every part of the moment, and I was smiling harder than a kid with priority in the surf lineup.

Javi waited at our usual meeting point, his silky black waves tucked beneath a wreath of flowers. With his frayed shorts, glossy black studs, and mismatched vest, he looked more Lost Boy than Shakespeare character.

He bowed deeply as I slowed to a stop. "I bid you good morrow."

I slid off the seat and returned a curtsey, my olive-green peasant dress catching dried oak leaves in its floor-length hem. "Your flower crown turned out fab." Slipping on my own band of faux florals, I eyed his empty chest while locking up my bike. "No camera?"

"Nah, some things are better left undocumented." He winked. "Plus, I don't think it's the easiest thing to secure on a roller coaster, and I plan on riding both of them at least ten times."

We hopped onto a pair of rotting wood train tracks that served as the unofficial border to the Santa Cruz Board-walk—arms wide, one sneaker in front of the other, cheeks squinched from suppressing our laughter. The tiniest slip of a chuckle and one of us would suffer the devastating two-inch drop into a mix of sand, gravel, and bird poop.

Javi made it to safety first, holding out his arm until I was close enough to loop mine through. "Where to first, my lady?" He directed us around a group of dudes in minotaur masks, board shorts, and unbuttoned shirts, who had all stopped to gape at something in the middle of the walkway.

"I hate to pull us away from this grand performance"—I jerked my chin at the crop top-wearing pixies taking selfies around a maypole who seemed to be stopping traffic—"but I need to stuff my face with a Boardwalk dog. Stat."

Javi steered us in the opposite direction, nodding sagely.

"Good idea. Therapy can be a fun sucker. You need to replenish your energy with something fried."

"You have no idea. I'd rather eat my feelings than another word of that therapist bullshit." It was high five worthy, but my stomach plummeted alongside the rooftop roller coaster riders the instant I said it.

Javi tugged on my hand, drawing me to the check-in table, where my worries dissolved to nothing but a speck of powdered sugar on a mountain of funnel cake.

After collecting our wristbands and almost making it past the photographer—who forced us to pose under the deflating balloon arch—we lost ourselves amongst the merrymakers, the PA system's Top 40 drowned out by clapping hands, melodic flutes, and clanging tambourines.

The crowd pressed in, all the buzz in activity luring us farther down the esplanade. Even without counting the hired courtiers, there seemed to be *a lot* of people for a closed event.

Then I remembered: we shared this evening with the graduating class of the other local high school.

Not everyone embraced Shakespeare, hence the group of half-tied togas and farm animal onesies that strode by, but everyone sure embraced their chance to be different. To welcome this next chapter as a whole new person, with a chance to actually live and fulfill their wildest hopes and dreams. Even the Boardwalk's Paleolithic mascots—creepy cave man statues the size of full-grown humans that were sprinkled throughout the Boardwalk even though they had nothing to do with the amusement park's theme—received a *Congrats, Grad!* garland or wig.

Walking along the sidewalk games, I was careful to avoid the eye of the persistent jester and the call of Hippolyta's storefront sales pitch. Javi, on the other hand, found himself trapped between a neon counter and two Amazonian's bosoms, and almost gave in.

"Let's at least get my corn dog before we lose all our money." I pulled him deeper into the midsummer night sea of seniors.

Javi slapped his hand over his heart. "Lose? You think I won't win?"

I chuckled at that, having played and yes, *lost*, enough games of dime toss with him to know we'd go broke.

We reached the far end of the park, and I finally felt the air, not sweaty bodies up against me. Short of thrills, out here, the majority of attractions closed because they served young kids, the crowd started to let up and darkness found its place between the unlit rides.

Sporadic red flares dotted the black with the quick drags of those that flocked to its sooty pockets. My vision strayed from the smokers and glued on to a shack beneath the scaffolding of the Big Dipper. Its infamous words glowed angelic against the twilight sky: *Hot Dog on a Stick.*

Javi gave my shoulders a victory tug. "Well, I'll be. It seems you have led me to a feast fit for a king."

We darted for an open window, warm and inviting and beckoning our hungry souls, when one of the adjacent shadow huddles stirred and broke into five towering, beefed-up individuals.

"River," the head of the pack crooned before us, his wide upper body dimming the snack shack's neon bulbs.

My body became stiffer than a board.

Ugh, that baritone drawl lined with a sexual vitriol. I had the misfortune of being able to recognize it anywhere: Chet Jennings. Star of our rival water polo team. Prick of the century.

Zero attempt was made to hide the loathing in my voice. "I should've known you'd be here."

"Nice of them to combine our Grad Nights, right? It's like we're one big happy family." His cronies snickered into bottles they no longer bothered to conceal with paper bags. Each of them, utter clones of the six-foot, steel-eyed, bastard in my direct path.

Javi scoffed. Couldn't blame him. I bit my tongue, hoping the nip of pain would stop the anger from rising and bursting out of me.

Even with half of Chet's face shaded by dusk, I could make out the ire flickering in his glazed-over stare. He turned to Javi, letting forth an inebriated snarl, before his wavering stance fixed on me again.

"So how are you, River?" His smile was wicked, uneven.

I didn't return it.

He reached for my waist, maybe my wrist, but didn't get, either. I recoiled from his touch, from his intentions, from his nasty acetone breath, and as I tried to squirm away, his hand brushed my chest. Ugh. He'd never even have considered talking to me if it hadn't been for our unfortunate fling at a house party following the homecoming game. I knew I was nothing special, but I guess by his standards Javi and I were decent enough to get singled out for a night as playthings for the varsity rulers. I should have been suspicious of the hearty welcome, the drinks thrust in our hands, the games of flip cup that resulted in the chugging.

Lucky for Javi, he'd spent the rest of that evening vomiting under the stars. Unlucky for me, I'd spent it half-aware, twisting in the sheets under *the* Chet Jennings.

An honor, he'd told me while he wiped away my tears, readying for another round. Until the Voices found me, and then I was no longer Baby. But Crazy, Psycho, and Slut.

You've got issues, he'd said.

Thank you, I'd whispered as the stifling air retreated, as my senses left me for a welcome blackout.

It took one look for Javi to know what had been done. And he still didn't forgive himself, would never forgive himself, for not being there to protect me. For being stripped of his will, and I of my clothes. I'd cried into his barf-stained shirt, in the backyard of whoever's house we were at, until the sun wrapped us in its hug.

But this time, Javi was here, and he stepped forward, answering for me. "We were great, until you came along."

This time Chet moved to my friend, his bone structure even more cutting with his wrath, like it had been carved with indifference, as he sized Javi up. "That last time I saw you, you were puking into my jacuzzi. That cost my parents a lot of money to clean."

Oh. So *that's* whose house we'd been at.

Chet inched a step closer. Javi stood his ground.

"Fucking lightweight," Chet growled into his face and slammed a palm into his chest.

Javi stumbled backwards, but I caught his arm, planting his feet alongside mine.

I glowered at the over-toned, sandy-haired "specimen" peacocking in the night before us. Positioning himself so the shadows lengthened his square chin, and the setting sun sharpened his cheeks, and the testosterone curled his fingers and lip.

All a front for some scared, small, little boy inside who couldn't get validation outside his unwilling conquests. It was sick.

"How'd that last game go for you again?" I tilted my head. "Your parents disappointed you didn't score enough points? Or do you just count the ones you score in the bedroom?"

The idiots in Chet's wing let out various yelps of surprise, their stilted laughter stoking his fragile ego. I could practically see the rage simmering in his reddened face.

"Get out of our way." I wielded my words like a knife.

"Or what?" he breathed.

Then I struck. My hand screamed at the impact, bright pink in its wake.

I was about as shocked as he seemed to be. But these feelings, this fury…they had been brewing for months now, roiling beneath my skin. Channeled into bitten cuticles and screams the ocean swallowed up while surfing.

I'd never slapped someone before—but it felt damn good to release that rage.

In the aftermath, I swore the stars flickered in my honor, the wind caressed my hot palm, and the silence, it actually gasped. Words hung in the air, and wouldn't this have been a moment, if the Voices decided to show—for a second, it felt like I could command them to with the sudden flare of power that thrummed through my veins.

Seconds that felt like hours passed before *someone* decided to speak. Chet.

"Enjoy your dinner, bitch." He motioned to the building behind him. "You do love those sausages in your mouth."

"Well, they're bigger than yours." I grabbed Javi's hand and dragged him towards our destination. Unable to resist, I added over my shoulder, "By a long shot!"

"You. Are. My. Hero!" Javi exclaimed as we got in line to order, the bro horde howling—one sulking—away. I didn't listen to what he was saying, didn't so much as flinch when the person in front of us stumbled into me, their sparkly nylon wings leaving a trail of glitter on my arm.

A hollow feeling growled inside me, one separate from my hunger.

Two corn dogs and a basket of fries later, we took our next course to go and moved west with the sun, the funnel cake so fresh and crispy that the dough still burned our tongues.

Wrapped in my world of fried food luxury, I almost walked right next to the water ride with my piping hot dessert—a rookie move. Javi yanked me away to dodge an overhead wave from Logger's Revenge just in time, the group next to us not quite as lucky.

"There are two types of people," he commented as we settled along the outskirts of the chlorinated puddles to watch. "People who enjoy the splash zone and people who avoid it all costs."

I frowned. "And people who slap others—"

"Who stand up for themselves and don't let the bad guys win," he corrected. "Are you okay?"

I sighed, ignoring his question. "I think we know where we fit in." I looked over at him, sticky battle wounds from our epic meal speckling his face. "Ah, you've grown out your sugar-stache, I see."

"My facial hair regenerates faster than Wolverine." He licked his thumb, using it to try—and ultimately fail—to get the powdered sugar off his upper lip. "Dang it, I forgot a napkin."

"Here." I removed one from the stack I had pressed into the bottom of my plate. His stare burned into me as I wiped the side of his mouth.

"You get it?" Had he even taken a breath?

"Yeah." I shoved the crumpled napkin into my dress pocket, fidgeting with it longer than needed—it seemed like the best place to avert my eyes because his gaze hadn't left me yet.

And then he blurted out, "Want to get our fortunes read?"

"What?" My brain stumbled for a connection.

He pointed behind me. "That lady over there in the corner—there's no line at her booth."

I followed his finger and sure enough, nestled beneath the dripping log ride, near the creepy Cave Train, sat an eccentric older woman in a knotted headband and matching robe with an intricate celestial pattern. Her hand-written advertisement looked as pathetic as the discolored, collapsible furniture she sat in. The whole booth—and Javi was being generous when he called it that—appeared to morph out of the attraction's faded underbelly.

My stomach plunged with the riders free-falling on the Double Shot in the distance.

A psychic. That's what he'd been staring at. Not me. My emotions must still be running high. I hadn't seen his attention flicker anywhere else, but the abrupt change in subject was all the proof I needed.

"Fortunes by Madame Myrian." I managed to read the peeling vinyl words on the banner loosely draped across the front of the table, its corners pinned down by rugged, sky-blue crystals. My nostrils flared. I think I caught a hint of sewage. "Looks like a bad omen."

Javi pretended to think hard on it. "Obviously let's do it."

Without any time for consideration, he grabbed my hand, the soles of my feet skidding on the sidewalk as he power walked us over.

The fortune teller remained unmoved as we barreled towards her, resembling more of a wax figure than a real person. Her skin could have been crafted out of leather—aged and etched with the most symmetrical frown lines. Her fishbowl glasses magnified her pupils so they were all that filled the lenses. Her brows indented in concentration and if I didn't know any better, I'd say she was using her mental strength to reel us in.

There wasn't so much as a blink from her until we reached her display.

Her fingers, adorned in thin silver chains that cascaded from the bangles on her wrist, were the first to move, reaching for the deck of tarot cards in the center of the table. The rest of her slowly came to motion, as if the energy flowed from her hands: pointy elbows reset against the astral tablecloth, narrow shoulders rolled and arched. Her jaw protruded forward, the gears revving each muscle until her entire body became animated with life.

"Hello." Javi crept closer, as if the psychic were a stray cat he didn't want to frighten away. "How much for a reading?"

The woman held up her palm, flashing a grin that was one rotten stump away from being toothless.

"Five tokens," he translated, with a light elbow to my ribs like we were in on some big secret. He murmured something along the lines of "deal of the century," but I was too entranced by the shadows behind her to catch it. Seeming to stem from her spine, they fluttered and furled, casting wraithlike shapes that didn't match any of our surroundings. A violent tickle erupted on my back, as if buried under my scars, deep beneath my skin.

"Come on Riv, indulge me." Javi broke my trance, and as I batted a hand at my back, the sensation ceased.

I turned to him. "Seriously, Jav, its Grad Night, and this is what you want to do?"

He *knew* what he was doing batting those unfairly long lashes, and it worked like a charm on me. Pretending to consider his plea, I shot another glance at the open-aired booth.

The shadows fell still and nondescript. Huh. Must have been a trick of the light.

"Alright, fine." I let him think I was giving in, but to be honest, I was now a little curious myself.

Madame Myrian nodded and pointed to an empty chair. Javi obeyed, making a dramatic show of stepping forward as he entered her circle of fate.

Tarot cards twisted and bridged atop a sheer black tablecloth with a gilded zodiac wheel, their silvery white edges glistening like tiny mirrors in the setting sun. Suits dropped one by one into a cross-like sequence, a mosaic of swords and wands and every color of the rainbow. Myrian translated their secrets, or I supposed she meant to, but her words were unintelligible against the latest dispatch of screams from Logger's Revenge.

Javi leaned in closer until his body stretched halfway across the table.

Not feeling the same urge to close the gap, I inspected the spread from the side, pausing on a pair of cards with images reminiscent of Adam and Eve and the Grim Reaper.

These were just symbolic representations, of course, but my pulse quickened about what kind of conclusions would be drawn from their meanings. Not wanting, or qualified, to read too far into it, I swiveled around to people-watch instead.

Or…I would have if anyone was there.

Tucked between the industrial-strength power cords and desolate employee breakroom, we'd separated from the herd. It hadn't fazed me at sunset, but the string lights over the midway didn't shine where we were, and darkness started to seep into every crevice.

Already around us the lines were thinning, and the remaining few stragglers boarded the Cave Train or spent the last of their tokens at the mini arcade or sprinted towards the primary entrance of the park—a sign the beach concert was beginning soon, if it hadn't already.

The fleeing footsteps reverberated over my body like I was being trampled beneath them. Each resounding *thud* had me clutching my hair a little harder as the noises around me grew sharper and the scents and stains and shades of color of the Boardwalk started melding together. I meandered away from the reading, with a weight in my stomach that threatened to take the rest of me down.

Even though there was no one else around, it didn't feel like I was alone.

The second voice sizzled with the cornbread's oily batter wafting from the row of carnival-themed cafes. "Watcher, go back to the cards," she urged. "Tell us what you see."

I clutched my stomach. *Breathe breathe breathe*—for a second, the air got caught in my windpipe, when a game stall's overhead door slammed shut.

The first voice rang out in the clang of the metal, her shrill tones mocking me. "Or just keep standing there. We've obviously got all the time in the world..."

"Is this you helping? Because it's definitely not working." The second voice tried to reason against the Down the Clown's insufferable laugh track, but the screechy combo just brought goosebumps to my flesh.

My breathing came in short bursts. I wanted, no *needed*, them to stop. I clamped down on my tongue—if I opened my mouth, words might not be the only thing that'd come spewing out.

"What? It's not like she's in a rush to figure anything out." The first feigned offense, her voice softening as the metal door stilled.

"But *we are*," the third belted out in sync with the riders braving the Fireball's pendulum swing.

"She doesn't understand our world. Maybe she can find meaning through her own." The second voice refuted the others, still paired with the creepy clown game's recorded instructions. For the love of God, could she pick another sound!?

"How long must we wait for her to come around? It's been ten years and she has shown no interest in the truth." The third voice chipped at my brain, using the sharp clicks from an air hockey puck. "We need to accept that no matter how hard we try to steer her, she will never be her mother."

Her words stung me like a thousand angry bees. Not just because they were lined with venom, but because in my core I knew they were every part true. "You think I don't know that? You're preaching to the choir," I finally whispered back.

The second voice cut back in. "Watcher—"

Watcher. Their little pet name they'd never cared to explain. Hm, was it because when my mom saved me from the rip current all I could do was *watch*, helpless, while she got caught in it?

My nails dug into my palms. "Don't fucking call me that!" I didn't bother to conceal my voice.

Now that she'd moved on from the clown, the second voice brushed against my senses with the nearby janitor's rhythmic sweeping. "Please, we're down to the wire. The time has come to accept your fate—it isn't what it seems. Listen to us before the transfer of power completes."

"The time has come to move on," the third voice corrected with the hard clank of the puck slamming into the goal.

Saliva bubbled over my teeth. "GET OUT OF MY LIFE!"

"That's not the worst idea you've had," one of the Voices bit back. "We are better off without you."

BETTER OFF WITHOUT YOU.

BETTER OFF WITHOUT YOU.

At that point, I didn't know who spoke it. I didn't even know where it came from.

It honestly didn't matter. Maybe they'd never said it outright before, but they'd been thinking it for a long, long time. All of them.

My stomach twisted painfully, but I assembled what little bit of mental strength I had and fired back, "Good, then *leave*."

Violent flapping rustled the air, like a group of spooked pigeons scattering, as an invisible bind released me. It felt like a hand had been clenching my throat. My legs folded and my knees struck pavement as I took a ragged inhale.

Any bit of will, any wall of resistance, crumbled. I planted my palms and heaved.

Nothing cut the night except my weakened gasps, not even the hum of the generator. Or the sloshing of the salty waves meeting the lazy flow of the river, or the screamers on the distant rides…

I raised my head, half expecting to see a circle of implicating fingers or the flash of a phone or the reflectors of a security guard. Or, if lucky, Javi's outstretched hand. But none of those things greeted me when I rose to my feet. Instead, I met a stillness I couldn't explain.

The world around me mimicked a wax museum and the people, its mannequins.

I slowly spun in place.

Park employees' mouths gaped open while taking food orders, and their bodies hovered over control panels. Their shiny, unblinking eyes reflected the carnival lights. The few attendees who hadn't changed course for the concert were frozen in place, some caught in stride, others gripping arcade game joysticks. Rides hung mid-fall, gears stuck on the tracks, their multicolored bulbs stuck in the middle of a sequence.

I hurried back over to Javi but he too had been struck— in eyebrow-lifting, forehead-crinkling bemusement. His fingers lay in an identical pattern to Madame Myrian's, gripping the lip of the table. My heart thundering in shock, I dared a glance over to her. Her oversized violet tunic draped her wrists, swallowing her whole except for her neck, head, and hands, but it was her unchanged indigo stare that made me catch my breath.

It bored into me, like it *saw* me, all the way to my soul.

Her presence felt more real in this alternate state than it had when I had spoken to her.

"Myrian?" I waved a hand in front of her face. She didn't flinch, didn't bat an eyelash. Then the tarot spread stole my attention.

The entire deck had been spread across the table into a position that resembled…wings.

Most cards were facedown, and the back of the deck featured an angelic figure drawn with metallic wispy lines that made it look like they were built of light and power. The faceup cards were all of one suit, golden cups: one overflowing, two intertwined, three being clinked together. Four, five, six—seven of them—centered on this symbol.

Any uncontained liquid depicted in the images seemed to ripple, like it was *actual* water. I bent closer and heard the faintest *whoosh* when something splashed the back of my head.

I craned my neck to see where it had come from, and another droplet hit my nose—trickles of condensation falling from the winding tube of the log ride above me.

Before I had time to realize what was happening, the waterway started flowing full force, piercing the absolute stillness around me. And in the blink of an eye, everything else roared back to life.

CHAPTER 4

The cave train let out its steam and with it came a declarative *choo choo!* signaling its arrival into the boarding bay—and my arrival to reality, too. Riders disembarked from their time-traveling voyage into the attraction's eclectic version of the Stone Age, dusk settled amongst the stars, a hint of fresh caramel apple mixed with the stench of the estuary…

Life returned as if it had never paused.

But it did. It *did* pause. So why did everyone seem so nonchalant about it? I didn't need a mirror to tell me I looked like a fish out of water. My gaping mouth did *not* match their beaming smiles.

"River?" I got the impression that was the third or fourth time Javi had said it.

"Sorry, yeah?" I faked a tone of indifference. He saw right through it.

"Youuu okay?" He squeezed the sweet spot between my thumb and index finger. Clearly, he hadn't experienced anything out of the ordinary. A quick sweep of the few people in eyeshot confirmed it—no one else had, either. Just me again.

My nails shot to my mouth and took the brunt of my stress.

"Why wouldn't I be?" I lied, avoiding the concern in his gaze by returning to the deck of cards. All had been reverted to a normal pattern, in the shape of a V, the extras stashed into a neat pile.

No wings. No cups.

I released a breath, relieved to see the Grim Reaper's faded silhouette again, instead.

"You look like you're about to chew off a finger." He gently guided my hand away from my mouth. "And you're hovering over me like my *abuela* when she senses something is wrong."

"Oh." I stepped back to put a few inches between us. "My bad."

This time he grabbed my whole hand and pulled me even closer to him. "Hey. You've got a little something on your chin." Heat flooded my face. Oh God, there must've been puke—dried puke from the break-in-time-that-couldn't-have-happened. He raised a brow and eyed me suspiciously. "Everything good?"

I brushed my chin and attempted a smile. "Yeah, thanks. Did you get what you wanted?"

"I did." He strummed the edge of the tablecloth and dropped a couple bills in Myrian's tip jar. "Thanks for the reading."

Judging by the complete sense of vacancy behind Madame Myrian's eyes, she didn't hear—or care—that we were done.

As we turned to leave, a calloused hand gripped my wrist and I boomeranged backwards, my shoulder nicking the sharp edge of a crystal as my body slammed into the table. Tarot cards fluttered in the air, until a petite, rumpled frame loomed above me and blocked everything else from sight.

Risen from her chair, the psychic hooked her stare on to mine. Her gleaming irises were so black and shiny, dilating wildly, and the receding sun cast a devilish veil across her weathered face.

Pinned in place by Myrian's sudden—and unexpected—strength, there was nowhere for me to look except directly into the hollow of her haunting expression. And her expression said it all: She knew that I knew she'd witnessed the blip. She had seen me.

She had seen *everything*.

Those taut lips started to spasm, hacking and spitting, twitching with frantic purpose. Her garbled words intensified, growing louder. Sharper.

I willed myself to focus on each syllable flowing from her lips, and soon, with repetition, the words became a bit more coherent.

"*Quarto vigil*," Madame Myrian bellowed. "*Quarto vigil*," she repeated again. And again. And again. Without stopping for breath.

The fortune teller's throat croaked from the lack of air and her sunken cheeks bloated with rage. Something controlled her and propelled the chant forward and monopolized each of her muscles in its wake. A shocking familiarity swept over my body, pushing my fear away.

As I was readying myself to ask if she'd heard the Voices too, a tug on my free arm stole my attention. Javi.

"LET HER—whoa!"

The distraction broke us apart.

Myrian's grip lifted, and whatever spell she had cast, or whatever spell had bound her, ceased. Javi and I tumbled like a sideshow's milk bottles onto the gum-specked promenade.

Lucky for me, I didn't hit pavement. Not so lucky for Javi, I landed on him.

His arms stayed wrapped around me, a blockade against the littered ground. Our chests lifted in unison with each breath. His cheeks flushed—probably from the fall. I'm sure that's why mine burned, too. In fact, I'm *sure* it wasn't because I was literally on top of him, and our pulses seemed to be syncing with each rattled beat. For a few more winded inhales, neither of us moved.

Then he whispered, "Let's blow this popsicle stand."

Yeah—good idea. After getting up and securing myself on my own two feet I moved to help him, arm outstretched. His words ghosted on my lips, and with a smile due to the irony, I asked, "Hey, you okay?"

He wriggled his eyebrows in response, tucking me into him once he was up.

"That's my line," he muttered into my sun-kissed highlights, giving me a light squeeze, when his grip suddenly tightened. "Jesus, Riv, you're shaking."

I pushed off his chest, curling my hands behind my back, trying to hide that every limb and bone within me was indeed trembling. "Am I?"

"Yes." He took a tentative step forward. "You sure you're okay? I know tonight's been wild, with Chet and then whatever that was—"

"I'm fine." It sucked to lie, but even worse was seeing the recognition of it flash across his face.

He tapped my arm, the goosebumps disappearing under the imprint of his touch. "C'mon, let's go catch the band. We don't want tonight to be a total bummer."

"Music cures all, they do say." I deigned a final glance at Madame Myrian's unlit space. She'd reverted back to her glazed-over look, her body locked into position no different than any of the other odd cave-people sculptures found throughout the Boardwalk.

Blinded by the colorful neon lights, we emerged from the Boardwalk's crevices, and the park's amusements summoned me with an insincere playfulness. Festive music played from the scrap metal interiors yet warped into a tuneless loop. Shopkeepers bowed their top hats but hid their expressions within the shadows of their brims. Game hosts beckoned with bloodred painted smiles that smeared across their lips and teeth. The calm face I wore, also a lie, drawn with a hint of a frown and a tinge of rosy panic.

Attempting to make things normal, I said, "Thanks for saving me—it's, like, your job."

"I know, what are you going to do without me?" Javi grinned.

I didn't want to talk—even think—about that. Didn't want to think about what happened after tonight or what would happen a few months later, when our summer drew to a close. When he'd box up his board games, comics, skateboards, and Santa Cruz tees, and head for his new life as an undergrad at Santa Barbara.

While I stayed and repeated a class at the city college. Just to get my stupid diploma.

I scoffed at a green-and-gold *Future is bright!* banner, the pirate mascot stamped next to the words as unimpressed as I was. My future wasn't bright. My future was shit.

I only had things to lose. Like Javi.

I knew how intangible some of our greatest aspirations were—slay a sea monster, surf in the Arctic Circle, get out of Santa Cruz and see the world—but when dreaming them up with him they somehow felt unleashed, alive, and possible.

That's exactly what Javi's dreams had become when he received his acceptance package. Mine died when I watched him read the letter. I'd known it was coming—I'd given up on getting good grades, hardly able to hold a C, but it still felt like the veins had been disconnected from my heart. He hadn't even left, and I already grieved him.

He must have sensed it. "You know, you can visit me at UCSB."

I knew. It wasn't the same. But I just nodded, eyes locked on the whirling spotlights from the stage coming into view ahead.

"What was up with that fortune teller, by the way? What did she want?"

The image of her empty onyx stare made me shudder, even if we were a solid six rides away from her.

"She kept repeating the same thing over and over." I was definitely going to butcher it. "*Qua…quarto…vigil?*"

"*Quarto vigil?*" Of course, it rolled off his tongue in perfect form. "What is that, Latin?"

"Sounds about right." I harrumphed like a crotchety old lady. "I don't know what it is, or what it means."

"Let's Google it." He whipped out his phone.

"My guess is that she had a breakdown," I continued as he swiped and tapped, "and took it out on the closest person. Me."

"I know the feeling. Kidding!" He threw his hands up in surrender, the bright background of his screen shining between his fingers.

I stopped in my tracks, hating myself for needing the validation. "I'm not that bad, am I?"

"Of course not." He shot me a devious smile. Great, so, I was.

"Well, since we've got an unreliable fortune teller on our hands here, my reading is most definitely shit." He folded Madame Myrian's business card into his pocket. "Won't be needing this."

I bumped his shoulder with mine. "Aw, were you hoping all her predictions might be true?" We resumed walking, forgetting about the unfinished phrase in his phone's search bar. "What did she tell you, anyway?"

The hair-lifting bass from the concert muted his response.

At least the organizers didn't tie the live music to Grad Night's theme. I'd heard enough flutes and bagpipes and tambourines and the soundtrack to *Midsummer Night's Dream*.

We leaned against the metal railing overlooking the stage and scanned the beach for a good spot to sit. Spotting one, we broke through the perimeter of the swaying crowd, plopped down onto an unclaimed woven blanket, and burrowed our toes in the cool velvet sand.

I attempted to calm my fretting nerves by belting out the lyrics to some popular nineties song, letting the music sweep the incidents of the night from my mind—but in between the long breathes a chill ran over my spine, and unease broke the cracks of my forced excitement.

This wasn't the first fight I'd had with the Voices, so I didn't know why this one shook me so much. Maybe it was because time and space had also glitched…but had it? Or had I just imagined that? I couldn't say for sure—the hard line of reality was always a little blurry for me.

Grooved rings indented my skin, interrupting my anxieties before they tossed me into a pit of distress I couldn't climb out of. Javi's palm layered the back of my hand, fingers weaving through mine. He squeezed lightly. "Do you know what time it is?"

My nose crinkled. "Midnight, I presume?"

Chuckling as if I'd said the cutest, most endearing thing in the world, his dark brown eyes lit up like fireworks. Drawing in closer, he whispered, "Happy birthday."

He draped his arm around my shoulders, and I tilted my head so it tucked under his chin. For a second, the rush of blood was the only thing that filled my ears, racing as fast as my heart. It was just a hug—just a birthday wish. One I hadn't acknowledged yet because I was too caught up in my own head.

"Thanks," I whispered back, never wanting to let go of my best friend.

CHAPTER 5

Pebbles and splintered seashells crunched beneath my feet as I hopped on my cruiser and biked away from Grad Night. Bits caught on my tire's rubber spikes as I pedaled along the trail that lay sandwiched between the old rail line, just beyond the Boardwalk's reach.

Using the chirp of the insects as my instrumentals and the click of the gears as my beat, I hummed a tune from a night that already felt so distant, as if the entire evening had been one out-of-body experience.

My knuckles strained against the handlebars, and for a second I imagined Javi's resting there, too. I replayed our goodbye from fifteen minutes ago: his fingers threading between mine, his lips brushing my cheek, his *happy birthday* whisper in my ear…I released a slow breath, but it did nothing to ease the tension in my chest.

To be honest, it was totally unclear what I should do about this divergence from our friendship, which felt as off the rails as the uprooted train tracks I passed.

Our future stopped in August when he blossomed, and I remained. We had less than two months left before he'd split for SB. I didn't want to sabotage it.

At least I wasn't alone in being tortured by this. Judging by the glint in his eyes, the crumple of his forehead, the way his shoulders sagged when I declined his invite to walk me home…he definitely felt it, too. The question remained: should we say goodbye, or should we give in to this—whatever *this* was?

My sigh clouded in front of me, mixing with the damp thickets of fog. It ushered the earth behind its misty curtain, devouring the streetlights and singing crickets. Soon the wimpy glow from my front basket's headlamp was the only shine left to indicate if I hurtled towards home or off a cliff.

Pretty standard for a late-night trek near the sea, but tonight it was suffocating, like slogging through quicksand. I hopped off my cruiser, towing it next to me as I waded through the sphere of gray. Its tendrils were as thick as a wall, hardly parting for my legs, devouring my footsteps. A shiver rippled down my spine.

Up ahead, an oblique shape parted the fog. I concentrated on its outline while my light bounced off its surface, and a rectangle that was placed vertically solidified out of the haze. Peeled black-and-red paint, the only imprints left of an old warning sign, came into focus, the words *Stop! Turn Back! No Foot Path!* popping against the grain.

The San Lorenzo River truss had been out of commission for years. It had been a popular crossing for the east and west sides of town until the decayed floorboards and exposed metal hinges forced its shutdown. Rumors that the ousted members of an old blood-drinking cult that was prevalent here in the eighties shuffled across the planks, waiting for fresh meat like a horde of zombies, didn't make it sound any less sketchy.

But I needed a straight shot home, and this saved me about twenty minutes.

Plus, I'd taken it plenty of times before, just not in the middle of the night. Not when the fog was this thick. Not when my anxiety made me mistake the swirls for more sinister things—nope.

I swallowed the fear that lodged in my throat and stepped onto the corroded platform.

The outline of its steel frames arched like the roof of a chapel, nails so big they looked like scarab beetles crawling up and down the pillars. Avoiding all the sharp ledges and eroded strips of wood became a twisted game. My bike thumped alongside me, dragging along the wet lumber, growing heavier with every push.

Something stirred ahead—or was it the dampness I cut through, creasing and drawing back in again? I slowed to a halt and listened while the moisture clung to my body.

Armed with nothing but my flickering LED bike lamp and cell phone, I held down the flashlight button until it turned on and shone towards the nearest support beam. A hermit crab skittered out of sight.

I swore, hoping that damn crustacean would be my first and last encounter on this trestle.

One by one, my hairs stood on end as the fog grew more restless—I swore it whispered my name—swore it cackled in my ear, and beckoned me deeper, and tricked me into thinking I was seeing things. My muscles tightened, bracing for the onslaught of Voices.

But none of the sounds or shapes or smells manifested into a version that hijacked my brain. None of the Voices rose out of the evening acoustics to haunt me. Which might've been weird, but frankly, I was too drained to care where they were.

Then a shadow a shade darker than the rest of the trestle dropped from overhead. It cut the mist like a knife, emerging a few tracks away, with a stillness that asserted predator versus prey. I think my heart completely stopped before stuttering back to life at double time.

I swore to God if it was Chet, I might push him off. My fingers tingled with adrenaline.

"Who's there?" It was as guttural as I could make it. Which wasn't saying much. Ugh, and my voice cracked.

Unaffected by my bark, the human form inched closer, drifting rather seamlessly, as if they floated on the wind—as if they commanded the vapor that flapped at their sides and used it to drive them forward.

Not the grace I expected from a drunk water polo behemoth—but still.

"Don't come near me!" Improvising, I flung my cruiser to the ground, just killing the calm game. It landed horizontally between us, forming a barricade.

They stopped at the edge of my bike frame. A black combat boot appeared and struck a spinning spoke, putting an end to the *click click* it made.

What would they silence next? My beating heart?

I shoved my phone at the figure, and they pulled back their hood, revealing an angular face hardly touched by the summer sun, with the most striking hazel eyes I had ever seen. A guy. A guy about my age. Well…*that* was certainly a surprise.

Green dominated his light brown irises, with specks of gold so pure they belonged in a pan sifter's dish. He observed me, brow furrowed behind tufts of black or brown hair—hard to tell in the dark, even with my flashlight shining in his face—as if in an attempt to hide any emotion.

His lips curled up, angling ivory cheekbones into a menacing grin. Like he was detecting if *I* was the threat. Me. The one at least a solid foot and a half shorter than him.

In a concerted effort to look intimidating as hell, I held my head higher and willed my facial features to set into a shield of indifference—while he stood with the coiled tension of a mountain lion before it unleashes itself.

"What are you doing here?" He spoke in a cold, hard tone with a subtle lilt to his R's.

I opened my mouth but reconsidered my response—I was feeling ballsy. So, instead of condemning myself right off the bat, I decided to do some digging of my own. "I could ask you the same thing."

"This trestle's off-limits." The silver cross that hung from his ear dangled with the tilt of his chin, as his gaze swept me up and down in one long, fluid movement.

A wave of heat erupted through me, following the path of his stare. I took a step closer to my bike—closer to him—hoping the brisk air would cool the sudden fever. "Yet here we are, both trespassing. What's your excuse?"

It wasn't too dark for me to catch his sneer. "I was looking for something."

"Pretty odd place to search in the middle of the night. Don't you think?"

He shrugged.

"Well, did you find it?" I pressed.

"I think so." His gaze didn't waver, whether due to my lopsided flower crown or his own curiousness. Even as I neared the middle of my bike, still lying on its side, parallel to my feet, his eyes bored into me, dead center. "The fog, did it lead you out this way?"

"Believe it or not most people try and do the *opposite* and avoid places totally hidden by thick layers of fog." I paused and crossed my arms, all a show of indifference, because my mind was racing as fast as my heart. "But it's a good shortcut…" I trailed off, as my light landed on a lump protruding from behind his shoulder. A backpack, obviously. One that blended like stitches into his all-black ensemble, with a tufted top.

The warmth flooding me moments ago completely left my body. That wasn't a backpack. It was a quiver. Packed with arrows.

Being armed with pepper spray was one thing. Waltzing around Santa Cruz with archery equipment? Excessive. What was he going to do, shoot a misbehaving starfish?

Every fiber in my being urged me to turn around. I should have done it. Right then and there, I should have picked up my bike and gone. But I was curious about his venom, whether it actually stung, so I stayed and buried the doubt. "Were you at Grad Night?"

"Why?" No emotion. Not even a flicker. Did he ever blink?

I motioned to his arrows. "Your gear, it looks like part of a costume."

"Oh, these." He rotated the onyx quiver so it splayed across his chest. Intricate silvery-white patterns swirled up the sides, like they'd been threaded out of moonlight. With a tilt of his head, he admired his props, revealing a similar motif inked beneath his low, open collar, snaking on the flesh right over the bone.

"Let me guess, new age Oberon?" I said it like there was no other answer, because dressing as a character from Shakespeare was the only rational explanation as to why he was walking around with hunting weapons.

Smirking, he gave a slow bat of his lashes, as if he read my mind and wanted to throw those concerns back in my face. "Ryder."

"I don't know that Shakespeare character."

His voice remained flat. "It's my name."

"Oh. Well, Ryder, do you go to school around here?" If he did, there was no way it was mine. I obviously didn't know all nine hundred-ish kids there, but a guy like him, he'd never skate by unmissed. Especially if this wasn't a costume, and I was starting to think it might not be.

He smirked again, the prominent freckle on his cheek lost to his extended dimple. "No."

So—he wasn't at Grad Night. He wasn't in costume. And he didn't go to school around here. The thunderous roar of the ocean crashing onto the beach wasn't loud enough to mask the awkwardness.

Salt drifted in the air and mixed with the mist. I licked it from my lips. "You know…the polite thing to do would be to ask what my name is." My eyes darted to my bike, the small talk a distraction while I gauged how difficult it would be to rip it out from under his treaded shoe, hop on, and split.

"I know all I need to about you." He wiped a drop of condensation off the sleeve of his leather jacket. It interested him way more than talking to me. Well, good. I didn't care about him or his stupid weapons, either.

"So, you're a psychic, too. You should meet my friend at the Boardwalk." At this point I'd say anything to avoid the silence. Why was I even still there? "Yeah, she's a dear old thing. Bit of a wild card. You'd love her."

I bent to get my cruiser, huffing to myself while I jerked it off the ground, concentrating on Ryder's boot and how it wouldn't even *move*—when my foot got stuck in the chain and I completely toppled as I tried to stand. The whole bridge shook under my clumsy ass.

One of Ryder's calloused palms grasped mine, and the other the handlebars, and in an effortless lift, he pulled me upright. Tarnished rings stamped into my hand, and tattooed fingers left traces of heat on my skin. It thawed the chill that'd overtaken my bones and stayed long after I retracted from his grip. My nostrils flared at a sharp, woody smell, reminiscent of pine.

"Thanks." I denied myself a smile, though one diffused below the surface.

His mouth twitched. Close enough to a response.

Sitting on my bike, I craned my neck to meet his face. Another flicker of those golden-green eyes and I felt dizzy enough to whip out my kickstand. The unshakeable depth of his stare was like peering into the latticed canopy of a redwood grove. It gave me a mild form of vertigo, but I didn't want to look away.

My motor skills sputtered as I tried to kick off. I swerved, getting nowhere, but I at least landed on my feet. For no other reason than my worthless curiosity, I decided to ask, "What were you looking for, by the way?"

He paused on his answer, as if picking the right words. "The path to the river."

I pushed off, gesturing behind me. "There's a flat one at the other end of the trestle. It's basically connected to the sidewalk. You can't miss it…"

As I shakily biked away, I swore I heard a heady flapping on the wind.

CHAPTER 6

The weight of the vapor blanketed my body, hardly parting for me as I pedaled through it, veiling the world with a layer of fog that felt as secluded as the thick of the forest. It was honestly a miracle I made it across the trestle without hurtling off it.

Once my tires thumped on solid ground and I turned inland, the wall of gray dissipated. One unsteady hand gripping the handlebar, I checked my phone notifications, my eyes darting from the screen to the road: generic birthday wishes and gifs from Javi and questions from my dad that I'm sure he sent not even a second past midnight.

Where are you? one message from him read.

And, You're late.

The latest, If you're not home in 5 min you're grounded forever.

He was lucky I wasn't going to be out until sunrise like most of the others. Chill dad, grad night, remember? I managed to type without crashing.

I accelerated up my drive, pedaling against the slope. A snort of relief escaped me as my familiar two-unit complex came into view. Its tan exterior walls, seventies brown trim, and lattice shielding the balconies with vines hardly visible in the hazy light of the moon.

The automatic light announced my homecoming and busted the trash-diving racoons. They hissed, dodging my cruiser as I tossed it to the side yard's refuge.

I dashed up the stoop and through the front door, the entryway lit in expectation. My dad would be in his office waiting for me, poring over some research in lieu of pacing, because the window behind his desk gave a full view of our street and the entrance onto our landing.

Holding my breath, I kicked off my shoes, ascended the dozen steps, and glided into our flat. Those text threats didn't scare me. They were very much empty, like the flasks on his desk that he tried to hide when I reached the threshold of his study.

Already well into the night, he was well into the whiskey, and my texts had probably doubled before his eyes. I exhaled, the tension so thick it coiled around my limbs and absorbed any confidence I'd built up.

He peered at me through his reading glasses, a red tint to his stubbled cheeks from too many hours in the sun. Restless fingers tapped a mahogany antique desk, the silhouette framed by a stained-glass window that fed my childhood spirit stories with its stars, knights, and angels. Light from the passing vehicles seemed to mobilize its features, illuminating his face, and polo, in the soft hues of its primary colors.

His frown lines grew deeper as he stared me down.

"River, can you come in here?" A shaky hand folded a stack of crinkled essays, the other swift to close a drawer that rattled with empty glass bottles. The effort was futile—it made me wince and wish the steaming French press was the only aroma that wafted out into the hall.

I dragged my feet over the threshold's carpet, the shaggy beige pieces sliding between my toes. His hands rested in the inner parts of his elbows, not quite crossed: his fighting stance for our verbal brawls.

As I took in the knitted brows, the downward lips, the clenched fingers on his sleeves, I tried to recall the moment when things between us got so…disconnected. I didn't think there was a specific one I could blame. Every year since my mother's death his drinks got stronger, and our relationship weaker, and now it crumbled right in front of me.

I avoided his eyes—I couldn't face them yet—and focused on a slug paperweight instead. The bronze mascot pointed at me from his tabletop perch with a cheesy cartoon smirk, holding a *Professor Corbin Harlow, I DIG you!* sign, and bearing the brunt of my nervous stare.

"Do you know what time it is?" My dad filled his coffee mug to the brim, his tone flat and failing to assuage the anxiety I had within.

"Yes." No reason to argue against something as foolproof as time.

"Do you want to explain what happened?"

Sure, the night was full of terrors and trespassing and a brooding guy to boot.

Ryder. Just his name had my fingers twisting, my feet scuffing the carpet of their own accord. And when his golden-green stare flared in my mind…I tightened my arms around my torso, like they could protect me. I nodded in answer to my dad's question before my mouth did something stupid: smile.

"It's Grad Night, you know, the official graduation party thrown by the school? They talked about it at the ceremony. Remember?" I tried my best to keep my voice even as understanding dawned on him. "I reminded you about it over text. Did you check your messages?"

He eyed the phone that at some point had leapt from his pocket to the floor. With an audible groan infused with that oaky edge, he stumbled out of his chair to pick it up.

I bit the inside of my cheek. The tears wouldn't win—not today. I'd hold them in even if it drew blood.

"I'm sorry." He pressed on his knees to stand. "How could I forget."

I grimaced at the answer to that.

"It was a beautiful ceremony. You made me very proud." A sliver of that pride slipped from his already glassy eyes, and it started to soften the blow. Even if that diploma was still up for grabs, he didn't mention my shortcomings, and in that endless sea of parents I'd found him clapping and cheering like I deserved every stride across that stage. "And I was listening, I just…forgot how late those things run."

His ambient smile dampened the frustration in the air, his arms widening for a hug. I looped around his desk and dumped myself into his embrace. The grief dissipated the longer I stayed, as if every extra squeeze wrung it out a little more.

"I shouldn't have been so hard on you," he said into the top of my head. "After all, it *is* your birthday." His arms left my shoulders as he glanced at his watch. "I know we're only thirty minutes in, but I want to give you your present now."

With a wistful smile that had my heart breaking all over again, he unlocked a hidden desk compartment and pulled out a small velvet pouch. It had no label or visible branding, just plain black with a silver cord. His fingers jerked, seeming to hesitate for a second, as he passed it to me. I stared at the peculiar bag as if it might bite me, then emptied its secrets into my palm.

A surge of prickling energy flooded my veins the second the lapis stone touched my skin. Folding my lips to conceal a gasp, the power traveled through me like a river and rushed my ears with a gurgle that sounded so similar to the syllables of my name.

All the air whooshed out of me as the sensation slowly receded, and the pins and needles faded, leaving my muscles tender and sore. I glanced at my dad to see if he'd noticed, but he was fiddling with his secret drawer again.

With my insides feeling a bit like churned butter, I ran my thumb over the back of the necklace's circular pendant—smooth and silky as water, while the raised edges on its other side indented my palm. I flipped it over. A rippled water droplet with two four-pointed stars lining the upper lefthand corner brocaded the stone's surface. It glistened with a blue so mixed and multihued, it could have been crafted out of the element itself.

"It was your mom's." My dad addressed me with an inscrutable sable stare, running his fingers through his wavy chestnut hair. "She never took it off. Until…"

Like a plague of locusts, guilt swarmed the frail buds of joy, leaving me—and the entire room—feeling raw and consumed. I'd already taken the most important gift, her life. I couldn't take anything more from her. It didn't seem right.

"It's beautiful but…" I shoved my hand forward. "I don't deserve it."

My dad didn't falter, staring deep into the necklace's sparkling center.

"It was her eyes. One look and I was drowning. They reminded me of the sea on a winter day. Mira saw the world through a different lens, and she let me in." He pointed to himself as if in disbelief. "Nothing got old for her, even the simple every day. Her love for us, her love for life…it renewed something in me."

Sometimes, like now, I saw a flicker of that zest animate his entire being. It lasted half of a second, so quickly I wasn't sure if I imagined it, because the real truth was it'd been lost long ago. Or maybe it'd just been numbed by his drinking.

"I know I need to let you grow and be your own person and let you experience life…be free. It's what Mira would have wanted, it's why she…" He shook his head, unwilling to finish the thought.

At this point I was happy to hear anything.

"I see so much of her in you." He cleared his throat thickly. "And I can't lose her again."

I swallowed a sob.

"She told me over and over she wanted you to have this when you turned eighteen, as if…deep in her gut she knew something might happen to her." He squinched his eyes shut. "I know I'm a forgetful old guy, but I'd never forget this."

Silence, such deep, cataclysmic silence, hung on the air with his words.

And still, I thought about rejecting it. Not because of her, but because I didn't deserve it—her sympathy, her love, whatever the necklace represented. Yet...I pulled back my hand, clasping my fingers around the pendant, and held it close to my heart.

I STARED AT my bedroom's ceiling, the glossy surf posters lit by the atomic yellow glow of celestial stickers, as I replayed my dad's words. My mom's—now my—necklace settled against my chest. I spun its silver chain and cuddled further into the warmth of my geometric-patterned quilt.

Light from a passing car slipped through the cracks in my blinds, illuminating my room, and I flipped onto my side. Old photos, like the one that stared back at me from the frame on my nightstand, and distant memories, like the rare one tonight given by my dad, pieced together an image of the woman I'd never see again. *The woman I'd never live up to,* a little voice started to tell me before I banished it from my mind.

My own self-doubt was loud and clear, but I expected much more commentary—a feisty outburst from the first, maybe a spark of interest from the second, or some wry humor from the third. There was none of that. There was nothing.

Closing my eyes, I took a controlled breath in and focused on every sound: the slatted blinds clinking on the breeze, the water pipes humming in the walls, the pastel sheets creasing around me…Nothing else materialized, except the whine of a mosquito flying around my head. I swatted at it and huffed.

"Some still feeling sensitive over what happened earlier?" I didn't try to hide the bite in my tone. "Oh, you didn't actually leave—because that would be a miracle." Silence answered me, pressing in on my senses, louder, harsher than any auditory episode. I sat up abruptly. "Did you?"

I took my annoyance out on the duvet, flattening the fluffy barricade around me with dramatic strikes and puffs. The blue pendant settled at the base of my neck. Every fiber in my body lightened with its touch as if I'd drift up into the clouds. Not from nerves. Not from grief. From the opposite of it. Happiness?

No, happiness was a pipe dream. But this was pretty close.

I held on to the feeling, whatever it was, letting it lift me high above the seeds of worry, as I drifted off to sleep.

THE DARKNESS SWALLOWED everything. My quick breaths, my cries for help, the echo of my footsteps. Nothing, no one, escaped this black hole of a place that sucked all color, all life from existence.

A flash cut the void—a star born out of the nothingness. It pierced my vision with pulsing white blotches.

When those settled, I blinked, and faced a large white door.

Tentacles of light crept through its cracks, dancing over my face and downturned lips. Fighting my hesitation, with trembling fingers I grazed the lines of thin text carved into its frame, written in a language I didn't understand or recognize. I pressed a hand to the center of the door. It swung open.

I peeked through the opening at a forest.

Colossal redwoods guarded the woodland, so tall and broad they could be the children of Goliath. A stream divided the grove, the dense branches an awning over the lazy current like a vaulted church over its pews. With a glance back to the darkness affirming I had nowhere else to go, I crossed the threshold.

The sun kissed my cheeks, and an earthy scent tickled my nose. Before I had a chance to really take in the beauty of the forest, a film of fog wisped in, graying out the sky, turning the air harsh and rotten. My cheeks suddenly burned with an icy cold that singed the tiny hairs in my nostrils. The trees shuddered, a generous portion of their leaves drying to a crisp in piles at the bases of their trunks, as if all of winter had happened in a single moment. The stream went still, stagnant, its inhabitants flopping along the banks.

Death was here. And I brought it. Spread it with every breath.

I turned to go back, but the door had disappeared.

Something fluttered in my peripheral vision and a buzzing rang in my ears. A pesky gnat or a fly or a—sprite? The fairy creature flapped its iridescent wings before me, baring miniature fangs. Its empty, black eyes held no flicker of life, like they'd been molded from the void I'd just escaped.

With a cobalt flash, it flew into the trees, leaving me stunned—and determined to catch it. Fear and wits forgotten, I sprinted into the thick of the woods, but soon lost its glinting blue trail.

Every breath stung my lungs and my ego. I almost dropped to the ground until I noticed the lagoon, and the guy standing on the opposite shore.

My heart already thudded wildly but now it felt like it might burst.

Ryder.

He was dressed in his all-black ensemble, with his hood flipped off, and the floating fish circled his reflection like a garland of death. As I stared, his head snapped to me and he pointed at me with a bloody arrow, his irises so vibrant, like they had stripped the green from the foliage.

It took forever to find my voice. "What are you doing?!"

In answer, he stretched out his arm, readied his bow, and slowly drew back the string. Crimson stained his wrist. The smirk that had once made my knees buckle now twisted into a sinister grin.

"The end is nigh, River—the transfer of power has been completed." He released the words with an arrow, headed directly for my heart.

CHAPTER 7

I BOLTED UPRIGHT, CLUTCHING MY CHEST, CHOKING for air, my hands slick with sweat.

My mom's necklace lay atop my heart, hot on my skin, the heat radiating to my core. Instinctively, I tugged it away from my chest and it cooled against my fingertips.

No trace remained of the strange sensation except a red mark on my chest, and that soon faded into my overall flush. I dipped my head back so the fan above my bed cooled my temples and cheeks. Steph, Carissa, Kelly, all the greatest surf legends greeted me from the barrels of the biggest waves on the posters taped onto every spare inch of my ceiling.

Half-open drawers and messy furniture tops around me almost threw me into another fit of terror. I'd meant to clean my room days ago but…priorities, surfing being the main one. Now my clothing was piled on the carpet like a fabric tsunami had hit.

Shielding myself in a cocoon of cool percale bedding, I checked my watch. Six AM. I forced my eyes shut, but the sting of my throat thrust them open, raw from the nightmare or the circulating air. My fingers found my water bottle on the nightstand. Empty, of course.

Tossing the sheets aside, I slid my feet into my cozy fleece slippers and shuffled down the hall. Pots and pans clattered in the kitchen—my dad must be getting a head start, a *really* big head start, on his annual birthday tradition. I lifted my nose but didn't catch the waft of his famous paprika potatoes.

As I inched closer, something bit into my foot. I jerked back on instinct. A dirty fork lay in the middle of the hallway. Why was that there…? My thoughts trailed off as another glisten of silver caught my eye.

Scattered utensils littered the floor like shrapnel, leading to the checkerboard tile, which was splattered with food. My toes left the carpet and a spoon skimmed across the granite island. What the…?

Cupboards flew open, and the culprit wasn't my tall, ungraceful dad surprising me with anything. It was the cobalt sprite from my dream.

Hoping reality would come crashing down harder than the plates now striking the ground, I pinched the inside of my arm. I didn't wake; I didn't snap out of anything. My wide eyes darted around—because *this* was my reality.

The realization unrooted me and I started backing away. Slow, cautious. "OW!"

A piece of glass from a splintered baking dish tore my skin.

The sprite's head swiveled to face me, but its body stayed forward—some real exorcist shit. Keeping its distance, it hissed and bared its slimy fangs, black eyes swollen and lightless beneath a prominent hairless brow ridge.

Daybreak illuminated the creature's leathery skin; a sickly blue, stretched so tight over its bald head I could count the veins in its scalp. Its glittery undertones shimmered in the spotlight, reflecting off the surfaces like a disco ball. My breath caught in my throat as it raised the spikes on its spine and hissed. Snapping its neck into place, it shot out an open window, and the dawn beamed it up like an ET.

The silence set in quicker than the disbelief. Quiet, yet also deafening.

I stared at the wreckage, done by something born of nightmares—because that's what this was. No matter how hard I'd pinched myself to try and wake up, that's what this *had* to be.

A dream. A bad, bad dream.

Or…maybe it wasn't all in my head. Maybe I'd imagined the sprite, but then that meant *I* had made this mess. Maybe if I just picked an excuse my brain would stop churning, move on, and accept it.

A sting on my foot interrupted my panicked thoughts. My attention drifted to the tile and the small puddle of red that grew slowly beneath the soles of my feet.

Hobbling to the sink, I lifted myself onto the counter and put my toes under the faucet. A flare of pain shot through me as the water cleaned my minor wound. I picked the shards out of a callus, the glass clinking in the aluminum sink and somehow, at the same time, inside my skull. Crisp coastal air blew in through the window, brushing the curtains and raising the hairs on my arms.

With bated breath I waited for the Voices—I was sure

this'd be their moment. But the sounds of the water and the wind and the reel of anticipation became nothing more than what they were.

"Not so fast," I said aloud, hoping it'd induce a response. When it didn't, I closed my eyes, ground my molars, and tried to lasso the noises with my mind instead, focusing on the dips and pitches, grabbing at the *cracks* and *hums*. A whisper had to be just one frequency away—it always was.

Ah ha! I heard a voice, hushed and invoking.

"C'mon, c'mon, c'mon." False alarm. That was my own.

When I opened my eyes, lightheadedness hit me so fast I almost fell off the counter.

I managed to swing my legs out to keep that from happening and, once stable, rested my head against the side of a cabinet. I picked at my cuticles, flustered, tired, mostly desperate for some sort of explanation—it didn't even have to be a rational one. I just wanted to get their take on what was real or an illusion. But no one wanted to speak to me.

Ignoring the throb in my head and the hole in my foot, I began disposing of the evidence. I grabbed a bottle of bleach and a trash bag, and with yellow-gloved hands I cleared the debris from the floor. Tile by tile, the traces of my encounter with the sprite disappeared.

Now at least things *looked* normal. Without the chaos I went back to wondering if it was a hallucination or reality, and which one I'd be more okay with.

"River, what are you doing?"

A gasp slipped out of me at my dad's sudden presence. In the middle of cleaning, I hadn't heard him come in.

Caught yellow-handed, I fumbled with my words. "Um, giving the kitchen a deep clean?"

"This early? On your birthday?" He crossed his arms. "I thought you'd sleep in. I was going to make breakfast burritos."

I clasped my hands. "As a token of my appreciation, you have a perfectly clean prep station." My smile was so fake my lips felt like they'd split.

He eyed me, a bit suspicious. "Well, since you're up… help me chop these." He threw me two bell peppers and opened the fridge, mumbling, "That's weird, I could have sworn we had half an onion in here…"

I, perhaps a little too eagerly, accepted his offer as sous. Dicing the veggies as slowly and purposefully as possible was a good diversion from his comments on the messy state of the fridge and the garlic that also seemed to have disappeared.

Soon the smoke from burnt sausage and the sizzle of bacon filled our cozy galley. It snuffed out my dad's lingering wariness, watered our eyes, and made both our stomachs rumble.

As my dad measured coffee grounds, I sat down at the table and packed my tortilla with eggs. Hurried footsteps struck the stairs—at least this intruder used the front door.

Javi's eyes glinted with hunger. "Ah, just in time." And at least he was human.

It should have made me smile, but all I could think about as he waltzed in and sat down, flipping those black wavy strands out of his eyes as he filled up a plate, was that it might be the last time he interrupted a birthday breakfast.

Because who knew what next year at college would bring and if he'd find himself preferring to stay in Santa Barbara instead of coming home for the summer, for my birthday.

Even though I didn't want to dwell on that, my frown stayed put as I teased him. "Great timing, Jav. The hard work's over and the feast is about to begin."

"Perks of being the guest of honor." His wink combatted my eye roll as my elbow landed on a rogue potato that had rolled off his over-stuffed plate.

I peeled its mushed interior off my skin and threw it at his forehead.

"Bullseye," he said mid-chomp. That got a stifled laugh out of me.

Gobbling up a cheesy bite, he leaned in and whispered, "You okay this morning? You seemed a little tense when I walked in. Is it what happened with Chet yesterday?"

I chewed a bit more aggressively at the sound of that d-bag's name. That's not what bothered me, but I didn't have the guts to say what did: *It's not Chet—it's you.* And it stirred something in me to see him walk in like he owned the place. I hadn't realized how much I was going to miss it.

So, I deflected. "No, I just…I had the weirdest dream last night." A cold shiver worked its way through me as I envisioned the fairy-sprite-creature thing's bald head rotating almost full circle. I eyed the other side of the kitchen as the teakettle whistled, and my dad poured the hot water into his French press. "You know when you wake up and it feels like you're still in it—like you're in some sort of illusion?"

Javi held up his fork, wiggling it to his words. "Ah, lucid dreaming?"

"Hmm. No."

"Sleepwalking?"

"No."

"Still half-asleep?"

"Maybe I was." I shook my head. "I mean…I woke up to a blue sprite the size of a crow, raiding my kitchen, after all."

He snorted, and I swore a droplet of orange juice spewed out of his nostrils. "River, you kill me sometimes."

"Yeah…" Hadn't meant for that to be a knee-slapper. "Pretty wild."

"Surf report looks good today," my dad announced as he joined us at the table, tendrils of steam wafting from his mug. The caramel streaks in his hair glinted in the light as it curtained his forehead and he dove into his food, too. "You guys want to head to the Point after this?"

Our chipmunk cheeks stopped any verbal answer. Javi nodded and I gave a thumbs up.

"Great. I might need to leave early to work on my syllabus—classes begin next week." My dad turned to me with a look of sympathy. "When does summer school start for you again, Riv?"

"Monday." I bowed my head in dismay.

"What about you, Javi? When does school start?"

Javi spread his arms wide, as if they were wings. "I'm a free bird till September."

This subtle reminder of his imminent departure hit me

square in the heart. I tried to let it slide; I knew he hadn't meant to irk me. "Lucky you," I muttered.

The grief dug deeper, churning in my gut, bunching in my shoulders.

My dad shot me a look. "You should be happy you still got to participate in graduation, Riv." Oh, here came the parental lecture I'd sorely missed. "And that they're letting you retake economics at the City College over summer."

"Only cause the high school isn't offering it," I mumbled into my burrito.

Javi spun his torso towards me. "Look at it this way, you can check out the campus ahead of fall semester, get a feel for where everything is. That's what my sister and I did." I'd already heard this story, but the way he lit up when he talked about college…I let him tell it anyway. "Her roommate at Berkeley's from SB, so she got to introduce me to some people she knew there, too. Now I won't be going in totally clueless."

I forced air out my nose as I tried to keep my irritation in. I really didn't want to hear a "bright side" right now. A serving of cold, hard truth would go down much better.

I failed a class. Now I had to repeat it. Just to get my high school diploma—a piece of paper that had come so fucking easy for the rest of my class. With their golden tickets and the next four years mapped out at the school of their choice.

I wanted to be happy for him, wanted to plan out my visits, wanted to flip through the brochure and learn all about the life that awaited him. Javi was going to break out of the bubble, something we'd always dreamed of, but still.

The only thing I could muster right now was a glare,

especially when he said, "Maybe you'll meet some new people, too."

"Easier said than done." It came out harsher than intended, but my insecurities had entered the chat. If it were that effortless, I wouldn't be mourning the loss of my best friend before he even left. Because most people, whether he believed it or not, weren't drawn to people like me. How could he not know that? How could he not see what a unicorn he was?

My fingers replaced my food, every nail I spat out a visual score of my stress. A prick of blood dripped from my pointer's cuticle. I wrapped it in my oversized Nirvana tee as a makeshift tourniquet and loosed an exhale, forcing my shoulders to release some tension.

I shouldn't be blaming Javi for my lack of friends—I should be blaming the Voices. They ruined my social life just like my senior year, growing more and more restless over the past few months like they had some divine version of senioritis. Concentrating had become a mere art form—it's a miracle I passed anything with them around.

Almost as miraculous as this permeating silence of theirs.

The soft pings of intuition that'd been trying to get my attention finally broke through— the Voices hadn't just been threatening to leave during our fight at Grad Night. *They actually did.*

My spiral must have been written all over my face because Javi changed the topic. "Hey, Corbs, what's the worst that can happen at college if I decide to surf instead of going to class?"

"Is that a trick question?" My dad's laugh lines went slack, and I could tell a little part of his teaching heart died at the thought of giving Javi advice on how to ditch.

For the first time that morning, I felt an upward tug on my lips. I answered on my dad's behalf, "The opportunity cost is missing the lecture. Attendance doesn't actually count, and you could easily get the notes from someone else. I say when the surf's up, go for it."

Javi's grin was worth my dad's frown.

Now *those* were some economics I'd ace.

I CLUTCHED THE frame, marveling at the picture inside of it. "Javi, when did you even have time to develop this?" Despite rinsing off, I still had remnants of sand stuck to the undersides of my ankles. I brushed them off with my feet, the tiny pieces of grit dispersing into my living room's shaggy carpet.

"I snuck away after the first hour of surfing," he answered, his chin grazing my shoulder.

I grinned, my muscles tingling as I replayed the best day in my head. For three plus hours after our breakfast burritos, I had sparred with the ocean, chasing the wipeouts just as much as the waves.

Surfing was so addicting.

When he'd disappeared from the lineup, I figured he was chilling at the lighthouse, where we always met. But the texts I read, after I got out, said he was passing on post-surf tacos to run a couple errands and promised to meet up with me later. When he'd really been developing *this*.

"I love this one." His breath caressed my ear. "It looks like you have wings."

The corners of the driftwood frame indented my fingers as I studied the picture within it, one he'd snapped only yesterday. It was a photo of me, fresh out of the water—but he'd captured the moment so well I smelled the brine of the air, felt the rays on my skin, saw the arched shadows splaying from my back. Like wings. It was a beautiful trick of the light that met the angle of the surfboard I'd been balancing on my head.

"Thank you. I love it."

"Please, Riv—" It came out hitched, like his words were getting away from him. "Don't forget me while I'm gone."

I snorted, even though I couldn't seem to get the proper air behind it, like I was catching some of that breathlessness. "I should be telling *you* that, Jav. I'll just be here." Leaning against the central breakfast counter, I gave a mocking salute to my connected living room/kitchen that we stood in. "Not as sexy as UCSB. But hey, at least you know where to find me."

My response tethered whatever hovered on his lips, and instead, he gave me a peck on the cheek. An unspoken promise he wouldn't forget.

Heat bloomed from the touch and swept over my face, and I hooked his pinky with mine. "You can't get rid of me that easily."

"I'd never think about trying." His grip shook with his voice.

I'm not sure how long we looped pinkies like that, but I wasn't going to be the first one to let go, and I don't think he wanted to, either.

CHAPTER 8

A SPRITE WOULD HAVE COME IN HANDY THAT MORN-ing, considering my alarm never went off.

Without any possibly hallucinated creatures destroying the kitchen loud enough to wake me up at the crack of dawn, I slept way too late. Now I sprinted up the stairs to the City College, praying for no pit stains in my cropped striped crew neck, as I jumped over the eroded steps.

The humidity smeared my Chapstick, and the shorter layers of hair that framed my face tangled in my mouth. When I got to the top of the staircase, I pulled up the map to find the best route to class and picked a path that seemed to go in the direction I needed to be heading.

I entered a gray-slatted building, my hurried footsteps echoing through the empty hall, curious glances and my feverish reflection staring back at me from the tiny windows in the classrooms' doors I swept past. Behind the Plexiglass, labs with white coats and microscopes made it clear this was not where I was supposed to be.

Cool, cool, cool. I'd just continue to wander around aimlessly and miss my first day, no big deal.

Pavement replaced the linoleum as I exited out into a

shady courtyard. Concrete benches arranged in a half-moon lined the perimeter, backed by trellises of morning glory flowers. It would have been a peaceful place to study if it wasn't enveloped by a cloud of smoke.

Its current patrons crowded in front of the exit path, their stream of laugher and swearing stifled by coughing and hocking loogies—one landing near my shoe. Ew.

Cringing a bit, I glanced around the courtyard for an alternative route or a map because the one on my phone was hardly legible when I zoomed in. Going back the way I came would just put me in circles. Ugh, I should've listened to Javi and toured the campus before my first day… My hands balled into fists. That was it, I was going to have to grow a spine and cut through the smokers, even if they looked like they'd bite.

A guy turned away from the group and blew a plume right in my face. It watered my eyes and tickled my nose. I bit back a cough, but it was too late, and one came bursting out of me. As my palm covered my mouth, the others turned to look.

Ten. Ten older guys and girls stared back. All of them dressed the same—greasers, but with a James Dean edge—abundantly pierced, tattooed, wearing band t-shirts, hair slicked into messy comb-overs that made anyone want to run their fingers through it.

All eyes were on me as I took a deep breath. "Excuse me—hi—is the seven hundred building that way?"

One guy responded with an endearing burp, while the girl next to him brought a fist to her lips, her striking blue eyes squinting from trying to withhold her laughter. The rest gaped at me as if I just told them punk rock was dead. The way my cheeks flushed, I felt like I might've. Standing on the outskirts shifting between tippy-toes did not send off the vibe of confidence I needed.

Before I changed my mind, I beelined through the group, not daring to lift my head any higher than the knee holes in their jeans. They parted for me only a second before I'd plow into them. One person was a little too slow—my toe caught their half-laced boot, and I dove headfirst into the concrete.

I ate more of that fall than my own birthday cake.

For a moment, the shock kept me from moving—kept me from feeling anything. Slow as an earthworm, I crawled to my feet, resisting the urge to cry or scream as embarrassment flooded me. I'd be surprised if the welt protruding on my forehead didn't spell out the word *loser*.

Common sense yelled, *Get lost!* while impulse thought, *How bad?* The smart thing to do would be to leave and not look, but of course I did the opposite and stole a quick glance, because I was sure they were just dying to know I was okay…

They weren't. Their dismissive stares pierced me like laser beams. Someone scoffed.

"I'm good!" I threw my hands up to prove it. Not that they were asking or cared.

Eager to split, I almost tripped over another pair of Doc Martens as I scampered away.

For those few mortifying seconds, I forgot why I'd been

running in the first place, then the light bounced off a plastic room number plaque. I was still scrambling, but at least it was in the right direction.

Finally, I found it: 707. The door to my class practically glowed.

My plan? Slip in, take a seat in the back row—after all, this was college. Chances were the teacher wouldn't even notice. Beaming with giddiness, I reached for the handle. What could be worse than the humiliation I just endured?

A classroom filled to the brim. Students taking tests. Everyone looking up at me in silence from their desks.

That's what.

The wiry, grayed professor tilted his silver spectacles, observing me through agitated blinks. His scorn destroyed my short-lived joy at finding the classroom, replacing it with the hot shame I thought I'd escaped.

Sorry, I mouthed, narrowly avoiding the school-style booby traps in the aisle: backpacks and pen caps and outstretched ankles—my own almost hooking on a skinny metal desk leg. I followed the professor's finger, fighting the urge to give him one of my own, to the single empty seat. Settling into his direct line of fire, I realized why it hadn't been taken yet: it was front row, dead center.

He gestured to the engraved tumbler he held. *MR. HESS.* Then with his free hand, flashed me four fingers, followed by five. *Forty-five minutes,* I assumed.

Would the entire semester be taught in mime?

Nodding in acknowledgement, I took out my calculator and opened the pop quiz on my desk, the smallest motions met with passive-aggressive throat clearing. At this rate, I was on track to get kicked out for breathing, so asking to use the bathroom was definitely an offense.

After skimming the questions, centered on stats (which I assumed was to make sure we understood the basic fundamentals of econ) I returned to the first problem: *Create a value table then graph the result.* Easy.

My brain went as blank as the whiteboard.

Pencils scratched around me. Mine hovered above the paper. An eraser tapped, and my foot moved with it. Numerical signs spotted my vision—looking at economics equations had the same effect as staring at the sun. In my mind I knew the Voices wouldn't come, but my body still tensed and flinched at the tiniest noise as if they'd show any minute. I must've wasted fifteen just untangling my senses to find some sort of groove.

True to his word, Mr. Hess's alarm rang not a second past the allotted time. I plugged in the remaining coordinates, barely having enough time to finish writing my name at the top before a mottled hand ripped the booklet out from under my pencil tip.

"Time is u*p*, Miss Harlow." I'd honestly have been happier if he taught in mime, then I wouldn't have had to contort my upper body to avoid the spit from his dramatic over pronunciations.

He addressed the class. "We'll break for ten and go over the answers when you come back." No one flinched. "Or we could start now and fit in a review of supply and demand?"

Despite the sarcasm, I was sure he'd be more than happy to oblige. Everyone seemed to feel the same, our chairs skidding against the floor as we jolted from our seats.

"And if you're smart, you'll be back by the ninth minute!" he called after us as he went to lean against the front of his desk. "Um, Miss Harlow? Where do you think you're going?"

I careened to a stop. The remaining students filed around me into the great outdoors—or the quad. Hey, it was better than nothing.

"Are you forgetting? You already had your break this morning when you were seventeen minutes late to my class." He stroked his goatee. "You'll be staying and reading the syllabus."

Sunshine slipped in as the last student left, teasing me with its warmth. The door clicked shut, taking the buttery rays with it. I scowled at the flickering frosted lights above my head.

"Yes, Professor." I sat back down, letting out an exasperated sigh.

Mr. Hess stared at me with a tight-lipped smile. Condescending ass.

I lowered my head and pretended to read, flipping the pages every now and then for emphasis. It satisfied him enough that he finally left his post to write the next part of the lesson on the whiteboard, and I went back to my not-reading.

When the door opened, my ears perked up, and I shot a glance over my shoulder. A guy with a fade and matching slit through his eyebrow crossed the threshold, carrying a disposable cup. Steam billowed from the lidless top—there must be a café close by. Dimples punctured his cheeks as he held in a smile, making me keenly aware of my own expression, which had slipped into a frown. It took too much effort to correct my resting bitch face, so even though I wasn't mad, it stayed.

A slender redhead wearing a fringe vest and rose-tinted glasses, with a fresh daisy tucked behind her ear, strode in behind him. I bet she took a lap around the community garden—I had thought I saw tops of sunflowers during my mad dash through campus.

A pair holding hands came next, lips swollen, clearly fresh out of a make-out sesh. One of the girls popped her collar to conceal a reddish mark stamped onto her neck.

My fingers drifted to the same area on my body, tracing the spot Javi had nuzzled into during Grad Night after wishing me a happy birthday. I shivered, banishing the memory from ever resurfacing again. That was fine, because an image of Ryder replaced him, lips suctioning the sensitive skin below my earlobe. Oh my God. No. No…One wasn't right, I needed two for this job, one on each side of me. Javi reappeared and trailed simultaneous kisses…I shook my head and the fantasy dispersed just as Mr. Hess cleared his throat to bring order to an already orderly class.

My faced burned. There couldn't be a more inappropriate time for either of them to pop into my thoughts like that. Intercepts. Origins. Numbers. Numbers. Numbers. I reached for the boring, formulaic, and *not sexy at all* to quiet the pent-up lust twirling in my gut.

Beet red, I slunk lower in my chair and wrapped my arms around my stomach, as if that could contain my questionable urges.

I never did get past that first sentence of the syllabus

before the monotonous voice of Mr. Hess interrupted my daydream. Well, if I needed a buzzkill, that right there did the trick. At least his droning was good for something.

WHEN TWELVE O'CLOCK hit, I wasted no time, just up and walked out.

Mr. Hess's final words faltered on his lips as the rest of the class joined me in leaving, his glare trailing me until I reached the sanctuary of the courtyard.

Taking a moment, I slipped on my headphones. A balmy breeze tickled my bare skin and parted my hair, the fresh air fanning the nape of my neck. The temperature must have risen to at least ninety degrees during that four-hour lockdown, and sweat was already dotting my inner elbows and knees. I'd love nothing more than to ditch the rest of the afternoon and post up in the heat with Javi, but as my luck—or lack of it—would have it, duty called me elsewhere. Work.

Nothing sounded worse than whipping up frappes at Kona Koffee. Ugh, I wanted to be a *customer*, enjoying the day, the one ordering a complicated drink. As if on cue, Javi texted me his sympathies with a selfie on the beach.

Damn him.

And to damn me even more, the ocean never left my field of view as I trudged towards the street, sparkling blue peeking out around corners of buildings and massive oak trees.

The bus pulled to the curb as soon as I got there, hissing

as the brakes engaged and the doors squeaked open, revealing a compartment full of people packed like sardines.

I groaned at the idea of elbowing through the crowd just to spend the next twenty minutes standing, and swaying, and trying not to fall—especially on top of somebody.

But if I didn't catch this one, I'd be late for my shift.

After tapping my metro card, I hopped onto the lowered platform, the automated swish of the door causing me to leap into the person in front of me. Spotting an inch of free upper railing, I grabbed it and hung on for dear life as we barreled down Soquel Drive.

The molting eucalyptus trees struck the roof like a summer storm, leaves collecting in puddles near the gutters that departing passengers jumped to avoid. As the steady traffic merged to go around us, twinges of jealousy curled my toes with every roof-racked surfboard that went by.

Closer to the city center, the hints of nature thinned out, replaced by streetlamps plastered in stickers reminding people to "Keep Santa Cruz Weird." Art murals covered sidewalk power boxes with whales, starfish, and seals. A man strolled beneath the shade of his pink umbrella, outfitted with matching pants and a feather boa.

A gaggle of tourists huddled at the crosswalk, squealing in excitement as they waited for the electronic signal to flash their cue. A figure stood apart—still as a shadow, their face shielded by a hoodie layered beneath their leather jacket, indifferent to the animated gestures of the crowd around them, even after getting bumped into multiple times. I was in a t-shirt that barely covered my shoulders, and I was sweating. They must have been hot as hell.

My stomach lurched. Not with the bus, but at the thought of those forest green eyes that'd swept over every inch of me like a tide the other night.

I craned my neck as the bus bounded forward, hoping to catch a glimpse, until my upper body leaned so far into the aisle the lady across from me gave a very scornful *ahem*. As I shifted back into place, the stranger flipped off their hood and an audible breath escaped me, like both of my lungs had been torn from my body.

Just another guy, wearing all black, walking around downtown.

The air stung my throat when I finally remembered to inhale. I'd met Ryder once; there was no way I'd just start seeing him all over town. In fact, I'd probably never run into him again. And I didn't need to. Didn't *want* to. I turned the volume higher on my alt rock playlist to drown out the restless beat of my heart—which worked so well I almost missed my stop. I paused the song long enough to catch the final call, and with jelly knees hopped off just in time.

Keeping a low profile, I whisked through the entrance of Kona Koffee. Espresso grinders, business conversations, and feverish typing adding a soundtrack outside my headphones.

Someone unrecognizable measured coffee grounds, poorly, spilling the grainy residue all over the granite counter. Even though her back was to me, something about her ear gauges and the checkered ruby flannel tied around her waist seemed familiar.

She flipped a stained rag over her shoulder, ran a hand

over the slick hair that crowned her bronde undercut, and spun to face the register.

"Ah, River. Meet your new co-worker, Shanley." The store manager, Tom, emerged from out of nowhere. He had a habit of lurking in the background and sneaking up on his employees, trying to catch them in fireable offenses. Great use of time. "You'll be training her today."

The rubber mat I stood on became a glue trap, freezing me in front the Order Here sign, as I stared at the girl who happened to have witnessed my humiliating courtyard performance—starring one. Icy blue eyes swept me up and down, a flash of recognition, and pity, lighting up her heart-shaped face. I wanted to die or hide in a hole.

But I was at work, so I could do neither.

CHAPTER 9

I CHANNELED COOL, CALM, COLLECTED, BUT INSTEAD of being any, blurted out, "You work here?"

Shanley's ringed lips spread in a smile across a dramatic jawline. "I could ask the same."

"Yeah. Sorry." I cringed after I said it, not actually meaning to apologize.

"No need to be sorry. Nice to meet you." Her palm, dry as sandpaper, shook mine. She gripped lightly, handling me like I was a porcelain doll, but she was capable of breaking me in one squeeze if she wanted.

"It's nice to meet you, too." As we let go, I noticed a faint set of scars notched on her knuckles.

"Well, isn't this sweet. I don't think our customers were anticipating coffee and a show." Tom harrumphed and tapped his foot, obviously annoyed at not being the dominant force in the room. Which was a joke next to Shanley's easy confidence and the canines she flashed in a grin—he practically shriveled in her presence. Still, he bit out, "Perhaps you can move this lovefest behind the counter so we can address the line out the door?"

I turned to him, already expecting the infamous lip quiver. About a five on the scale of combustion. Not life-threatening for me yet.

Frickin' Tom. His unhappiness roiled inside him until it permanently set like the yolk of a hard-boiled egg. Fitting, considering the shape of his head. I had to say, I enjoyed poking cracks in his shell.

Nevertheless, I jumped into the line of duty even though Tom was exaggerating and there were only two people waiting. Shanley joined me in greeting customers, repeating the script with a forced smile: *welcome, what can we get you, what can we get you, what can we get you.*

When our faces and voices no longer contradicted our lack of enthusiasm—about one hundred drinks later, it felt like, I muttered, "It gets old pretty fast." I handed her a portafilter full of compacted grounds. "Do you want to brew the espresso? I'll steam the soy milk."

With a gleam of amusement, she twisted the spoon-looking device into the machine and pressed the double shot button as I held the bottom of the stainless-steel pitcher under the steam wand.

Right. "It's not rocket science, huh? Ow!" It wasn't the best moment for me to nearly burn the skin off my fingers. They screamed in red-hot pain.

"Are you okay!?" Shanley's smirk turned to concern, and she turned the dial on the steam wand to off.

I waved my scorched hand. "Let that be a lesson in what *not* to do. Always hold the pitcher by the handle when steaming anything."

Despite the pain and embarrassment flushing my neck, I let out a laugh. Shanley laughed with me as she turned on the faucet and guided me towards it.

"Put your fingers under here. I got the next order." I flinched as the water rushed against my tender skin, until the velvety stream eased the swelling and the heat no longer radiated to my wrist.

Tom Boiled Egg glowered in my periphery. I was surprised he hadn't jumped at the chance to correct me, which in his mind was more useful than helping make drinks. He shoved a box of rolled gauze at me. "It's better now. Quit slacking and get back to work."

Fighting every impulse to roll my eyes, I wrapped my hand in the clingy fabric as he bellowed something about the deterioration of the community's youth. I'd rather burn my other hand than listen to his griping, its shrillness reaching decibels the Voices hadn't even mastered. By the time the Open sign finally flickered off he *still* hadn't stopped nagging.

The closing checklist hung beneath the soft glow of a wall lamp, lit like a shrine, the laminated list of procedures about as long as my econ syllabus. A warm feeling of contentment curled up inside me at the thought of restocking chai.

It wasn't every person's fantasy to be saddled with the grunt work while their boss left them high and dry, but if it meant we no longer had to share the vicinity with him, then bring on the inventory.

Like clockwork, Tom Boiled Egg resigned for the evening.

"Unfortunately, I have to leave," he announced, not even trying to suppress his victorious smile. "Shanley, River will show you how to close. Training can be overwhelming, so if she's too slow or not explaining things, refer to the handbook. You seem to pick things up easily."

Nice burn, Tom. My forehead scrunched at the flagrant dig. It wasn't new, this failure to believe I possessed the capacity to teach anyone anything. He'd held on to this mantra since the day I started when I had an episode twenty minutes into my shift.

Do you have a disease? he'd asked, wrinkling his nose in disgust. He'd probably wanted to fire me on the spot, but I'm sure some sort of legal implication stopped him. It was bullshit. I tossed the metal frother I was shining in the sink, hoping its resounding *clink* made it very clear I had heard him.

"I'm sure she can handle it." Shanley's retort was the epitome of untroubled coolness, just like how I'd wanted to sound earlier.

I downplayed the excitement that upturned my lips and stole a glance at The Egg. A vein popped above his eyebrow. His shell flushed red.

"Uh—I—are you sure?" His programming must not include a reaction for this failed attempt at alpha bonding.

"For sure. River's a rock star." In egregious defiance, Shanley gave me a wink.

My cheeks lifted in response thanks to my knightess in shining flannel, taking a stand against this workplace monster.

With his anger smoldering from the inside out, Tom's

human characteristics melted away until he resembled nothing more than a mass of cringing bones. He was so tightly wound his fists lost their color, the tendons in his neck protruded, and his pupils flared with devoted hatred.

Not at Shanley; it was all directed at me: the subordinate forever ruining his mood.

"Okay then," he managed to choke out. Tom Boiled Egg paused at the exit, his final grimace an omen of what to expect at my next shift.

"Piss off," Shanley said under her breath as he slipped into the night. The second he disappeared from view, she threw off her apron and hopped onto the counter, the ripped knees of her jeans baring more skin as her legs dangled over the edge. A growl thrummed in her throat as she rolled her head, relieving the tension from taking hours of drink orders.

I flicked my eyes between my coworker's colorfully muraled arms and the store's entry, wanting to kick off my shoes and join her—but the last thing I needed was another reason for Tom to yell at me, and we had way too much side work to do.

"Is he that out of touch?" Shanley asked, no longer cracking the joints in her neck.

"Yep." I grabbed a rag and idly wiped at the water marks, waiting for him to barge back in.

"How do you do it? How do you deal with him?" Her arched brows rose higher.

I shrugged. "It's part of the job."

"You can stop monitoring the door. He's not coming back." The finality of her tone had me believing her, whether it was true or not. My shoulders started to unroll when a jingle from the entrance had me standing straight up again.

Tom—or worse, one of those people that demanded service after we'd closed.

My head whipped in their direction. As I took in their ebony hair, the way it curled over their forehead, the bounce to it matching their steps, and the sparkle in their brown eyes—which seemed to burn brighter as they locked with mine—my horror dissolved completely.

Javi slowed his pace as he reached the grab-n-go display. "Don't kill me."

The air I'd been holding in left me in one long, relieved sigh, deflating my upper body. "I was literally just thinking, *the audacity.*"

His laugh was one that crinkled his eyes and his nose, so infectious I couldn't stop myself from smiling, too. "I'm not here as an asshole customer—you've got enough of those." Plopping a clear plastic bag on the counter filled with pink-and-green sugary snacks, he added, "I've come bearing gifts."

Watermelon candy. I salivated instantly. "What is this for?"

"A little something to sweeten your first day of summer school." He shrugged, like it was no big deal he was constantly going out of his way to be a decent human, when the world clearly didn't have enough of those.

"Thank you." I examined the goods and reached in, offering one to him. "Mmm…Take one now, because I'm definitely going to devour this entire bag tonight."

The slight dimple on his chin deepened the wider he grinned. "That's the spirit."

I felt another gaze on me, outside of Javi's, as I took down a second handful. "Oh!" I spun towards my coworker, whose cheeks were tight as if she'd eaten something sweet or sour. "Javi, this is Shanley."

"Hey," she chirped, lips falling into a smile way too easily.

"Hey," he repeated, dragging his fingers through the waves of his hair to get the strands out of his eyes. "I know you guys are closing. Just came to drop that off."

Shanley waved a hand. "No worries, man. Stay as long as you want."

"Ah, I got to get going anyways." Before he reached the door, he turned on the heels of his black high tops, the same ones I wore, to pause and raise a brow at me. "See you to-morrow?"

"Yep." The word came out muffled as I covered my mouth and chewed what remained of my gummy.

He slipped out the way he came with a flash of teeth in acknowledgment, the wheels of his skateboard rum-bling against the pavement like distant thunder in the night. Picking at the last pieces of candy, I let myself slouch against the counter and cross my arms. A yawn slipped past my lips.

"Tired?" Shanley jumped down from her perch and fired up the espresso machine. "You know, we do work at a coffee shop."

"Yeah, thanks." A bigger yawn this time.

"That your boyfriend?"

I almost choked on a mini watermelon. "No," I spat between coughs, "No. Definitely not. Javi's my friend. My best friend."

"Your *best friend* went out of his way to come to your work and bring you your favorite candy?" The frother dampened her voice, but the insinuation was louder than the whistle of the steam.

I threw up my arms. "He was probably in the neighborhood!"

"Okay." I caught a stilted laugh as she blew out the word and passed me a fresh almond milk latte. "So, what classes are you taking at CC?"

With everything that had happened since I'd started my shift, I completely forgot we'd crossed paths earlier. Well, more like *I* crossed *her* path when I ate it in front of her and all of her friends.

"Econ 101." I blew on the piping-hot liquid and took a tentative sip, ready to move on from the topic of me and Javi. I knew what we were, and maybe it was complicated, but I didn't need anyone else telling me so. "Good milk-to-espresso ratio. Frothy. Not bad, Shanley." I raised my drink in cheers.

She grabbed an empty cup, clinking it against mine. Then her brows drew together. "Wait, you're taking economics on purpose!?"

My cheeks burned. "I have to. In order to graduate. High school," I added.

"Hey." She shrugged. "You're way smarter than me. I don't think I ever got as high as geometry. Well, I definitely got high, but not in class."

My forced laugh could've cut glass. "Spare me the sympathy jokes."

I knew what I was. Diploma-less. A sham. Pathetic.

Maybe it was the openness of Shanley's stance or the nonthreatening crook of her smile. I knew that she saw right past my bark but took the hint.

Shanley sidestepped the subject, and me, as she crossed the floor, took the checklist off its hook, and twirled it around her finger. "Alright, which one of us is cleaning the bathroom?"

"I will." A moment of solitude, even amongst dirty toilets, didn't sound so bad.

"No, I'm kidding. I'll do it." Then in a stage whisper, she added, "There's poop in there."

I snickered. "Tom must have laid an egg."

"What did you say?" Shanley's eyes widened. Her lips remained parted, like the thoughts were there, but she was stuck on how to convey them.

Forgetting this inside joke was very much inside my own head, I couldn't tell if her feral stare meant she was offended—or impressed. After a moment her wildness faded into a peculiar grin, and a few short yips turned into an uncontainable howl of laughter.

Whether it came from a place of relief or insanity, I jumped in, filling her in on my petty nickname for him, until we were both so consumed with laughter that we clutched our stomachs for air.

"Tom Boiled Egg! That's great." Shanley wiped her eyes and headed for the restroom.

After the giggles ran their course and my face ached

from smiling so hard, I tried to focus on inventory, but my mind drifted elsewhere. It'd been four full days without the Voices, and while the world was much more manageable without them—predictable, coherent—it also felt like it was missing an element or a color.

I couldn't decide if that was a good thing or not.

Sure, I'd made a few more friends in their absence, if that's what you'd call Ryder and Shanley. I held a bag of Sumatran dark roast in one hand (earthy, wild, bitter) and a Costa Rican light roast in the other (sweet, easy, mildly acidic), weighing them alongside my new friendships.

"If we inhale any more of these chemicals we're going to turn into zombies." Shanley's voice scattered my thoughts as her oversized gloves landed in the bin next to me. "I'm also late for a show. What do you say we roll, girl?"

As I went to reference the checklist, she stole it from my hands and threw it in the trash. Clipboard and all. "We're done with this."

This time *my* reaction stalled. Unlike me, she wasn't bothered by how her actions might or might not be interpreted. She was bold, whether people liked it or not. And Tom would definitely *not* like what he saw.

As hard as I tried, my eyes couldn't resist a sweep of the coffee grounds beneath the appliances, the still-soapy kitchen gadgets, the empty napkin container.

For anyone but Tom our cleaning might've not been a big deal. Then again, what's one more infraction for the girl who already topped his shit list?

"Screw it." I tossed in the towel, the yellow microfiber soaring into the laundry cart.

The flash of Shanley's teeth gave me the approval I needed to carry out my rebellion against the eggheaded overlord.
I grabbed my backpack from the office and switched off
all the lights, ignoring the smudges on the pastry case as I
threw on my corduroy drop-sleeve.

Faint stripes of light fell in zigzags over the laminate
from the headlights of passing cars. They doubled Shanley's
shadow, making her appear broader than the doorframe
she waited in front of. I followed her *after you* motion out
into the courtyard, illuminated by the waxing moon. Heat
steamed from the gutters, grunts came from shady corners,
and stores lay abandoned for the night.

"I'm going this way." Shanley gestured towards the
grouping of nightclubs at the opposite end of the street.
"Keep standing up for yourself, River. Mutiny suits you."

"Any time you want to schedule an uprising, just holler," I said as we parted ways.

"Let's make it easy and arrange it now," she called, walking backwards to face me. "Say same time, same place? Er,
uh, next shift?"

"You got it!" I yelled before she disappeared behind a
neighboring bakery.

Smiling to myself, I turned the opposite way, taking the
alley of graffiti behind Kona Koffee, a charming passage of
dumpsters that flanked the pee-soaked wall.

The construction site on my other side hadn't seemed
threatening when I came to clock in. But this late, devoid
of workers in their orange safety vests, it was nothing but a
crater of darkness. I picked up the pace and swung my backpack around, my breath clouding in front of me. Strange,

because it was the peak of summer, and although there'd been a chill in the air, I hadn't exactly needed a parka when I'd left Kona Koffee. Now the cold curled my fingers, so numb I couldn't pinch them together to unzip the front pocket and grab my headphones.

I choked on an icy inhale, as if the rising steam from the gutters had wrapped around my throat, trapping the air. My gut somersaulted, turning tight and acidic, as a whisper on the wind tickled the thousands of nerves in my ear. I groaned through strained teeth as the patter of tiny paws scraped the worn asphalt, fleeing a presence that couldn't be seen—the goosebumps on my skin feeling more like dozens of rat claws climbing all over me.

That idea seemed to take hold, causing me to low-key panic: I wiped my arms, my neck, my legs—but my hands didn't brush against anything furry, nothing fell off me and scurried into the crevices, despite the squeaks and scrapes growing steadily. My spine curled as water droplets trickled out of drainpipes and burst against the asphalt, reverberating inside my skull.

I cursed all the innocent little noises that made the night so lovely and intriguing—my eardrums on the verge of bursting at the shout of my own voice. Soon, there was nothing but a vortex of sound all around me.

And that could only mean one thing.

CHAPTER 10

ONE, TWO... I SENSED TWO VOICES OUT OF THE three.

Sensed, not heard, because they were barely audible, as if they couldn't break through the normal static of the universe to reach me. Meeting it head-on—that deep-rooted fear I'd fought so hard to ignore—turned my blood to stone. Something wasn't just off. Something was wrong.

Every inch of me froze, including my lungs.

A desperate cry gurgled in the trickles of a drainpipe, loud and unsteady, like someone was applying pressure to my ears, on and off. A forlorn wail slipped through the incessant yowls of a prowling feline, so rough and unbearable that every hiss and whine curdled my blood.

I parsed through all the noises, praying their choppy wavelengths would yield *something* I could read. But they just built and split and sputtered, exhausting my concentration, as I hyper-analyzed every little variation of sound.

The outside world fluctuated in and out the harder I tried to focus. My legs folded under me, and as everything grew louder, oppressive, unending, I curled into a fetal position, clutching the sides of my head in the middle of the alley.

I lay flat against the ground, hiding from the sound-storm like it was violent, whirling, desert sand—hoping to meet the Voices, *dying* to hear them reaching out for me, as I was for them—when a human-shaped glowing apparition flickered through tears that had started to form. It billowed against the night with a rhythmic crackle that shushed everything else around me.

In the silence, I mustered the strength to stand. The alley and the darkness swirled around me as I took a step towards the figure, my foot thudding into the asphalt, heavy as an anchor dropping into the ocean. Feeling like the slightest wind would knock me over, I tried to blink through the dizziness and balance myself by clenching every tooth and bone. But before I had a chance to try to walk again, my knees once again struck pavement as the apparition exploded into flames.

My lungs ignited as I gasped at air that was heavy, burnt tasting, like it'd been torched—like someone had come down the alley with a flamethrower and I was sucking up all the fumes while being burned alive. My eyes fluttered to stay open, searching for the source of the white-hot light, but there was no visible blaze. The phantom had disappeared. The flames were gone. Yet somehow…I was still burning.

I screamed at the heat pushing my body further into the ground, grit scraping my cheeks. Every inch of me ignited. I pounded my fists until the indents bled, until the pain numbed, and I could no longer feel it, could no longer feel myself.

Then…there was nothing.

Hours, days, decades later—I had no clue how long had passed—someone picked me up and carried me through the sky. My muscles immediately went lax, the breath whooshing out of me as I drooped against them. It was over. Death had come for me, finally, and carried me like a princess.

A raw scent—pine—entered my nose. Mmm. Death smelled good.

Wait a minute.

Despite my tender skin, and mind even tenderer from the phantom burning I'd just endured, my eyelids showed no resistance when I shot them open and peered into the dark expanse. The blackness was punctuated by stars and planets and—nope, I wasn't facing up, I was facing down—that was gum and glass I was staring at.

I flopped, frantically waving my limbs as the gravity of the situation hit me. I wasn't floating in the hands of a saint. I was being carried in the arms of a stranger.

I glanced at nails, stained in Sharpie, bunched into my corduroy shirt, the smokey-lettered knuckles wrapped around my torso, the strange tattoo that resembled an N and an S wrapped in a snake head on the web between their thumb and index finger.

Instinct took over from there. I didn't direct my legs to kick or my throat to scream, they just *did*.

"Watch it!" My courier huffed.

"Let me go!" Slipping out of their grasp, I dropped to the ground and bear-crawled away. "Who are you? What do you want?"

Pressed against the brick wall of a building—a safe distance, enough—I surveyed my…Abductor? Savior? Whatever they were, suited in black from head to combat-boot toe. If their leather jacket hadn't reflected the face of the moon, they'd pass for the grim reaper.

Death isn't that stylish, but I knew another creature of the night that was.

When he flipped off his hood it came as no surprise. If anything, it explained the bank-heist ensemble, the after-hours loitering, the fluttering in my chest…

This time the ocean's mist didn't block the moonlight—instead, it revealed the parts of him my imagination had once filled in. Like his untextured waves, the darkest brown, longer strands curling around his ears. And the twin to his freckle, mirrored on the apple of his cheek on the other side of his face. And the glyphs on his clavicle, that area a minor shade lighter than the rest of his visible, ivory skin.

I might've been staring, and he seemed to relish that. Damn him.

Still, I demanded some answers. "Ryder. What are you doing here?"

"Great running into you, too." He snickered and considered me, hunched on the ground. "And I mean that almost literally."

I declined his bid at formalities and pushed myself to standing, having—and hating—to clutch the wall when my stiff limbs refused to bear my weight at first.

It was slightly less humiliating up here, even if I had to crane my neck to meet his eyes. Arranging my face into a scowl, I crossed my arms. "Stalk much?"

He raised an eyebrow. "We do live in the same town."

"And take the same shortcuts?" I wiped the dirt off my thighs.

"You know, this is the second time I've saved you, and I don't think I've heard thank you once." He tilted his head, as if waiting for the gratitude to come singing out of my mouth.

My ass. It may have been cute the first time around, but were we really doing this again? He evaded my questions like he did the city streetlamps—at some point, he'd have to come into the light. Or I'd just straight up walk away.

"Saved me? Oh please, you ran into me on a train trestle at midnight." I resisted the urge to march towards him and poke him in the chest, deflate it a bit. "Do you even know my name?"

He rocked on his heels and for a beat looked away before settling into stillness again.

I scoffed. Of course, he didn't know my name. He hadn't asked. He hadn't cared. "It's River."

"River." He repeated it purposeful, slow, like he was savoring it on his tongue. Ending with a softer R than a local would say. British, maybe? The accent faded the more he spoke. "Well, if it weren't for me, you'd either have walked off a trestle by now or been flattened by a car. You could just say thank you."

"Neither of those situations called for you to fly in like Superman." I combatted his glare with my own. "Is that your thing? Because if it is, I'm the wrong girl. I'm not helpless, it's called an episode. I can't control it—neither can you. But I guess you got to be the hero after all. So… thanks."

Ryder's look hardened. "I'm anything but a hero."

Something in his face told me he was done with this conversation. Well good, 'cause so was I. Without a good-bye, he stepped backwards. It didn't take long for him to blend in with the shadows, unfurling at his shoulders as if they might become wings and he'd take flight. Not even halfway down the street, he disappeared altogether.

By the time the adrenaline started to thaw my frozen muscles, my lungs worked to catch up on that whole intake-of-oxygen thing. Then again, I imagined his arrogance would leave anyone breathless.

A loud *bang* came from the construction site on the other side of the alley. Flinching, I turned towards the sound but held firm where I was standing. There was a solid chance Ryder was messing with me and I wouldn't indulge him, no way.

I squinted into the darkness, trying to find the source of the noise in the vacant pile of beams. "Ryder?" I called. "I know you're there!"

There was no sign of him.

Kneading the raised flesh on my arms, I continued towards my original destination—the bus stop—when I heard it again. Another crash, this time closer. As in right next to me, just beyond the screen-in fence. Was he following me again? I didn't wait to find out.

"This isn't funny," I said as I increased my pace and ran towards the main road. The beep of swiping metro cards was music to my ears, even as hydraulics lifted the vehicle away from the curb, ready to depart.

I'd be damned if I didn't join the last group of people

stepping onto the platform for final boarding—I was over this. The freezing air choked me as I shifted into a sprint, and even though the succession of crashes from whatever pursued me grew hot on my tail, I didn't look anywhere but forward.

Ignoring the driver's scowl, I waved my hand between the doors before they could seal shut, then darted to the very back. When the bus finally lurched forward, I pressed a hand below my collarbone to slow my thundering heart.

Collapsing into a sweaty rumpled slump in the gray plastic chair, I rested my head against the window and stole a glance at the unlit concrete. I assumed this'd been the work of Ryder, just to mess with me, until a pair of glowing red eyes glowered back from among the beams. I blinked and they disappeared. Or had they even been there?

A more ominous idea formed—maybe my brain was progressing from hearing things to feeling things—to *seeing* things.

My muscles trembled, and my heart leapt so fast it felt like it would bruise my rib cage.

The stuffy heat inside the bus compartment wrapped around me as the construction site disappeared into the distance. With my appendages now thawed and working, I unzipped my backpack and crowned myself with my headphones. Sweat lined my fingers, staining the screen as I pressed play.

The melancholic guitar riff temporarily washed away whatever I was running from. Fear. Reality. My own fucking mind. I wasn't even sure what I was trying to escape anymore. Because the Voices had already escaped *me,* and I never thought they'd do it—pick up and leave.

But they did—they had abandoned me.

I pressed my palms into my eye sockets, then brought my fingers to my mouth until I bit the little nail growth I had back to nubs. Chewing, chewing, chewing, like every sliver of keratin I spat was one more worry I shed.

Where were the Voices? Better yet…*what* were they? Something more than a figment of my grief? Something that summoned sprites and red eyes and invisible flames…? I bit the inside of my cheek—it was a question that'd hovered on the tip of my conscious, but I'd never allowed myself to fully think it. Because that would mean…so many things.

So many things I didn't dare tackle yet.

The next song riffed through my headphones, slowly diffusing my tension as the acoustic strings lured my paranoia into a slumber. Two of the Voices had returned earlier. Well, tried to. Hints of their inflections had lined the sounds in the alley, but they came out low, mumbled, like a hand covered their mouths to prevent them from speaking.

I wanted to say it was for the best—that three's company, and four's a crowd. That the missing one, the third, the most brash and resolute that they were better off without me, was the one I could do without. But I couldn't, even if I'd told them otherwise during our fight at Grad Night.

Something leaden weighed over my heart. My necklace. I balanced the pendant in my palm, pinching its raised pattern into my skin, a tide of calm washing through me.

Tomorrow. Tomorrow I'd reach inside the darkest, hollowest parts of my skull and figure out what happened to the Voices—what was happening to me.

I yawned past a growing, gnawing concern that I'd likely have to visit my most forbidden memory. I didn't have enough brainpower for that, not after this hellish evening.

For now, I let the bus rock me and my eyes grew heavy, even as unease prickled alongside my limbs that had already fallen asleep.

CHAPTER 11

Last night's pain rolled into the morning, seem-ing to seep into the atmosphere, coloring all of Santa Cruz Bay. By late afternoon, storm clouds gathered on the hori-zon, waiting to tuck the skyline into their sheet of gray.

I watched the cumulus collect while I nestled into the hide of the chair I'd designated for myself in my therapist's office, the only thing about this purgatorial sentence that welcomed me with familiar and comfy arms.

My phone distracted me from descending into my own layers of Limbo—which I should have been doing, in search of the Voices, to get answers—but I aimlessly scrolled in-stead. A text popped up. Javi.

What are we doing today? **he asked.**

Just got out of class. Now I'm at therapy, **I typed.** Then I have work. Ugh. **Cupping my jaw, I made a sad face and snapped a quick selfie. He hearted it immediately after I sent it.**

Fine, valid excuse. What about tomorrow?

My thumbs pecked feverishly. Summer school in the morning.

This whole summer school thing is really ruining our plans.

I sighed. IKR? I can meet you at the lighthouse after class tomorrow?

Deal. Not to give you fomo or anything but… **A perfectly curated pic of milky cold brew, a bean bag, and a stack of comics taunted me from the screen.**

The jealousyyyy. BRB crying.

Javi flooded the thread with cry-laugh emojis.

I exited the app, turning up the trancey track resonating through my headphones so it was no longer background noise. Continuing to avoid the oath I'd made to myself—the Voices could wait. A little more daydreaming wouldn't hurt.

The door to the office opened, but I didn't notice until Dr. Fairmore's apple cheeks and indigo cat-eye rims came into my view. "How are you, River?" her mauve tinted lips mouthed, words muffled by the music. "Doing okay?"

Eh, just missing some telepathic Voices and have potentially been hallucinating. Oh, and my best friend leaves for college soon, my last episode almost killed me but other than that, fine, totally fine. Actually, the endless list of not-okay things had me rubbing my temples.

I removed my headphones just in time to hear, "I saw the surf's up."

Oof, nobody says that except total rookies and characters on TV shows. An irrepressible cringe scrunched my nose. The motion seemed to jump from my face to my therapist's, like she knew how forced and awkward it came out.

"That was corny," she admitted, her natural rosy undertones flaring, searing her cheeks. With a self-deprecating shake of her head, she took a seat in the armchair across from me.

My heart sputtered. Did she—was she—cracking jokes with me. At her own expense?

When her color evened out, she addressed me again with a cool expression that slightly raised her brows and lips. "Anything specific you'd like to start with, or do you want to pick up where we left off?"

The wall clock filled the silence. I listened intently: to the ticking, to her mulling, to the scrapes on the leather seat from my restless fingers. She'd done this last time, disarmed me with her unexpected humanness. Kind, but not lacking confidence. Focused, but not in a creepy way that made me feel like a science experiment. Expectant, but not demanding answers. Although her straight posture and unwavering gaze did make it clear she demanded my respect. I could give her that. She'd actually earned it. I still hated therapists, but I found it hard to hate her.

I averted my eyes towards the window, feeling defeated. The wind had picked up and brushed the first drops of rain into long slashes against the glass. My exhales grew longer, the heaviness lifting from my chest.

Maybe she really was different than the others. Maybe I should give her a chance. Our last conversation had seemed to draw out the Voices.

The bud of an idea formed: if I let her in, could it coax them out of hiding?

"River," Dr. Fairmore stressed my name like she had

already repeated it, "is everything alright? You seem distracted."

The aged leather lounger must have memorized my exasperation, because I flung myself back into a perfectly indented shape. "Sorry, I just have a lot going on."

"Do you want to talk about it?" Dr. Fairmore spun a hammered medallion, its white gold chain dangling to her ribs—the same one from our last session, the angel with the trumpet. "This is what I'm here for."

She closed her file. It was the smallest flick of her wrist, but the gesture was louder than anything she'd ever said. It was an invitation to be, to speak, to do whatever I wanted, with no scribbling pen to take my words out of context just to plot my next diagnosis.

Time to test my theory.

Tugging on the pockets of my high-rise jeans, I swallowed and began. "Summer school, work, it's been a lot. Less episodes"—I pressed my lips together, fighting the truth; like being tortured by invisible flames and seeing monsters in the night was any better—"which is crazy…"

"Why is that crazy?"

"Because with the…" I gulped. Here goes. "Anniversary of my mom's death, you'd think I'd be experiencing more of them. Not less. And now they're…it's like they're gone."

Curiosity lit the amber flecks in Dr. Fairmore's brown eyes. "What do you mean 'gone'?"

I sighed, trying to ignore the flicker of concern that furrowed her brows for a literal second. I was looking for that—something in her body language to derail me so I didn't have to go through with this. *Stop it*. Stop it stop it stop it.

"As if that part of me has *poof!* vanished." My fingers balled and extended, mimicking a firework burst. "Something I've wished away for so long, but without them…the world doesn't feel right. It feels wrong." I gnawed at my lip. Maybe I was giving too much away.

Dr. Fairmore let my words hang in the air for a beat. "When did this start?"

"Last week, around my birthday." I replayed the final convo with the Voices in my head.

GET OUT OF MY LIFE!

That's not the worst idea you've had. We are better off without you.

Dr. Fairmore leaned a little closer, resting her forearms on her knees. "Let me ask you something, River. Why is this upsetting to you? Is it not what you wanted—what you've been working towards—for your episodes to lessen, in frequency or severity?"

Fair point. It's what my file said. It's what I'd always said. I wondered when I'd actually stopped wanting that. "Because I-I feel like…some faulty version of myself. Like I lost the main thing tying me to…"

"Your mother." Her voice cracked on the words. She took a sip of water and cleared her throat.

I dipped my chin but couldn't bring it back up. A tear slipped, whether in sadness or in shame, and I didn't try to hide it. Because it was all true. No one else had witnessed her death—except us, me and the Voices—and as they took their first breath, she took her last, like her final exhale had formed them.

"River." When I met Dr. Fairmore's gaze, she trembled with a hesitation I didn't think possible. All I'd seen from her was confidence. "There are…ways to get them back."

Her words almost knocked the wind out of me. Were we talking about the same thing?

Did she know? She had to know. I didn't ask her to clarify.

Instead, I sucked in a ragged inhale, trying not to show how breathless I'd become. Still, my voice came out raw. "How?"

"Allow yourself to feel. And listen"—the word sent a full body shiver through me—"to your emotions before pushing them away. That's where the power lies—where you can confront the things you have pushed deep down inside of you."

I was ready to, oh God I was ready to. But I was also scared. I reached for my necklace, a beacon of warmth against my ice-cold skin. My heart thumped beneath it so fast I swore the pendant jumped.

Dr. Fairmore cleared her throat. "Can I see your hands?"

The ones I'd been wringing in my lap, those ones? "Why?"

"So we can do a breathing exercise. Sometimes a moment of peace is all you need to reconnect to your truest self." She presented her hands, casting twin shadows that grew above our heads and folded around me. But the space didn't cool. If anything it…warmed, the billowy shade a cocoon until it retracted back into her shoulders.

I blinked. A few times. Just to make sure I wasn't hallucinating. Must have been a shift of the storm. The shadows were gone, but her palms waited before me. A quick once-over revealed no claws or talons or any other indication they'd be tearing me to shreds.

Before I could stop it, I placed my fingers atop hers, flushing at how bitten and nubby my nails were compared to her manicured tips.

That weird sting of familiarity I'd felt the first time I'd met her struck me again. I shook it away, obviously just desperate for some form of connection.

"Close your eyes." Her voice lost its tremble, poised and self-assured again. "Lower your head to take the strain off your neck. Good. Now take a deep breath."

With trembling lips, I sucked in the air, staring at the blank space beneath my shut lids. I willed myself to latch on to this untapped quietness. But I'd never felt so vulnerable in my life. I was as good as naked.

"Think of somewhere peaceful that totally relaxes you. Imagine yourself there."

There was only one place capable of that. Patterns from the natural light filtered into the room, ebbing and flowing before my eyes even though they remained closed, swirling until they settled into a mirrored horizon—glassy blue above and below: the ocean.

"Exhale. Envision something you'd be doing in this special place."

A board appeared, the bright white deck popping against the water's blue-green. I slid onto its middle, lining up my belly with the stringer. And paddled.

Muscles burned as they lifted me—"Another big inhale"—into a crouch where I rode, and I reigned, and as I entered the barrel of the wave…I simply became. I simply *became* the element.

Something soared with me in this frosted green cathedral. Power, like I'd never known it. It coated me like the salt spray, kissed me like the rush of the wind, spoke to me like the roar of the ocean. Here, that power had an outlet. Here, that power had a voice. And here, I'd muster the courage to tread the last memory of my mom—and I'd find the others.

Every fiber in my being told me this was it, as the weighty tug of reality pulled me back to the dreary office, and I opened my eyes with a gasp—like I'd actually surfed the perfect wave when the reality was, I hadn't left the chair.

CHAPTER 12

Twisting in my chair, for probably the hundredth time since class had started, I tried to register the words scrawled by the harsh strokes of Mr. Hess's dry-erase marker. But the rain—which had turned into an epic downpour after my solo shift at work last night—and the feeling of entrapment that came with it, made it all the harder to concentrate.

I bit out a sigh. No point in trying to follow this lecture on resources during the boom-clap of thunder. I had more important tasks to see to, anyways: finding the Voices. Closing my eyes, I attempted to replicate the guided breathing I had done with my therapist the day before, imagining myself in a place that brought calm—far from the fluorescent lights overhead.

Shielding my brows with my beanie, I tried to escape them, but every flicker interrupted my concentration, making it damn near impossible to leave the classroom behind.

I blew air against my lips. The summer storm—unusual, but not unheard of—trapped us indoors beneath the stained, moldy ceiling, so even the break offered no relief.

Growing restless, I went to lean against the window and watched the raindrops hit the concrete.

Focusing on one at a time, I followed their journey from the heavens to their final contact with Earth. The impact rang in my ears as if they weren't liquid at all, but marbles or diamonds, plinking down faster and faster. I tucked my hands into my long-sleeve shirt and brought them together, hunching my shoulders to cocoon the warmth.

Ferocious gusts bent the trees; some branches gave in, littering the outdoor hallways. Lightning struck, exposing the quad and all of its silhouettes: rose bushes, basketball nets, some idiot at the three-point line staring down my class.

Wait, what?

Squinting, I fixed my vision on the centermost part of their hood. A mask against the incoming elements, or maybe a way to conceal their identity.

A chill swept over my skin, pricking each hair on my body, and my stomach dipped—nice try at going incognito, but even within this level of darkness, I caught that piercing green gaze.

When I crossed the door's threshold, I knew I was defying all common sense. I didn't need to see any more of the person beyond the façade, though; my intuition already recognized his tricks.

The first step drenched my pale rose thermal to a dark maroon. Righteous anger surged in me after the next, when it became more like swimming, my beanie nothing more than a wet rag on top of my head. This close I could trace his distinctive jaw, jutting from his disguise.

"What are you doing here, Ryder?" I meant to sound demanding, but of course my voice came out weary, due to him or the effort it took to shout over the storm.

I took a final step towards him. And this close I could count the water droplets clinging to his lashes.

He barely turned to look at me, focused on something in the distance. "I don't know."

"You mean you thought you'd take a stroll in the middle of a hurricane?" I raised my palms to the sky.

"No, I had this feeling…like I needed to protect you." Even with his voice dampened by the rainfall, I could make out how strained each syllable sounded.

"Seriously." I wrapped my arms around my body, my shirt crinkled and logged with water, hardly protecting the skin beneath. "You're really bad at taking a hint."

A flash lit up the court again. The stroke of light underlined his cheekbones and revealed the panic in his eyes. It cast the quad's shadows across his shoulders and reflected off his drop hoop earring, the cross swiveling in the torrent.

"I know I'm breaking all the rules being here." Being out here, with him, I was breaking some of my own. He let the rumbling thunder pass before he continued. "But I had to make sure you were okay."

"I think I'm equipped enough to handle a rainy day." Never thought I'd be so thrilled to retreat to Mr. Hess's economics trenches.

When I turned to leave, he grabbed my wrist. "I'm not letting you out of my sight."

I looked down at his grasp. "You need to let go. *Now.*"

He may have unlocked his fingers, but it wasn't at my command. It was when a lightning bolt struck a utility pole not even six feet away. My arms arched above me to cover my face from the eruption of sparks.

In one fluid motion he moved his grip from me to his bow, and had an arrow drawn into aim. What, was he going to shoot a lightning bolt? Only Ryder.

From under my hands, I watched each classroom go black, one after another. Darkness swept across the windows, closer and closer to us.

"We need to get out of here," he said, his voice low and urgent. The tendons flared in his neck and clenched fists, and when he finally met my gaze…gone were the arrogance and the wry gleam in his eyes and the smirk he wore so often I figured it was permanent.

The classroom, dry, in both temperature and substance—and way less dramatic—almost lured me to forget Ryder's plea. But the second we locked eyes, all of that seemed to have fallen away. Staring up at him was like staring upwards into a forested canopy: disorienting in a good, heart-pounding way.

"I need to grab my bag—"

He shook his head, cutting me off. "There's no time."

With my phone and what little cash I had in my pocket, I guessed I didn't need the extra five pounds of books weighing me down…I tugged at the headphones still looped around my neck, the ear cushions sopping wet. "Okay. Where do we go?"

He dropped his shoulders and softened his stance. For a second try, he reached for my hand, and this time I laced my fingers between his. I flinched as a light shock zapped me at the contact. His touch was electric.

"Follow me." He gave me a squeeze. "And whatever you do, don't look back."

I didn't follow his advice. Obviously not right away, but as I shadowed his footprints across the snaking concrete, I turned and saw…a school with a power outage?

Class would be let out early. My classmates would be stoked. What was the problem?

Ryder steered me around the terraced stairs and through the muddy fields, never dropping his pace or his eyes, or my hand. We darted into student parking, shielded by the rows of Toyota Priuses, and stopped at an old Chevrolet pickup.

Low and long and painted all black, aside from the red accent on its rims that matched the cross-shaped logo on the front of its silver squarish grill—it was the type of car that turned heads wherever it went and had collectors selling kidneys for it.

With all his lurking it had never occurred to me that he could drive. Couldn't say I was mad about it.

Since it was too old a model for a simple click to unlock it, he fumbled with the keys. With his focus there, I snuck another glance behind me, scanning the football stadium behind us, eyes cataloging grass, metal, and rain.

Stands stood empty, sidelines a ghost town, despite the scheduled scrimmage. A yellow goal post towered above the end zone, while its twin on the opposite end of the field remained dark and obscure—covered, I figured. That is, until it mobilized and barreled towards us.

"River, get inside!" Someone jerked my hand—Ryder. I jumped back from his touch. I'd almost forgotten about him with the obscure heap of dark matter rushing at me. He was already in the truck, leaning over the passenger seat, fighting the epic wind to hold the door open for me. Before my instincts could push me further away, he pulled me inside, and it slammed shut.

Inside, the rain hit like bullets spraying the roof. I wasn't sure I could breathe. My eyes stayed locked outside the window, frantically sweeping the parking lot's shadows for any sign of what I'd just seen.

"What was that?" I wiped my face with my sleeve. "It didn't look like the average storm cloud…"

Ryder failed to respond, too busy turning the key in the ignition and slamming his palms into the wheel, when a dreaded *click* signaled his failure to start the engine.

Impeccable timing, really.

Because that's when a mass built like a linebacker landed on the hood. My screams filled the silence.

Whatever this was, it wasn't human. It stood on two legs, but too many limbs jutted out of its back and stretched into the rain. Fluid oozed from its mouth, staining its teeth, as it let out a growl so deep and threatening it made the car shake. Glossy red streaks smeared over death-gray limbs, bloated from decay and rage. I couldn't shift my gaze from its beady red eyes, not even as Ryder swore and frantically jerked the key.

The car still wouldn't start.

Totally fine, because any minute my mind would rationalize the situation, and this pallid beast spreading its featherless wings would actually be something like a pelican with rabies.

Can birds get rabies?

Its bill opened with a shriek that competed with my own, revealing rows and rows of sharky teeth. I flinched at the wave of saliva it spat onto the hood of the car, sizzling like acid where it struck.

So, reality was playing hard to get.

Finally, the engine caught, and the shadow creature lost its footing as Ryder launched the car in reverse. Fortunately, I, the very unsuspecting passenger, caught myself on the dash before diving through it headfirst.

I gritted my teeth. "A heads-up would be nice."

"Buckle your seatbelt." Undeterred by my near-death experience, he swerved in and out of the open spots, the Chevy's tires not the only thing screeching throughout the lot as the creature followed us.

"What the hell was that, Ryder?"

"A teratorn," he said as he smoothly inspected the mirrors, then the street.

I raised an eyebrow. "Tera-whatta?" I didn't want to come off frantic, but you know, a Pterodactyl-looking monster had just chased us off campus.

"Tera*torn*." His dramatic pronunciation brought out his accent. The windshield wipers beat a frantic rhythm as we fishtailed onto the main road.

I twisted in my seat, craning my neck to see if it was still there. "Well, what's it doing here? Doesn't seem like it escaped from the zoo."

"It's not from this dimension." His head quirked to the

side as if my disbelief was wholly inappropriate for the situation. "It's a demon."

My whole body swiveled towards him. Somehow his words were harder to comprehend than the actual thing that was chasing us. Dimensions. Demons. And said with such indifference, like it was nothing special, like he was used to this.

Like this was *real*.

This was a far cry from the mischievous sprite that had crashed my birthday. This thing had *actual fangs*. Ones that could tear me to shreds in a matter of seconds. I slid deeper into my seat.

"It shouldn't be here."

That was comforting, Ryder. "Then care to explain why it is?" I snapped.

His lips slightly pursed and opened, seeming to be stuck on what to say. Clearing his throat, he offered nothing but empty words. "That…might take a while to explain." I wasn't sure why it was so hard to comprehend how clueless I was, when the majority of people would act the same. "The ward's there to stop it. Unless it was summoned…"

"Sounds casual." I narrowed my eyes, the angry creases in my forehead practically digging into my skull, feeling as out of the loop as the other drivers waiting at the traffic light beside us. Must be nice, sitting in their normal cars, thinking normal thoughts, heading to do normal things.

I tried to channel that vibe. "Hey, looks like we may have lost it." Unsuccessfully—a reverberating thud shook the roof, catching in my chest.

Before I had a moment to panic, an explosive force

crashed into the windshield, hairline cracks spreading from the center of impact, fractal and delicate like a spider's web. My heart raced with the rhythm of the rain. A barbed tail flailed outside the window beside me, coming for its second score. One more hit and the glass would shatter completely. Ryder reached for his arrows, but it wouldn't be quick enough—he had been as stunned as I had.

Neon reflected in the top right corner of the windshield, the only piece that had remained intact. "Green light!" I yelled.

Ryder jammed the pedal into the floor and our companion flailed off the roof, its cries as sharp as the shards that had started dropping into our laps.

I clamped my hands over my ears, but the scream blared past them, spearing my bones like the monster's throat was a megaphone for the underworld. And maybe it was. We careened onto a road that funneled into the mountains. I crossed my fingers we'd be harbored by the trees.

"I can't see," Ryder barked, eyes scanning the ruined glass. His demeanor had hardened, like any slip of emotion might cost us precious seconds again.

He stuck the upper half of his body out the window to get a better view, toes pressing the gas, fingertips steering. I wanted to reach over and take the wheel and let him do his thing—but I slumped helplessly in the copilot's seat, hands pressed against the sides of my head as if to keep it from rolling off.

The sad reality was, I couldn't even *offer* to drive. I didn't have my license or permit. I'd tried to get it—Javi had even tagged along with me to the written test. But when my finger met the touch screen, the DMV's noises built and warped until every shoe scuff, every paper shuffle, every murmur turned my concentration to dust. I'd walked out without looking back.

A beach cruiser was all I needed. Until now.

It wouldn't be long before the teratorn caught up to us again. I shuddered at the thought, wanting to slink so far into the cushion I'd disappear. But I couldn't; I had to do something.

I checked the rearview and as my eyes caught on the monster's clunky form, I scooted towards the middle. "Ryder, it's gaining on us!"

He began to lean in for his quiver. "Take the wheel!"

"I can't! I don't know how to drive." I cringed at the look on his face, which spelled our defeat.

"Do you know how to shoot an arrow?" he yelled, still halfway out the window.

"No? And this doesn't feel like a good time for archery lessons!" I yelled back.

"They say the best way to learn is by doing, so grab them out of my bag!"

The same black leather pouch he paraded the other night leaned against his empty seat, glowing ceremonially in the dash's backlight. Its crescent-shaped tip grazed my thigh—I hadn't even noticed I'd scooted that close to the driver's side. I reached for the strap.

"I have them." It took an enormous amount of willpower to stay calm. "Now what?"

"You're going to have to join me out here."

Shit. How did I *not* realize that climbing out the window would be a requirement when I agreed to this? Rewind; I no longer wanted to help. My legs lifted me despite my resistance.

Ryder's eyes lit up when I folded the upper half of my body over the top of the cab on the opposite side—and held on for dear life.

"Alright," he said, "listen closely. First take the bow and hold it with whatever hand you don't write with."

I attempted to control my shaky left hand.

"Next, place the nock against the string—the end with the fletching. Pull back, using whatever fingers feel most comfortable. Then aim and release."

The equipment sloshed in the water running rivers atop the metal as I scrambled to bring the two pieces together. Sagging feathers, drenched wood, no notches I could see or feel in this unrelenting downpour. I went for it anyways, connecting the bow with the feathered end, and pulled back. The arrow didn't even catch air; it simply slipped into the truck bed.

"Damnit!" I braved a look at my driver.

What Ryder lacked in verbal acknowledgment he made up for with a glare.

Ass. It was my first try!

My next attempt didn't go any better.

As the arrow disappeared, I was thrown back into my seat—Ryder had jerked the wheel to get us off the main road. I clutched the quiver to my chest, the stiff material rising and falling with my rapid breaths.

The sky, absent beneath the redwoods, cracked with thunder. Blanketed by the canopy, the rumble bounced off the tree trunks and echoed throughout the forest. The storm howled and hissed, and I swore it snickered. The world was truly against me. A ball of hopelessness lodged in my gut.

"What's the problem in here?" He'd slipped into the cab for a quick second to shift us into another gear. Before I could open my mouth to answer, he was heading up again. I let out a stressed sigh.

There were many, Ryder.

For starters, the Voices had split, and they were probably the only ones who had a clear explanation as to what was happening to me. Oh, and per his little pep talk, I was being chased by nothing other than a demon. A *demon*. Not to mention with no license and with every lost arrow, I was further proving my worthlessness.

Not that I was anything special to begin with…

The despair felt as deadly as the teratorn, and it started to consume me. My neck drooped, my throat burning with self-pity. As my eyes, wet with tears and rain, fluttered shut, I went to rip the pendant from my neck. It burned as if it were metal that'd been sitting in the sun.

I yelped as it seared my flesh, but the physical pain brought me back to the moment—the truck barreling through the redwoods, the guy perched atop the driver's window ledge screaming for my assistance—the moment I had just been ready to quit.

Giving up on myself had been the obvious choice because I was a failure in every sense of the word: I couldn't drive, I couldn't use a bow, I couldn't graduate high school…I couldn't save my mom. I looked at the heated mark from my necklace, the swelling already reduced.

Maybe this was a chance for me to prove otherwise.

With the demon closing in, it was now or never.

Treating the cushion like my surfboard, I balanced on its springs, maneuvering the jerky bumps and swerves as I would a restless, angry ocean. Arms out, the gear looped around my elbow, I joined Ryder, the midsummer monsoon rain beating into my soaked clothes like pellets. Squinting, I stared past the truck bed, the harshness of the storm turning branches into trolls and roots into ogres and boulders into monsters. Every shape, every shadow of the Santa Cruz mountains turned into something sinister.

I grabbed another arrow, its glittering silver-white tip catching my eye. Weightless in my hand as if carved from stardust, but sharper than a steel blade.

My target hovered above the asphalt's yellow stripes in a glide. Its outstretched wings covered the width of each lane as it sped towards the exhaust, dangerously close to the truck bed. I almost choked on its stench, so rotten it stung my eyes, but I blinked through the burn and tried to ignore it.

Claws scraped metal as the teratorn kicked its legs out and drew upwards. I aimed for the center of the dark mass, hoping its heart lay in the middle of its chest. If demons had hearts, that is—it was more likely to be born of necromancy and decayed cartilage. Thin, avian limbs swung forwards, slamming into the bumper. The sudden jolt threw me off balance.

Yet another arrow plummeted to the ground.

The creature snapped its jowls and moved closer, teeth closing on the air. Up close, I could see every sickening detail—the clotted blood pumping through its infected follicles, the skeletal arch of its back. I fumbled with the remaining projectiles when the hooked edge of a wing grazed my cheek, and the monster circled back around.

"It's preying on your fear—don't let it toy with you!" Ryder called out, as if detecting the shift in me. "You can do this, River. I know you can."

A chill hugged my bones despite his encouragement—which, by the way, would've been a lot more helpful to hear earlier than ordering me to shoot something that wasn't even supposed to be real, with a weapon I'd never used, and grimacing that I couldn't ace it on my first try—like, not everyone is blessed with natural marksmanship. Oh, and all while speeding down a two-lane road, which he now skidded across.

I flailed to hug the body of the truck, and the slick quiver whirled around my wrist and its contents came dumping out. When I crooked my head to see what had happened, my headphones slipped off my neck and went tumbling down. Leaving a cold, empty imprint around my collar. My insides went hollow as if my organs had been ripped out and fell with them, slamming into every speed bump along the way.

"NO!" The force of my shout almost scattered the raindrops.

Ryder's swears covered the entire alphabet.

I whimpered. "My headphones." One of the only defense mechanisms I'd had for so long. To me they were more than curved pieces of plastic—they were an extra appendage.

One arrow remained in my palm. Its notches pinched my hand as I squeezed. I'd kill this beast for what it'd taken from me. Our final shot. Our last hope. I pulled back the string, waiting for the perfect moment of release.

Ryder turned in my peripheral as I launched our hopes and dreams, compacted into the sparkling pale point. It soared towards the monster like a shooting star, as if in slow motion.

And with a blink time sped up, the arrow twisting in its spiral and suddenly…jerking left. Without even a graze against the monster it vanished into the mist.

We lost.

Mother Earth bellowed, the thunder echoing along with the teratorn's shrieks. It landed on the truck bed and cackled at my miss. This whole chase had been a game, one it'd knew it'd win. My shoulders collapsed in defeat. I counted the spines on its throat, stared at the endless rows of denticles, winced at the open, maggoty sores gaping from the empty pockets that might have once contained feathers.

Slumped over the top of the cab, I closed my eyes and waited for death. I'd suffered most of my life—I hoped it'd be short and quick. I thought of the ocean. My happy place.

As my pulse dwindled, my breaths evened out, and my entire body relaxed in acceptance. The raindrops striking the truck and spraying my cheeks became the heavy crash of the break. The water splashing off the hood and trailing through my fingers became the velvety flow of the current.

The wind whistling through the trees and whipping my hair became the wild force of the waves.

I opened my eyes as the ocean's power washed over me. The teratorn licked its marred beak, salivating at what would be my last exhale. Faces of my loved ones flashed before me, as if they were already fading from my mind. One in particular got my attention, and the frail threads of a veiled memory popped up.

We couldn't have asked for a better day—it was one of those where the morning fog had delayed the crowds and when it had finally dissipated, my mom and I had the beach to ourselves. The swell wasn't overbearing; it provided just enough push to send me sailing across the shallows on my boogie board. As I'd left her grip for maybe the dozenth time and glided towards shore, a sneaker wave overcame me, the thick froth unhooking my leash from my ankle. Out of fear or shock, I swam against the current—against everything I had been taught—my mom's calls and splashes padded by the fierce roar of the water as it carried me farther.

What was she saying? Something like…take me instead?

And I'd let it.

"I hate you," I gritted out, my voice turning the memory to vapor. To no one really. I'd say the teratorn, but I knew I meant me. Anger and something metallic, bitter, like regret, coated my tongue and thrummed in my veins.

The monster's hungry maw stretched open in response, with a sickening smile, as it swooped in for my head. In one bite it'd be taken right off my neck. I stared straight into its killing jaws, not unnerved, not afraid, but so energized by my wrath I might explode before it even got to me. Then the opposite happened.

A random bolt of lightning cleaved the clouds and the leaves, searing the teratorn's flesh. Intense, white light abraded its scalp, the energy electrifying its core, petrifying its being.

I jumped back at a sound—a haunting bellow from deep within the demon's gut, harsher than the thunderclap seizing the air around me—and slammed my waist into the window frame. Its chorus of agony cut off abruptly when it exploded into a million pieces, covering me with a film of clumpy ash and the stench of rancid egg.

As if winning its own battle against the darkness, the sun disintegrated the cloud cover and shone deep into the forest, remnants of the demon filtering through its pale streaks.

Ryder's hollers faded in and out, so distant from where my focus lay—fixed on the black tar stain in the back of the truck, where I had just witnessed the impromptu cremation.

CHAPTER 13

It should have been me. My blood, my bowels, lodged into the steel grooves. But I was somehow still standing—frozen in place, sweat slicking my temples, stringy-haired—absolutely filthy. My brows grew heavy with exhaustion; my throat burned and threatened to close. I still felt the adrenaline tingling beneath my skin, and the memory, it was like the wake of a speedboat, rippling through my thoughts. Nothing made sense.

Ryder had quieted along with the forest—aside from his frantic looks. I felt those, even this dazed and confused, but I didn't react to his silent pleas for me to get down. I was content where I was, hanging over the top of the truck. Plus, there's no way my knees would bend and cooperate.

The Chevy's engine thrummed through the stillness. Its tires crunched on the narrow dirt road, that at some point, we had turned down. Ryder slowed so the bounce over the potholes didn't fling me off the side. The redwoods blurred together, despite there being no way we surpassed ten miles per hour. Dizzy, I tore my gaze from the leaping tree trunks and focused on the smooth metal directly in front of me, wondering how far he'd divert us into the wilderness.

He revved around a corner, splashing through a puddle. Mud flung through the air, settling on the bumpers and the back of my pants and probably in my hair. Hopefully they had showers wherever Ryder was taking us. A flock of roaming chickens squawked and ruffled their feathers as they darted away from the incoming tires.

"Welcome home," he offered.

I never got the impression Ryder came from the whole white-picket-fence situation, but I hadn't expected something as off-grid as this.

The driveway dumped us at a multitiered home that was built into the trees as if it were just another sequoia.

Deep copper trunks fused with the walls and shady crowns shielded the roof. Twigs scraped the windows like fingers, shedding remnants of their leaves onto the six or so balconies. A lookout tower on stilts stood tall and watchful in a grove of oaks, connected to the main house by a pretty badass rope bridge. It was the most epic treehouse I had ever seen.

My nine-year-old self would be reeling with envy. I wished I had the stamina to explore every nook and cranny, but…baby steps. The first order of business was discussing the teratorn, not gawking at the woodwork.

A break in the branches revealed a small glade where the sunshine funneled down and ignited the dust, the specks floating through the air like effervescent forest fairies— which could be plausible at this point.

We rolled up to a gabled barn, its sliders opened wide, exposing rafters and a loft strewn with hay. A large bay hollowed out the middle of the building, tools lining the walls and grease staining the floor. I shifted as Ryder braked, still clinging to the roof of the truck, staring at the rooster weathervane, admiring its rusty feathers...alright, I was avoiding him. But the metal bird was good company—it asked no questions, it didn't cluck orders, it had no social obligations to meet. Yet waiting around in park seemed to amplify the silence and his implicit curiosity. Uggghhh. I couldn't stay up there forever.

Slinking through the window, I slumped onto the cushion. His eyes were on me before I spoke. My neck felt so light, like something was missing—my headphones. That alone made me want to cry.

"I yelled at it." It came out flat, unconnected, like this never could have happened. My nails found their way to my mouth and my teeth clamped on.

"You what?" His voice matched my disbelief.

"I was desperate," I said in between bites. "I didn't have any other great ideas."

Ryder gently pulled my hands free, guiding them down to my lap. "So, you yelled at it." He didn't break the physical contact, his calloused palms wrapping around my knuckles. "And...poof?"

"And then it got struck by lightning?" I said into the floor, embarrassed to admit it out loud because it...it just...

"That doesn't make sense—"

"No shit," I cut in. None of this did.

"What I mean is, lightning itself won't send a demon back to the underworld."

I huffed, exasperated, but mostly tired of talking, already and this conversation didn't seem like it'd be over soon. A couple days ago, these things didn't exist outside of comics and sci-fi movies. It was supposed to be fiction. Make-believe. Not real.

Yet I'd been there; I'd witnessed it. And so had he. But only one of us was having trouble processing it. "You're the expert, dude. I'm just telling you what happened."

We glanced at the bed of the truck. Smoke melted into the post-rain air, rising from the char where the creature once stood. As we both turned to face forward, he watched me beneath lashes so long they could sweep the floor.

Then all he said was, "'Dude?'"

What, like he'd never been called that before? "Yes." I doubled down. *"Dude."*

He chuckled, giving my hands a light squeeze. Somehow, his heat managed to break through the layers of my crusty exoskeleton. "Let's go inside and chill out. You need a bath, *dude.*"

When he said it, his accent dropped the U a few pitches, reverberating in my lower belly. The truck may have stopped, but my pulse shot right back to the chase. Good lord. It was just a *word.* Heat bloomed in my face. I didn't need to check the side mirror to confirm I was blushing, hard. When I met his gaze as he opened my door, his smirk said it all.

Ugh. Could we just go back to discussing demons?

I took his outstretched hand, my legs a little shakier than I'd like to admit, and he helped me to the ground. "We don't have to talk about any of it right now if you don't want to."

An attempt to reassure me, clearly. It might have done so, if the rest of the world hadn't started to spiral around me. After one puny step I teetered for support. He caught me and guided me into the crook of his chest. I leaned in, my arms instinctively wrapping around his waist—*not* because he was solid and comfy and his touch was sanctuary—but because everything was spinning. Until it wasn't, because by then, I'd passed out.

WHISPERS FLOODED MY mind. Had the Voices finally come home? In my foggy state, head still pounding, it could have been two or all three of them. My mind raced to wake the rest of my body, which clearly wasn't ready to stir—my legs leaden, fingers tingling, throat tight and parched. It took a few moments, but my bleary vision adjusted to the late afternoon, and my ears perked at the voices I'd heard: two guys, hints of their accents slipping under the crack of the door.

I pulled off the comforter someone had placed over me and swung my legs off the bed someone had put me in—cringing at the stains left by my dirty clothes, and how overall crusty I was. I tiptoed towards the entrance of the bedroom, pushing the door ajar just enough to catch a glimpse of Ryder and the silhouette of whomever he was talking to.

If it hadn't been for their terse exchange of words, the crackling fire would've drawn me out.

Although his face remained in shadow, Ryder's intensity burned as bright as the flames in the hearth. Normally the hunter moved with grace, but something added tension to his stride, like he carried an invisible weight.

"Just some girl," Ryder said to the figure in the room.

"Why'd you bring her here?" the guy questioned, the timbre of his voice similar to the deep bellow of a foghorn.

"I had no choice. We almost got killed by a teratorn." Ryder's pacing halted.

The response that came was angry as the spitting fire. "Teratorn don't just come up for air from the underworld; they need an anchor. Who would waste that energy on a mortal girl? And more importantly, why would you risk *our lives* to save her?"

"I don't know, I-I got caught in the crossfire." Ryder's pacing resumed.

"These childish games are derailing your first real mission. If you can't fix this, I will." The figure stepped closer to Ryder, his brawny, straight-backed shadow completely engulfing him. I had to crane my neck whenever I tried to meet Ryder's gaze, so I couldn't imagine how tall this other guy was. "No more messing around."

"I won't screw it up, brother." My stomach fluttered on that detail. "The oath was taken in blood. I still have time to find them."

The floorboards creaked, and another pair of boots entered my narrow field of view. "It's been two weeks and you don't have eyes on your target?" Something slammed in the room, a fist perhaps, rattling a piece of furniture. Brother's rage made me shiver.

"No," Ryder murmured, barely loud enough for me to hear. "I haven't found them yet."

The flames snapped. He turned to face the bedroom and I jumped back, going until I hit a wall. I really hoped he hadn't seen me or noticed the fact that the door had been slightly opened—but who was I kidding? With that hunter's precision, the one that saw every movement no matter how big or small, I'd been caught like a fox in a trap.

I clenched my jaw, molars grinding at the base of my skull. My chest bloated from the air I held hostage, too nervous to breathe. I remained there for several heartbeats, which thundered wildly in my ears, waiting for him to call me out. But he continued talking, whether he noticed me or not, his words now muffled by the space I'd put between us.

Eavesdropping post abandoned, I slid down the cold, bare wood, allowing myself a sigh of relief. I landed on my butt, bracing my elbows against my knees, and let the last words I heard sink in.

This friendship clearly wasn't built to last, as he readied to drop me to continue his search for another…target? Friend? Potential girlfriend? That I wasn't sure of.

The conversation I'd overheard raised many concerns, but above all else, the reference to me as *just some girl* made my heart sink. For whatever pathetic, superficial reason, I'd held a glimmer of hope that his wild, depthless stare was reserved for… me. That it wasn't just part of the hunt. That it meant something different. But it didn't. I didn't. So, whatever.

Pale yellow light trickled in through the cracks of yet another door. This one closer, to my left. It flickered with a soft, rhythmic pulse. I brought myself to standing, the wood around me creaking and groaning as if recording every time I so much as shifted.

I pulled on the handle and peered into the room. My soul might've left my body as the promise of relaxation hit me: cozy candlelight flickered off the ivory walls, pooling over the lava tile. A fresh towel lay draped over a stool, next to a steaming clawfoot tub filled with *bubbles*. An earthy, floral scent diffused from a ceramic vase in the corner. I breathed it in. *Lavender.* When my feet crossed the threshold, I expected my toes to be hit with a flare of coolness. But the tile was warm, as if it was…*heated.*

Maybe I was just *some girl*, but that girl needed a bath. With no hesitation, I pulled off my clothes and got in. After a morning of hell, it felt like heaven.

CHAPTER 14

THE SETTING SUN FILTERED THROUGH THE PORT-
hole windows and turned the space into a colorful oasis as I
circled the bedroom I'd initially been brought to and blotted my wet hair with a towel.

A folded black crew neck had been placed next to the
abalone vessel sink like a peace offering. Even if the hem
passed my thighs and it turned me into a shapeless heap,
at least it was free of teratorn guts. And it smelled like fresh
laundry—enough to mask the reek of the clothes I'd had to
slip on beneath it, my jeans starched and ashen.

Slashes of pink and orange sherbet hues tunneled in
from the skylight, the color splashing the black-and-white
nature prints and reflecting off the industrial bulbs in the
two metal light fixtures hanging on each side of the ceiling.
Each item provided a clue as to who lived here—and with
the black and leather touches, the boot-shining kit in the
corner, the underlying scent of pine on the pillows, it became very clear—this was Ryder's room.

Crossing a gray shag rug that felt like butter between
my toes, I gravitated towards two club chairs that faced the
largest window. A square pouf sewn with a UK flag cover

served as an ottoman—well, that answered *that* question. He was British, maybe.

Nestled between the furniture was a small table with a stack of jacketless books and a pair of framed photos. I picked one up, curious about the memories they contained, and a pint-sized version of Ryder looked up at me with sun-streaked hair and a bowl cut. His gap-toothed *Cheese!* held an innocence I wouldn't have believed him capable of if I hadn't seen this photo. Others huddled near him—mom, dad, brother?—and smiled into the camera. Hands on each other's shoulders, fingers clasped, matching shirts tucked into their khakis. I smiled back at them. With retro sunglasses and awkward tan lines, their pinched cheeks holding back laughter, it could have been any old Santa Cruz family not cursed by demonic projections.

But there was one weird thing: their shadows.

They seemed to stretch, almost billow, across the fence. Something from outside the shot must have caused it, although…it did kind of look like they spread directly from their backs—

"Do you have to do that?"

I flinched, almost dropping the picture. "What?"

"Look at things." I turned to find Ryder leaning against the doorframe with his arms crossed, his right finger tapping the rounded muscle beneath his sleeve.

"I didn't hear you come in." I set it back down. "Who are they?"

"A reminder of what used to be," he said flatly, retreating into the hall.

I followed him out onto the woven rug that had served

as a track for his pacing, and the fireplace eclipsed me with its heat. Pressing my hands to the warmth, I could have watched it burn for hours, spellbound by the dancing flames.

Could have, but a mug of tea was forced into my grip and a warped tree stump nudged my knees from behind. Ryder enjoyed his herbal blend on one, waiting for me to take the other.

He was putting me in the hot seat. Literally.

Lucky for him, I was too tired to challenge the gesture. And hot tea by the fire sounded so…pleasant. Mild. Just what I needed. But that described everything this situation *wasn't*.

I took his silent instruction and sat on the smooth surface, taking an indulgent sip. "So?"

"So."

"So…" I paused, derailed by the art drawn onto his right forearm. Stories that'd been buried by layers of night and leather now glistened, unearthed in the firelight. And they were as mesmerizing as the flames.

I explored the verses, the symbols, the pictures trailing to his triceps and into the barrier of his t-shirt. Then back down to the unblemished back of his hand, to the lone old English letters on his fingers and the two stenciled in his thumb's web.

"Um," I mumbled, tearing my eyes away from his tattoos. "I guess I'll start. What exactly am I walking into?"

He stirred his tea with a tiny silver spoon. So posh for a hunter. "I'm not understanding."

"I mean it's got be like Armageddon out there. Someone

lets a demon loose and it flies around terrorizing the locals? We've had some weird shit happen here, but not that weird. I can only imagine what's trending on Twitter—"

"River." He stopped short before continuing. "There are no other witnesses. They're—"

"DEAD!?" And what did that make me, an accomplice?

"No." He waved his free hand in attempt to quell my hysteria. "They're only human."

That only escalated my fever pitch. "Yeah, and so am *I*. And so are *you*. And I happen to think human life is worth something. I assumed you did, too. Unless you really just want to…" *Kill me* sounded a bit ridiculous, but really? They're only human? I took the living space in more thoroughly, glazing over the reclaimed wooden furniture and the large woven tapestry, straight to the twig-inspired lamps and the steel fire poker. Weapons, if needed.

"No." He facepalmed, dragging his hand downwards like he could wipe the expression off his face. "Not 'only human' as if they don't matter. What I meant is they're people not born with Source in their blood—you know, magic."

"Magic?" The word soured on my tongue.

His hand remained on his face, cupping his jaw. "Is it that hard to digest?"

"I…" The flames popped, guiding each one of my wispy neck hairs up. The noise felt heavier than the air, pressing on my ears, crushing the drums. My skin got hotter, itchier, with untapped energy just like it had during my last session with Dr. Fairmore, and when the lightning bolt struck the teratorn. Folding my lower lip into my teeth, I clamped down as if I could bite back the overwhelming fear and confusion. Ryder wouldn't know what to do if I had an episode now, and I didn't want to explain, even if my mind was starting to feel like it was sizzling on top of the embers.

"You see things for what they are." He set his drink down and clasped his hands together. "And most people in this world do not."

I latched on to his voice, to his conviction, as if it was the only sound in the world, like it was my favorite song blasting through my headphones.

"Why does it feel like I'm the first person to tell you this?" Creases were drawn into his forehead. He'd been documenting the delay in my expressions, which to him probably looked like I was struggling to believe what he was saying. Which, yes, but I inclined my head.

He had no idea I'd almost lost myself to an episode.

"Because you are," I whispered, my voice shaking as badly as my hands.

Everything in the room seemed to still at that—our breaths, the blood in my veins, time itself—until his rough palms cradled my fists.

"Well, I'm a good tutor, as you know. Take a look at this." He guided me to a window and pulled the linen curtain aside to reveal rows of ripe veggies in planter boxes, water storage tanks, and undeveloped trails that led through the redwoods: his backyard. "Source is as vital as the air we breathe. It runs through everything. Seeds the size of a lentil grew into those towering trees. And eggs, little shells of life, hatched into the circling hawk over there and into the hens nesting in that coop. A spinning ball of gas millions of miles away feeds the days and the plants and our moods."

I took biology 101; I didn't need the review. The magic I saw stemmed from the passion in his gestures—not just the flurry of pointing, but the delicate touches to my lower back he didn't seem to be aware he was doing—the pure enthusiasm in his tone, the excitement flaring in his vibrant green eyes. It totally transformed him to speak about nature. *That* was magic.

"It's a miracle." His whisper echoed across the space between us, which thinned into more of a sliver with each exhale—I couldn't tell if I was inching towards him or he towards me. I remembered his words—*just some girl, just some girl*—but my heart would not stop racing. "Everything has a sixth sense. Humans are just born with a mental filter that catches and rejects anything supernatural before it can pass through."

Geeking out on the magical intricacies of everything sounded lovely, but we had more pressing things to discuss. "So…the teratorn. No one saw it."

He nodded. "Except us."

Us. A term that roped me into the supernatural minority.

"And whoever decided to summon it." There was the harsh truth I'd been waiting for.

I picked at a cuticle. "Who would do that?"

"I don't know." He shifted his weight. "It wasn't my bidding."

A rush of intuition burned in my throat, clenching my heartbeat, freezing my lungs. The blood flushed to my head and his words echoed, branding my mind with molten strength.

"I didn't ask if it was." Impulse drove my feet backwards, away from the window—away from him. Ryder followed my slow but determined steps until I was backed against a wall. He stood so close his breath warmed my hairline. The heat gave way to a hellish fever, yet every one of my hairs stood on end. I hadn't even considered what he said as an option. But now…did he just admit he could command something like that?

Maybe he *had* seen me through the slit in the door and wanted to quiet my suspicions. If anything, though, this raised them tenfold and left me with the impression he conjured demons—which definitely came with a pretty gnarly warning label.

Trying to keep my breaths even, I tore my gaze from the gold flecks in his eyes, glancing up at the domed ceiling, but it too felt like it was caving in—just like the rest of my life had.

"I have to go to work." I was surprised to find any words, especially ones that seemed logical enough. Enough to get me out of there, at least. Even if it wasn't my scheduled shift. Even if I had no idea what time it was.

"Now?" Ryder inched back, reluctant to give too much distance, as if I might flee. "It's almost seven PM."

"Yeah. I…uh…" *Think, think, think.* "I'm training the new employee how to close."

Ryder read my movements like tea leaves, analyzing each blink, swallow, and shoulder fidget. If I caved to my body's impulses and grimaced, what would that reveal?

I didn't want to lie, but I needed to be real with my-self: he played with the dark side, he'd figured out my school schedule—I'd be damned to give out my home address.

"Won't your parents be home soon anyway and want to know why some strange girl is sitting in their living room?" I was trying way too hard to be conversational. *Don't lay it on so heavy, River.* "Your brother already seems a bit… unimpressed."

"He's always like that." Ryder broke his stare and went back to the window, the last light glistening on his hardened gaze. At this angle it cast a glassy film over his eyes, as if this was all just a front and he was about to be real and break down—or maybe that's what I was hoping for. He sniffed, and in a moment the look shattered, disappearing with the rest of his emotions.

"Well, I know my dad would be pissed," I continued, forcing my voice light. "I should actually touch base with him. Have you seen my phone?" Not because I was freaking out or anything.

He pointed to the mantel.

"Thanks." I delivered the same lie to my dad. Next in line, Javi…Shit. Javi. He'd waited for me at the lighthouse after class. How would I even begin to explain I'd ghosted him because I'd been chased off campus by a sharky-mouthed, blood-spewing demon?

And worse, that I'd fled with a guy wearing combat boots who didn't even consider me—I gulped—fully human?

Hey! **I typed.** Sorry I bailed. Got called into work. New girl no showed. Def owe you a trip to watermelon ice cream.

Three dots indicating he was typing flashed, then disappeared. Flashed, then disappeared. I waited another minute. Nothing. And then, No worries. WITH A PERIOD.

That was it. He hated me. Our friendship was ruined.

I pinched the upper bridge of my nose. At least this proved the theory Ryder used to explain everyone else's ignorance. No one saw the teratorn—but us. I rolled my eyes at the convenience of that.

Javi's response stung, but I'd find a way to make it up to him. Ice cream and comic books to start. *After* I decompressed and hid from any potential demonic accomplices.

"We should get going then." Ryder broke my attention from my screen. "We don't want you to be late." Oh, I sensed some skepticism.

"Right." I slipped on my Vans and followed him outside.

A full moon rose into a burnt tangerine sky. Pine needles, golden under its fading light, crunched beneath my shoes. The mud had dried. No sign of rain clouds. The heavy air clung to my skin, hot and sticky from the burst in humidity. I tried not to think about the last time I was outdoors, which had to have been almost eight hours ago, hardly functioning on any level, just so, so done, caked in ash and demon blood.

A fierce wave of lightheadedness rushed through me, and I battled against the sudden wobble in my legs—and in a harmonic spin with the Earth's rotation my body hurtled into the wall of the truck bed.

Squeaky-clean. No teratorn guts. Not even a chip in the paint.

"Cleaned it while you were sleeping," Ryder answered my unspoken question. Damn, he was getting good at reading me. I straightened my features. "Water, a dash of vinegar, and lemon essential oil. My little secret."

I snorted. "How organic of you. How'd you do this, though?" I waved at the smooth glass of the windshield.

"That'd be me." The declaration rumbled like the voice of God, then I noticed the oil-stained jeans sticking out from under the fender.

Ryder jumped. *Actually jumped.* He hadn't even been this spooked over a demon. "Leif, you scared the shit out of me."

The mechanic emerged from beneath the car, rolling back on the chassis. "Reflexes a bit rusty, eh?"

Ryder's jaw locked as he ran his fingers through his hair. "I thought you already left."

"Your suspension needed some extra juice." Leif lifted his hand, his blackened fingertips smearing the lubricant all over Ryder's as Ryder helped him to his feet.

Immediately, I recognized the shaggy blonde mane now clasped into a bun, the hazel irises now a dominant green, and the height on him—still two inches taller than Ryder. The boy from the family photo was now a man.

"River." Ryder's hand grazed my lower back. I tried not to lean into the touch. "This is Leif. My brother."

Leif raised his eyebrows at my clothes and his chin at my hello, skipping the how-you-do's. Eyeing me with an incisive stare as sharp and predatory as his brother's, which convinced me he knew my secrets just by reading my gestures. His interest didn't linger, and he moved to his workbench, grabbing a rag to wipe off his arms. Unlike Ryder, he rocked a full sleeve of tattoos, a colorful canvas of conquests and dreams.

"Consider your truck as good as new." He clapped his hands and grabbed a weathered leather jacket, throwing it over his white-ribbed tank. The umbra cast by his shifting shoulders spanned past his silhouette, a spooky trick of the light that caused shadowy extensions to unfurl from his upper back. I'd seen that before. A few times, actually. I again recalled the picture in Ryder's room.

As Leif popped his collar, a small yet recurring emblem stood out in his tattoos: NS with a serpent's head near his thumb. Too soon it disappeared within the other designs as he hiked his leg over the wide saddle of his classic motorcycle. Nearly mistaking the turn of the engine for a mini explosion, I jumped so high I was pretty sure I left my skin for a second.

"I'm out of here then." Leif bumped his brother's knuckles and took a final glance at me, eyes boring past the surface. "You two should get going as well."

"Right." We answered at the same time, jittery, as if needing to prove our innocence.

We must have looked like bumbling fools rushing for the doors and fumbling with the handles as we clambered into the car. Neither of us made a peep as we trailed Leif down the dirt driveway and out onto the main road. He saluted us as he turned his iron hog left, and we skidded to the right.

"You work at the coffee shop downtown, right?" Ryder asked.

Don't remember providing that detail, but I must have at some point, I thought, as I nodded yes. After that, the silence kept—which I was fine with. I had too much anxiety to say anything coherent. I stared at the side of the road, hoping to see my bulky wireless headphones, because without them I couldn't turn my brain off. I mean, how does one go from learning econ to magic and not feel overwhelmed?

Magic. Not just pulling rabbits out of hats. Magic capable of incinerating living beings.

I gnawed at my lip. My necklace hummed against my fingertips, a temporary wash from the stress. I peered over at my driver, who paid more attention to the rearview mirror than he did the actual road. It didn't ease my fear that a pissed off demon could manifest out of thin air at any moment.

"I do want to say one thing." The tiniest tremble entered my voice, so minor no one but Ryder would have noticed. "I think it's pretty suspicious all this started happening around the time I met you."

"All of what?"

"All of this weird stuff." Although I peered out the window, his reflection dominated my view. He maintained his focus on his task. I tried to do the same. "The other day I woke up to a flying gremlin, today I was chased by the Creature from the Black Lagoon's cousin. I can't tell the nightmares from reality anymore, and there's one common denominator in all of this: you."

Ryder tightened his grip on the wheel. "These things don't materialize overnight. It takes decades, or an obscene amount of money, for a human to interact with a piece of dandruff from another dimension. So, unless you've invested in some 4D spectacles or are suddenly a scholar in Source…" He tilted his neck towards me and raised his brows despite the obvious answer to that. "Maybe you've been a part of this world all along. You've just been taught not to notice."

"For eighteen years I've been getting along fine and dandy," I argued, "then you show up and shit hits the fan. Any other suggestions?"

"Really." Ryder shot me a disbelieving look, lightning fast, before focusing back on the stretch of road in front of us and behind us. "In that entire time, you've experienced nothing?"

"Besides the tarot reading from hell, no." I held in my lies as tightly as I clenched my fists. I hadn't explained the Voices to anyone—the shame held me back from opening up—plus, I'd been able to do life fine-ish the way things were. But now…now the Voices were gone, and the same old wound still existed. Now it felt like everything was crashing in at once and if I didn't change the topic I might get buried. "We're focusing too much on me here. I still don't understand how you tie into all of this. Why haven't I met anyone else like you? Where are all the other Ryders?"

"They're here," he said.

"What, in hiding?" I waved at the endless stretch of forest.

"No." He tightened his jaw. "The Nephilim walk among us."

They had a name. Even if I couldn't pronounce it, my

heart leapt faster than the blur of trees passing by. "Are they all as stealthy as you? Is that why I haven't seen them?"

"You've seen them, but you haven't noticed."

"How so?"

"Your eye has clearly been trained to overlook their abilities. As if it were only human."

That. Phrase.

He glanced over at me, probably to make sure I didn't mistake him for an ax murderer again. "But angelic DNA is dominant. Those traits can't stay dormant forever."

"What does that mean?"

He smirked. "It means you're part angel, baby."

I heard what he said, but the words didn't register. They went right over my head. With the freaking halo I had, apparently. Angels. Demons. Magic—Source. I took a deep breath to try and stifle the panic.

"How does that even happen?" I twisted a strand of hair, not sure I wanted to know the answer.

"Well, when an angel and human love each other very much…"

Not *those* details. "I actually took sex ed, but thanks for being so willing to give me a refresher." I rolled my eyes. "Aren't angels supposed to be in heaven or something like that?"

He laughed softly, running his tongue along his molars. "Figures you'd bring that up. Heaven, hell. Good and evil. Those concepts are for mortals, not us." He scrunched the hair on the crown of his head, pulling the unbridled strands out of his eyes with the hand that wasn't driving. "The angels *are* in another realm, and they used to come to

Earth on assignment. Some stayed for the mortals—those were our ancestors, and unlucky for them, they were totally star-crossed. It's forbidden for an angel to get romantically involved with a human."

My heart seemed to have inched up my throat, and I had to gulp it back down. "What happened to them—the angels that fell in love with mortals?"

"They were punished, banished." Ryder shrugged. "No one really knows for sure."

"Do angels not come here anymore, then?"

"Supposedly a few. But we never see them."

It felt absurd to be having this conversation as the trees cleared and we sped past a liquor store, but at least the return to familiar civilization grounded me so I could ask the important questions. "What kind of assignments?"

"Someone's suddenly curious." Yeah, well, it wasn't often he willingly provided me info, so I was taking advantage of it. His smile had faded, but the left corner of his mouth still twitched up. "Deliver messages, provide strength and comfort, mete out judgement…"

"So, what does that make you then? My guardian angel?" It was supposed to come off funny and sarcastic, but it came out exactly how I felt: scared, overwhelmed, and done. Totally done. Doner than I was earlier—and I hadn't thought that was possible.

Ryder shifted in his seat and hunched his shoulders. I could literally see him retreating into himself. "I don't know what I am anymore."

His emo response would've annoyed me more, but I sighed, because that made two of us.

If Ryder was right and I was Neph…Nephli…ugh, whatever it was, part-human part-angel, did that mean my parents were, too? Obviously, it would. But were both? Was one? Did the other know? Was my mom condemned for love? So many questions spiraled in my mind.

Something occurred to me. "Do the angels, do they ever…communicate in other ways with you?"

He raised a brow. "Like…"

"Like through sounds or your mind or I don't know, handwritten letters?" I figured I'd make it as general as possible so as not to reveal myself, but my voice came out small, mouselike with embarrassment.

"No."

Wow. Sharp and to the point and not even a breath between my last word and his. Any hope I had shattered, but I had to think the Voices would've said *something* if they were literal angels. A knot formed in my stomach and prickled my senses, irritating those vertical scars on my back. Maybe they did—at one point or another they'd mentioned powers and apocalypse and I'd been too scared and stubborn to listen, and…I would hear them out now if they just came back.

Before I could stop myself, I blurted out, "Are you saying I've been surfing alongside these beings and serving them drip coffee this whole time without realizing it?"

He nodded.

I envisioned the impassive employee at the Boardwalk ticket booth counter, the girl with the choppy bangs in my class. The longboarder dude who paddled out next to me, the quadruple-shot-extra-foam-two-pumps-sugar-free-vanilla-latte drinker who never tipped. They had all seemed normal. Was it a mask?

"What are they doing here?" I caught myself. "What are *we* doing here?"

"Trying to get by, like the rest of humanity." Why did he sound. So. Indifferent.

Meanwhile, I was on the verge of hyperventilation. "Sounds complicated when you've got monsters spawning out of nowhere. I'd say life is a bit more dangerous on your side of the tracks."

"Demons," Ryder corrected. "Which are really the tortured souls of corrupted angels. And they don't spawn—they're summoned, remember?"

"That's beside the point!" I snapped, even if his disclosure made my heart skip a beat. Like, how did he think that would make it better?!

"Well demons aren't born, they're made! And that doesn't always happen," he added.

"Then why is it happening to me?" I couldn't disguise the strain in my voice anymore. Was I becoming a demon—is that what was happening? "You have an idea, Ryder. I overheard you talking to your brother when I was in your room."

I may have confessed to espionage, but forcing an honest answer was worth the risk. I waited on the edge of my seat for his response, my fingers drumming the sides of my legs.

Minutes passed, and flaky paint soon replaced the stripped bark as the buildings started to outnumber the tree trunks.

Fully out of the forest now, the low howl of the wind faded to crosswalk beeps and the tune of the pedestrian shuffle. The neon bulbs of downtown rose ahead like a sun. Blocks from my drop I was nowhere closer to solving the mystery of this guy—or myself.

When he didn't speak, I forced myself to needle him, which wasn't hard considering how annoyed I was. "Seriously? I can tell you all about me, but when it comes to you, not a peep?"

As the car slowed to a halt, Ryder gave his most honest response: the silence that defined him. He didn't owe me anything anyways, and how could I forget: to him, I was *just some girl.*

"Screw you." I jumped out, stopping before I slammed the door. Over my shoulder, I called, "By the way, if you're my guardian angel, then I'm officially firing you."

CHAPTER 15

Not going to lie, I was pretty proud of myself, snapping at Ryder, until my ankle twisted with the jump out of his truck. The whimper definitely undercut my badassery, but it wasn't my fault my fury had cancelled out my brain's ability to judge the truck's deceleration.

Real cool, River. Real cool.

As the thrums and hums of downtown filled the air around me, the Chevrolet's sputter mixed with the urban sounds—the last thing I'd let myself do was look back, so I couldn't tell if Ryder bounced or stuck around.

Not sure why I cared anyway.

Stalking through the door of Kona Koffee, my anger kept me from focusing on much else. That's why when I heard, "River, what's up?" It completely stopped me in my tracks.

I may have blamed my exit on training her—I didn't think she'd actually be here. Closing by herself, after working there for like…a day.

I forced a smile that hurt my insides. "Hey, Shanley. I needed a minute. Is Tom around?"

"Nope." She shook her head.

Phew. My shoulders dropped as if releasing an invisible weight. "Thank God." I flung myself to the closest bistro table and plopped into a curved plastic chair, resting my foot on the one next to me, unabashedly making myself at home.

Shanley took note of my sprawled-out posture. "You look like you could use a drink."

I didn't have the chance to decline or accept, but I was glad she made the choice for me because I did need a coffee. Stat.

Whipping out the grinder from the countertop rinsing station, she got to work, stopping everything to help me in the final stretch of her shift. Her hustle, something she'd been lacking during our last shift, melted my cold, angry heart.

"Any preference?" She held up my milk options.

"Almond, please." This time my smile was genuine.

She'd gotten the system down pretty fast: tamping the espresso grounds, locking the portafilter, steaming the milk without burning herself. I hated when people watched my every move behind the counter, but I couldn't turn away from her—her flannel twirled around her waist as she spun to grab things, bopping the buttons and tapping the granite as if the only way to tame her energy was to keep moving.

Either she'd had too much caffeine, or something was different…

I bit out a sigh. I was probably being paranoid. I mean, I'd just been told that angels and demons existed—how could I not second-guess everything? And the longer I watched… the more unraveled she became. The instruments shook with her erratic moves. Under-eye bags dug like craters into her fair face, visible even in the dimly lit room. She'd been a little unkempt when I'd met her, but that was different, on purpose—part of her style. Tonight, she smelled a little huskier, her hair looked a little patchier, the blackness of her pupils dominated the blue.

She grabbed an opaque brown bottle from the mini fridge, dipped her head, and took a pull. The flask perspired onto her fingers, like the sweat sprouting from her hairline.

It was struggle city over there.

"You feeling okay?" I tried to be nonchalant.

"Yeah, just out late last night." Shanley offered a tight grin.

"Ah, hair of the dog that bit you then." The goal had been to make her laugh, but not the forced kind she barked out as she handed me the drink. I deflated a bit. "Thanks."

My gaze lingered on her irises, which seemed to lose themselves in the moonlight before she went to sanitize the equipment for the second time that night.

Palms pushing off the tabletop, I attempted to stand. "Here, let me help."

"I don't think so, girly." She pointed for me to sit. "You've got an ankle to nurse and a mochaccino to sip."

She'd caught that? It was the *slightest* limp. But I lowered myself into the chair because this was exactly what I needed right now—a comradery with no strings attached.

"What are your plans tonight?" she asked as she dipped beneath the counter.

"Well, it's a school night, so probably nothing. You?"

"You got to let loose sometimes, Riv." She popped back

up. "My friends and I are having a bonfire at Davenport Beach. You think you can hobble yourself to it?"

It'd definitely warmed up, but I still found myself saying, "Even after that downpour today?"

"Especially after that downpour today. We were about to cancel and then the rain let up." She pointed to the stretch of cloudless sky visible outside the windows. "I'm not letting this night go to waste."

She had a point. I couldn't deny I was tempted. But… "I would, but school. Remember?" I'd already failed economics once; I didn't need to do it again.

"You don't strike me as someone who lets authority dictate your personal life." Shanley inclined her chin. "Come with."

Taking a sip of my drink, I cycled through excuses—curfew, homework, Dad, finding out what happened to the Voices, learning more about my part-angel lineage. For a second, I closed my eyes. I had so much shit to sort through. What was one night to live and forget about all of it?

"Sure," I finally said. "Why not."

"Awesome." The enthusiasm spread across Shanley's cheekbones with a peach flush. It hid last night's boozy imprints, making her glow. "You're right though, we do have a problem," she said straight to my sagging crew neck.

I followed her gaze and pulled at my potato sack of a shirt—Ryder's. My hands balled into fists. I wanted to burn it, along with the rest of my outfit that was caked in demon.

"Not to worry." Clearly sensing my stress, Shanley waved a hand as if she could erase it. "I know someone who can help us." Sweet of her to say *us*, even though she meant *me*.

After a few punches into her cell, she returned to her closing duties, using the machinery as her drum set. Every so often she'd stop and take a few ragged breaths, shaking with a whole-body twitch. Then she'd lift her shoulders, roll her neck, and sigh. And every time I tried to stand up and run over, she'd wave me off and get back to it like there'd been no interruption.

While we waited for a miracle, because that was what it would take to fix this mess, I stole a glance outside.

The asphalt sparkled in the full moon's light, a disco ball of glass and calcite. Stray bar hoppers stumbled into trash cans that had been ransacked by the gulls. A motorcycle revved a couple blocks over, the vibrations carrying all the way to my seat by the windows.

Other than that, it remained pretty quiet.

No hot rods lurking in the shadows. No prehistoric demon birds dropping from the sky. No guys in black clothes and combat boots.

Then my miracle arrived.

She stomped across the plaza as if it was her personal runway in her thigh-high boots and fence-net tights. Kicking loose soda cans, blowing hot pink gum bubbles, wearing a suede jacket like a cape over her shoulders. Her bare arms flared with each authoritative strut, her skin as pale and radiant as the moon that shone down on her like a spotlight.

"Hey, babe," she said in a sultry tone to Shanley when she entered, tossing her jet-black bob and cherry-patterned sack of tricks aside before going in for the European double kiss.

Wrapping her arms around this mystery woman's waist, Shanley tucked her fingers into her flared, leather shorts' back pockets, and turned them both towards the taken bistro table—to me. "Mau, I want you to meet River."

"Hey, kitten." She batted her wide-set eyes, irises dark as a desert night, cat liner swirling out from her smooth, creaseless lids.

"Hi there." I waved from the corner, feeling a bit like fresh meat.

"She's coming to the bonfire tonight." Shanley's mouth stretched into a grin so wide it exposed prominent canines. "Can you work some of your magic?"

I tried not to flinch, but hearing the M-word was like taking a sip of a too-hot drink.

Mau's heels echoed off the concrete as she left the rubber mats behind the counter. "Let me get a good look at you. C'mon, don't be scared."

I rose from my chair, cringing as my butt peeled away like it'd been stuck to the surface. I wished I would've checked a mirror before I left Ryder's, or at any point before being put on display here. Mau didn't seem to notice, or at least didn't seem care, as she circled around me, humming in deep introspection.

She brought her palms together, her amethyst nails steepled against her bright red lips. "I can work with this."

Oh great! My stained jeans, scraped cheek, and hair that probably looked like a rat's nest didn't sabotage my potential for whatever it was that came next.

"Hand me my bag." Mau gestured to her friend and then returned her focus to me. "Now, kitten, this may hurt a bit, but I know what I'm doing. Just call me your fairy gothmother."

Signaling my consent, not that I had a chance to protest anyways, Mau pulled at my roots and suffocated me with dry shampoo. I winced as she got out her tweezers, seeing stars after a hefty plucking. A cool towelette calmed the burn, and per the artist's directive I rubbed in some primer and tinted moisturizer. She pulled out an earring gun.

I shielded my lobes. "I already have them pierced but thank you."

Her finger rested on the trigger. "Care for another one?" With her free hand, she tucked my hair behind my ear, exposing my cartilage.

I shook my head no. The scorches from her curling wand had been enough.

"Suit yourself." She handed me a pair of oversized gold hoops instead.

Hair sprayed, face contoured, and tied into my clothes—Mau knotted the bottom of my t-shirt so it fit snugger, and it cropped even higher—I breathed in the scent of vanilla and coconut. She'd really worked magic. Then she tossed me a piece of fabric. "Try this on, but put it under the hand dryer for a sec. Let's keep the high tops; those are sick."

I went to the bathroom, beyond thankful tonight's invitation didn't require an attempt to walk in some surprise stilettos. If I had to ditch my Vans, I'd never agree to this.

Letting out a breath in the urinal-equipped room of freedom, I peeked in the splotchy mirror. Despite Mau's clear preferences for dramatic winged liner and a bold lip, I still looked…myself. Myself with tamer brows, a hint of bronzer, a silkiness to my golden split ends, and a powdered beige sparkle to my lids. I ran a finger along my cheek—the scratch left by the teratorn's claw completely invisible behind a few dabs of concealer.

After I smeared some tinted gloss onto my lips, I held the pleated skirt Mau had gifted me beneath the heat to let it iron out the wrinkles and laced the bows on each side. Smooth enough, I slipped it on, and it sat a little higher than my belly button—but it still didn't reach my top.

Bearing an unusual confidence and an equally exposed midriff, I made my grand reveal.

Shanley had her companion pinned up against the register, too invested in the taste of her neck to notice my entrance. I cleared my throat and they parted.

"Not bad for using an automatic dryer." Shanley beamed. "Babe, she looks incredible."

"Thank you." With my arms awkwardly stiff at my sides, it might not have sounded too convincing when I said, "I like it." But truly, I did. I was just used to a more boho look. This was jarring, and sexy, and it was different. But for a night, it allowed me to play someone else—and after the day I'd had, someone else was exactly who I needed to be.

"Looks like my work here is done. See you there." Grabbing her designer duffel, Mau strutted out, giving me, her muse, a final, "Bye, kitten."

I watched my fairy gothmother parade across the courtyard until she disappeared.

Shanley appeared behind me in the window's reflection, twirling the mop. "Ready to rock 'n roll?"

Decked in a smile and a makeover that rivaled Cinderella's, I grinned. "Ready as I'll ever be."

CHAPTER 16

Shanley patrolled the rows of cars parked every which way in the dirt. After circling a few times, she backed her Honda up to another's bumper, leaving less than an inch for them to reverse.

A bush impeded my own exit. Worried I'd scratch her car, I opened the door a crack and shimmied through the sliver of space. I didn't think she noticed—she was already out, her gaze glued to the stars. I smoothed the wrinkles from my skirt and joined her. There were no streetlamps out here, but the hoots and hollers gave a clear path to where we should go.

Her bright eyes reflected the Milky Way's glow. "Ready?"

I nodded, though my stomach dipped in equal parts fear and anticipation as we trotted down the bluff. I tried to match Shanley's eager strides; her excitement provided a shield against my anxiety—but that hit me the second I fell behind.

What if she forgot about me once we hit the party and left me to fend for myself? Large group settings weren't my strong suit. All the overlapping threads of conversation tangled in my mind and made it hard for my thoughts to reach my lips. In similar situations, Javi had been there for me to grab on to when it all got to be a bit too much.

I couldn't exactly latch on to my new coworker's arm for the night. That'd be weird. I sucked in a breath. Three hours to midnight and with no cell service, my fate was written in the stars above. I'd be alone, I'd be stuck, there was no way I'd make curfew—

My worn soles slipped on a loose pile of rocks and skidded out beneath me. The whiplash snapped me out of my spiral, almost doing the same to my neck as my limbs twisted awkwardly to keep me upright. I found my footing just as Shanley glanced over her shoulder and slowed so I could catch up. Her face, alight with excitement as she waited for me, only made me feel worse.

Alright, River, enough.

I agreed to do this. I was here. I would make the best of it.

Returning the grin, I scurried to her side, and we trekked through the brush and gritty outcrops. Shadows from the sheltered cove below rose past the limestone cliffs. We neared the bottom as the thickest part of the overgrowth tapered out, and found the party gathered around a raging bonfire in the middle of the sand.

Fire spinners burned circles into the night that remained on the inside of my eyelids long after I walked away. Couples fled into the natural grottoes, tending to their own budding flames. Some sprawled on the circumference and drew tribal patterns across each other's chests.

An artist beckoned me over. "Can I paint you?" She was lathered in a palette of reddish clay, the dried texture staining her skin and the tips of her dreads. My eyes traced the moon cycles over her abdomen. A *yes* ghosted my lips, but as I turned to my host, I realized she wasn't next to me.

"No thanks," I quickly said. I trudged around the red Solo cups littering the shore, careful not to let Shanley escape into the sea of bobbing heads—until one of those heads jumped into my path, crouched like a panther, and I lost sight of her anyways.

He broke out in a capricious roar, russet drawings branding his exposed pecs: a motif of animals and crescents. Perspiration beaded the back of my neck, as the swollen muscles in front of me trembled and flexed…just like they had after taking me upstairs at the last party we were at together.

I closed my eyes to escape the visual, but the ale on his breath smelled too much like his vodka aftertaste had. And the salt in the air felt too much like the tears that had streamed down my face, during and after.

When I opened my eyes, the memory faded, but he was unfortunately still standing there.

"We welcome the moon!" Chet Jennings declared.

"Please tell me you're not a regular here." He'd already killed the vibe; I didn't need him taking out my new friendship, too.

"Maybe not, but can't I appreciate the full moon for what it is?" He stepped closer. "A big, influential mass with a gravitational pull that even you can't seem to resist."

Gross, now he was penning metaphors about his dick.

Without a single nod of appreciation to the "lunar" bulge in his pants, I moved to go around his arched silhouette. Brute strength pinned me in place, and his dilated stare pierced me with a feral hunger that morphed his boxy face into a grimace. I wriggled against his grip, but he twisted my arm when I fought.

"What are you doing?" Anger plated my voice. "Let go."

He sniffed my collarbone. "You look delicious tonight, River."

His disgusting attempt at flattery snuffed out the confidence I'd built up, and I suddenly felt way too bare in my makeshift crop top. "Don't touch me." I used my free hand to push him off, but it had the opposite effect, and he wrenched me closer.

Flush against his rock-hard body, I couldn't look away as he mocked me with a broad grin. Saliva collected at the corners of his mouth. Frothy, foamy. Gross. "One school away, it's as far as we've always been. And lucky for you, it's as far as we'll ever be." He waved towards the mountains separating us from the valley. "I'll be at a private university over the hill starting in August. Just one. School. Away."

"What are you even talking about? You make zero sense." I tugged to break out of his grasp, but he held my wrists and curved them towards his chest.

"C'mon, let's kiss and make up."

"You are sick." I'd rip those lips off with my own damn teeth before submitting to him. Would have the first time if the shots hadn't left me nearly immobile, too far gone to say yes or no or slow down or stop. I might've even unbuttoned my pants myself—but deep down I knew I hadn't wanted it. By the time that realization surpassed a slurry rush of emotions, I'd already felt the lubricated condom.

The spacious clearing suddenly felt too tight, like the rock walls were caving in. The sky hung too low, like night was just a painted ceiling and the stars would combust on top of me. I had to get out. There were too many nooks and crannies here, too many sea caves he could pull me into. Where the hell did my plus-one go?

As Shanley's name left my lips, the grip ripped from my arm and a blurry mass bowled into the party. Sending people scattering as it neared, it knocked already swaying bystanders to their asses like bowling pins.

The wind rustled my lungs. It had all happened so fast. But at least my arm was free, and my captor was huffing on the ground.

Shanley pointed to the whimpering heap in the sand. "Don't come near her again!"

Chet hissed, swatting at those naïve enough to try and help him to his feet.

I crossed my arms, unable to hide the tremble in my voice. "A little late."

"I'm so sorry." Shanley tapped my elbow. "I thought you were right behind me."

"I was, until I got caught in a drunken mousetrap—" I broke off to duck from a sailing champagne cork. "Clearly we have different meanings for *bonfire*." My fingers found their way to my mouth. I chewed nervously. "Out of all the beaches on this sprawling coastline, why does Chet Jennings have to be at this one?!"

I shuddered at his name, and I hated myself for it— that even his name, *his name*, three simple syllables, had this much power over me. "Do you know who that is?"

Shanley shook her head, a few strands of her blonde hair, woven with ashy brown undertones, shaking loose to frame her temples. "Absolutely no idea, but he sounds like a prick. I'm sorry." It came off genuine enough for me to relax my arms to my sides. "Honestly, I don't even recognize half the people here. It's usually our small pack of twenty or so every month, but in the summer, it can get out of control."

Twenty? Not that night. Maybe add another zero. I nudged a discarded beer can, fighting the urge to pick it up. "You do this every month?"

"Yeah. And don't worry, we clean up." Shanley must have noticed the scrutiny, given her wink that followed. "Anyway, before we were so rudely interrupted, I found some of my friends. I swear they won't bite. And we'll make sure that idiot…"

"Chet," I offered.

"We'll make sure he doesn't, either."

The thought brought a shiver. I didn't think she realized how literally she'd spoken, what he'd do to me if given the chance. But I wanted to believe her, especially because I still felt his glare stabbing me in the back.

With a sigh my shoulders dropped, effectively giving in to her reassurance. She smiled and tucked me into her side, giving me a one-armed squeeze before steering us a friendlier route.

The group split for Shanley like a royal procession, but they paid their respects in beer, not roses, to their queen—bottles and red cups being thrust in our path, ready for her to clink.

For someone who claimed she was clueless on the headcount, she reciprocated every greeting. I sauntered beside her, offering a nod when anyone said hello, awestruck by what was unfolding. The high and low fives, the pats on the back, the mock howls she received from literally every person.

Rippled indents spread beneath our heels the farther we treaded down shore, my Vans sinking into the ground that had been kissed by the waves a short while ago. A motley crew of six perched on a cluster of barnacled stones and hopped down as we made our approach.

The fresh ocean air vacuumed the veil of smoke and revealed the strawberry moon. It rose above the waterline, igniting the salt crystals into infinite rows of string lights, reflecting across the surface in shiny strips and glowing shards.

Strands of bluish white glistened from the horizon to the bridge of Shanley's nose. The cool moonlight illuminated a smile that shone brighter than the constellations—it flushed away the haunted look she wore from the day before, practically transforming her into a whole new person.

It was hard not to catch the mood.

Met with howls instead of fist bumps, Shanley returned the primitive welcome, and they sang together as a pack. I pursed my lips in a show of solidarity but refrained from joining in.

This party grew more interesting by the minute. I wasn't sure if that fascinated me or scared the shit out of me. A little bit of both, I decided, as a chain of people with merlot-stained teeth awaited me with eager grins. Unsure of what the appropriate response would be, I let out a belated "Woo!" and, odd ceremony completed, the exchange of names commenced.

Maverick, with a paisley kerchief tied around his dusky forehead, spoke to me between puffs of his cigarette. He explained that earlier in the day he lost a bet to Des, a busty chick with a green flat mohawk that trailed to her pale, exposed shoulder blades, which led to a tattoo of Smurfette on his butt.

He offered to show me—

"Maybe next time," I said.

"Hey, kitten." Mau flashed a sly grin next to a shirtless and very sunburned guy named Kenny rocking bear trap nipple rings. I continued down the line. Despite their air of ruggedness, Shanley kept her promise: they didn't bark or bite.

With my elbows propped on the seaweed draped over the rocks, I felt like I could hang! There was enough distance between our small group and the larger gathering, where the chatter and laughter of Shanley's close friends ebbed and surged with the waves, but its crescendo didn't rattle me into silence—that was just me being shy.

I leaned in closer to catch Des's side of the story, but another conversation snagged my attention.

A somber trio built like marines and gruff like unshaven frontiersmen had marched towards the group during intros, pace set by the thuds of the bongo drums. Two stayed tight-lipped, scanning the beach, while Kai, Shanley called him—the one in front, the one in charge—rattled off a monotonous download of the night, as the flares of the bonfire reflected off his ochre biceps.

Normal shenanigans, I determined of the bits and pieces that made it to my ears. Until Kai's tone changed, and instead of reporting overenthusiastic party crashers, he was getting riled up about bastards and bites and *Chet*.

Unease flooded me.

If this news bothered Shanley as much as it did me, she made sure it didn't breach her expression. "What do you mean he bit a guy named Chet?" she muttered to Kai, her face still beaming. It wasn't a question. It was an order, a command.

Kai masked his emotions, his hooded eyes revealing nothing of concern. "The wrestling turned to brawling. Antonio nipped him right on the shoulder."

Shanley's smile didn't waver as she continued through her teeth, "It's the full moon, Kai. Anyone bitten tonight will turn."

My stomach dropped. Full moon, bitten, turn? I didn't like where this was going…

"Antonio's drunk." He rolled his muscular neck, puffing his chest. "And that idiot was asking for it."

"And Antonio couldn't fucking control himself?" There it was. The slip of concern I'd been waiting for. I really hoped this wasn't a problem. "This is a problem." Damnit. "Take care of it, General. Before shit really goes south."

Kai's response was drowned out by the noise in the background—now garbled. Grating. Screechy. I pressed down on the little flap of cartilage on my ear, effectively covering the canal, the slight pressure warding off the throb building in my head. If I hadn't sensed the abrupt spike of tension in our group, I'd assume the Voices were coming.

Given the tight-lipped faces of everyone around me, they heard it, too.

Des rose from her rocky perch. Watchful, waiting. Mau stilled, her angled lob swaying over her shoulders. Nostrils flared, Kenny inhaled in slow, methodical huffs. Mav put his stog out between his fingers.

A blood-curdling shriek severed any remaining discussion, and everyone's focus whipped to the center of the gathering. The bongo players stopped their music. Even the bonfire seemed to sputter out. A rush of panic flowed through my veins as a raucous howl responded—different from the playful yips of Shanley and her friends. Its guttural resonance gave me goosebumps.

Cries broke out. Not of joy. These were cries for help. For a tense moment, time seemed to freeze. And then everyone around me scattered, disappearing with a wave of kicked-up sand into the chaos.

Uh…should I be following? Dozens of people, scared and shoeless, darted towards the bluffs. Puddles of them collected at the bottom, unable to scale the steeper parts. The madness nipped the heels of those who fled, herding them away from the path and into the rocky cliffs.

Eyes wide as the moon, I turned to Shanley, the only person who had stayed with.

"River, I need you to listen to me." Her palms, swollen to the size of baseball gloves, cupped my shoulders.

I flinched at her distorted mitts. "Are you okay?"

"Get away from here. Now. Go back the way we came." She jerked her head towards the trailhead we'd entered from on the other side of the clearing. "Quickly! My keys are in the glovebox. Drive yourself back to town."

Judging by the hysteria that took over her face, so genuine it spooked me, this seemed like advice I'd be stupid not to follow. But with no license or any real practice behind the wheel—that was twice in one day it had failed me—the best I could do was hide in the back seat and wait it out.

What *were* we running from, exactly? I would absolutely die if she said teratorn. Maybe it was just the cops? Most here looked under twenty-one. Then I remembered what Kai said.

"What's going on?" A chill shook my spine and laced my words. "Don't tell me: Chet did something dumb."

"Please." Shanley's voice was strained. "Just leave!" With that, she spun on her heels and sprinted towards the commotion, leaving me alone.

Water tickled my soles, seeping into the cloth of my Vans. The tide was coming in, stinging my feet with its persistent, cold laps. But I didn't budge—the shock turned me to ice and froze me in place.

What had caused everyone to go full apocalypse?

A low, tormented wail cut the night. I peered into the shadows, distorted since the bonfire had flamed out. Most had escaped, but there amongst the stragglers I tracked a lone figure who chased instead of ran. A figure with a square jaw and sideswept hair the color of butter and too many abs for a six-pack.

Chet.

His form danced with the night, contorting in a way that didn't seem humanly possible.

I grimaced as muscles split and he writhed against bones that seemed to fracture and reform—unable to look away as he bellowed and raged while his jaw twisted, nose elongated, like a snout was forming out of his face.

The chill that had danced along my body was now uncontrollable.

He wasn't Chet anymore. He was a wolf…A werewolf who drew his nose to the sky, taking in the moon with what seemed like pious admiration, sniffing with dramatic heaves. Fur sprouted in patches but bloomed in the moonlight along his unnaturally tan skin, golden tufts growing behind his vertical ears and between the webs of his hands—now paws.

Chet had always been a wolf. But now he dressed the part, too.

Faded celestial symbols stained his jacked, hairless chest, remnants of the reddish clay cementing the tips of his bushy mane. Symbols he'd lain down to receive half-naked, taunting whoever got the torture of painting him, I'm sure.

The thick ocean haze quickly started closing in, its billowy tendrils cloaking the seafront and muffling the distant screams. If I didn't leave, I'd be trapped here between the rising tide and the werewolf, who, by nothing short of a miracle, hadn't noticed me yet.

I leapt into the mist. It broke apart in plumes, shielding the bluffs, throwing off my sense of direction. I pressed my heels into the sand. As long as my ankles weren't sopping wet it meant I was headed towards dry land. Using that knowledge to guide me, I broke into a jog, smack-dab into a column of shadow. I ricocheted off it and tumbled to the ground.

It edged forward, the temperature dropping as it shaded my body. Weird, shadows didn't move like that…

It was Chet.

Still on two legs, his face disfigured into something more canine. Sharper. He hovered over me and took a big whiff. Oh my God, he was smelling me. This couldn't get any worse. I'd gladly take a teratorn over this.

He scraped his back claws into the silt while his front claws cut the night with an audible whir. I flinched as the trail of air brushed my face and he sneered, no longer flashing straight, blindingly white veneers but teeth sharp as daggers.

A heavy *boom* crashed behind me, the water rushing to where I was sitting and stinging my hands—the surf break was closing in. It threatened to swoop me up and deliver me right into the enemy's clutches. His hot breath was so close it caressed my neck. I needed a distraction, a way to get out from under him…

Armed with nothing but chipped turquoise nails and my own set of canines, sharp enough to tear the skin off an apple, *not* the skin off a throat, I dug my fingers into the sand. I threw a fistful in his face. He yelped and scratched his eyes, allowing me the seconds I needed to crab-walk out of his reach. I clambered to my feet, and knowing how ridiculous it looked, I put my dukes up.

Shoulders hunched, I readied myself for his imminent attack. He rose to full height, at least two feet taller than his human form, snarling, spitting, salivating at my fear. But I didn't escape a demon just to die by *his* hands. I wouldn't go down without a fight.

In a mirrored dance, we both tilted forward, but Chet didn't strike. Eating time instead of me, he toyed with his prey, licking his chops, feasting on our little death game.

The rules were obvious: If I ran, he'd run faster. If I charged, he'd charge stronger. If I screamed, he'd scream louder. The odds were not in my favor.

A growl interrupted our choreography. Too busy trying to psych each other out, neither of us had noticed the other being enter our circumference.

Snared in its shadow, I couldn't tell where this new were-wolf's true outline ended and where the darkness began. I stood my ground, for no other reason than I was rattled to my core. Unlike Chet, this newcomer wasn't adorned with red tinted swirls and whorls across its chest. But they did have something feminine, like two little replicas of the moon, tucked beneath the ends of their overgrown neck hair. Breasts.

This werewolf had breasts.

They curved half-hidden beneath her silky mane, which flowed much fuller and longer with hints of bronze, brown, and gray. While I remained frozen in fear, like petrified prey, the she-wolf's presence clearly didn't faze my sandy-haired aggressor. He rolled his four sets of claws and made a snort—a sound of dismissal.

And then with a snarl, the werewolves became a swiping mass of claws and fur and teeth, nothing more than a spin-ning lump of fur, blurring into a single form.

I inched to sneak past, but their fight veered into my path, threatening to knock me down. If I fell again, chances were I wouldn't make it back up. I retreated, the frigid water now up to my calves.

As the fighting began to detangle, I wondered what kind of death the winner would hand me. The iron hate in Chet's eyes promised he'd go slow with all that immortal time he'd likely been granted. With the other werewolf it was harder to know, but I hoped it involved one swift killing blow. And there was always the off chance the ocean would take me. My knees shook against the force of the undertow pulling the sand out from under my feet.

With the losing werewolf pinned to the ground, the victor settled its icy gaze on me. I couldn't quite let myself feel relieved that Chet had been defeated as she ground her incisors deep into his yellow collar—after all, those jaws would be tearing into me next.

The precision of her bite released the tremor I'd been trying so hard to hold in, knowing that once I unleashed it, it'd spread to the rest of my body and open the floodgates to the terror I'd been able to keep on lock—until now. All while those eyes, a piercing blue that I had seen before but at the moment couldn't place, drove me towards the rising current. Water almost knocked me over and submerged my thighs, just like the anxiety that threatened to drown me, too.

Call it déjà vu, or had I been here twelve hours ago? Clawing at life's final moments, searching for help in a pile of lost causes. Summoning another lightning bolt was laughable at this point. I'm pretty sure that had resulted from sheer luck, not some secret powers I had. It also helped that I'd had a wingman, one who casually packed a quiver and probably—no, definitely—would know what to do with a couple of hounds from hell.

My bottom lip, which now stung and tasted of blood, bore the brunt of my panic. I wiped my mouth on my sleeve. The werewolf's nostrils flared wide, purposeful. Hungry at the scent of my blood. I was a goner. Tears fell and mixed with the salt water, searing the skin around my eyes. At first, I attempted to blink them away but then gave in to the burn and kept them shut.

I didn't need to see what came next.

Cold pain lanced my fingers and toes. It spread through my veins to the rest of my body: the onset of hypothermia. I'd felt this before—and the memory came as frigid and fast as the rip current that'd carried me away from my mom when I was eight years old. Much too quickly I'd succumbed to the open water, my muscles leaden like anchors. And the cold…it wasn't just the crisp ocean. It was the air above me, suddenly harsh and stormy even though it'd been the definition of picturesque. Familiar arms wrapped around me the second mine could no longer move. My mom and I should've both made it out—she'd pulled me far past the siloed flow of the current—but something had held her back.

A deafening roar collided with the crashing break, forcing me into the present—the shapeshifters had grown impatient, their thunderous roars an omen of death. It sounded like dozens more had joined them.

The one beautiful thing about this bitter end was that I didn't need to imagine my sacred place, the ocean. I was already there, wrapped in its nippy cloak, its undulating fury an extension of my own. My numb hands dropped to my sides, extending out to meet the ocean's spray, even though by now I couldn't really feel it. I couldn't really feel anything. Except anger.

Lots and lots of anger. So much hot, fiery anger it could have thawed me. I couldn't get it out of my head: that I'd just *waded there*, dumbstruck, while the ocean flooded my mom's throat and turned her cries to gargles. *Why?* Why didn't I do anything? Then. Now. Ever.

When my eyes snapped open, I didn't see werewolves. Instead, a surge of water flew past me.

I tripped backwards, expecting to be submerged by the tide, but landed in squishy damp sand. The mighty flow of the current muffled my gasp as the ocean parted around me without so much as a splash. The threat before me tumbled into the twisting tide. A wave, big as the beach itself, flooded the crescent clearing with the force and speed of a river overflowing, devouring everything in sight.

Except me.

Breathing hard, I eased to my feet and paced next to the towering element and looked up. Translucent at the top, it deepened in color with each descending layer, ending in a rich midnight blue at the bottom. It stretched high, but not as high as the cliffs. Six feet, maybe, at my back and my sides. Ahead, it sloped downwards, giving me a clear line of sight to the bluffs—like I was caught in the crest of the wave just before it would break and speed towards shore.

Shadowy figures waded through the surf. I couldn't tell if they were werewolf or human.

My hand quivered as I reached for the water's surface. It jolted back instead of flowing across my fingertips, like my touch was a magnet repelling it. I did it again and it receded.

It hit me then: these fluid walls weren't here to keep *me* in, they were here to keep *them* out.

The water shuddered, a small wake of it slipping forward—this would only hold for so long. I needed to find a way out. I made a run for it.

The Pacific Ocean parted at my strides, recoiling with each drive of my knees and swing of my arms, as if we were dancing, me leading, the ocean following. With each salty inhale, it was beginning to feel a lot less like divine luck and more like it was me—like *I* had summoned the water, and the lightning.

Either way, I was getting the hell out of that cove, away from Chet and the beasts that wanted to kill me. The water shook, struggling to retain its form as I leapt over tidepools and cut across the beach. Whatever magic controlled it must have been pushed to its limits, the water's glassy shell punctured by leaks that started out small but grew bigger the farther I traveled through it.

Behind me, the ocean covered my footprints and surged forward, as if attempting to lasso my feet. I didn't let it distract me, using every ounce of energy I had left to propel my legs forward until I reached the base of the cliffs.

The trail on this side of the cove appeared steeper, fissured by landslides, rugged from infrequent use. Scaling it would require all of my extremities, not just my feet. As I flexed my stiff fingers, the ocean shook off the final remnants of magic, releasing a small tsunami headed right towards me. There was no time to absorb what was happening. The burst of power rushed at my heels and I scrambled over the scree, latching on to craggy slabs and exposed roots as every muscle in my body worked to outrun the stampede of water. Its rumble was omnipotent, like a prevailing wind and a heavy rainfall and a fire crackling all at once. I felt it in my ears and my brain just as much as my bones.

I hoisted myself onto the top of the bluff and immediately doubled over, my breaths short and stabbing and not giving me nearly the amount of oxygen I needed. Gripping my kneecaps, I lifted my chin as the swell lapped the edges of the high ground and withdrew just as fast as it had come.

It was over.

My right hand curled into a fist over my heart. I peered at the ocean below, rolling and splashing like nothing was out of the ordinary. All my emotions flooded me at once, and I wasn't sure if I should cry or laugh or scream. I'd escaped. I'd actually escaped.

A blood-curdling shriek suspended my short-lived relief. Was my mind playing tricks, or had the monsters recovered? After today, anything seemed possible. There was no chance I would stick around to see.

Adrenaline spiked in my veins, and I sprinted through the gold-tipped grasses, scanning the flat field of brush and briars to try and recall which way I had come in. Getting out of the cove had been my priority; I hadn't thought of where I'd end up once I reached the bluffs.

Desperate to find an outlet to society, I fixated on the faint yellow light peeking out from the cypress grove ahead. Hypnotized by the illusion of safety, I charged through the prickly branches and spilled out onto the two-lane highway, skidding to a halt at the frantic honking. I didn't know what I thought I'd find there, but as quickly as my hope rose, even more quickly it was slashed by the semi-truck barreling towards me, its headlights speckling my vision like a mosaic.

It screeched past—or that might have been the air leaving my lungs. As the entirety of the day and my exhaustion hit me, I sank next to the defaced white line on the side of the road, the taillights fading with my adrenaline. I tucked my knees beneath me and recounted my misfortunes to the constellations. I'd stretched myself as far as I could.

Even resting against my thighs, my hands would not stop shaking.

Chances were slim that someone would rescue me. This road was quiet. I was about a mile from the makeshift parking lot. And I was pretty sure everyone except the wolves had left.

Shanley didn't seem like the type to leave me hanging, but she hadn't signed up to be my human crutch, either. And if monsters prowled these parts, well, that was even more reason for her to split.

But she'd given me a warning when she told me to get away from the bonfire, like she…knew what was coming. I remembered her panicked words, but I also remember thinking there was so much left unsaid in those blue—*glacial* blue—eyes…

Eyes that pierced me as she locked on to another's throat.

Air rushed my lips in an audible gasp.

Shanley wasn't just *aware* of the threat—Shanley *was* the threat. Shanley was the darker blonde werewolf.

My stomach might have actually dropped out of my

body. A chill cinched my spine and radiated across my flesh. The quirky mannerisms I mistook as a hangover, the wolfy innuendos, the weird obsession with the moon…it all made sense now.

Well, kind of. I was still having trouble grasping the fact that these things were real. And I still wondered if she'd meant to eat me. No matter what her intentions were though, she *did* save me.

Unsure if I wanted to hate her or thank her, I pulled my cell phone out of my skirt's tiny pocket, amazed it hadn't fallen out. Irritation grumbled in my throat. Dead, of course.

Tempted to smash it on the pavement, I dropped it into my lap instead and reached for my mom's necklace—another item I was shocked had made it through the night, still clasped around my neck. The lapis zapped my fingers, scorching my collarbone as it thudded back onto my chest. Wincing as the pain dissolved, I couldn't help it. I *laughed.*

Nothing was funny about my predicament, but there I was, laughing hysterically. It startled me so much I clasped a hand over my mouth to hold it in, but it leapt forth past my fingers. Who harnesses lightning and the sea, kills a demon, challenges not one but *two* werewolves, and is ready to give up because they have to walk a couple miles in the dark?

People who aren't born with Source in their blood. Ryder's voice echoed in my head.

"Source." A concept with the power to mold me or break me, it left my lips in a cloud and dispersed in the moonlight.

You see things for what they are. And most people in this world do not.

A crossroads lay before me, and not the literal one I'd stumbled onto.

I could hide from the truth and treat my afflictions like I always had: as an inconvenience. Although supernatural creatures and episodes that made my skin feel like it was on fire were no longer just annoying disruptions. The other, honestly more terrifying, option was accepting that I was different. I was something else entirely. I was—

Nephilim. A word so loaded it caved in my shoulder blades and prickled the scars raised along the skin there like slashes. I took a ragged breath, wanting to think it away before it spread to my lips. Because if I spoke it out loud it all seemed too real: that I was part angel. And no one was here to fight me on it. No one was here to call me crazy. No one was here to confirm or deny it.

Maybe that's what I needed. I shuffled on my scraped knees, untucking my legs. I was so tired of running.

So, I rose from the ashes and walked, accepting my place on the other side of normal. Already, I felt less alone.

CHAPTER 17

So far, the other side of normal seemed pretty …normal.

I still had miles of pavement to go, but I expected something a little more…climactic. A dramatic unveiling of a wizard guide, maybe? Angel wings sprouting out of my back? Or what I was really hoping for: a visit from a certain three telepathic Voices? Since honesty was now the name of the game, I'd be lying if I said a little part of me hadn't deflated when that didn't happen.

My senses piqued at a rustle alongside the desolate highway, and the skin on my arms rose. Maybe the skeletal limbs swaying off the overhanging trees were about to reveal—nope. The ocean breeze tousled my hair, scattering the roadside debris, but nothing more. I sighed.

No wizard guide. No Voices.

At least the darkness didn't bother me like it used to. Its affiliation with the unknown used to be unnerving, but tonight we walked hand in hand. Tonight, I belonged amongst the shadows of the supernatural. Tonight, I was more than just a midnight rogue.

I trekked next to the painted white line that ran through

the maritime forest parallel to the beach, unflinching as a car flew past—the first I'd seen in at least ten minutes—nearly drenching me as it zoomed through a puddle. Droplets splashed my legs, reminding me of this morning's rainstorm, which already felt so far away.

As the chirps from the crickets started to settle around me, the hum of tires broke the silence again. This time the headlights came *at* me, burning away the blackness, casting my path in a blinding yellowish light.

Shielding my eyes, I ducked my chin as the vehicle came towards me, then hauled past. A futile attempt at turning invisible, but I wasn't about to hurl myself into a bush of what looked like poison oak—wouldn't that be the cherry on top of such a lovely day.

The weight of the wind shifted with the squealing of tires as the car cut across the double line. Its engine jumped in frenetic spurts, like my heart, as it 180'd beside me. Between the diesel and burnt rubber, something familiar hung on the edge of the night.

The passenger door swung open. "Get in."

I faltered, only briefly, to recognize Ryder's starlit jawline. My face tightened, shattering whatever sense of calm I had. A blast of cool mint diffused from the interior, the heady scent trapping any good comebacks. I needed to keep walking, or I might do something stupid, like get in the car.

Letting the bullfrogs speak for me, I picked up my feet and my jaw, which had been hanging open. His truck followed.

"You're freezing cold. I can see your breath."

Nope, that melodic British accent *would not lure me in.* I held my head high. "I thought we were done with this."

"What?" he retorted. "Keeping you out of danger? That might be easier if you didn't put yourself in situations where you're alone in the pitch black, on the side of the road."

"Well done, Ryder." I rolled my eyes, not stopping for his reaction. "You've managed to conveniently find yourself in the right place at the right time again. How do you do it?"

"It'd be a lot easier if you gave me your number." Ugh. I sensed a smirk.

"That's not happening." *Do not look. Do not look.* "And don't change the subject."

This time the ribbiting orchestra answered on *his* behalf.

"Oh, that's right." I let out a bitter laugh. "You never give away your dirty little secrets, but you expect to know all of mine."

My traitorous eyes drifted left, just shy of the door that still hung open. The truck crawled beside me in a smooth straight line, despite the fact that I knew his gaze hadn't left me. My heart pounded against my rib cage, and not because I was worried that he might crash. He'd driven in far more dangerous predicaments.

"I'm not going anywhere. It's not safe out here. I'll drive next to you all the way back to town if I have to."

"Thanks for the warning." My thumb and pointer cupped my chin as I tilted my head. "You don't happen to mean giant-gathering-of-bloodthirsty-werewolves kind of not safe, do you?"

I needed to see his face when I delivered that tidbit, and immediately wished I hadn't turned to look. The golden specks in his eyes glistened in the moon's alabaster glare. Teasing, pleading—I whipped my head forward before that alone convinced me to get in.

"What's the matter, cat got your tongue?" I crossed my arms against a sudden chill that tickled my spine. "Or should I say, wolf?"

"No, I-I'm impressed."

I searched for a hint of sarcasm, scowling when I didn't find it. I kicked a pebble. "I'm not as helpless as you think." As either of us thought, really.

"Please get in the car and we can talk about this."

I stopped walking then, to meet his gaze, and his truck slowed to a stop. "Talk. Like…actually have a conversation? The kind where I get to ask a question, and then you say something back, and you don't just leave me hanging?"

To say the silence was unexpected would have been naïve of me. Yet when he cleared his throat, it had me waiting on bated breath. Several moments passed and nothing came of it, except a familiar wave of disappointment. I should've known better than to believe it'd be any different. So, call me naïve.

And call me ready to go home. I'd walk the entire continent before accepting a ride with him. Maybe he knew that, and that's why he finally answered when my toes pointed north.

"I know what it's like to navigate this world alone. I don't want you to."

My feet halted as I turned to face him. "Which world, Ryder?" I knew the answer. I just needed to hear him say it. He shifted the truck into park.

"The one you're looking for." Not the most monumental admission but it still counted for something—or maybe that was the excuse I used to let myself step towards the car. Nothing but the thrum of his engine, my racing pulse, and his words hung on the night.

"The one I've found," I corrected.

The car stereo illuminated the twitch of his lips and the dimple indented across his right cheek. "I didn't think you'd accepted it so quickly."

My cheeks flushed, tingly and warm. Why did his stupid smirk make it so much easier to forgive him? "Well, when you've been chased by demons and partied with half-naked were-people, you don't have much choice."

His eyes widened, just a bit, while another sort of tension seemed to form between us. "See, we have much more in common than you think."

"Fine." I waved my cell. "Got a charger?"

He held up the USB cord and patted the empty seat. I assessed the way his palms scraped the material, hands worn from nocking arrows and demon-slaying. I sighed. This might very well be the death of me, but it sure beat the company of the mosquitos. And I needed a charge.

Reluctantly, I scooted in and plugged in my phone. The warmth of the cab flooded my skin, thawing my bones. I could have melted into the springy cushion. Ryder responded with a smile that actually felt genuine and not sarcastic for a change, one that creased his eyes and revealed every single one of his teeth, including a cute little crooked one near his bottom canine. It made me melt even more.

Sleep became my next opponent. I battled against the

motor's steady rock, and the hot air defrosting my finger-tips, and a comfy warmth pooling in my belly. But to yield to the exhaustion meant forfeiting what might be my only chance to hear his side of, well, everything.

Was he at the party? Did he see my powers? How much did he know? If I didn't push for answers, I'd never get them. And after all, he promised a conversation. I'd start out small, ease him into it.

Then I blurted, not chill at all, "Tell me this isn't a coincidence. Are you following me?"

His grin vanished. "I'm a hunter. I have a knack for these things."

"Things?" The disbelief in my voice begged him to go on.

He sighed. "Tracking, pursuing, targeting…"

"And humans are on your list? You do realize how creepy that is." The headlights from a passing car illuminated his profile, washing along the crinkle in his brow. I stared at him, waiting for my answer, not caring if it made him uncomfortable.

He tweaked his shoulders. "You're not human—well, not fully."

I crossed my arms and narrowed my eyes. He knew he was evading the question. I'd jump out of this car so fast…

My look must have said it all. "Okay, so I may have stuck around after I dropped you off."

I shot him an *and?* look.

"And I saw you leave with that mongr—coworker of yours."

And?

"And I know what that crowd gets up to on a night like this." He must have said that last part under his breath because he *knew* what kind of reaction it'd spark.

"Wait. You knew I was going to a remote beach with a bunch of literal party animals, and you didn't think to do anything about it *before* I got there?" The audacity of it blew my mind.

"So now you *want* me to rescue you?" The laugh in his voice made me shift in my seat. This was funny to him now?

"This is ridiculous." Frustration startled me out of my fatigue. Death traps warranted a heads-up. Tripping in alleys did not. Ryder was so obsessed with his own self-importance he failed to see the difference. I couldn't believe this.

As I opened my mouth to, I didn't even know, maybe scream, he said, "The Santa Cruz pack is on a No Hunt Order. They have been for over thirty years, ever since the turf war with the vampires in the eighties. A tourist will go missing every now and then, but they don't usually mess with the locals."

They don't *usually*? My fingers dug into the leather seat. I couldn't decide what freaked me out more, another blood-lusting species—vampires, *really*!?—or Ryder's nonchalance about it.

"Yeah, well one of their pack members broke that streak tonight and *attacked* me." The same opportunistic prick who'd cornered me at Grad Night. And did even worse before that. "And by some crazy twist of fate I made it out alive." I kept the whole controlling-the-ocean thing on the DL. At this point, it was a tidbit he didn't deserve to get.

And I still didn't even understand exactly what had happened myself. "No thanks to you."

He went silent before he asked, "Are you…okay?"

"I'm fine. Thanks for asking. But—" Despite being unsettled enough to check the area in case I needed help after he literally threw me to the wolves, he what, ignored the screams? Blew off the dozens of people fleeing the scene? In his words, he was a hunter; he should've been able to sense the chaos, even from the road. I shook my head, my thoughts and emotions tangling my words. "Your timing is just weird," I finally muttered.

"Funny, I thought it was just right." His tone was flat.

"Didn't your parents ever teach you that vanity isn't a virtue?" I snapped.

"My parents died when I was four, so my priority was learning how to survive." His throat bobbed, like the words stuck there. "Virtues don't make the top of the list in survival skills."

Well, now I was the asshole. "I'm sorry. I-I didn't know."

"But instincts do." His green eyes flared as they met mine. He spoke as if he hadn't heard me. "And my gut keeps leading me back to you."

My spine straightened at his admission.

The wall he'd built around his emotions had held up so well I'd doubted it'd ever break. For days I had chiseled at his stony exterior and hadn't even made a dent. In this moment outside the city limits, heated from our perpetual bickering and raw from unexpected truths, I'd finally gotten through.

What now? I reached for his hand atop the stick shift in

the cheesiest, most cliché move possible, and yet it couldn't have felt more perfect.

In an instant, the unsolvable riddle of Ryder became so easy to read. His dark humor, his arrogance, his self-importance: it all had that touch of grief. We shared an identity most were lucky enough not to. Left. Lonely. Incomplete. With my other hand I clutched the lapis between my collarbones, longing for its familiar comfort.

"I lost my mom." I was surprised to hear the words coming out of my mouth. "It…was a tragic accident that happened when I was eight. We were at the beach and"—I held my eyes shut for a moment as a rush of words tangled my tongue—"I got pulled out to sea. She drowned trying to save me."

"Death isn't something most people are comfortable with, but it's all Leif and I know." Ryder's thumb stroked my pinky, and I went rigid at the slow movement. "You start talking to me about the meaning of life? That's when I make a run for it."

"Yeah, I noticed."

"And-I'm-sorry-too." He rushed through each syllable like it might curse him, the apology clearly not a common phrase in his vocabulary. "About your mom. And…that I left you."

I accepted with a subdued "thanks," not wanting to overplay my gratitude and have him retreat again. Because this, having someone to talk and relate to for no other reason than it just seemed natural, felt good. And the more we talked, the more I wanted to know about him.

After a moment I asked, "Are you and your brother close?"

"He raised me after our parents passed." Ryder gripped the steering wheel tighter. "We don't play pranks on each other or have video game nights or even regularly eat dinner together. But he taught me how to hunt and how to shoot an arrow, how to thrive in the forest."

Life skills that, sure, maybe someone learns in Cub Scouts, but survival skills starting at four years old? What about blueberry pancake breakfasts and building forts and learning how to surf? Even if Ryder had *wanted* to experience that, he'd never had the chance to. It was kind of sad.

"I owe Leif everything. He's more than a brother; he's the closest to a father I've ever had." Despite the praise, Ryder's voice rang cold, no hint of the warmth that I'd expect to hear from someone sharing stories about a loved one.

I found myself staring down at my pendant, my fingers worrying the stone. "His opinion must be really important to you then." Without my consent, a memory popped into my head: *Just some girl,* he'd reassured Leif.

"It's more than that." His gaze remained fixed on the road. "Without him I'd be dead."

A deafening quiet settled between us, the air heavy and charged. I didn't press further, partly because the echo of what he'd said to his brother started to sink in again. If I was *just some girl,* then why hadn't his thumb stopped tracing the side of my hand? Why did it arc wider, with a hint of pressure? And *why* did my pinky flutter in response? Why did it rub back with a mind of its own?

Soon the middle of nowhere led into outskirts, and outskirts became boulevards. The night sky, once dotted with stars, now washed out by the city's glow.

We slowed to stop at a red light, the streetlamps illuminating our path like an airstrip.

"Well, here we are, just two lost souls." Ryder toggled the gear shift, the jerky movement causing my hand to slip from his. "What do you want to do?"

I glanced at him suddenly, taken aback by the question and the low drawl to his voice.

What did I want to do?

Crawl into bed and hide under the covers. Return every fantasy book I owned. Cry-laugh about my night to Javi. Uncover my powers. Follow a werewolf.

What did I want to do?

The dashboard's clock read ten thirty on what felt like the longest day of my life. There was an obvious choice: go home and make curfew.

Aside from needing to change out of my damp shoes and still having bits of sand and salt on my legs, staying out meant surrendering more than my freedom: it meant surrendering my old identity. So *why*, when I opened my mouth, was *take me home* not what came out?

"Screw it." I thrummed my palms on my thighs. "What did you have in mind?"

CHAPTER 18

Y OU'VE NEVER BEEN ON A ROLLER COASTER?!" MY
shouts filled the truck, and the back of my hand smacked
Ryder's arm harder than I'd meant to, but shit. Out of Nephilim and werewolves and Source magic, this had to be the
wildest thing I'd heard all day.

And yet the demon hunter sitting right next to me had
looked at me point-blank and said he wanted to ride the
Dipper.

I took a breath to contain my disbelief, but my voice
still pitched up in surprise. "What do you usually do for
fun?"

"I don't know." He dipped his chin, as if trying to hide
how his lips curved into a grin. "Hunt."

"That can't be all you do. Don't you have friends?" Not
that I had them in abundance. "What do you do with
them?"

Both his hands clutched the steering wheel as we cut
through downtown, the shrill cries from the bar hoppers
and after-dark renegades drifting through our open windows. I hadn't taken my eyes off him, and a light flush crept

up his neck. Ryder actually looked *sheepish*. And he still hadn't answered my question.

It shouldn't be a shocker that this moody drifter, who looked like he walked straight out of *The Matrix*, was kind of a loner. But really? No one? Who was his Javi? I knew Leif wasn't. But he had to have *someone* to scream his lungs out at the top of the Double Shot with. Someone to go on long drives with. Someone to laugh with, and cry with, and hug when everything went wrong in the world.

His silence hit me hard. I almost reached for his hand again when he released an audible breath as the twisted amusement park architecture rose into the full moon's sky.

It was open late because summer, and shrieks escaped in regular intervals from the Boardwalk's rides. Circus riffs swelled in and out with every entrance gate we drove by. As we glided into the main visitor lot, my grin inflated my cheeks as his fingers tapped the leather, and he sat up a little higher. Was he nervous?

Ryder got out first when we parked, his gaze fixed on the rooftops and the smattering of attractions atop it, while he waited for me to join. After I got out, we walked to the crosswalk, our arms so close to touching I could feel his heat radiating off him, to the ticket counter nestled in the building beneath the teal tracks.

"Two roller coaster rides, please." The neon lights reflected in his wide green eyes.

The lady behind the counter stared at him blankly, then returned to buffing her nails. He turned to me, flabbergasted.

"That…" I clapped my hand over my mouth, holding

back the giggle that threatened to undo me. "Oh my God, that is too cute." I bumped his hip with mine, shifting him to the side. "Two ride passes, please."

The park employee barely glanced up. "Twenty dollars with the after-dark discount."

I went for the bill tucked in the hidden pocket of my skirt, but Ryder cut in. "Let me pay." As he slipped his credit card under the plastic barrier, I swore his hand trembled—maybe that was just a trick of the amusement park's whirling lights.

"Here's the plan." I snatched up the goods and turned to him, placing the wristband on his wrist and gently sticking the ends together so they didn't snag the hair on his arm. Despite his warmth, goosebumps appeared on his skin. "First rides, second food. Always in that order. Safe to say you've never had a corn dog?"

"I...I'm a vegetarian." His response made me falter with my own paper bracelet, which I usually had no problem putting on even while I was walking.

Perhaps I hadn't heard him correctly through the rally cries of the midway. Yet when I whirled on my heels to question him further, he stared at the cracks in the ground as if he was counting them. A vegetarian. Ha! I'd assumed he ate steak and eggs for breakfast and teratorn pudding for dessert. This night was full of surprises. *He* was full of surprises.

"Oh my God," I just said again, looping my arm through his as I led him down the path, fully embracing my role as tour guide as I pointed out the various carnival games: "I swear the milk bottle towers are rigged." And the

Surf City Grill's delights: "Their famous popcorn chicken might not appeal, but the deep-fried artichoke hearts are to die for." And explained the importance of a roller coaster's seats: "The front obviously has the best view, but the back is where you feel weightless." I caught our reflection as we ambled past the mirrored windows of Fantasyworld Comics. The double dimples set next to my full-faced smile stopped me in my tracks. I looked so…happy.

Then the guilt hit me like a breaking wave.

It's not like I couldn't hang with anyone else, but I knew this would sting my best friend a bit. For a moment, I imagined his rich tawny hands pulling me to the nearest ride, his soft curls lifting with the wind, his thick black brows that always seemed to be raised in amusement.

I did a double-take, and it was someone else entirely who reached for my waist, slaying the illusion of Javi.

The coax of Ryder's fingers, and an eruption of screams, pulled me back to the moment. Both rattled my bones, but it was the righteous roar that shook the doors of the comic bookstore. Our chins lifted to the looming red-and-white structure as an electric-blue cart and a dozen hands flew overhead, taking the screams with it.

The corners of my lips twitched up. "You ready?"

He opened his mouth to respond, but I didn't wait to hear it.

Pulling his arm, we snaked into a faded orange building and followed the curved wooden interior. The line went quickly since it was already so late, and Ryder's warm ivory cheeks paled as the group in front of us boarded.

I gave his arm a reassuring squeeze, clutching on to

his bicep as I raised to my tiptoes to whisper in his ear. "You chase big, bad demons and you're scared of the Big Dipper?"

Now he really looked like he'd seen a ghost.

The ride attendant motioned us over and I darted to the very back seats. "Remember what I said?" I reminded him in a singsong voice.

Ryder forcefully swallowed and wiped his brow, tucking his long legs to fit into the tight space. Beneath the lap bar his chest deflated, keeping our bodies, and his terror, restrained. It was kind of cute to see him squirming like this, over a roller coaster of all things.

A warped *choo choo* signaled our departure. I threw my arms in the air. The cart lurched forward. "Hands up!"

He looked at me like I had gone absolutely insane. "What?"

"Hands UP!" I yelled, and with that, we plunged down into darkness.

Our screams echoed through the tunnel, dissipating in the moonlight as the coaster pulled outside. Breaths tight in our chests, ears stinging with the cool wind, we chugged up the first hill, the track powered by hydraulics and adrenaline.

Being at the top of the Big Dipper stripped life to its simplest form. Here, everything escaped us, except our basic instincts and the energy of the climb.

It was that involuntary reflex that caused me to reach for my neighbor's hand, just before the tipping moment. Half expecting the familiar form of Javi's, I latched on to Ryder's calloused palm instead. Free from the pressure to play it cool, he didn't flinch away, holding me tight until the free fall stole the air from our lungs, and gravity broke us apart.

The rest of the ride was chasing that initial plummet. Which, after the day I'd had, you'd think I'd be good off that. The stomach-twisting turns and heart-stopping hills made my heart pound with the same rush I got running from the teratorn and the werewolves, but I shrieked with joy, not fear.

We lurched into the station, laughing, gasping for the breaths that'd been stolen from us.

Ryder brought his fist to his chest. "I don't think my heart beats that fast when I'm hunting demons!" he shouted, oblivious to the onlookers hunched over the railing.

I buried my cheek into my palm to hide my smile. "You never forget your first drop."

"I definitely won't now." The gold flecks in his eyes burned bright with enthusiasm.

There was something deep behind that stare that seemed to take in every inch of my face. Him looking at me like that…it was like a stroke of lightning and a gentle caress all at once, the moment awkwardly shattered by the attendant freeing us from the lap bar.

We staggered out of our seats, Ryder carving a less straight path, bumping his shoulder with mine. That electric current ignited between us once more, and I couldn't help but think, what happened when the buzz wore off? When we left this paradise for the cold hard world—hands down, rush gone, back to two strangers in the night?

As we made our way to the viewing area that showcased a collage of pictures taken of everyone screaming their lungs out during the ride, his hand brushed my elbow, gliding to my lower back. I'd be a jerk to move away. He was clearly unsteady from some roller coaster-induced vertigo. Right? So, what was my excuse when we finally stood still and waited for our photos, and that hand wrapped around my waist…Maybe it was me who needed the support—because the world seemed to be tilting around me.

Deep down, I knew the shaky legs were temporary. That the dopey grins would dim. And still I couldn't stop the smile from squeezing my cheeks when I spotted our picture on the screen. Our shared joy looked so convincing of a real friendship it'd fool the most cynical bystanders, us. But that picture wasn't reality; it was pretend. The high would fade and we'd be back to what we were, no matter how many purposeful touches he snuck in…

It'd be better to just end it now and go home. "Now that we've got that out of the way." I slid out of his grasp. "I've got to bounce."

"Oh no, we're just getting started." He followed my backwards steps.

I stayed just out of his reach. "Nephilim or not, I still have homework."

"C'mon," he pleaded behind lowered lashes. "You don't have time for one more ride?"

No. I didn't have time for *this* ride, or whatever literal ups and downs we were sharing. Or this conversation. But the second I met his intense green hazel gaze I found myself debating the consequences. Again.

Sure, the threat of missing curfew didn't mean much since I had turned eighteen. But I did still live at home and was technically still a high school student until I got the official piece of paper that said otherwise. House rules, although loose, did remain standing—unless I wanted to sleep somewhere other than under my dad's roof. Okay that was a little extreme; would an extra twenty minutes really change that much?

"Please?" he said, voice low and longing. "You're already going to be late."

My lower back still tingling from his touch, I made the mistake of meeting his eyes, and the words slipped out. "Fine. What's on your list next?"

Our heads slowly turned to the circular steel structure at the opposite end of the park.

"How about the Ferris wheel?" he suggested, gesturing down the path. The hanging lights bathed the concrete in a warm, cozy iridescence, and the music seemed softer over there.

Nope, nope, nope, shouted the logical part of my brain. At this time of night, the Ferris wheel was reserved for people trying to escape the prying eyes of others so they could vape or make out or admire the stars. We were doing none of that. Which was why I had every intention of taking him to the gravity-defying Rock-O-Plane instead.

"Okay." *Damnit, River.* At this point my heart required a muzzle because it kept butting into all my decisions. Maybe we'd get lucky and there'd be so many people waiting we'd have to give up and head to another ride. A backwards, upside-down, super-spinny one…

Of course, when we got to the Ferris wheel, there was no one in line. With jittery limbs, I hoisted myself towards the torn pleather cushion. Ryder caught my hand and guided me onto the seat, sliding in next. My stomach rocked with the pink metal basket as the wheel lifted us closer to the heavens.

On our first loop, we stopped just shy of the peak, thank goodness, because that's where the "magic" happened. I didn't need that added temptation. Plus, being sandwiched between an old couple ahead and gawking tourists behind did take some of the edge off.

"Does it always feel like this?" Ryder broke the silence. A first.

"What?" The layers that framed my face tossed lightly in the wind.

Ryder watched the hair dance across my cheeks. His arm twitched like he was thinking of brushing a hand across my face, and my heart thumped in response. "Hanging out with you."

I let out a barking laugh, hoping it'd distract from the tremble in my voice. "Uh, hectic? Stressful? Death-defying? Yes."

With a ghost of a grin, he shook his head. "No, interesting. Exciting. Amazing." And then he whispered, almost to himself, "I don't think I want to let you go."

A pain cinched my chest. We'd eventually part—he'd made that clear to Leif. I still didn't understand what or who he was looking for; I just knew it wasn't me. That thought broke away as we teetered downwards, and the acceleration brought us earthward. Whizzing past the loading dock, we did another full rotation, and ended our second lap parallel to the roofs of the game stalls. Our shoes dangled so close to the tacked-on prizes I could count the bottles on the Ring Toss.

"It seems pretty lonely, this wizardry, or whatever you call it." My tongue knotted on the word. "Nephilim." I sensed Ryder's smirk and gave his arm a playful backhand. "I've been asking myself, what am I really giving up by giving in? Will I be able to have a semi-normal life? Will I still be able to surf? And have days where the only thing I do is binge snacks and comics? I haven't even graduated high school—I know, I sound stupid, but is it like…demons or diploma?"

He chuckled. "Of course you can do all that."

Suddenly feeling shy and exposed, I glanced over at him, hoping he wouldn't notice the blush blasting my skin. His eyes stayed on the horizon, where the ocean blended into the night sky, the midnight blues fading into each other seamlessly.

When his lips straightened, he said, "And you're not stupid. You're far from it. For what it's worth, I was home-schooled. I definitely didn't finish my schoolwork on society's acceptable timeline, whatever that is. To be honest, I don't even think I got a diploma."

"That's different," I muttered.

"Well, isn't that what you want? A piece of paper to tell you you're as good as everyone else?" Valid point. "Let me tell you now." He closed the space between us, leaning so close that one slight rock of the cart would push me into his lips. "You are."

The gears started shifting, the spokes started spinning, and we plummeted again, back to earth and into each other.

When I fell exactly where I thought I'd land, his mouth was soft, warm. Welcoming. I knew it was coming, but the kiss still surprised me. I froze, savoring the cushion of his lips that pressed so gently against mine.

Only when the Ferris wheel bounced to a halt did we break apart, and it hit me where we had stopped—at the top, a light breeze swinging us back and forth. With no one in view ahead or behind, we might as well have been alone at the top of the world.

Ryder's concentration hadn't strayed from my face. I met his gaze, and he caressed my cheek, his finger lingering on my chin. His bones, used to crushing monsters, trembled slightly, like they strained against the tenderness. My body, giving in to its desires, leaned further into his chest.

He bent his neck, bringing his face down to meet mine again, and I inhaled him with every quickened breath. In the spirit of letting fate run its course, I'd been running too long from this. I just prayed my insecurities, the emotional scarring from my past, didn't seize the moment. Because I did want this—I wanted him, wanted his intense but intimate contact, wanted my lips to kiss him unrestrained once they joined his.

They did.

My fingers skimmed the shape of his shoulders, brushing the dips and curves of his taut muscles, tracing the nape of his neck. I buried them in his hair, each strand like fine silk, flowing against my skin like a river.

Folding my legs over his, he guided me onto his lap, pulling me even closer. My hand caught between our bodies, and we let out breathless laughs as I slipped it free then wrapped it around his back. That smile of his quickly turned hungry, and it was all too easy for me to give in. Mouths desperate for the other's, chests shuddering in rhythm, we pressed close together, becoming so intensely intertwined that I thought we might flip the basket—and I wouldn't have even cared if that happened.

His hand slid into the pleats that covered my thighs. I flinched at first, then arched into the touch. Our tongues collided and clashed in fierce, purposeful circles as his other hand moved beneath the cotton that clung to my stomach, the knot that had been tied there earlier in the night coming loose under his fingertips. They kneaded their way to my ribs, to my spine, to every muscle on my back, strumming the raised scars across my shoulder blades.

The fingers that had been lingering in my skirt grazed my underwear. It was impossible to contain a gasp. Impossible, as a hint of rough skin slipped past the fabric, as they teased the sensitive edges beneath it, as I felt everything and nothing, again and again.

Every inch of me burned and soared, and I was torn in a million directions, not even sure where to focus: On his lips on mine with the slight nip of his teeth as he pressed me deeper into the kiss. Or on his hands, each tracing the shape of my body in a way that made me shiver. Or on the way I sat draped across his lap and how he made me tingle with the simplest rock of his hips. Every sound, every touch, every scent was *him*.

With the way my stomach dropped and the wind tousled my hair…his kiss made me feel like I was falling. I peered through the gaps of our tangled limbs and—oh God, we actually were! The real world very much returning as the Ferris wheel started up again and we departed our corner of the stars. I shot back to my seat, our limbs detangling and separating. Ryder's swollen lips glistened. He didn't rush to wipe them.

Judging by the raised eyebrows from the people *now* waiting in line, the dangling stuffed bears hadn't been our only audience. I wished I could say I cared, but the butterflies flapping in the deepest part of my belly destroyed any sense of decency.

Not holding back our smiles, we jumped off the ride and his hand squeezed my ass. We reentered the Boardwalk, testing things out as a pair. Walking a little closer. Laughing a little louder. Tripping over our feet, pushing stray curls behind each other's ears. Noting the many alleyways and unlit corners that had the potential to host round two. It didn't matter if this was short-lived or what he'd told his brother or that he was invested in someone else. I didn't care that I hadn't fully processed what and who I was or that I still needed to find the Voices. In this moment, this hunger, this *need* was all-consuming, and it was the only thing that mattered.

To *both* of us.

Spotting an alluring employee alley next to the Haunted Castle, we beelined into its dim silhouette. The taste of him burned through me, igniting me even more. I tossed him against the defaced wall, my body thrumming with the promise of releasing those butterflies as I closed the short distance between us. Connected from chest to thigh, that need of his became very, very obvious...

A voice called my name. Impossible, considering how deep we pressed into the shadows, into the late hour, into each other. I must've been imagining things. Our breathless gasps had to be distorting the sounds—it came again.

"Hey, River!"

I might as well have been doused with cold water.

"River?"

Not even turned to see him, I sensed his confusion. Heat bloomed in my cheeks. I really, really didn't want to face him right now, but I couldn't stand frozen against Ryder's lips forever.

CHAPTER 19

J AVI!" I SQUEALED, PITCHING MY VOICE UP TO FAKE
enthusiasm I definitely didn't feel. I cringed from the inau-
thenticity.

"Who's he?" Ryder drawled.

"Who's *he*?" Javi fired back.

I'd fight any demon rather than deal with this. Realizing the entire front of my body was still pressed against
Ryder's, I flinched back a few steps, not quite sure what to
do with my hands now that they weren't dragging through
his hair.

"Javi, this is my f..." He wasn't my friend. And he definitely wasn't my lover, even if his saliva sealed my lips. What
was he to me? I shook my head. Didn't matter. What was
I saying again? Oh, his name. That's right. "This is Ryder.
Ryder, this is my best friend, Javi." That did little to calm
them—I could practically see the raised hackles, the animalistic glint in their eyes as they assessed each other.

"How do you guys know each other?" Javi bit out,
breaking the tense moment. Aannddd the interrogation began. I gnawed on my lip. Our indulgence had been a lot of

things, but I wasn't totally sure it was worth landing in *this* situation.

"We met at Grad Night." It wasn't a lie. Not technically.

Javi barked out a cold laugh. "That's strange, because I was with you the whole night, and I don't remember bumping into Neo from *The Matrix*."

My eyes widened and a full-body flush heated my skin. He did unfortunately bear a resemblance to somebody out of a sci-fi movie. I glanced over at Ryder, who didn't seem the least bit concerned by the comment. His arms stayed crossed as he leaned against the wall with his foot kicked up behind him, eyeing Javi as if he was nothing but a mouse.

Thank God he left his bow in the car.

"After, as I was walking home." Remaining calm and unflustered in a moment like this was truly a superpower. One I didn't have, my voice unsteady.

"How is this any of your business?" Ryder cut in, dropping his heel from the wall, finally deciding to speak. It wasn't even really a question, but pure indifference.

Javi's eyes glimmered with rage and something else I couldn't acknowledge. "Because, like River said, I'm her best friend." He redirected his glare back to me. "What's going on with you?"

I tensed. "What do you mean?"

"You're not texting me back, you ditched me after class, you're galivanting around with a guy that wears combat boots, for shit's sake." He waved at Ryder's outstretched legs. "There's a new season of *Stranger Things* premiering tonight. WE NEVER MISS *STRANGER THINGS!*"

His words stung, but my insides curdled at the look in his eyes—the rich oaky eyes I'd been avoiding, now shiny and tinged red, because I knew they'd make me truly break. I hadn't meant to ditch him. I didn't *want* to lie to him. But still, I did. And now, he'd found me with a stupid lovestruck grin plastered on my face…Ugh. I dug my fingers into my palms. I couldn't look guiltier if I'd tried.

"I'm sorry, I…" I stepped forward to console him, stopping short as he shifted his focus to the ground, looking at everything and anything except me. A lump constricted my throat. "Jav—" My voice cracked, but the damage had already been done. He wouldn't raise his chin an inch to look at me.

"Here, I got this for you." A comic book landed at my feet. My eyes darted to the metallic image beneath the clear wrapping. Silver Surfer. The dagger to the heart.

By the time I looked up, he had disappeared into a herd of people being ushered out by park employees. I winced in the spotlight of the art deco lampposts, blinded by the fluorescent bulbs and the tears that prickled my lashes.

It was closing time, which was fine by me because I suddenly couldn't stand the aroma of corn dogs and deep-fried Twinkies. I'd lose my mind if I had to listen to another repeat of the Haunted Castle's melody.

I brushed my hand across my eyes, pulling at my lids, hoping to dash the tears before they could overflow. Setting my sights on the throngs of tourists, I went to follow Javi, but a rough grip gently caught my arm. I didn't make it past the building's edge.

"Come on, River." Ryder skimmed his fingers along my shoulder. The spark had faded from his touch. "It's a lost cause."

Turning to face him, I snarled, "That *lost cause* happens to be my friend."

"That's not what I meant." His palms rubbed my biceps in long, soothing strokes. "Look, you're not going to get through to him tonight. Chasing after him might make things worse. He's obviously upset and you're…" What, a hot emotional mess? He trailed off at whatever face I made. "Let him cool down for a bit. You both should."

I let out a sigh, ragged from being on the cusp of bawling, and scooted away from his touch. The last thing I needed was for Javi to come back and see me being comforted by *him*. Though in my heart, I knew he was gone.

As much as it had killed me to watch him slump away, I'd let him for a reason: I didn't know what was happening to me, but it involved dangerous things—things capable of shredding a body in one swipe or maddening a mind irrevocably. How could I expose him to that?

I couldn't, not until I got a handle on things. Doing so after an argument over "Neo from *The Matrix*" wouldn't help my credibility—not in the slightest.

Shaking my head, I snatched Javi's gift off the ground and trudged to the parking lot, my eyes fixed on my own two feet. Ryder didn't try to reach for me, he didn't even walk next to me. He must've gotten the hint and stayed a few paces behind me.

The comic book crinkled under my arms, locked and crossed over my chest. A brush of skittish energy pulsed in tandem with my heartbeat. There was another reason why this was so hard for Javi—one involving feelings I'd tried so hard not to acknowledge because love had the capacity to kill us just as much as it could save us.

I stepped onto the train track that ran parallel to the park, balancing my footwork and the echo of Javi's laughter as his memory screamed *the floor is lava!* That alone made my eyeballs burn. Hopping down, I blinked the tears away, knowing they'd flow freely once I hit my pillow.

As we approached the glossy black truck, Ryder caught me off guard when he opened my door before his. Faltering *slightly* at the unexpected chivalry, I slid onto the bench. My phone lay on the floorboard's carpet, connected to the USB. With the turn of the ignition the screen glowed to life, and in came the dreaded Dad texts. Since it was now after midnight, I prepared myself for a decade of scolding, but a "phew" slipped between my lips.

Ryder raised his eyebrows.

"My dad's faculty dinner is running late." *Really late.* Like drinks until two AM kind of late. Ryder's expression remained unchanged, so I added, "He's not home. Or I would be screwed." He nodded at that, a mutual understanding. His brother, or in his words, the only father figure he had, must be the same way.

An acoustic track riffed from the stereo, calming my restless nerves. My gaze flicked to Ryder mouthing the lyrics, tapping his fingers to the song. Despite the warmth blasting from the air vents, goosebumps broke out along my arms as if the singer plucked my skin instead of the guitar strings.

I was sitting next to an angel. Well, part angel. But in

this moment, as he drove me home in his old Chevrolet pickup, Ryder couldn't have looked more mortal. He didn't have wings, and while the gold flecks in his green stare ignited something dangerous and molten in me, he didn't have actual fire in his eyes. Then again, neither did I, and based on what he'd told me I was also part angel. Nephilim, apparently.

Why would my dad—why would the *Voices*—hide that from me? Like, what was the point? Sure, the concept was a little jarring, but to keep me in the dark to just have me find out, *on accident*, eighteen years later and have my view of the world totally upended? I had a really hard time believing everyone was as oblivious as me. Someone had to have known.

My head drifted backwards, my lids growing heavy. It's not like I would've listened anyway.

In what felt like the blink of an eye, we arrived at my house. How did he know where I lived? I must've…told him or something. Regardless, I was home, and I was spent. He slowed to my curb. I squeaked out *goodnight* before I could even debate staying in the car, slinking to the middle seat, and thanking him for the ride in a way that seemed completely inappropriate for what had just happened with Javi. A chill greeted me as I stepped out of his car and dragged my feet to the door.

Halfway to the porch intuition drop-kicked my stomach. I stopped in my tracks. Kissing may have been off the table, but this didn't feel like the right ending for tonight. Doubling down on destiny, I strode back to the truck.

"Hey." Resting my elbows on the base of the open window, I took a deep breath. "I get out of class at two tomorrow. I have therapy after, but do you want to…" I still had a second to reconsider, but I was done thinking, and he was the only Nephilim I knew. The words jumped out of my mouth: "Hang-out-when-I'm-done?"

"Yeah." His reply came quick, cushioned by a smile that made his mouth dimple and raised the two beauty marks on his cheeks. "I can pick you up from school and take you."

"Okay. Cool." I stood there, not sure what I was waiting for, the corners of my lips lifting in response. "Can you leave the demons at home this time?"

I took his smirk as a yes, but I wasn't quite sure I believed him.

CHAPTER 20

Sure enough, when the clock struck twelve, my chariot awaited. My gut tumbled at the sight of Ryder's truck sitting in line with the rest of the cars in the five-minute curbside pickup.

As I approached the passenger door, he lowered his chin, peering at me over round, metal-framed Ray-Bans. "Miss me?"

With my cheeks flushed from the dash across campus, you'd think I did. I rolled my eyes, my attention snagging on a box that had an image of an object in the shape of a semicircle with padded ends on top, sitting next to him on the leather cushion.

I stopped reaching for the handle. My heart skipped a beat.

"W-what's that?" I stammered. I fully knew what it was.

Ryder dipped his head back and let out a deep, carefree laugh. "It's not going to bite you, River. Get in and see." He winked and flashed a full smile that was equal parts rare and reckless.

Catching my ghost-white reflection in the side mirror as I opened the door, I *did* look like I was about to face a teratorn, not a gift. I climbed in and tossed my bag—which thankfully was still in the classroom when I got there this morning after I'd left it mid-lecture the day prior—to the carpeted floor as he handed me the present.

"You lost yours during our little chase." His words barely reached my ears as I opened the box and weighed the headphones in my hands. They weren't bent and worn in and covered in surf stickers, or even the color I'd pick. But they…they were perfect.

I looped the black headband around my neck and my shoulders immediately relaxed, like they had missed the familiar imprint.

"Thank you," I breathed. I'd been bummed when I'd dropped mine yesterday, but with everything that had happened, aside from pouting and scanning the mountain road for a flash of their deep teal, I hadn't even had time to reconcile their loss. It was such a sweet and thoughtful gesture, and I could've just…*kissed him.*

"You're welcome." Ryder's eyes brightened as he took me in. "I have one more surprise for you. Hopefully you'll still be thanking me."

I put the headphones next to me and reclined against the padded leather seat. "Oh great, what does that mean?"

"You'll see." He nodded to my seatbelt. "Buckle up. You know, that's a very bad habit of yours." Yeah, then why did he make it sound so good?

I tugged the clip, snapped it into place, and teased back, "With you behind the wheel, no kidding."

He shifted into drive with a closemouthed smile that squinted his eyes. The fog from that morning had me in my favorite sweatshirt, but now I was overheating. I shed the extra layer to a peach racerback tank, the wind fanning the flush from my cheeks and whipping my hair in my face. A small stretch of eucalyptus and oaks passed by in a flurry between off-white weatherworn buildings.

We stopped at an intersection that led to the highway. My brows furrowed in curiosity.

Sensing my confusion, he said, "We're not going far," and turned inland instead.

"Good, 'cause I have a little under an hour until therapy." My doctor's office was about ten minutes away, but I had no idea where he was taking me—or what we'd be doing. Only a quick recollection of last night's activities had my mind, and my pulse, racing.

Before I could ask any more questions, or get any more ideas, he turned onto a residential street, slowed to the curb, and parked. I crossed my arms, suspicious at the nervous stroke of his thumb against the braided steering wheel, the slow unfurling of his spine.

"Spit it out. What are we doing here?"

He answered with a hint of a smile. "Welcome to driver's ed."

"You're not serious." My jaw fell open. "You want to teach me how to drive?"

"If you're going to be running from demons, you need to learn how to get away." He leaned in, chin almost grazing mine. "Your lack of driver's education almost killed us last time."

I shot back against my seat. "That wasn't all there was to blame!"

He crooked an eyebrow.

I sighed. Indeed, with a dash of luck and a bit of fool's hope, we had narrowly escaped the teratorn. Realistically, I should've been the one driving us to safety and he should've been the one driving the arrows into its heart. I'd done neither.

And yet somehow, I'd been able to channel Source, and *I* had landed the kill shot. *I* had met the monster's jaundiced stare, had watched its ruptured blood vessels spurt…

Reading my bewildered expression, he added, "Don't worry, we'll get to target practice." A breeze kissed my burning chest as he cracked open the door, and it fluttered in the hair tucked behind his ear. "But first you need to learn the basics. So, take the wheel, baby."

My fingers trembled as I scooched into his seat and placed them at ten and two. He was right. Even if a part of me died of embarrassment…I needed to be prepared. No more running. No more hiding. No more defecting from the truth.

"You're so stiff." He strummed my shoulders through the open window. "Loosen up a bit. It's not like you have a demon behind you. Yet."

My raised middle finger volleyed his wink. "Thanks, that helps a lot."

"Alright, check your mirrors." He hovered just outside the door, resting his forearms on the window's base. My eyes, more gray than blue today, darted from the way his muscles flexed against the metal and across the three reflective surfaces.

"Put your left foot on the clutch and your right foot on

the brake," he continued. "You do know which pedal the brake is, right?"

I hoped my glare made it obvious I did.

"Good girl." It came with an explorative gaze that started with the pedals and followed my bare legs, ending at the waistband of my shorts. "Turn the ignition."

I did. He left my side and walked around the hood, the truck dipping as he slid onto the passenger seat. The heat in my cheeks flared despite the fresh air circulating throughout the cab.

"Shift to first and release the brake." Ryder's coarse palm cradled mine, and together we moved the gearshift. His callouses scraped my knuckles, and every single hair, every part of my body responded to that touch.

"You still with me?" That damn unrelenting smirk—and why did it have to highlight the two lone freckles marked beautifully across his jaw?

I nodded, the knob already slipping beneath my sweaty palm. As I went to remove my foot from the brake, his next question stopped me. "What happened to your fingers?"

"Oh…" Tensing, I peeked at my irritated cuticles and the jagged edges of my nails. I was so used to picking and chewing until the anxiety faded, the gnarly state of them didn't ever really bother me. But now all I could think about was how raw and ugly they were. How obsessive it looked. "I…uh…I bite them."

"Down to the very nub," he murmured, bringing my hand towards his mouth. I sucked in a breath as he pressed his lips to my thumbnail. A bolt of awareness shot through me.

"It's—it's a nervous habit." I tried to remain steady as his lips slowly caressed my pointer, gently melting into every bit of uneven skin.

His words were now muffled against my middle finger. "What are you nervous about?"

Right now? That once his lips were done with my fingers, they'd trail to my mouth, and I'd be totally okay with that. In fact, I'd say fuck it and ditch my appointment just so I could see what other parts of my body they'd like to explore.

I gulped, but it did nothing to clear my hoarse throat. "Um, I have these episodes—I mean, I used to. I haven't had a full-blown one in a while. They take over my senses and I…" My voice trembled at his mouth parting on my ring finger, a brush of hot moisture submerging the skin. "I guess this is just one of my coping mechanisms."

He took my marred pinky into his mouth, suckling the tip. When he withdrew, our gazes locked. He didn't release my hand, not until he leaned in so close his jaw grazed the baby hairs around my hairline. The move shattered my inhibitions, and I was seconds away from grabbing the front of his shirt and redirecting his face to mine. His voice was a torrid whisper against my ear. "Ease up on the clutch and slowly press on the gas."

At that point he could have told me to get out of the car and dance like a chicken and I'd probably have done it. Without thinking, I did as he said, and the truck lurched forward, making such a god-awful screech it might as well have been a piece of metal dragging over my skull. A searing blush hit my cheeks, not just from almost hurling him through the windshield.

His laugh reverberated in my belly with the revs of the engine, as he drew back into his seat and buckled in. "Slow and steady, River." He draped my name with a velvety coax, gentle and beseeching. A tone I'd never heard out of him before, but one I now craved. My foot tapped the pedal again. "That's it," he murmured encouragingly. "You got it."

Soaring down the street at a whopping five miles per hour, I did it. I was driving. Despite myself, I relaxed a bit. "Javi would be stoked to see me right now."

"Javi." There was no obvious bitterness when he repeated his name, but there was a tinge of something, like… sympathy. "He's in love with you, you know."

I blew through the stop sign, fully expecting middle fingers and angry honks. Once free of the intersection, I slammed on the brakes. "What? Javi's my best friend. He doesn't love me. I mean he loves me, but not like…not like that."

He chuckled. "Keep telling yourself that."

I glowered at him, uninterested in debating what he'd stated—so matter-of-factly. And *so smug*. He was wrong, of course.

Attempting to retain my focus, I stared ahead at the road, the trees' silhouettes breaking the bursts of light as I drove us through the quiet neighborhood. Each time the sun cleared the shadows over the dashboard, it illuminated an unbidden memory of Javi. Simple ones, at first: dances and holidays and matinee movies. But those quickly snowballed into ones that stole the air from my lungs. Holding me the night of homecoming, after the incident with Chet. Never saying no to a surf sesh, even on days when the rain and unruly waves pummeled our skin and our vision. My birthday gift, the photo he took of me simply in my element. All his photography, really, that seemed to center on one subject—me.

I shook my head. No. I wouldn't twist these pure, harmless moments to fit Ryder's very false narrative. We were friends. Best friends. Nothing more, I reassured myself, as I slowed for a crosswalk, my heart ramming against my rib cage.

"Since you're basically ready for Formula One..." Ryder's drawl unwound me, just a tad—my fingers still curled around the wheel in a death grip. He dipped his head towards the odometer. It read fifteen miles per hour. "I'm going to start calling shotgun from now on."

My attention veered from the road as he stretched his arms behind his head, to the cut of his taut, inked biceps— gaze lingering on the tattoos protruding from his short black sleeves that snaked all the way down to his fingers: an urn, an evil eye, a kettle pouring skulls, a runic cross, the serpent's head entwined with the Celtic N and S.

After my eyes darted to the road to make sure we weren't about to crash, they instantly flicked back to a flash of color that flickered just beneath his shirt cuff and wrapped around his muscle. It was the only mark not drawn in monochrome, hints of white and vivid blues sticking out with specks of pewter droplets bursting from the flowy aquamarine outline of a traced-on body of water.

"Is that—" I began to ask, until the engine sputtered viciously, and the entire car started to shake.

"Clutch and foot on the brake." He quickly maneuvered us into neutral, the tattoo falling behind his t-shirt again. If he sensed my curiosity, he ignored it and soon, I forgot about it too, as he directed me into the flow of traffic.

CHAPTER 21

CRUISING THROUGH THE RESIDENTIAL COMMUNI-ties had been one thing—turning onto one of the busiest roads in town gave me heart palpitations that mimicked last night's escape from the werewolves. It'd been easy-ish to focus on the road when there was nothing but the hum of the tires, the chirps of the birds, and my pounding heart filling my ears. But now there were so many competing colors and sounds and restless activity that I was one swerve away from crashing.

And the digs from Ryder that I hovered over the wheel like a grandma didn't make the transition easier. I glared at him, but he was too busy taking in the sun with his eyes half-closed and his arm out the window to notice. My irritation flared even more. How could he even make those annoying comments when he was basically asleep next to me?

I pulled into the complex of my therapist's office, the usual fluttering in my chest hitting me hard when I saw the brown stucco building and drove through the two-level garage. Breath shallow, I channeled all of my energy into my grip on the steering wheel, the tips of my fingers turning white. About to jump out of my own skin, I took a ragged inhale, and it reminded me of my last session with Dr. Fair-more, and the breathing exercise she'd had me try.

Not able to close my eyes and mentally transport myself to the ocean, I rolled my neck, inhaled a lungful of fresh air, and held it in for ten seconds. I gradually released it, shocked at how not-sweaty my palms were, how not-racy my pulse was, how not-bouncy my legs were.

I released a laughy breath at the simplicity of it, but shoot, this little breathing trick was effective. Even a simpler version, like what I just did. Dr. Fairmore would be stoked to hear it.

For the first time ever, I was actually excited to share something with my therapist.

No longer sprawled out in his seat like I was his personal chauffeur, Ryder scanned the lot for an open spot as I turned down the last row. He pointed at one towards the back, free of any neighbors. One where we wouldn't be boxed in. The better for a stealthy escape, I guessed. Actually…I had no idea what motivated any of his decisions.

I hitched the e-brake and stepped out, leaving the head-phones on the seat. As I tamed my unbrushed beachy waves in the circular side-view mirror, movement fluttered to my right, and the passenger door clicked shut. I stopped preen-ing. "What are you doing?"

With his keys in one hand, the other running through his hair attempting to subdue the locks spilling over his forehead, Ryder donned an expression as perplexed as mine. "There's a waiting room, isn't there?"

Not this again. I'm sure my face said it all.

"What, you thought I was going to wait for you in a hot

car for forty-five minutes?" Ryder's brows dipped inward, quizzical. "They have air conditioning in there."

My eye roll might've made it a tad obvious I'd rather not have him as my plus-one. But I didn't have time to fight him on it. "Please, leave the arrows in the car, would you?"

He responded with a boyish grin that I didn't trust at all.

We marched towards the units on the ground floor, leaving the shade of the garage for the dry heat of the summer day. Something flashed in my peripheral, metal in the sunlight. Twisting in its direction, I wasn't surprised *at all* to find the source on my companion's waist. From his very low, hip-hugging waistband that had me looking right above his—

"What's that?"

"What?"

I pointed to the brilliant white buckle that glimmered from his belt, the material so similar to that of his arrowheads.

"Oh, this?" He pulled on the clasp, repositioning the seam of his pants. "A belt buckle."

I narrowed my eyes at the half-truth he'd given. "Then why is it shaped like it could fit around your knuckles?"

"Because it can. They're brass knuckles," he added in his irritatingly nonchalant way.

My jaw dropped. "Those are *illegal.* I said no weapons—"

"You said no arrows." He pointed a finger at me. "You didn't say anything about other weapons."

"Oh my God," I muttered. Before I could ask more about their color and why he'd felt the need to bring them along, a cool blast hit my face and shoulders as we entered the lobby. We sighed in sync, savoring the chill. Ignoring Ryder's prideful smirk, I sent him to a corner to lavish in his imaginary superiority so I could sign in at the front desk.

Meeting the receptionist's smile—a first—I passed over my insurance and scribbled down my name, actually engaging in small talk. I could almost pass off as happy to be there. What was wrong with me?

"River Harlow?" an assistant read from her clipboard. I sauntered over to the threshold between the waiting room and hallway that led to the individual offices. "Dr. Finis will see you now."

"Great—wait, who?" I stopped dead in the doorway.

She unpropped the door, ushering me in. "Did you not get the email? Dr. Fairmore's on leave. In the interim, Dr. Finis will be meeting with all of her patients."

What. This pressure chamber of a corridor became about ten sizes too small, the spiel about my therapist's absence lost to the too-loud thud of our footsteps and the blood drumming in my ears. I'd obviously heard wrong. Dr. Fairmore wouldn't leave me. I saw her *two days ago*. She was here. She *had* to be. As the panic grew, it clenched the inside of my chest.

The sconces seemed to flicker, and I lowered my gaze to the floor. Starting with my forehead, I trailed my fingers over my scalp, glacially slow, so that my arms acted like shields from the world that was crashing down.

I didn't want to be surprised. I didn't want to be hurt. But that's exactly what I felt like, and that's exactly why I'd avoided opening up all these years. That, and the fact that no one else had ever convinced me I was more than just a patient who needed fixing. With Dr. Fairmore, I wasn't just somebody. I wasn't just a girl. I was River, and the guilt and the episodes and all that came with them made me stronger, not weaker.

A subtle, but growing, tug in my gut told me this next person would be nothing like her. The final door creaked opened at the end of the hall, as if expecting us. The buttery streaks from the familiar wall of windows vanished when I entered, the passing clouds dampening the room to gray.

"River." A middle-aged woman, who I assumed to be my therapist, greeted me from Dr. Fairmore's desk. With a smile so crooked it made her neck veins pop out and her lashless, black eyes bulge. It had to be mocking. No one was ever *that* excited to meet me. "Riiivveeerrr." She drawled out each syllable, tasting the vowels on her tongue. Her contorted fingers, like they'd been fractured and never reset, pointed at the chair opposite. "Sit."

I trudged past my favorite recliner, sentenced to the hard wooden seat.

That exaggerated smile stayed plastered to her face, her ashen skin stretched so tight her cheekbones could've broken through her sickly pallor. "I'm sure you've heard Dr. Fairmore had an emergency and had to leave town."

"I'm missing the details." I flinched as the door shut behind me, leaving us alone. "What happened?"

"Oh, I can't disclose that." Dr. Finis dabbed the excess saliva pooling at the sides of her upturned lips with a tissue. She tossed it into a small trashcan already overflowing with the white paper squares stained with pale dots of black and red liquid. My nose wrinkled at the sight. "But what I can tell you is she won't be coming back."

I lifted my brows at the framed milestones on the bookcase, the cross-stitched artwork in hoops. The color-coded anthologies, the handloomed woven rug, the chic knick-knacks that lined the shelves.

"The receptionist made it sound like this was temporary." I considered pointing out how odd it was that someone would leave all their belongings if they had no intention of coming back. But that would give me false hope, which I was done with.

"Don't you worry, I'll be seeing to your problems now." Her voice was sharper than a knife and pricked my hair follicles up. I leaned back in my chair and glanced towards the busy atrium, hoping to catch the eyes of someone walking through it.

A hollow *thud* snapped my attention to the fists that had slammed into the desk. Dr. Finis rose with unnatural quickness, flicked on a tabletop lamp, and headed for the windows.

"We don't need any distractions," she hissed. An aggressive pull on each curtain panel killed the natural light. Whirling back to the desk, she settled into command, draped in shadow and unspoken threats. "Much better."

The darkness hollowed her eyes like clouds eclipsing the sun. Her craggy, bruised nails hit the mahogany surface in impatient thrums.

After a moment she relaxed, that same shady grin adorning her face again. "River." There came another chant of my name, like I was a little glass doll on a shelf for display. "Daughter of Corbin Harlow and Mira Rae. Mother deceased. Isn't that unfortunate."

Despite her words, I found no trace of sympathy.

She cleared her throat, the sound guttural and ragged against the stillness of the room. "Remind me, how did she die?"

My eyes widening, I shot back against my chair as if the question had slapped me across the face. "Can't you just look at my file?"

"I like to hear things from the source, not try to interpret a far less competent person's scribble." Her hand slithered to a folder lying atop the stack. She opened it and said, "We're going to start out fresh." Then she ripped my medical chart in half.

There was something seriously wrong with this woman. I shifted in my seat, the notes from my last visit drifting to my feet. Feeling like I might end up on the floor with it by the end of this, I cleared my throat and said, "My mom died in a drowning accident."

"An accident you're responsible for." There was no question to her tone, but it had to be one. There's no way anyone would just come out and say that.

I straightened, holding my chin high despite the grief pushing me towards the lowest of lows. "Dr. Fairmore says I'm not."

"Well, Dr. Fairmore's no longer here." Her voice shifted to a higher pitch that scraped against my mind like nails on a chalkboard. "And, of course, you're responsible. If it weren't for you, your mother would still be alive!" Her cackle flittered through the room with such force, it rustled the hairs on my arms and shuffled loose papers, scattering any confidence I'd had.

When I didn't respond, her laughter stilled, and a heaviness settled on the air, thick with sorrow that threatened to drown me and breathe life into Dr. Finis. She stared at me, leering and panting, eyes rimmed with black tears as if she'd laughed off her mascara—but she hadn't been wearing any makeup.

"Don't act so surprised," she croaked. "Those little voices of yours would agree with me, wouldn't they?"

The shock hit me like a dart dipped in poison, shutting off each motor function until I was nothing but a wide-eyed bag of muscle and bones. How did she know? The Voices wouldn't have been mentioned in my file—unless she'd gone through ten years of records, back to the very beginning. Even then, though, at eight years old, I'd been too young, too *traumatized*, to explicitly state what was happening. If I'd said I heard voices, no one took it literally, and I'd suffered in shame and silence since then. Until my last session, when Dr. Fairmore alluded to their presence… Had she shared that info with Dr. Finis?

A bolt of anger electrified my veins and brought the feeling back to my fingers. I curled them in. That was *my* secret. "What are you talking about?"

Dr. Finis's verbal venom was working; she knew it. "Tell me, what else do they say to you, River?"

A cautionary instinct temporarily constricted my throat, halting me from spewing every curse burning inside me. This is what she wanted. A reaction out of me. Because if her claims were untrue, then why would I get so worked up? I took a measured breath. I needed to deflect.

"This is entirely inappropriate." Like, did we need to switch spots?

I figured I'd be met with a condescending laugh. It was the ghost-white palms slamming into the tabletop and the way she thrust herself forward that had me leaning so far back in my chair it lifted its two front legs. The wood creaked against her weight as she extended her neck, her hair slithering across the surface like thin black snakes.

Clearly her teeth hadn't seen a toothbrush in ages, the enamel so rotten and her breath so sour it singed my nostrils when she whispered, "Says the murderer."

In the face of such bluntness, my patience crumbled. It was already wavering, but now the walls came down and fury rose in its place. Cold and vindictive. I knew what I was. Unfortunately for her, I was ready to stop running from it.

"You're right. It is my fault." My words came out small in the large, dark room.

The doctor curled her lip. "What?" Her tone remained flat.

"I. Killed. My. Mother." Each letter should have stabbed until the guilt flowed like blood, emptying me out. The confession should have ruined me, but it somehow released me.

If the doctor's words were venom, my acceptance was the antidote.

Bring it on, serpentine woman.

Dr. Finis released a grumble too similar to a growl. Her

withered fingertips drifted with ear-splitting friction over the desk to meet mine—which at some point had gripped the edge. Her touch was stiffer than a corpse's, so cold it froze my blood. But I didn't dare draw away.

"Is that what you wanted to hear?" I remained unflinching, despite every neuron in my brain firing at me to run.

"Where is your fear, River?" Her jaw jolted open and shut as if it were detached from her body and someone else pulled a string to move it.

"It's not…" A foul stench clogged my thoughts before I could finish. I'd gagged on that smell once before—burnt rubber and teratorn guts. My head swiveled around the room, but I didn't know what I was searching for. An answer? A distraction? A demon? The air stung my widened eyes as I turned back to the doctor, her skin more waxy, saggy than it had just been when I was looking at her a second ago. It seemed to melt off her bones.

I tried to pull my hands away, but she gripped them even tighter.

The realization I'd been ignoring from the moment I walked in reared its ugly head. This woman wasn't human. She was something different. Supernatural. Evil.

"Where are *they*, River?" The question bellowed from deep inside her throat. It rattled the picture frames, the pens in their holder, but I wouldn't let it rattle me.

An unsettling calm, like what came before a storm, brewed beneath my skin—as the clip of a memory, one that'd been buried so deep it didn't seem real, overtook me.

I'd barely gotten my head above water when my mom ricocheted back into the rip current she'd saved me from.

The waves swept around her like limbs, dragging her farther, deeper—until every part of her was submerged except her angled chin and contorted, gaping mouth. But she'd told me to stay, so…I did. Then the sky parted as if Death himself had come to snatch her, in a beam of wind and shadow and rain. Shafts of light broke through the nearby clouds, casting a silhouette within the storm—human-shaped, but with billowy arches jutting out of their back. Wings. The shock and icy cold froze me to the bone, but I couldn't take my eyes off the figure; it looked so much like her.

I shook my head. She was *sinking*. Right in front of me. It couldn't have been her.

My mom had died because I just *sat there*, treading water. Anger launched me out of the memory like a slingshot.

On a tight inhale, I met Dr. Finis's hungry, death-black stare. The fury remained, but I schooled my features as the energy that had started building prickled and parted into each finger and toe, to the very core of me. Power, unchecked and instinctive and so similar to the rush I got when surfing, pressed against my body, searching for a way out. I thought it might shoot out of me.

Her death grip tightened, scaly fingers coiling around mine, demanding an answer. I didn't know where the Voices were. But I did know one thing as I thrust my hands forward, trying to throw her off me. "They're not HERE!"

I knew this feeling. It welled up inside of me when I reached my breaking point; not just here, or with the ter-atorn, but throughout my life. I just hadn't known what to do with it—magic. Source. It beaded my senses like the sweat lining my upper lip as years of heartbreak, hate, and humility gushed out of me. It pulsed outwards in a gilded wave, not just from my fingertips, but every pore that dotted my skin. The pressure in my skull throbbed, one painful pulse away from utterly wrecking me—but I couldn't stop, not even as it twisted each nerve, and felt like it might tear my limbs from my body.

The curtains whipped to the sides and the day flooded in, momentarily blinding me. The magic ceased as the backs of my hands shot to my brows, shielding me from the brightness and the thuds and shrieks that came from somewhere in the room, but I couldn't see.

I shot to my feet, tripping over my chair as I scrambled to get away from the area until the light settled—which it didn't.

My vision adjusted, but it was just as bright. I locked eyes with Dr. Finis, still behind the desk, but she wasn't sitting; she wasn't even standing. She was *dangling*, pinned to the bookcase like a wall mount by a dozen brilliant gold threads that seemed to splinter off from the sunbeams. They wove through the air, from her to the windows, swaying in an absent breeze. She clawed at the light, but it wrapped around her wrists, her ankles, her neck, her gaping mouth, translucent but strong as rope. Books fell off the shelves as she rammed her head back and tried to force the muzzle free.

I didn't move. I couldn't, as if I too were bound by the glistening strings.

Feathers black as a crow's, torn and singed, wafted to my feet. One landed on my toe, the faint tickle enough for me to twitch in response, coaxing my body out of shock. They were everywhere, like someone had shredded a pillow, but didn't have an obvious source. I collected one and stuffed it in the back pocket of my shorts, hoping it'd make it out of there intact.

Which meant I had to, as well.

The doctor angrily thrashed as light flooded her mouth, and more feathers erupted from behind her back. I didn't have time to consider what that meant. The sunbeams were dimming, losing their grip. The golden threads shuddered and then, one by one, they started to snap. Which meant I needed to stop acting like a deer in headlights and get the hell out of there. As I turned to book it out of the room, a raspy voice starved of oxygen stopped me in my tracks.

"We will find you, River Harlow." Dr. Finis gulped and gargled as if she were drowning, fighting off the golden gag. "This isn't the end. This is only the beginning."

My necklace singed my clavicle, the short stab of pain keeping me from spinning around to face her threats. I flung open the door and hustled down the hallway, not daring to look back to see if she pursued me.

CHAPTER 22

Ryder hopped out of his chair, dropping an out-of-date gossip magazine as I bolted past him in the waiting room. I felt him on my heels as he jogged to catch up to me. "What happened in there?"

Busting through the automatic doors, I didn't let my focus drift to anything but what was ahead of me. "She humiliated me, threatened me, tried to destroy me."

"Isn't that what therapists do?" There was a lightness to his question, as if it were a joke, but I was *not* in the mood.

I shook my head, dispelling the image of Dr. Fairmore before it could cool my heated thoughts. No. She was just like the rest of them. "Yes," I said coldly, my breaths getting faster even as my strides slowed. "But something else happened in there—" Struggling to get that last part out, I stopped in the middle of the garage, doubling over and gripping my knees. It felt like an invisible hand clutched my throat.

Ryder placed his palm on my curled spine. "River, are you okay?"

Pins and needles struck every one of my senses, harsh and jarring and heavy.

What happened to his sixth sense, his hunter's instinct that had saved me more times than I cared to count?

I managed to whisper, "How did you not see this coming?"

The caress along my spine slowed. "What happened in there?"

When I didn't answer, the ground slipped out from beneath me, and sturdy arms cradled my body, tucking themselves around my back and under my legs. Out of frustration I went rigid, but after a few steps I relaxed into his arms. Ryder really needed to stop sweeping me off my feet or he might think he was actually helping. But to make that point I'd have to actually stop him. I lifted my head to do just that, then let it fall back. I was too winded to argue, and this little nook between his neck and his shoulder against his soft cotton tee unfortunately felt nice.

He carried me through the garage, towards the back, past his car. I twisted in his grasp, eyeing the Chevy, his responding squeeze meant to assuage my confusion as he stepped onto an unmarked gravel path between the columns. It led to a courtyard nestled within the neighboring complex, lined with three concrete benches sheltered by individual arbors crawling in orange and pink honeysuckle. He gently placed me down on one of the benches and took a seat next to me, his eyes lightened by the vines breaching the wooden frames.

A fountain, sculpted into an angel of all things, stood in the middle. I grimaced, pivoting away from it. Water trickled in the background—calming, soothing. The peacefulness of this spot, at complete odds with the chaos next door, brought feeling back to my limbs and words to my mouth. I repeated my earlier question. "How did you not see this coming?"

"What?" he asked flatly.

Shifting to my side, I reached into my pocket, relieved to find the feather. Somehow, it hadn't burned to a crisp like the rest of them. "What does this mean?"

Ryder took it by the quill. He held it to the light, and I was able to see the deep, purple lowlights to the onyx vane. It was stiff, unlike the flowy plumes I'd find spilling out of my down comforter.

"Is it from a Nephilim? Demon? Something else I don't know about but can already tell you I don't want to?"

He lowered the feather, twirling the translucent shaft between his fingertips. "Remember how I told you demons are the tortured souls of corrupted angels?"

This—this was exactly what I didn't want to know. I bit down on my bottom lip.

"This is from one of their wings."

"So. My therapist is a demon." Any more pressure on my lip and I'd break the skin. "Fan-fucking-tastic." Ryder's mouth twitched and I swore if he laughed, I'd smack him. I gripped the bench's roughened edge. "I couldn't see any wings," I told him, like that'd refute his claim.

It didn't. "She has them, but they don't manifest in this dimension. Here, they're more of a shadow. Kind of like… phantom wings."

Out of everything Dr. Finis had the potential to be, a demon was honestly the least farfetched. If he would've explained to me that she was an angel, or even just a mortal, that's when I would've stopped believing him, because there was nothing decent or human about her.

As I stared at the chipped wings of the stone angel carved around the tiers of the fountain, my thoughts inevitably trailed to Dr. Fairmore. Her eyes a brown so rich at certain angles they were almost black, but nothing like the bottomless pits of Dr. Finis's. Even if Fairmore knew or had a hunch about the Voices, even if she'd left me high and dry…There was no way she was a demon. No way.

"The only way you'd see her wings is if she was injured, by Source, that threatened to return her to her dimension or kill her. Which brings the question…how'd you get this feather?" He leaned in so close I could count the golden flecks in his eyes. "I'll ask again, River. What happened in there?"

His gaze was so overwhelming I had to look back to the fountain, or I'd be spilling my whole life story. "She knew too much." I ran my fingers along my hairline, sweeping away the shorter layers falling into my face. "About my mom, my episodes, parts of me I haven't shared with anyone. Then she got super aggressive, tried to force it out of me, and I did that…thing."

His voice was tight. "What thing?"

I scuffed my sandals on the packed gravel. "You know, that…yelling thing."

Ryder raised his brows in understanding. "She got struck by lightning and exploded?"

"No, she got taken out by a beam of light." Catching my hands as they flew to my mouth, he lowered them to my lap, his grip unwavering. "Which I'm…pretty sure I summoned."

"How? Did you use the same words?"

"No, but I had…similar feelings." And visions. Even fully removed from the situation, the anger still simmered. And the grief, well, it was unrelenting.

"Which were?" His thumb stroked my knuckle.

I wasn't sure if it was Ryder's subtle touches or if I was in that weirdly blissful, short-lived period between adrenaline and shock…For some reason the rawness of this moment, the surge of my emotions, it all stripped away my fears. And once the words left my lips…I couldn't stop.

"Anger, frustration. Grief, guilt. So much of it, it overwhelms me. I can still feel it now, thrumming beneath my skin." My digits curled over each other in an uncomfortable bend, but I continued. "I don't think me literally yelling has anything to do with it. I think it's the point I reach to actually get to that place, where my feelings don't have anywhere to go…except out."

When Ryder didn't respond, I decided to shift my gaze from his fingers, still clasped over mine, to his eyes. They peered at me with such an intense yearning. I couldn't tell if it was me, or the information I had, that he sought so badly.

"Most Nephilim have abilities," he finally said. "But I haven't met someone that could wield the elements at that kind of scale, like, ever."

Lucky me. "So, what kind of abilities do you have that makes you so special, *hunter*?" It was meant to wipe the smugness off his face, but it only made it worse, and that was the kind of look that undid me.

In an instant, his breath was a warm caress against the sensitive space below my earlobe.

"Maybe it's my impeccable sense of hearing." There's no way he heard my heartbeat, even if it raged against my ribs. "Or my supernatural reflexes." Even if he caught that rogue piece of hair before it met my chin, there's no way he sensed the pleasurable shiver when his calloused fingers brushed my skin. "Or my ability to detect the faintest flicker of pain, or fear or…" A huskiness entered his throat. "Excitement."

That…Oh God. There's no way. Even if it rippled off me like pheromonal perfume. I gulped. *Evil therapist. Demon. Evil therapist. Demon.*

He chuckled, and I knew right there and then my cheeks had turned beet red. I willed him to stop looking at me like that, like he had fire in his eyes and in his…Ugh, Ryder, just get back to the subject before we switch to one that involves a lot less talking.

"We're not technically required to do anything with said abilities, or the title that comes with them." He leaned back, giving me some breathing room, but remained closer than he had when we originally sat. "Although the Sainthood definitely encourages it…"

I didn't miss the hint of venom that coated *the Sainthood*. "What's the Sainthood?"

The lines in Ryder's face hardened, causing him to look as chiseled as the stone angel before us. "A council that preserves the Order of the Nephilim and performs the duties…" He shook his head. "More like rituals, that enforce our Law and Judgement."

I wanted to ask about these rituals, about the whole other world that seemingly existed before my very eyes and yet had somehow stayed hidden from me for eighteen years.

"So, when is someone going to come and get the demon that just tried to kill me?" I had to hit the important stuff first. "There's bound to be a repercussion for that…right?" When he clicked his tongue in answer, incredulity may have gotten the best of me. "What are they good for, then?"

"Depends on who's funneling their cash," he gritted out. "Mostly they walk around with a damn archangel complex, just because their power was decreed from Above."

"From Above." I glanced up into the sky, bright and burning. "As in the Supreme Being Upstairs?"

"The one and only." He closed his eyes and dipped his head back for the briefest second, as if this topic frazzled him as much as it did me.

"Trippy…" I murmured. It was worth a pause, but not one that'd smother me in panic. I myself was part angel, after all. "So, you're a hunter because the Sainthood told you to be?"

His shoulders rolled, flexing inwards. "I'm not a hunter to appease anyone but myself."

"Why does it all matter, then?"

"Because these are instincts we're talking about. What happens when you ignore those? When you ignore who you are, who you were meant to be?"

I got the feeling he was no longer speaking hypothetically. "Spontaneous combustion?" I offered with a grin.

His flicker of a smile disappeared way too soon. "Pretty much."

We were already so far down the rabbit hole I didn't stop myself when I asked, "So what the hell am I? What's my title?"

"Besides a beautiful girl with the power to shoot laser beams out of her hands?" Well, they weren't exactly *laser beams*, but he did make it sound pretty badass. "The one person on this earth that's genuinely surprised me."

A flash of heat warmed my cheeks as he blew out a laugh and tucked his bottom lip into his teeth. I pulled my hands out of his grasp, the air cool against my fingers.

"There's something I haven't told you." I was surprising myself at this point. "The thing I did today, it happened last night when two werewolves cornered me at the bonfire."

Ryder's forehead crinkled in question. "You channeled lightning? Or a beam of light?"

"Water." An unstoppable surge of energy washed over me as I recalled the wall of ocean that I'd somehow constructed and the force of it flooding the beach. I shuddered, suddenly as chilly and numb as I'd been standing on the bluffs before he'd found me—found me, in the dead of night on the side of the highway.

Frustration boiled inside me once again. "And now *I'll* ask you, Ryder. For the final time, I hope. How did you not see this"—I waved in the direction of the other building—"coming?"

He sighed, lowering his lashes. "I was…distracted."

"What, by the latest Hollywood boob job?" Chances were, he wasn't reading the tabloids, but the snark would keep the panic from closing up my throat again.

"I'm sorry." He ran his tattooed fingers through his hair just for the strands to fall right back to his temples. "Sometimes these things slip through the cracks."

Sorry wasn't going to cut it.

"Forgetting to put away laundry. Missing a homework assignment. *Those* things slip through the cracks." *Not* life-or-death scenarios involving threats from the underworld. I threw my hands up. "You're a hunter, Ryder. Isn't the first rule of thumb to never let your guard down?"

Waiting for him to own up to his mistake was like waiting for the apocalypse. Imminent, but likely never to come in my lifetime. I peered at him out of the corner of my eye. He remained facing forward, chest caved, shoulders hunched, too proud to say the words. I let him sit there like a dog with his tail between his legs for another minute.

"What do we do next?" I huffed out air through my nose. "I imagine dialing 911 is out of the question. What's the equivalent in Nephilim world? Do we try and bring it up with the Saints?"

"No." It broke his stillness, and I swore I caught a glisten to his eyes. "No, we don't need them…" He blinked and it was gone. "Look, you don't know why these things are after you. But is there anyone who might? Anyone who has more info on your ancestry? About where you came from? Someone you trust?"

Not where, but who.

I clutched the lapis pendant around my neck. What other secrets sat locked away in my dad's den? It'd be an awkward conversation…but I guess I could just ask him straight up: *Are you or mom an angel?* I bit out a sigh. If he'd known about my lineage and never told me—why would he divulge anything now, just because I asked nicely? Pinpricks of anger struck my heart. I took a deep, steady breath, inclined to think the chances he knew anything about this were slim to none. I couldn't let the other, more nauseating, possibility sidetrack me.

Why couldn't I just look into a crystal ball? It'd be so much easier than breaking and entering into his office—

My musing provoked a memory, and suddenly the idea didn't seem so farfetched.

"Have I told you about the tarot reader?" I asked even though I knew I hadn't. He shook his head to confirm. "At Grad Night, the night I met you, I had an episode—like the one I had that night in the alley you found me in. Anyways, it's almost like this psychic experienced it with me. Afterwards she grabbed me, all possessed, and started chanting something over and over."

"You've mentioned these episodes," he drawled, continuing to watch the playful splash of the fountain. "What exactly do they entail?"

I bit the inside of my cheek, my mouth quirking to the other side. I'd never explained this out loud—the whole truth of it, that is. But after what I'd experienced with werewolves, demons, Dr. Finis…The idea of holding on to this secret any longer weighed so heavy on me it felt like it'd sink me to the molten core of the Earth.

There were no words to adequately explain my episodes. But I'd sure as hell try, because I needed to get this off my chest, needed to tell somebody, needed to feel…less alone.

"My episodes," I repeated uneasily. "It's like… the world is speaking to me. Directly. Sometimes I listen. Sometimes I talk back. Sometimes all my senses blend together so the only thing I taste, touch, smell, and see are the voices on the air—but also aren't—because I'm the only one who hears them. It's…overwhelming. I usually end up blacking out or my brain kind of"—I thought about how I tripped during graduation, which, wow, that seemed so insignificant now—"stalls."

His face betrayed nothing as he flicked his eyes to me. "How do they manifest?"

"In anything and everything that makes a sound." I shut my eyes for a beat, the hairs on my neck prickling in anticipation as I listened, fully knowing they weren't going to come. "In…the crunch of my shoes against the gravel. In the steady laps of the fountain. In the low howl of the breeze that keeps whipping my hair into my face." I let the unruly waves tickle the bridge of my nose. "To you, that's ambiance, to me…one second, it's white noise, the next it's screaming at me."

I waited for Ryder to laugh, to shove off the bench, to brush me off as crazy. But he stayed, unmoving, next to me, not looking anywhere else but at me. "And you think this psychic heard these voices, too?"

My breath hitched as he studied me, like I was different, but in a good way—in a way that seemed to intrigue him. I cleared the knot bundled in my throat. "I'm not sure exactly, but she kind of short-circuited during Javi's reading, right after I had an episode, and that's when she grabbed me and started chanting."

"What did she say?"

"*Quart…vigi…Quarto vigil?*" I butchered it for sure. "Any clue to what that means?"

"The Fourth Watcher." Ryder's brows tilted in. "That's Latin. It's the old language of the Nephilim."

Surprise twisted my features. No one but the Voices called me *Watcher*. How did she know? I'd always brushed it off as a petty nickname. But...did it mean something more? My stomach sank like I'd swallowed a hundred steel balls.

"Hey, you okay?" Javi's infamous line. It sounded so different coming from Ryder.

I forced my expression to one of indifference even though I was anything but. "What's a Watcher?"

"Powerful archangels supposedly tasked with keeping humanity safe from demons." He wiped invisible dirt off the flat stone seat. "Nothing but an urban legend, clearly."

"Oh." I wrung my hands, fighting the urge not to put them in my mouth so he'd try and grab them again. "Why... why would she call me that?"

He strummed his fingers against the edge of the bench. "I think we need to find her and ask."

I dug deep for an excuse but came up with nothing, because there was nothing left to do but face this. "She had a temporary structure for the festival. But...I know who can help us find her." I sighed, cringing at what that meant.

We stood to leave, the courtyard's fountain grabbing my attention as I went to follow him to the garage. I stepped over to its basin. The water had turned dark and oily. Red.

"Ryder, do you see this?" My gaze tracked upwards, to each pool of liquid, to the cement wings wrapped around the tiers. He stilled beside me, obviously seeing how the angel's face had shifted; not frowning but not quite smiling, her lips pulled, brows tilted up. She was crying.

The angel was crying tears of blood.

CHAPTER 23

Javi chewed his tapioca pearls while he considered my request.

I picked our favorite bubble tea place to meet—somewhere casual, neutral—because nothing says I'm-sorry-let's-not-fight more than boba.

"Yeah, I have her business card. Why do you want it?" he asked mid-slurp.

Okay, I knew this answer. I'd rehearsed it in the sun visor's mirror. Yet here, in the act, I failed to remember what partial truth I decided to tell.

"I think she can help me uncover some things I've been trying to learn about myself." That didn't sound too off-script.

Chewing a mouthful of tapioca balls, he stared at me intently. "Don't you have therapy for that?"

"My therapist actually suggested it." The suspicion coming off him was stronger than the matcha in my drink. I took a nervous sip. It went down the wrong pipe, and I spent a good minute coughing, unable to look guiltier if I tried. "As a way to…get a unique perspective. You know, reframe." Which, kind of, because isn't that what facing my emotions meant?

His thick black eyebrows came together. "And you decided to start with the psychic who harassed you at Grad Night?"

My jaw quivered. I bit down to try and keep it steady, so hard that sweat dotted my upper lip despite being in a freezing-cold air-conditioned room.

"We have this thing called the internet." Avoiding my eyes, he tapped his phone's screen and started an aimless scroll.

"She doesn't have a website. I tried every search engine." It was true. An hour ago, I'd been curled up in the passenger seat of Ryder's car with the windows down, the music softly playing in the background and his arm resting atop my calves…while we input every rendition of *Madame Myrian* into the browsers' search bars on our phones—just so I didn't have to do *this*. I exhaled sharply. "There's no trace of her online."

Javi pulled a fabric bi-fold wallet out of his back pocket, and there between the Magic cards, old school IDs, and crumpled dollar bills, lay Madame Myrian's business card.

"Here." He slid the plain white card across the table.

My eyes narrowed as I tilted my chin and considered taking it or ripping it in half. Was it so bad to just give up now and go back to watching reruns of our favorite sitcoms in our sweatpants?

Javi took another long pull of his drink. "Do you need company, or is your *friend* joining you?" Condescension drenched his tone.

As much as I wanted to deny it, I couldn't stomach another lie. "Yes, he is."

"Figures," he grumbled into his tiger milk tea. "Well, I hope you find the insight you're looking for. Maybe she can even teach you a thing or two about being a good friend."

My heart lurched painfully. "That's not fair." Because I didn't want it to be.

"You know what's not fair?" His nostrils flared as his voice rose. "Always being by your side, answering every damn beck and call, and still getting the shit end of the stick. It's one thing to dip out on our adventures, but when did we start keeping secrets from each other?" He pushed the plastic cup away from him, jostling the ice. It tipped over, the light brown liquid seeping onto the tabletop.

"Javi," I pleaded, making a point to keep my voice low. "I don't even know how to start to explain what's happening to me. It's evolving and complicated and I'll sound insane."

"Try me, Riv!" He slammed his fingers into his chest. "I've sat outside almost all your doctor's appointments. I've witnessed a thousand of your episodes—and I've held your hand through them all. I've helped you off the ground. I've comforted you when you were drooling and muttering gibberish. I'm still here. Try me River, *please*."

The croak in his throat, the wrinkles in his forehead, the sheen to his eyes—I truly wished it were enough. Enough to say fuck it and bring him along for the ride and show him a world far trippier than the ones in his comics. But it wouldn't be the sunset we'd be riding off into—it'd be more like the apocalypse. Complete with vicious demons and bloodthirsty werewolves and half-angels armed with such wicked beauty they were perhaps the most dangerous of all.

Something else struck me then—what about the mental

filter Ryder had mentioned after the teratorn at his house? Would Javi even be able to see Source, or understand it? My mind had been on the verge of breaking at least ten times since I'd accepted this twist of fate—and I was *Nephilim*. What would it do to him, a human? It'd be life-altering, sure, but would it shatter him mentally? I was all too familiar with having a brain that operated differently. Even if I wouldn't change it, it was hard. Draining. I didn't want him to go through that unnecessarily. But I also didn't want to lose him. It was a no-win situation.

"I have one question." He broke my silence. "Does *he* know?"

I knew who *he* was, and for that, I hated my next words. "Yes, but…it's different."

Pushing up off the laminated table, he thrust his chair back. It squeaked against the linoleum, curdling my eardrums. "That's all I needed to hear." He paused after standing, messing with a crumpled straw wrapper. "We have half a summer left, and you're spending it with *him*. I guess our friendship—*I* mean that little to you that you can so easily toss me to the curb. By all means, be with whoever makes you happy, Riv. I just can't believe I was stupid enough to think it was me."

"You were going to leave me first," I whispered, trying and failing to hold back that festering piece of resentment. It gnawed at my integrity, killing any lingering decency. I didn't want to use that against him. I was a monster. I was…"I'm sorry."

I wanted to hear his snort-chuckle laugh, not his skateboard gliding away. Wanted to see his crinkled brown eyes, not his empty metal chair. Wanted his goodbye to insinuate a next time, not that he'd been hurt beyond repair. His absence left me with a haunting isolation, fueling the emptiness inside. I used to love being alone. I guess I got what I wanted.

"That looked rough." Ryder slid through my remorse and into the vacated seat.

If the bags under my eyes didn't give it away, my ragged breaths definitely did.

His hand reached for mine, ignoring the spilled tea. "You get it?" he asked, eager but quiet.

I nodded at the card next to the condensation mark where Javi's drink had sat, lacking the strength to do anything else.

"Sunset Court, Half Moon Bay," Ryder read aloud. "That's a few hours from here." He shuffled the edges of the card against the table. "Well, this'll take longer than expected. What are your plans tomorrow? Do you have class?"

I shook my head. Not on Fridays. "Hanging out with you." In any other situation the forwardness would make me feel cool and sexy, but it came out flat and didn't carry an ounce of thrill when my heart slushed in blended chunks like my drink. I had gone cold, stone-faced, utterly lifeless at the way things ended with Javi.

He's in love with you, you know.

I knew.

And the only thing I could do was squash that thought right out of my brain along with the maple leaves beneath my feet. Ryder had led me out onto the street, and we trudged past the weekly farmer's market, one of my and Javi's regular haunts. A place we'd taste test every cheese, sausage, hummus, and pitted fruit we were allowed before the commotion of the midmorning rush—aromas and flavors I loved to get lost in. But right now I couldn't stand them—I could hardly stand myself.

Which is why, before I went any further, there was one more thing left to do.

I ROUNDED THE alley's blunt corner, gripping its surface, the stone rough and firm against my fingertips. A solid buffer to catch me for when my knees undoubtedly buckled and I could no longer maintain my balance, let alone my composure. Once the cigarette fumes tickled my nose and my throat, I'd be too close to second-guess my decision.

The goodness of my heart hadn't led me to Kona Koffee—it was more like the glare from the glass door swinging open, the light hitting me square in the eyes. All but blinding me, it had caught my attention, and I knew right then and there, it had to be the final stop on my apology tour. As I'd peered through the windows, I didn't spot the soon-to-be recipient of said apology behind the counter. Which meant bathroom or smoke break out back.

I'd watched to see who came out of the restroom, Ryder at my side. "You can go. I'll see you tomorrow," I'd told him, once confirming their identity—not the person I needed. I'd stepped around my narrow-eyed companion, who'd moved to cross his arms and gripped the skin so tightly I could see the red mark of the indent. Yes, Ryder, I had the audacity to dismiss you, and I'd been feeling way too bitter to sugarcoat it. That stung him a bit, but I'd needed to do this next part myself. He'd get over it.

Disappearing behind my place of work, a twinge of fear curled my spine as bits of gravel and glass crunched beneath my feet. I hadn't forgotten that the last time I walked this dumpster-lined corridor I almost didn't make it out. Then Ryder found me. Shaking my head, shaking *him* away, I remembered what also found me that night. I shuddered, but the pit on my left fluttered with the yellow vests of construction, not a pair of glowing red eyes within unending darkness.

Chalky dust and metallic sparks billowed from the job-site and mixed with the alley's air, blending with the smoke from the cig's lit end, which its user dangled between their right pointer and middle fingers. Shanley took a drag and leaned against the brick, using her foot as a spring.

I took her in: The baggy jeans, the plaid flannel around her waist, the braless off-white tank behind the discolored apron. The plump rosy lips, the cool complexion, the fade beneath the tress of waxy dark blonde hair. Not the look of a stone-cold predator—but when her icy blue stare landed on me, I stopped cold, and all I saw was the monster within her.

"River?" she said. My breath lodged in my throat. "Hey." I expected a snarl of words, but they came out…subdued. The cig dropped to the pavement. She crushed the butt, not my bones, not under her claws, but her Converse.

An exhale slipped past my lips and that instinctual part of me that had me reacting like prey clicked off. Shanley wasn't the beast I needed to run from.

If anything, I was.

"Hey." I copied her stance against the wall. Not for cool factor, for sheer support. If the vision of a massive werewolf didn't bring me down, then my nerves most certainly would. My voice cracked with the blaring cement cutter as I went to say, "I'm sorry," but she beat me to it.

"What?" I spun on my heels to face her. "What are *you* sorry for?! I'm the one who caused this whole mess. If it weren't for me, Chet wouldn't have gone all bloodthirsty. I shouldn't have provoked him when we got to the party."

Shanley scoffed at the name. "*Chet* was going to do what he did regardless, because people like *Chet* have zero respect for others. I should have nipped the situation sooner"—no pun intended—"but I admit I'm a little rusty. We haven't had a situation like that in a long time, and even then…I wasn't even born, so I'm not totally sure how they dealt with it."

Right. Vampire takeover, eighties. No Hunt Order. Something I'd *actually* been briefed on. Although Ryder didn't reveal much outside of that phrase.

Shanley dropped her chin, her top locks a curtain across her brows. "It looks like I need to start screening the guest list again. Those bonfires have gotten pretty unruly anyways. Too many people, too many volatile young bucks. Way too much liability. I'm sorry," she repeated, stepping towards me. "You shouldn't have seen that."

I knew the lilt behind her plea meant more than just witnessing the hunger, the violence, the chaos of Chet's turning. Because that same lycanthropic spell had been mirrored in *her*—in her feral blue stare, in her raised ashy hackles, in her curled bloody flews, in her claws and fangs and growls—and she was my friend, not my enemy.

To try and ease any lingering tension, I said, "Eh, I've seen worse."

Shanley grinned, her eyes crinkling. "So, it seems you are one of us."

An assumption that'd already been made, I realized, when I'd seen through the façade of panic and locked eyes with that monster within. Or this convo would be going in a very different direction.

She leaned back against the brick, eyeing me with a suspicious smirk. "Didn't take you as this brand of misfit. What are you, exactly?"

My brain stumbled on the question. "Still trying to figure that one out."

"Well, welcome to the club. Hope the bonfire wasn't your initiation."

It was and it wasn't. The supernatural had always been coming for me; last night I'd just decided to stop hiding from it.

"So, when does my members-only jacket come?"

Her cackle was a blast of warmth, but it was my own laugh that really surprised me—for a minute there, I'd thought I'd never smile again.

It faded quickly. "Can I ask…where is he now?" The name didn't need repeating.

Shanley's gaze lingered on the activity across the alley. "He's awaiting his tribunal."

I raised a brow.

"The Pack Elders will sentence him, and those complicit, at the next new moon. If they have time for it." She ran her hand through her hair. "There's a lot of shit to sort through these days."

The weight of Shanley's tone, her fidgets, they didn't escape me. "What will they do to him? And those they find guilty?"

"Time will tell, but my ass is on the line. It happened under my watch, my rule." Another cigarette loosed, the lighter shaking on the path to ignite it.

I stated the obvious. "You're worried."

Shanley shook it off. "Best not to dwell on worst-case scenarios. As the Pack Leader, I'm always going to be involved." Her words didn't match the restlessness of her bouncing heel. The silence had me figuring we'd moved on from the topic when she added, a bit breathless, "If you want to testify…it'd help the case. It could also impact the type and severity of his punishment. Only if you're comfortable, though."

Wow. The only thing better would be delivering Chet his sentence myself.

I imagined his stupid pretty face on the stand, orangey tan faded from weeks out of the pool, sweat dripping from the fringes of his grown-out buzz cut, standing so scared and so small even at six feet tall compared to the pillars of wolfen muscle surrounding him.

Chet Jennings: water polo star, scholarship awardee. Those words would mean nothing there. *He* would mean nothing there. "What do I have to do?"

"Go in front of our Elders and some witnesses, and tell them what happened," Shanley blew out the smoke. "They'll want to know everything."

"Everything?" My muscles tensed.

"Every little detail." Each of her words could have been their own sentence, they came out so purposeful and slow. A warning or a heads-up, or maybe she was alluding to my trick, the whole summoning-the-ocean-and-flooding-the-clearing thing. Whoops.

Or maybe she was referencing my and Chet's obvious history. I didn't know if I could relive all that, let alone aloud, and in front of Elders—*strangers*. Even if I told every single truth, served my shattered heart as proof…What if no one believed me? What if his charm superseded it all? It seemed to always get him what he wanted.

"I'll think about it." I cut off my snowballing thoughts. "You still haven't answered my original question, though. Where is he?"

"He's in a holding kennel. Yes, you heard that right. Kennel." Shanley turned to me, and I swore the tip of a fang glistened in the sunlight. "Try not to hide your shock too much."

I couldn't even *if* I tried. The corners of my mouth twitched, fighting a smile.

"For all intents and purposes, Ch—*he's* just a pup. He has no control. Not that he had much before, clearly." She curled her lips over her teeth, up to the gums, lowering them quicker than they rose. "But now, it's like learning to walk again. He's flickering back and forth between man and wolf, and he's completely engulfed by his new urges."

"Sounds like the same guy to me," I mumbled as we walked in stride to the dumpster, where she tossed her cigarette butts. "How long can you keep him for? Surely not… forever?"

Shanley's look told me I'd be surprised. Then she shrugged. "Likely no, but his parents are too wealthy and aloof to notice his absence for now. At least he's eighteen, or this could have been really messy." And she added for emphasis, "We'd still hold him accountable."

I didn't know which night with Chet she was referring to now, but I nodded. As the dwindling afternoon light reflected in her eyes, I realized: she meant both.

"Hey." She slowed to a stop. "It wasn't your fault. You're not responsible for anyone else's behavior. You know that, right?"

"Thanks." I gave her a tight-lipped grin. Even with what I wasn't saying, Shanley understood the fear, how important hearing that was to me. "So," I breathed, "he's in the doghouse. Good."

The image of him crammed into a red-roofed, uninsulated shed with rusty water bowls was enough to bring us both to hysterics—exactly what I needed before venturing off to find the psychic and discover more about my half-angel heritage.

CHAPTER 24

SOMEWHERE ALONG THE STRETCH OF PAMPAS FIELDS, and me being fully zoned out, Ryder announced, "I need to make a pit stop."

Despite my restless night—the conversation with Javi and the crushing anxiety thrusting my eyelids open anytime a tendril of sleep attempted to coax them shut—I'd thrown on a pair of faded lilac Levi's, buttoned a capped gingham shirt, sprayed a couple pumps of surf spritz in my hair, and met my…friend? enemy? chauffer? at ten AM sharp at my curb.

We'd diverted from the Pacific Coast Highway for halcyon pastures, foxtail valleys, and grazing cows, and soon the coastline was all but covered by the rolling golden hillside.

Forcing myself back to the moment, to our mission, I figured Ryder's declaration didn't mean for gas or sandwiches, as my upper body bounced over the sandy potholes. "And what are we stopping for, may I ask?"

"Munitions," he said under his breath.

"Weapons?!" I clarified, hoping I'd misheard him.

He dipped his chin as he chuckled, then put his eyes back on the road. "Don't worry, we likely won't need them. But it's better to be prepared."

For demons? Werewolves? Vampires? Some other kind of monster that surely existed but I hadn't had the pleasure of being introduced to yet? I sank into my seat, crossing my arms. "Do I even want to know?"

The flare of mischief in his eyes told me enough.

The unpaved road got bumpier and bumpier, the dirt puffing up behind us, dusting the briny air in a drifting cloud. Boulders and oak trees wavered in the stretches of dried meadow before us, outlines fuzzy like a mirage in the heat.

A soft hum erupted above the tires' crunch—a low, almost infrasonic, vibration that ran from the grass's tips to the dash gauges. Scanning the horizon, I saw no source. In fact, the windless fields and cloudless blue sky painted the picture of a perfect day. Totally innocuous, yet the skin on my arms rose in anticipation.

"Do you hear that?" I couldn't be the only one. But Ryder didn't respond, he didn't even *smirk*, he just repositioned himself into a lazy lean and kept his eyes on the road.

The sound grew heavier, impossible to ignore, so intense it shook the windows, rumbling my seat and spiraling to my core. I shifted my gaze to the side mirror, ready to breeze over my reflection, when something stopped me.

Twisting in my seat, I craned my neck towards the road behind us and saw the source of the hum: a cloud of dust—not the spray of pebbles from the rotating rubber, but a small tempest made of soil, earth, and rock. It grew behind us, spinning larger and larger, hazing the air within the truck.

Coughing, I rolled up my window. "Ryder, how long before we get those weapons of yours?" I didn't take my eyes off the mirror.

He joined the surveillance in his own sideview, then put his focus back on the wheel. And that was that. No stiffening posture, no nervous tap of his fingers, no reaching for his arrows.

"They'll catch up before we get there." There wasn't a hint of fear in his voice.

"Uh…" I don't know what worried me more, the dust devil's increasing momentum or Ryder's clear lack of concern. "Well, *they're* gaining on us," I attempted to say, but by then the thunderous whirling drowned out my words and overtook the car.

Pebbles flung against the truck, so unbearably sharp and distinct they might as well have been impaling my skin. A bone-rumbling sound, like the rev of an engine, did just that, and my hands went straight to my ears. The air, thick with dust and panic, stung each inadequate breath. I brought my knees to my chest, praising myself for each attempted inhale and exhale while the noises blew out my senses and scrambled my thoughts.

To my right, a flash of silver and piercing spotlight penetrated the chalky vapor. They, whatever *they* were, trailed us so closely they rode our bumper, shrouding the glass in a beige film. The dust coated the sleek black hood and scratched my eyes, despite the windows being rolled up.

Two bulky chunks of metal escaped from the cloud and whizzed to the sides of the truck.

Motorcycles. That's what overtook us.

Then all hell broke loose.

Dozens of bikers hightailed past us, mocking us with cranking engines, head to pointed toe in leather, moustaches flapping in the wind, rocking braided tresses under their skull caps, riding so low their polarized lenses barely reached past the bases of the tall, arched handlebars.

I tried to ignore the catcalls from the riders next to me, but their hoots and hollers outdid the mufflers. Scrunched into a near-fetal position, I turned to Ryder for some affirmation, but he was too busy returning a gesture to a red-bearded, spiky-shouldered biker.

The rest of the gang roared past the Chevy, popping wheelies and blowing kisses. The dirt storm followed like a living, breathing thing, drifting where its rogue choppers took it.

Soon the sun's rays flooded the windshield as the last of the gang brought up the rear and passed us, taking the last of the swirling dust with them.

My hands dropped, one splayed above my chest. "What. The hell. Was that?"

"Dwarves." There it was again, that matter-of-factness. And his stupid, dimpled smirk.

"There's the information I could have used five minutes ago." I smacked his arm. "Your friends almost gave me a heart attack."

He played a smile and flinched away, like it actually hurt, but I was in no mood.

"I can't—" I sucked in a frazzled sigh, forcing myself to remain calm. "I can't *do* sudden, unexpected chaos like that. It overwhelms me." I massaged my temples. "I thought the engines might shatter my eardrums."

"Sorry," he cooed, trying to be cutesy.

I didn't need to be babied. I just needed him to get it. "Well, I told you I can get sensory overload," I snapped. "If we're going into something gnarly that I haven't seen before, you need to *tell* me first."

"I'm sorry." The teasing was gone from his tone. "Truly, River. I am."

I faced forward, sensing every time he looked at me. I'd counted twelve in the last two minutes.

"Did any of the noises speak to you?" he asked finally.

"No." I scowled. "That hasn't happened in a while."

We rode in silence. I continued to stare ahead at the picturesque fields, left undisturbed by the dwarves' magic. Ryder finally decided to speak after what may have been his hundredth glance at me. "You can roll your window back down. They don't leave any stragglers."

He took his own advice and let his arm meet the air, twirling his fingers in the breeze.

I didn't do the same, my mind caught on what I'd just experienced. "What is…what is even going on here?" A harsh laugh escaped me. "Like, what are all these species doing? Sprites, dwarves, werewolves, vampires…Are they all off fighting their own holy wars?"

"No, they're not." His gaze swept my cheek. "They're just collateral beings."

My palms rose with my shoulders. "See—what does that mean?"

"Humans and angels weren't meant to mix, at least romantically. It went against every law of nature when the first Nephilim were created. It literally altered time and space—ripped it apart, creating a secondary dimension that almost perfectly overlaps with this one, in what we call the Great Cataclysm."

My finger pulsed against my lips as I took it in. I hadn't expected him to tell me all this, but I sure as hell wasn't going to interrupt him.

"Even if the fabric of life is cut and reshaped with precision and purpose, it's impossible to predict all the trickle-down effects it will have on creation." Not ready to meet his eyes, I stole a glance at his hand atop the braided steering wheel—the tattooed one with the N and S stenciled between his thumb and pointer. My gaze shifted lower, to the fluid twist of his wrist, to the slight bend of his elbow. His body was lax, like his joints had been unlocked, like he might actually be enjoying this. Talking. "The other species? They were born of the Great Cataclysm. Born of two Earths. Like us."

Us. My heart skipped a beat. "And humans aren't affected because they…"

"Already live in the world that was created for them. How their Creator intended," he finished for me. "We may be part of them…but they are not part of us."

"So, instead of supernatural creatures, what do all these people see?"

"They see what you do. But, instead of taking it as truth, their mental filter kind of waters down the experience, and their brain spits up an excuse."

"Like extremely hairy men of shorter stature going for a joyride on their Harleys?" My mouth creased into an unwitting smile. If they hadn't been trailing us, I might not have looked twice or been attuned to their key, otherworldly differences—like how their helmets had thin slats for their pointy ears, or the way the dust around them twirled and twisted like a northern light.

"Yep." A soft chuckle slipped out with the word. "You won't catch them in the city very often, though. Mental filters or not, if their appearances became more frequent, sooner or later mortals would figure it out. Most supernatural beings want to keep their existence secret, so they live on the outskirts of society or blend in—harder to do with some species more than others."

The bonfire from a couple nights before flashed in my mind. I could say without a doubt there were humans there. I mean, Shanley had invited me before she knew I wasn't mortal. What had everyone running when Chet was turning into a werewolf—the cops? A belligerent dude? A stray wolf? And was it the same for them all, or dependent on the person?

Then I had another thought. "What about demons?"

"Demons are from another dimension that doesn't overlap with either of ours. In order to come here, they need to be called forth." The veins in the back of his hands popped as he gripped the steering wheel even tighter. "They need a leash from the underworld *and* a tether on earth."

I remembered his brother saying something similar. It froze my blood then just as much as it did now. "Who would do that?"

"Many people, River. More than you think."

One side of my lips curled up, scrunching my nose. "That's...pretty horrifying." Almost as bad as when he'd told me demons were really the tortured souls of corrupted angels.

I found myself back at a question I'd asked a couple days before, but I hadn't been totally satisfied with the answer. "What happened to those angels and humans—the ones that fell in love?"

He breathed in a sigh. "Well, a human can't join the angels because then they'd surpass Judgement. To be together, the angel would have to abandon their place among the Empyrean Throne and come to Earth, where they'd lose Source and immortality and essentially become mortal." And apparently raise little Nephilim babies. "*In theory*. We don't actually know if it went down that easy or if the lovers were ever rejoined."

Something about that last part didn't sit right with me. I gulped, the saliva burning my throat the entire way down. "What's the Empyrean Throne?"

"Empyrea's where the angels reside. They serve the Court of the Creator, who rules from the Empyrean Throne."

Wild. Utterly wild. "And...demons?"

"Chthonia, where they serve the Court of the Cursed."

"Who does everyone else serve?"

A muscle flexed in his jaw. "No one."

Ryder slowed the Chevrolet as we approached the base

of the foothills, the pale slopes cratered and brittle. The pinnacles emitted an almost metallic glow against the conifers and pines that grew sporadically on the peaks. I squinted to try and make out the forms carved into the sandstone outcroppings: aliens, peace signs, a symbol that looked like a cross between a sun and a compass, and…phallic doodles. I rolled my eyes.

In the fields below, scorched wood and broken billboards piled into mini pyramids, and rusty pipes littered the berm. The area no longer served as a grazing, golden field for cows but a graveyard of unwanted junk. Ahead, the trash was laid into a semicircle, marking the end of our dirt road. Nestled within the juts of the cratered rocks and the stacks of crushed cars was a run-down autobody shop.

It could have been abandoned—then I caught a flicker of movement as we crossed the threshold and the bustle of the yard enveloped me: the clink of a wrench, the hum of a lift, the whistled song of the mechanics. Dwarves serviced the vehicles with the rote of a hive, their bushy brows furrowing, blistered hands hammering, stocky arms hauling, bearded lips singing.

Half the roof's sign was hanging off, but that didn't stop its emerald flicker. The Wizard of Auto was rundown but reigned, and it was anything but deserted.

Ryder looped around the front of the working garage and pulled into a makeshift parking spot near where his leather-vested buddies posted up. Their motorcycles perched on kickstands, in a neat line like dominos, the inky metals glistening in the sun.

His hand met mine as I went to unlatch my seatbelt. "Wait for me here."

My face shot to his, the first time I'd looked at him straight on since my episode in the car. "No way, I'm coming with."

Hazel eyes flared, gold specks sifting against the green. "I don't have time to assess the situation." A tightness to his voice stopped me from what I was doing, and his fingers squeezed mine, hovering over the buckle. I took in the dwarves, their facial hair mimicking the colors of a changing autumn: rich chestnut, mahogany, ginger. Singing and shuffling and hyperfocused on their tinkering—nothing about this screamed danger. But Ryder did get reamed for blasting my senses, maybe he didn't want to make that mistake twice.

"Okay fine." I released the strap, scooting to the passenger door and propping my back against it. "But I'm going to get comfortable." He tracked the cross of my legs as I kicked my feet up, stilling as my shoes met his thigh. I wiggled my toes against his dark jeans. Too soon they met the air as he hopped out, a ghost of a smile on his lips.

Ryder strode to the pack of biker dwarves, a dark object in the shape of a crescent strapped to his waistband. It moved rigidly against his left leg's long, sweeping movements. Thin slits lined the edges, and through them I caught a flash of silvery white—it was so quick that if I blinked, I'd miss it. I narrowed my eyes. It was a sheath. For a knife. I sighed. Of course, he was armed.

As he strode by, each dwarf held out a fist and Ryder

went knuckle-to-knuckle down a half-formed line, turning grimaces into chuckles, scowls into sweet talk, and curled lips into broad smiles with obvious comradery. These were his friends.

Another person hung with the crowd, perched atop a splintered table, his shadow folding over his triceps. Boots on the seat, tatted elbows on knees, hunched in discreet conversation with two dwarves.

It was Ryder's brother, Leif.

The first time I'd met Leif, he was less than thrilled to have me at their house. What would he think of me being here, at their weapons depot? Oof. I sunk into the leather, hoping the dashboard would shield my cheeks flaring with heat. I watched him while he watched Ryder with their shared wild green stare, Leif's made even sharper with his dirty-blonde hair pulled into a tight bun.

The small group parted, and the chatter ceased as Ryder ambled closer to his brother. He wasn't greeted as warmly by his kin. No hints of enthusiasm softened Leif's tightened jaw. No dimples marked his clean-shaven cheeks. His gaze didn't waver from his younger brother's face. For a second, I was convinced he wouldn't notice me.

Then something in their exchange had them flicking their eyes towards the Chevy.

Towards me.

I mustered a motion that resembled a wave. It didn't get returned.

Could a demon just come and get me, like now? Leif's attention didn't linger on me long enough to catch the fifty shades of red I was turning.

When Ryder set foot towards the washed-out emerald building, Leif jumped down to join him, thank the freaking lord. They were off to see the Wizard, one that dealt weapons instead of spells, under the guise of an autobody shop. A path laden not with yellow brick but crushed sand and oil slicks. They snaked around the side of an empty lobby, out of view from the yard.

The minutes ticked upwards as I waited for them to come back. I didn't know how many more times I'd be able to retrace the doodles, swear words, serpents, and random N's and S's in thick block letters that were sprayed onto the corner of the garage's wall with my eyes.

My boredom rose with the temperature. I should've rolled my window down when I had the chance. Now it was locked. I fanned myself until it felt like my wrist might fall off.

A lonesome picnic table sat outside my door, the fresh air calling my name.

Wait here, he'd said. That didn't mean I had to hotbox myself, I thought as I opened the door and stepped out.

I welcomed the wind's immediate relief even if it carried dust, noise, and watching eyes. With a sigh, I gathered my hair off my sweaty neck, the strands knotty from the heat, curling it around my fingers and draping it over my shoulder. Situating myself beside the abandoned engines and the mounds of scrapped car parts, their bare edges sparkling like the tips of sharpened swords ready to slash anyone unlucky enough to graze them.

"We meet again—River, is it?"

Was it an inherited thing, this constant popping out of

the fringes and scaring the bejesus out of their conversational targets?

"H-hi," I said with the little breath I had left as Leif
sidled up next to me.

He smiled, a first, revealing his top row of teeth that
were brilliant white and straight. But with the vein popping
in his forehead and the unnatural squint to his eyes, I'm
pretty sure it was intended to disarm, not reassure me.

Leif drummed the tabletop. "What do you and Ryder
got going on today?"

Oh, just tracking down a potentially senile tarot reader
in hopes she can fill me in on the unfiltered, half-angel version of my past. A poke of intuition, sharper than the aluminum scraps, told me not to divulge that. So, I thought of
the next-best thing—a lie. "Uhhhh, going for a drive to…
Año Nuevo. To see the elephant seals."

"Ghastly buggers." He shook his head, the Cheshire
grin still plastered to his face. "You really wonder who they
pissed off to end up with a dick on their face, stuck in a
karmic cycle of blubber."

My patience wore thin in the heat, but I kept my expression bored. "What's with the small talk, Leif?"

He snickered. "That kind of outing sounds way too
wholesome for my brother."

I rolled my eyes. The chitchat was just a façade. I knew
exactly what he was doing here, curating his words to try
and get a rise out of me to see what might trigger a response
he could catalog and exploit.

"So, why are you hanging out with him? You in it for a
fake ID or a passport? A hit of cosmic acid? A mini chimeric

pet?" He motioned his thumb towards the defaced edifice that I was beginning to think served as some sort of black market. "Really though, what's a girl like you doing with a guy like him?"

Valid question, Leif. What was I doing with Ryder? I'd asked myself that on more than one occasion over the past week. In fact, I'd tried to walk away, but it seemed like the more I resisted the more tangled our lives became. Plus… there was no one else on this planet I could drop the words *werewolf* or *demon* or *Voices* in front of and be taken seriously. But I wouldn't admit that to his brother. I just shrugged. "He's not so bad."

"That's what they all say." Leif barked out a condescending laugh. "Hey, I've been searching for a necklace like that. Where did you get it?"

My hand flew to my chest, and in that mindless impulse I knew I had exposed my weakness. The shell he'd tried to crack with the dark humor, the obvious digs, the not-so-subtle manipulation—I had chiseled it myself with that telling flinch.

I sensed a shift in the energy, a prickle of eyes on the back of my neck. I pivoted and shot a look at the eavesdropping dwarves. They averted their stares, and as they turned away from me, I noticed a motif on the patches of their sleeves, one that also appeared on the web of Leif's and Ryder's thumbs.

"What does NS stand for?" I blurted out. "Nephilim Society, or something?"

"Ohhh," he crooned. "Ryder didn't tell you?"

I rolled my eyes. "What, like it's a big deal or something?" He smirked, and it wasn't cute or sexy or highlight any adorable freckles like Ryder's.

Leif leaned back on his elbows, stretching himself in a show of lean muscle that I was sure drove plenty of people mad. A cultivated ease meant to unsettle me—but it just made me want to punch him. "How about this: I'll fill you in on my little secret if you fill me in on yours?"

Tired of looking at his stupidly sculpted face cut like a damn Disney prince's, I crossed my arms and nodded. Maybe then he'd leave me alone. "Fine. It was my mom's."

His raised brows told me to go on.

"She died and she wanted me to have it, so my dad gave it to me for my birthday. It's a family heirloom." There. My hands rose then quickly plopped into my lap like it was no big deal.

Leif dipped his chin. His finger moved in lazy swirls across the top of the bench. "I'm sure Ryder told you we lost our parents, too."

More like I had to pry it out of him, but yes. I knew.

He peeled a piece of flaky paint. "How'd she die?"

"Nope, your turn." I didn't bother trying to hide the ice in my words.

"Fair enough." His silver dog tags clinked against the chain around his neck as he sat up. "It's somewhat of a society. More of a syndicate, really. You got peddlers, thieves, and assa—"

And then, at the literal worst time, someone called out, "What's going on?"

The sun funneled through the loops of the rooftop's sign, setting the Wizard of Auto's curved edges ablaze in an emerald light. From this angle, it caressed Ryder's frame and cast a wavering, horizontal shadow, spreading out from behind him like wings.

"Seems we've been interrupted," Leif muttered, his tone flat with annoyance. A hard pat landed on my back as he hopped down to his feet. I grimaced to avoid wincing. "Just getting to know your friend here, brother. Let me know when you're done with your escapades," I heard him whisper in his ear as he left to reunite with his gang, arm-wrestling by the assembly line of Harley's.

Ryder didn't so much as blink at his parting words. "You ready?" he asked me, a black duffel slung over his shoulder. Stocked with weapons, I presumed.

I nodded. Sensing goodbyes were futile around this joint, I saved myself the effort and went straight to his truck. We drove off, the dwarfdom sinking into the moonrocks, becoming nothing but a speck in the valley as we got farther away. The distance felt shorter, the highway came faster than it had when traveling in. I blinked and missed the boneyard of scraps and car parts, although it was miles long, and quicker than I could say *Wizard of Auto*, we straddled the line to the 1.

Perspiration slicked my palms and my hairline, even though both windows were down, and a cool ocean breeze filled the cab. I thought I'd been ready for this, to address where I came from, but I was moments from screaming *Stop!* Or *Turn left!* Or some inarticulate version of *Let's not go through with this.*

The blinker was like an ice pick chipping into my skull; every click had me closer to the edge. I let out a gust of breath, squinching my eyes shut, when rough, heated skin slid over my hand and snaked between my clammy fingers.

"Hey." The low drawl of an accent. "You ready to do this?"

No. But I couldn't turn back now, or I'd never go through with it.

Unclenching my eyelids, I met his wary, green stare.

It gave me the courage to say yes, and we turned right, towards our next destination, Madame Myrian's.

CHAPTER 25

WHAT'D MY BROTHER SAY TO YOU?" RYDER CASUALLY inquired a few minutes into our drive.

"He just wanted to know where we were going." Not a lie, but not the whole truth. The whole truth entailed Leif's scheming eyes across my collarbone as he tried to decode my body language for secrets. I still kicked myself for that slip of impulse when he'd asked about my necklace.

"And what'd you tell him?"

"I said we were going to Año Nuevo." The gentle clinks of the keys swinging against one another filled the silence that followed. I knew he was smirking without even looking at him. "It was the first thing that came to mind!"

He laughed and slapped the leather seat with his palm. "I'm not that wholesome."

"That's what he said," I grumbled.

"But you planted it in his mind." Ryder sighed. "So, we should at least do a drive-by."

My head swiveled towards him, but his attention didn't leave the two-lane road.

Confusion brought my brows together, flipped my lips into a frown. "Don't we have to get to Half Moon Bay?"

"We can spare a few minutes." He shot me an infuriating wink that made my heart race. "For our alibi."

I opened my mouth to argue, but that word had me thinking, watching the mirror for a certain motorcycle trailing in our exhaust. I hid the lapis, as if the cup of my hand could shield it from any threats. Leif's concern about our whereabouts started to feel more and more suspect as I replayed his interest in it—and the fact that we had to divert from our route in case he came to check.

I gazed at the flurry of trees on my right, green buds blooming between the red-black branches marred by a recent fire, the woodland broken apart every few miles by acres of lush golden farmland. Suddenly, the truck swung towards the crushed grass that lined the roadside and idled parallel to the lane's white line.

My stomach knotted as I glanced left, right, behind. "Why are we stopping?"

Ryder hopped out and strolled around the hood, coming to the passenger side. The sun highlighted the curve of his muscles as he crossed his arms and rested them on the base of my window. "It's your turn to drive."

For a second my heart stopped. "What? Now?"

"Yes, now. You need all the practice you can get. Now scoot." He shooed me with a flap of his fingers, then slid in. Panic swaddled me in a sheet of sweat as I brought my hands to the wheel. Groaning, I shot him a look that said, *Really?*

He patted the gear stick, waiting to blanket my hand with his. "Just to Año Nuevo. It's no more than fifteen minutes away. Although…" His chuckle was a harsh reminder of the last time we did this, and I went twenty miles per hour in a forty zone. "It's an easy, uncongested road. You'll be fine."

My pulse tumbled from my chest to my gut, drumming up an emotion almost identical to what I was already feeling but was too stubborn to admit: excitement.

A quick review of the basics—clutch, brake, shift—and this time I didn't wait for him to tell me to press on the gas and release the other pedals. This time we didn't stall or rev or lurch. Okay maybe we lurched a few times; the rolling hills were new. But for the most part we coasted, weightless and toasty from cruising with the speed and the wind. The ocean sparkled on my left, and the forested hills dotted the horizon on my right. And Ryder's stare, as vast as the world in front of me, danced over my body, my face, like the tendrils of light pouring in from the baby blue sky. The tension slowly eased from my jaw and my shoulders in the heat of his gaze, and the beautiful calm of the drive.

His thumb stroked my pinky, and I realized abruptly that he had never removed his hand from mine. It circled the side of my palm, providing a whole other sort of rush— one that had me contemplating looking for a turnout and putting this bad boy in park.

Which I eventually did, but not because of my completely inappropriate thoughts. We'd arrived at Año Nuevo, purple and pink lupine and heavy cypress bordering the empty visitor lot.

I hadn't even realized we'd made it. "That's weird," I said.

"Hm?" Ryder twirled his wrists.

"I lost track of what I was doing." I let out a yawn. He

caught it. "One minute we were on the road, the next we were here. Like I was on autopilot."

A sleepy smile raised his cheekbones, rosy from the sun. "It's normal to zone out when you're driving, especially longer distances. Relaxing, isn't it?"

"Yeah," I admitted, surprising myself. Tucking my shoulders behind me, I drew my arms back, a buttery satisfaction exuding from the stretch. "Ready to switch?"

"Turn off the car."

Objection bubbled in my throat. I'd thought about doing that one too many times on the ride here. When I met his eyes with a challenging stare, those golden-green specks blazed bright with excitement.

"Don't give me that damning look." He smirked. "I want to show you something."

"Now?"

"Yes, *now*," he repeated, exiting the vehicle. "Come on."

Weapon grabs were one thing, but biding our time like two seniors ditching math class when my destiny and potentially my safety were at stake?

I glared at him through the windshield, his fitted black t-shirt creeping up his lower abs while he waited outside and extended his long, athletic arms overhead. The tat with the flowing rapids of water snuck out from his sleeve again, while the light gleamed off the V lines carved into his hips. I blinked and he had already converted to his innate stillness, thumbs tucked into his belt loop, close to the knife at the waistband.

I wished there was a simple explanation as to why my feet hit the corroded asphalt and I strutted towards the guy with the emerald fire in his eyes. Why when he flashed a true smile, the kind that displayed his dimples, like right now, it made my insides melt and freeze at the same time. Why with a single gesture he made me feel like the ugliest parts of me were not only worth saving, but worth exploring.

This could get so damn messy. But I was ready to get my hands dirty.

Ignoring every red flag, I reached his side, and we trekked the crushed golden-granite path towards the ocean. We journeyed through the bushy headland, passing a pond layered in algae and surrounded by cattails, the mossy surface only broken by foraging herons. And then we descended crumbling steps framed by poison oak coils, until we finally reached an expansive beach spotted with blanched driftwood.

Shoes plunging into the dunes, we strode to the northernmost bluff jutting out to the sea. A fissure in the rock, invisible from across the sand due to its crags and jagged arches, revealed itself when we reached its base. The music of the ocean roared against walls smoothed by the tide. Only when the water shrunk far back enough in between sets were we able to cross through the tunnel to the other side.

And now we stood in a cove and waited.

"What exactly are we waiting for?" I shot Ryder a look, but his eyes didn't stray from the water.

And waited.

I tilted my hip, shifting my weight onto it, about to ask again. He shushed me with a light, teasing finger on my lips.

With a playful swat I knocked it away as we continued to stand, and wait, in this pristine crescent-shaped clearing, its naturally formed ramparts ancient and sacred—a mural of shells and fossils unearthed in the fresh copper soil from the small earth slides from the cliffs.

Tucked away here, we watched the water creep towards the soles of our shoes, rainbows reflecting in the tips of the waves that crashed on the diamond-flecked sand. The cove thrummed with a power that encased my skin like the salty brine on the tepid breeze, and then…a massive, opalescent blob jumped out of the ocean, and splashed back in.

I blinked, unsure of what I had seen. Before I could ask, I covered my mouth in shock, as a group of similar creatures followed suit—breaching, spinning, diving, much like a pod of dolphins, their lustrous coats of blubber shimmering with a pink and turquoise ombré sheen.

Elephant seals—the otherworldly kind. Or maybe they were the same mammalian species I'd grown to know and love, but I'd never given myself the chance to look past the surface and truly *see* them for what they were.

Regardless, they weren't ghastly; they were beautiful. Only a miserable fool would say otherwise. Tears pricked my eyes as they rotated through the air, nimble as torpedoes.

Right then and there, I knew that when I got to show Javi this world, this'd be the place I'd do it. If he ever forgave me.

A whisper tickled my ear. "What do you think?"

"They're the most beautiful things I've ever seen." I turned to my companion to find him fixed on me—not on the ethereal creatures springing out of the water, but *me*. I dipped my chin and let out a low, laughy breath, an attempt to downplay my tear-flecked eyes, the wonder written all over my face.

"I agree," he responded, guttural and absolutely yielding, his breath taken by the sight of me, just as mine had been taken by seeing the magic in the waves.

"Well…Leif was right about one thing," I said, filling the space with mindless words to cover the sound of my pounding heart. "This is way too wholesome for you."

"Well…" He took a step forward, the minty burn of his words coating my lips as a finger traced my jawline, then cupped my chin. "I know how we can make this experience a little less wholesome." The suggestion came in the form of a low, silken growl, stemming from the deepest part of his throat.

"Well…" I mimicked his movement, leaving nothing more than a sliver of charged air between us. "We wouldn't want to risk your reputation."

In one fluid motion, his hand dropped from my chin to my lower back. Resting on the slope, his fingertips slid into my jeans' back pockets.

I rose onto my tiptoes, and his entire body stilled as our mouths met.

The heat of embarrassment flooded me—was I about to be denied? My heels dropped an inch, and then his lips parted against mine and he scooped me into his sculpted chest. Whatever doubts I felt about him—about us—melted away as his tongue slipped past my teeth. I answered its patterns, my senses severed from feeling anything except the circular motions it made.

His touch was like the pull of the undertow. Once I was caught in it, it threatened to drown me, but I gave in to it without thinking.

We swayed, riding our own current towards the shelter of the bluffs. The brittle sediment crumbled beneath my spine as he hoisted me onto a natural ledge, and I curled my legs around his hips.

"Are you comfortable?" he asked like he was coming up for air from a dive far too deep.

"Yeah." My words trembled against his lips, the cavity intertwining our breathless voices with the ocean's bellows.

His hands followed the outline of my waist, slowly skimming the outer arc of my thighs. I gripped the hem of his shirt, and we broke apart for less than a heartbeat for me to pull it over his head. I took in his naked upper body, so imperfectly perfect, with its nicks and moles, defined in all the right places. My hands swept over the peaks and valleys of his muscles, across the scars along his back, so similar to mine…He was a blanket I wanted to wrap myself in, so I covered every inch of myself with his warm ivory skin.

The flimsy straps of my tank slid off my shoulders as his kisses drifted from my mouth. Stamping my jaw, trailing beneath my ear, brushing down my neck.

I dragged my fingers through his hair, the smooth strands of his grown-out locks the perfect part of him to hold on to as he sucked on my collarbone and pressed his hips into me.

A pounding wave broke with my moan as he pulled the bust of my top down and the cool brush of air peaked my nipples.

His eyes widened at the bare sight of them. "Arch your back for me a bit, baby."

I sat up a tad straighter, slightly bending my spine. "Like that?"

"Yes, oh my God." He cupped the lower swell of my breasts with tentative hands. "So, so perfect. I cannot wait to get these beautiful things in my mouth."

"I"—I gasped as he did just that, suctioning the rougher, pigmented part of my skin with a slight graze of his teeth—"I don't know about that."

"What?" he asked with a gentle tug that sent a shivery bolt through my heart and settled between my thighs.

My head shot back, every ounce of awareness honing in on that spot. "They're just your average boobs."

"Oh no, they are perky little bells, and you have the most exquisite nipples. Like I said, they're perfect." His tongue did figure eights around the hard, sensitive point as he massaged the other with his hand, his callouses a pleasant scrape against my tender skin. "Everything about you is." He switched, and I was seeing stars at the light nips and pressure as he fondled them like they truly were the most magnificent things to bless this Earth. "I haven't stopped thinking about you since the night we met." My lashes fluttered shut.

He returned to my mouth. I peeked through slitted eyes, knowing he did the same once I closed them, and my fingers traveled to his waistband. For a moment I let my imagination take me to a dark, sultry place within the shadows of the rocky overhang, where we were reduced to nothing but feelings and flesh. Where I succumbed to the increasing roll of his hips and spread for the hardness pitched between them, and the motion of our bodies swelled with the waves.

Where I was a tide of nerves and pleasure, a surge of magic and release, and Ryder was the gravity that moved me.

I had these urges—normal, human urges. But I knew more than anyone that bodies and minds don't always match up, and that night with Chet I didn't want it, no matter what the slickness between my legs relayed. I dismissed the unwanted thought, as intrusive as its namesake, and lifted the strap from Ryder's buckle, because this…this was different. This was *my* choice.

My fingers froze.

I wanted this. I did. My grip tremored as the belt's prong released and a swell of nervous heat overtook me. The rocky nook suddenly felt like a prison where my pain would be recorded on the walls with my nails. The tension heightened and changed, like the rawness had coiled into something jagged that would tear me apart.

Up against the wall, trapped beneath his chest, it'd be so easy for him to take me.

No one would hear us. He might or might not stop. I winced, slowing as he continued to claim me—then he paused, his swollen pout featherlight on my lips. I expelled a sigh, one of equal parts desire and relief.

He backed away, the fire tamed but still smoldering, taking all of me in. Every hair, every freckle, every rise and fall of my chest. I waited for the snarls, for the sexual slurs, for his anger from the sting of rejection. Instead, he picked his shirt up off the damp sand, pulled it down over his head, and outstretched a tattooed hand as he waited to guide me into the open air of the clearing.

I slid the straps over my shoulders and cinched up my snug top as my muscles began to shake. Ryder was unreadable as he stared at the uneven patches of skin on his palm, averting his eyes while I took what seemed like forever to get myself dressed. Then I accepted his hand and we headed for the narrow split in the bluff where we first entered the cove.

There was another kind of demon that followed our footprints, invisible and unrelenting.

Livid at myself and embarrassed for ruining the moment, I did what I do best: shut down my emotions and buried the old wounds.

The crushing quiet bored into me as we trudged through the sand. I wanted to spit out the most cliché line ever, *it's not you it's me*, to let Ryder know my freak reaction had nothing to do with him. Halting, I reached for his elbow, panting from the walk or the aftereffects of what had just happened. But instead of saying what I needed to get off my chest, I blurted out, "He asked me about my necklace."

"What?" Those powerful shoulders of his stiffened.

"Leif. He said he'd been looking for one like it." I bit down against the searing frustration that bubbled up inside me for deflecting.

Ryder slowly turned to face me. "Did you tell him?"

I nodded and took a deep breath, not realizing my hand had flown back to the pendant, clutching it tightly. My brain sparred with my heart. "I'm sorry I pulled away back there."

"You…" He sighed with a heavy longing, his stance softening. "You have nothing to be sorry for. One look at you and I…" His gaze drifted over my body before meeting my eyes. "I got carried away. I need to control myself better."

"You *did*, though." Without thinking, I fisted his shirt, twisting the soft fabric as I spoke. "You *listened* to me, Ryder, and I didn't have to say anything out loud. A courtesy that wasn't given to me the last time I…" A quiet sob cut off my confession. I squeezed my eyelids together in attempt to stave off the memory. But the mental anguish from that misogynistic, over-beefed jock hit me as hard and fast as the adrenaline from Ryder's kisses.

With a gentle coax, Ryder settled me into the crook of his chest, seemingly unnerved by the messy emotions that'd been on lock for so long and were now spewing out of me. I folded into his arms delicately draped across my back, dabbing my lashes against his tee.

For once, his silence didn't drive me crazy. I was grateful for it. He bent to kiss me one last time—a sweet, loving peck to my forehead. It felt like a promise. Or a goodbye.

I wasn't sure which.

CHAPTER 26

Y OU SURE THIS IS IT?" RYDER ASKED, KICKING A *For Sale* sign in front of the structure before us. In a line of Victorians splashed with pastel blues and manicured hedges, this Gothic outlier looked like it had been abandoned ages ago.

Maybe it had once been a brilliant eggplant—the sun had bleached the fish scale shingles that covered every inch of the exterior walls. The scrollwork—curling, swirling gold gingerbread trim—was half-eaten by the ocean's erosion. With cobwebs thick as curtains on the latticed panes of every gable, dome, and turret, the house seemed so out of place—and I found myself checking the business card for the dozenth time to make sure we had the right address.

I cut across the patchy dead lawn under the glaring gargoyle statuettes perched atop the multi-level spires, who watched for trespassers just as vigilantly as Ryder scanned for threats.

Propping myself up onto my tiptoes, I peered into a bay window along the circular lower tower. A glow caught my attention through the layers of lace: a neon *Fortunes* sign, flickering in the dimness. Score.

With a thumbs-up to my comrade, I ascended the porch, the paint splitting beneath my feet. My pulse quickened with every step. The door loomed over me, much taller than it had seemed from the base of the stairs. My head kicked back as I looked up at the cathedral top—it had the width and the height, even the smell, of a redwood sapling. It was huge. Curling my fingers into a fist, I rapped my knuckles against the wood. No answer. I knocked again.

I waited for the shuffling of footsteps when something else occurred to me. "There's no handle!" I yelled over my shoulder. Unless that too lay hidden behind some optical illusion. Still, I didn't see an obvious way to get in.

"Maybe a doorbell?" Ryder suggested from where the overgrown pathway met the sidewalk.

"I can't find that, either," I grumbled, skimming the archway. Thin, runic notches were cut into the doorframe. I tilted my neck to read them, but they were just as indecipherable sideways.

"Did you try knocking?" I didn't know how it was possible for Ryder's smirk to creep into his voice, yet that's exactly what I got from him. I hoped his *amazing* hunter's vision caught me rolling my eyes.

I studied the knots in the door, followed their emerging paths. They circled more like ring lines than splinters, forming a natural mosaic. The weirdest urge to press my hands into the wood overcame me. I gave in to the impulse, a smoky, violet haze billowing from beneath my palms. I jumped back, almost tripping off the porch's top step, as the tinted haze dispersed into the air.

My gaze shot to my hands. I flipped them over—they

still looked the same—still *felt* the same. So did the door. But when I touched it again, the hues erupted once more: wispy clouds of blue, lavender, silver billowing from the notches in the wood under each brush of my fingers.

A persistent tug on my intuition told me I had seen this before. Maybe I was reaching, but it reminded me of the portal I'd crossed into in the dream I had on Grad Night.

That doorway had inscriptions too, and tentacles of light, if I recalled. Aside from my touch, nothing special was needed for it to open and transport me to another realm. A realm full of magic and redwoods and…death. And Ryder. Who shot me with an arrow.

Frowning, I shook off the nightmare. "Ryder! You need to see this."

Thumbing the quiver strap that rested in the cleft between his pecs, he left his position at the edge of the lot. As he moved the overgrowth with his buckled black boots and long-legged stride, I gawked about as bad as the circling crows.

"Take a look." I gestured to the door, thankful for a reason to switch my attention from his black tee and how it hugged his brawny chest as he leapt up the stairs. "First of all, this thing is massive. Second, look at these patterns." My finger hovered over the swirling age lines. With every trace of the air, I focused on the knots. They became more and more symmetrical to me, like I could start pointing out shapes as I would in the clouds. "I don't think they're random."

Holding my breath, I guided his hand to the markings. Nothing happened.

Well, that was embarrassing.

He snorted. "This is what you wanted to show me? A big-ass door?"

"No," I huffed. Nudging him aside, I held my skin to the timber. Its grooves smoldered in color. "See?"

His eyebrows shot towards his hairline. I held my chin high in triumph.

"I must not have pressed hard enough. Let me try again." He lunged forward.

Nothing came from under his fingers' imprints.

I crossed my arms and gave him an expression I wasn't used to wielding: a smirk. "Guess I have the magic touch."

"You really do." He stared at me with wide, electric eyes, chest reclining on a long, unsteady inhale. For a moment, he looked like he might run. "And you've been right in front of me all this time. I wanted so bad to ignore it." He ran his hand through his hair and took me in like a panoramic view of a mountain—one he was supposed to climb. A petrified sort of awe that rooted him to the spot. I might've paused on his acknowledgment—at least I thought that's what this was—if we weren't breaking and entering.

I'd have to revel in the credit later.

Not sure where to go from there, I turned back to the door. "What if the key to get inside is a pattern on this door? Like some sort of code. And we just need to…trace the right one for it to unlock?"

My words seemed to snap him out of his daze. "That's a good idea, but we're not going to just get lucky and stumble across the code." He narrowed his eyes at what towered in front of us. "We need to figure out what the lines represent and narrow down a pattern from there."

I pulled the beige scrunchie off my wrist, twisting my hair into a loose, low bun. "There are so many to choose from."

Brows furrowed in concentration, Ryder rested his chin between his thumb and pointer. "Yeah, this could take forever." Ah, the king of encouragement.

The spiraled bark lifted more the longer I stared, defying its gravitational bounds. I rubbed my eyes until I was no longer seeing double and let out a sigh. Maybe if I treated it like a 3D image the answer would pop out? Javi and I had done dozens of stereograms in our lives, competing for who could see the illusion first—this'd be no different.

Despite my winning streak, after thirty dizzying seconds here, I tapped out cross-eyed and empty-handed. I spun my mom's necklace, directing my stress to the pendant. The brocade indented my fingers as I pressed into the dull lines—which strangely felt sharp.

"Ow!" Its raised, rounded edges had somehow punctured my skin enough to draw a drop of blood, but that's not what had the gears of my mind spinning wildly.

Holding my necklace, my breath, and the teensiest bit of hope that I refused to give in to too quickly, I drew the raindrop pattern of my necklace, ripples and all, with the two stars, onto the door. It glowed like bioluminescence against the red wood. So promising, until it wasn't.

"Damn. I thought I had figured it out," I muttered as the light faded into nothing.

"You might have the right idea…" Ryder's hand shook with the slightest tremor as it halted mere inches from my chest. "May I?" I nodded, and he scooped the lapis stone into his palm, tracing its design with an incisive gaze. "This is the Empyrean symbol for water."

A tidal roar reached my ears although I stood a mile away from the Pacific Ocean. A draft tunneled through the porch and caressed my skin like a chill, velvety current. Something about what he said clicked.

Gently releasing the pendant, he leaned into the door with his arm overhead, pressing his knuckles into the wood. "Since it doesn't work solo, it could be part of a greater combination." His eyes swept the door's gnarled patterns for meaning. "There are three other elements. Earth, air, and fire."

My heart thumped so hard it could've knocked on the door itself. "Do you know the symbols for those?"

"I do." He dropped his hand and took a step back.

"Okay." My nerves made it to my voice. "Where do we start?"

"Let's try ascending order. First would be earth, the basis of all creation. A circle with a star in its center, like the ones on your necklace. Like this." Ryder spoke with conviction, yet as he drew nearer, the trembling fingers he placed over mine lacked that assurance. He stroked my pinky with his thumb, a silent wish of good luck, and moved our hands to a larger knot in the center.

We traced a single round line, not lifting our fingers until the shape had been completed, then added a four-pointed star in the middle of it.

The drawing burned into the surface and flared with a stability unlike the flickering from earlier, like the door was accepting that part of the code.

"You were right." I stared at the geometric blaze, almost too dumbstruck to continue. "Which one next?"

"Earth rises out of the water, so water." I knew this symbol, but he still guided my finger, selecting a knot to trace over, a bit lower and to the left.

We watched, no less intrigued as the ultraviolet rays once again flared brighter.

"Now air, which breathes life into the first two pillars. Let's put it here." Still interlocked, together we traced on the symbol, his grip on me tighter than before. "Across from water."

Beginning with a four-pointed star this time, we used its bottom point to start a spiral that looped around it counter-clockwise, then snaked to the right and slightly below into a matching design. A final star was placed above the dip between the two.

Another element, bold, effervescent, lit up the board.

"The final glyph, fire, which reigns over everything. A flame with four stars lining its right side, below."

Ryder rotated my wrist as he moved behind me, draping his arm over my shoulder, the floorboards creaking against the thick soles of his boots. I was rooted, hardly breathing, as earth, water, air, and fire continued to burn in their places, an elemental compass directing me to my true north.

On the peripheral something plopped into the straw grass. I glanced back at Ryder and his gaze met mine, pupils condensing into pinpricks before my eyes. Tension stiffened his shoulders and every facial muscle stilled as his instincts seized control.

He prowled to the spindled railing and twisted over it to scan the roofline.

Then the whole house started moving.

One by one, the eaves slid off the roof, into a pile at the base of the home. Ryder dodged a mini cherub as the molding fell off the porch ceiling's plaster, the trim's cornices breaking apart at our feet.

A loud *crack* made me look upwards. The beams had begun to split. A tremor shook the foundation, dividing the deck, tossing Ryder to the stoop and me to the welcome mat.

I smashed into the door hinges, the receding nail heads tearing into my scars. The metal ripped one of my straps to mere threads and red sprinkled the floorboards, the blood and rust staining the side of my gingham top. Hoisting myself up the latched wooden entrance, I desperately knocked at the door.

"We need to get out of here!" Ryder called.

That was probably the better idea, but something in me told me to keep trying. That this might be my only chance. So, knocking became pushing, pushing became banging, but the door stayed sealed shut.

Closing my eyes, I prayed for something to click amongst the collapsing gothic revival, but my thoughts were weighed down by the frenetic whir of the sliding shingles. By the windows creaking and groaning and exploding into a thousand jagged pieces, my senses lying somewhere in the shattered glass. Around me, the entire building was caving in on itself like I had created a black hole at its center, and I was about to be swallowed.

"Quarto vigil." The fortune teller's phrase was hushed on my curling lips. "I am the Fourth Watcher." I exhaled sharply.

When I opened my eyes to face my crumbling reality, at first it seemed like nothing had changed. But as I reached to cling to the door, my hands grasped empty air. Because where the door had stood there was now a tunnel that swallowed the ultraviolet light we had brought forth on the wood. No floor. No ceiling. No old wicker furniture. A passage of darkness.

My gut nudged me forward. A voice called me back, the lilt of the accent so sharp and irresistible and growing so frantic that I almost listened. But intuition screamed louder, it could no longer be silenced, and I stepped into the epicenter.

CHAPTER 27

THE PASSAGE SIGHED IN RHYTHM, A SLIGHT WIND nipping at my hair and clothes, as if the house was taking a breath. My head swiveled to all sides, where the floor and ceiling *should have* been but swept over…nothing. Nothing but a black, infinite depth.

I reached for a wall, anxious to grab anything that might help anchor me. Air met my fingers. With the onset of complete darkness, a sudden chill crept around me, the goosebumps forming on my arms as pointed as the tip of a blade. I spun around and shot back towards the entrance, but it had disappeared, along with everything else.

My chest rose and fell in short, frantic heaves. Ryder was out there, and I was stuck here in this void, where there were no signs of life, let alone Madame Myrian.

Panic set in and my senses prickled on the cusp of turning silence into shrieks. Clenching my fists, I gnashed my teeth and willed myself to calm. I stood there, focused on each breath, until my eyes started to adjust. Tiny balls of light, the same purple-white as the markings on the door, dotted the black—as if the elemental symbols had fractured apart and now flecked this nebulous corridor like mini galaxies.

A scuttle came from somewhere in the dark, causing me to nearly jump out of my skin.

I turned on my heels, extra slow. Hardly steady.

"Myrian?" I could have shouted it at the top of my lungs, and it wouldn't have mattered. My voice was a squeak in this expanse. "Is that you?" My ears narrowed in on a steady hum, like a distant vacuum was on.

A brilliant orb appeared in the vastness, flooding the dark with a pearly iridescence that lit the space like a moon. Rippling with the fluidity of a wave, it sat atop a tourmaline pedestal that seemed to have been carved out of the shadows.

I gravitated towards it with short, eager steps.

Resisting the urge to touch it, I paced around it, transfixed by the milky matter beneath the glass surface. A draft swept the loose strands of hair from my face, and an outline emerged on the other side of the crystal ball. Stirring the air, pulling from the specks of ultraviolet light, until a proper shape materialized.

Buried in her violet robes, her thick auburn hair piled high, Madame Myrian observed me, her indigo stare enlarged and unblinking through her fishbowl glasses.

She bared a near-toothless grin. I was too shocked to return it.

Our relationship picked up right where it left off: in an epic stare down.

But I wouldn't mistake frailty for harmlessness, petite

for punchless, this time. Beneath the sunken cheeks and grandmotherly features, Myrian hid the strength of a lion. I reflexively rubbed my arm where she had grabbed me the last time I saw her.

"Hi." Really? That was the boldest, baddest thing I could think of? I almost facepalmed.

In answer, the psychic unclasped her fingers and pulled a stray thread from her clothes. I should have known I wouldn't get much out of her—she'd been a woman of few words at Grad Night. But those words haunted me.

Myrian's arms floated to her sides, the sleeves hanging off her sticklike arms cascading behind. Her hands hovered above the crystal ball, the silver stitching on her cuffs reflecting its pale light. A familiar pattern threaded the fabric— one that matched the charms on the crystal chain looped around her sun-spotted wrists and fingers. One I had also traced onto the door: the four elements.

Unease grew in the pit of my stomach. "Why did you call me the Fourth Watcher at Grad Night?"

She ignored me—shocker—and waved her hands over the sphere, just above its clear outer layer. The interior's cloudy liquid churned faster, following her wax-on, wax-off motion, gaining momentum as her hips and arms swayed in rhythm.

Spooky, for sure, but what was I going to do? *This*—unprocessed truth, truth so raw it hurt, truth so mind-blowing it came at the expense of my known reality—this was what I came here for. No more running. No more hiding. No more *thinking*. From here on out, I was doing.

"Do you know who I am? Where I came from?" I nodded to the crystal ball. "Or can you help me figure that out?"

A hum, similar to the eerie noise I'd heard earlier, came from Myrian's thinning lips. It intensified into sputters, progressing into consonants, finally harmonizing into language. A faint bolt of light broke from the orb, shooting through the glass barrier, attaching itself to the roof of her mouth. Her eyes flared with periwinkle lightning, each of her inhales draining a little more energy from the ball, then getting exhaled out as enchantments.

"Vultuuuus." Her croaky vowels shook me down to my nerves. *"Looook."* She beckoned me close.

I relaxed my fists, my teeth, my shoulders, every part of my body that'd been strung, and leaned over the orb—ready to accept whatever story the magic wanted to tell.

The liquid in the interior had thickened to a syrup, swirling, roiling, and turning, as if stretched by invisible hands. A flicker of color appeared, a flash of a place or an object, between its taffy-like folds. I craned my neck, my nose almost grazing the glass as I tried to make sense of the image forming within.

Heart jumping with the churning core, I lifted my chin to check in with the psychic. She shoved my head back down—and into the glass. Every muscle in me tensed, bracing for impact, but I went right through its glossy surface.

Although my head had made the initial plunge, every limb followed, like a dive into the ocean. Neither sinking nor swimming, I was submerged, the air inside chalky and thick as Jell-O. It densely draped over my nose and mouth, made each heavy breath feel like a swallow.

I turned to face the reality I had just left, wavering like a mirage behind a brumous veil. I shot my hand out, trying to breach the barrier, but the swirling mist just thickened around it.

Retreating, I compelled curiosity to eclipse my anxiety and took in my surroundings.

This place—whatever, wherever it was—seemed to be the diametric opposite of where I had come from. The light smothered the dark, swallowing the shadows before they could even form. Similar to before, there were no walls, but my footsteps echoed. No color, but the diluted sphere burned my eyes with stark, penetrating white. It was so bright. So empty. My senses revved into overdrive, bringing a wave of razor-sharp tingles to my skin. If Madame Myrian's home was the center of a black hole, this was the center of a starburst.

My legs slogged forward, each pull and shift lagging, leaving tracers in the air. It didn't take long for exhaustion to strike. I had barely moved a foot, but my body quivered like I had been sprinting for miles. When I collapsed into the nothingness, I swore others gasped alongside me. But then I was free-falling and the hint of a voice or two flushed into the bitter wind stinging my ears.

At first it was nothing but that feeling of weightlessness. But the farther I plummeted, the more my back arched, the more I felt like a cold, leaden slab of stone. I was spinning, twisting, screaming, with absolutely no control, as a force pulled me further down, until even just taking a breath seemed impossible.

It was like trying to fly without wings.

A brutal pressure slammed into my spine. Fierce, radiating pain shot up my back, across the scar tissue on my shoulder blades, down to my tailbone. The breath whooshed out of me, and I gasped fruitlessly for a full thirty seconds while my brain attempted to register that I'd landed. *Hard.*

The ground indented beneath me like a crater, dust wafting and settling onto my skin and clothes. A sharp inhale shocked my achy body, my muscles jerking at the sudden motion.

Groaning, I rolled to my side and tucked in my knees, peering at the world around me.

I'd landed on a desolate mesa so high it was surrounded by sheets of clouds. To my left, a tundra stretched into the horizon—no greenery, just miles of soil and rock. To my right, an eroded edge to a sheer drop-off. The icy wind roared with a hostile howl that chilled me to my bones. I'd never seen anywhere so gray and inhospitable.

The fog blanketed the view and seemed to suppress my emotions so the only thing I felt was sorrow. I drummed up the confidence to stand and when I reached my feet, a gut punch of hopelessness almost knocked me down again.

What was this place?

The ground vibrated with a seismic shock that trembled in sync with my nerves. Cracks as thin as hairlines traveled across the dry earth as it splintered beneath me.

I lost my balance, my already bruised tailbone catching my fall, the pain pulling a sharp cry from me. I didn't get up. Not as the air at the edge of the ridge distorted into putty. Not even when four distinct wormholes appeared, spinning in unison, like floating whirlpools carved into the sky.

There was nowhere to escape. Plus, my ass hurt too bad to run. I shrank into myself, hoping to blend in with the rock.

The vortex on the left started to speed up, sparking as if into overdrive. Ruby rays pierced its translucent helix, painting the gravel at its base in the dusky tones of an alpenglow as it spun faster, burned brighter.

Thinking it might combust, I nestled my face in my arms, lowering them only when a dark silhouette rapidly blotted out its center.

Red regalia blazed into being as a hooded figure stepped into a world of mist and sorrow. That wormhole dissolved to ash, scattering around the mysterious person's feet.

The figure entered towards the tundra, cloak billowing behind, her graceful gait simulating the dance of a flame. A runic design in a color that reminded me of moonlight was etched onto the lining of her puff-sleeved crimson shirt and full skirt, flaring with every swing of her arms.

Lean sable fingers clasped the edges of her hood before it could blow back and reveal her features, the movement riding up the hem of her shirt, revealing the tight band of skin around her belly button.

But that's not what stole the breath from my lungs.

What must have been a thousand feathered wings of the purest white outstretched from her back, gleaming in the desolate landscape. I gazed after her like I would at a fire: mesmerized and unmoving.

I was staring at a literal angel.

The next vortex in line was the only thing in the world that could grab my attention.

Emerald sparks erupted from its inner rings and showered the ground, some catching the backdraft and singeing the earth around my feet. I curled my legs in even more as mossy wreaths of energy coalesced into the flesh of another being. Green finery came to bloom as the figure ducked to exit, a muddy mound the lone trace of her journey here as the wormhole crumbled in on itself.

Cool platinum hair slipped out from the cover of this ethereal being's short, hooded cowl as she marched onto the dusty terrain. Her hand, so fair it popped against the stale, stark world like snow falling on an overcast day, twirled at a loose strand. A circular pattern in a metallic identical to the other angel's adorned the sides of her breeches and ribbed tunic.

The soil speckled the heels of her knee-high boots and clung with a magnetic attraction to the tips of her untucked wings.

"Akosua, I should have known you'd be the first to arrive," the newcomer said with a bite of sarcasm that made my ears perk as she joined her comrade in red.

"And here I assumed you'd be the last." Akosua's smoldering tone hit me like déjà vu. I racked my brain, but where would I have heard it? She inclined her head. "Cute boots."

The angel in green pretended to squash a bug. "I'm not the one whose ass is on the line. And thanks," she added, sticking her leg out, admiring them herself.

"Every time you cuss, Gaia, I swear a baby cherub dies." A playfulness lined Akosua's words.

Gaia exhaled heavily. "You say that about all my vices."

A gust carried their banter, blending their laughter with its sighs. I watched in awe, a curl of familiarity growing in my stomach and practically banging on the back of my head.

Plumes of daytime protruded from the third vortex, sheathing them in a buttery light. Like a rising dawn, it illuminated the sparse plain, near blinding as the helix accelerated and a winged human frame eclipsed the light. A breeze fanned her knee-length cloak, revealing the silvery white insignia stitched onto her amber bodysuit and matching leggings. She drifted out to join the others, lithe frame and feathers clad in rays from a sun that wasn't above her.

Gaia turned. "Fei, we almost thought you wouldn't make it." The shadow from her cowl still blocked her face, but I sensed the teasing in her tone.

"Please, I'm always on time. Some idiot released a demon over Shanghai." Fei stalked towards them as the wormhole released to the wind, she too shielded by the contour of a hood, aside from the slightest dip in her neckline that revealed her light fawn collarbone. "I'd never miss a meeting with my favorite Watchers."

The three of them together, and I knew in an instant.

These were my Voices, in the flesh.

Holy sh—maybe I shouldn't finish that thought; I was in the presence of angels. But the realization hit me harder than my near-back-breaking landing into their realm.

I was in complete shock and at the same time…I wasn't. I wished I could say it had never occurred to me this was a possibility—that the voices who hijacked the sounds of the world, and in turn my senses, weren't just a manifestation of my grief. That they were more than the darkest parts of my reflection that I was literally killing myself to keep hidden.

I'd silenced those ideas because it seemed like a way out of facing my reality, my grief. But deep down a piece of me had always known a greater meaning existed beyond their words.

Beyond me.

Watcher. Every whisper, holler, murmur…every spoken variation of the word over the last ten years replayed in my mind. Dizziness rocked me forward and my palms planted me firm as I stared at the loose pebbles, inches from my nose.

I took a ragged inhale and looked up. There was still another vortex left…

Azure ribbons poured out of the maelstrom, sparkling like the top of the sea, surging with the swell of its inner workings, crashing against invisible boundaries. It sprayed the rocks with a salty vapor and pattered the soil with rain. Rearing back, it strained under its own tidal influence until a figure was released with the small break of a wave.

Her drawn feathers shuddered, glistening as if touched by a spring morning's dew. The layered slip of her ultramarine dress flocked beneath her rich blue robe, submerging the rest of her body in loose, flowy fabric. Similar to the first three angels, I couldn't see the face beneath her hood, but I felt her purpose—a clear spark of recognition I felt deep in my fluttering heart as if it were my own.

Something in me pushed me to my feet, and I stumbled towards them, ignoring the intense burst of pain in my back.

As Akosua, Gaia, and Fei shifted to acknowledge the newcomer, the emblems on their seams reflected off the overcast sky. Emblems I'd passed off as standard patterns in the fabric, but these were something more. These were the Empyrean symbols for the elements—the ones I'd drawn on Myrian's door: fire, earth, air, water.

A cool, jagged surface worried against my fingertips. I glanced down, not even knowing when my necklace had made it into my palm.

Gaia curled her knuckles against her rounded hip. "Well, look who decided to show up."

"Sorry, I—" the fourth figure began, her gossamer sleeves rippling as her hand, a honey beige all too similar to mine, parted the front of her robe.

"Was doing ungodly things with lover boy?" Fei crossed her arms. "We know."

The woman in blue sighed loudly, ignoring the digs. "Akosua, you called this meeting. Why are we here, of all places?"

Akosua's voice rang with conviction. "Because some of us need reminding."

Tripping over my feet, I approached the conclave, my nerves, let alone the uneven rock, enough to mess with my equilibrium. The four of them kept talking, unmoved by my clumsiness. As I crept around the side, precariously close to the edge of the cliff, to try and get a better view of their faces, it started to sink in. They weren't just unmoved—they were completely unaffected by my presence. Because this was a memory.

A storm encroaching upon the mesa captured their attention, their conversation curtailed by the thunderous wails of its swift, dense clouds.

"Look at them." Akosua tsked and peered beyond the ledge. The fierce wind flapped long twists of her hair, a rich oak brown a shade darker than her skin, out from the hood of her cloak. "Their bodies have landed but their souls will always fall. You go mixing with mortals and you drop alongside them."

Them? I shuddered in sync with Fei's wings. "A testament of fate you—*we*—could also succumb to."

Akosua's voice was a whisper over the pitch of the screaming storm. "Which is why you cannot interfere the way you intend to, Mira."

I'd been waiting for someone to unmask the person behind the blue. But even if my gut had already told me it was her, I hadn't been expecting to hear my mom's name pierced by the same icy resentment Akosua usually reserved for me.

Fei clasped a gloved hand on Mira's shoulder. "How is an eternity of suffering worth a fleeting moment?"

My mom twisted to the woman in yellow. "It isn't fleeting. I'm in love."

The others groaned, shaking their heads.

"Love. Since when do the Watchers get to partake in such mortal pleasures?" Gaia's last phrase struck me—she'd used it against me for enjoying far less important things.

Unease bounced around my insides like a pinball.

"What about the souls you've sworn to protect?" Fei took my mom's hands. "What about your sisters; don't you love us?"

"Of course, I do." The others didn't seem super convinced. To be honest, neither did I, no matter how sincere she tried to sound. Not that I didn't think my mom cared but…I gulped, acid stinging my throat. I knew how this story ended.

"This temptation was written in Apocrypha. We knew it would come, yet you still give in to its lure." There was no denying the frustration in Akosua's words—it was her tone that gripped my chest, an aching, cauterizing sadness that no level of candor could conceal. "If you decide to pursue this, you will lose your place not just among the Watchers, but in Empyrea. It is Law, Mira. The greatest love won't change that. Three upsets the balance, and when you take away water, the elements, life…they simply cannot thrive. Neither can our Source or protection over the People of Earth, and that gives Chthonia the advantage."

A deep-rooted fear pooled in my gut like an iron shackle chaining me to the bottom of the sea. The gravity of this information swirled around me. I knew certain types of relationships were forbidden between angels and humans—and if they crossed that line, it was goodbye magic and immortality—but Akosua made it sound like there was something else to it…I eased closer to the ledge, my footfalls not disturbing the gravel or the ears of those gathered on the path.

"The world won't unravel because of this." My mom's laugh was like a playful splash of water that no one else engaged in. "We're not star-crossed lovers. We won't end up like them." It sounded a lot like denial. It surprised me to hear it.

Judging by Gaia's, Fei's, and Akosua's bowed heads and slackened shoulders, it killed them to hear it, too.

"We can only hope you're right." The Angel of Air released her grip, but the steel in her voice didn't soften.

"She's right. The world won't unravel." Gaia's voice was stale, no trace of the earlier snark. "It'll end up so much worse."

Akosua's gaze didn't waver from the inbound storm. "Chthonia will strike. Hell will truly be unleashed. And we'll be archangels without powers or purpose."

As I reached the mesa's rim, shadows intertwined with the sheets of hail and hurricane-force winds—the forms within the rain flailing, bending at awkward angles, shooting downward like stars.

The tempest swarmed the cliffside, its unruly gusts kicking up dirt and whipping my hair in my face, the frigid cold stinging my eyes. Erratic wails barreled into my ears, so unnaturally loud and thrashy, igniting every inch of my body in shivers. I tucked the sides of my head between my elbows as the shadows grew sharper, and it became clear these were far more sinister than ice pellets. They were people, angels, and the sound wasn't the wind echoing off the ravine: it was screams from them, endlessly falling.

Sentenced to a punishment worse than death, stuck in a vortex with no end or beginning, their broken wings and writhing bodies sent shudders up my spine. It was no wonder this mesa was so dead and gray. Their sorrow blanched the realm of all hope, drained the color from my face. Some angels fought against this unholy force, but it proved resistant to every punch, plea, and prayer. Others wept. A lot of them fell in a horrified stupor, limbs limp, skin raw and ruddy, as if they'd been plummeting for centuries.

I almost collapsed, my legs were shaking so badly.

Somehow, I gathered the strength to scoot to the edge of

the precipice and peer over. I choked on my breath at what coated the ground, some hundreds of feet below. Feathers, so many torn, drifting plumes, tinged with blood and earth. Skeletons crushed and fractured, skulls with bits of shredded muscle. Piles and piles of bones. The putrid stench of decay singed my nostrils and burned my throat.

Akosua was right. These weren't their bodies falling—those were already in rotten ribbons at the bottom of the ravine—these were their souls, trapped in eternal free fall.

Crumpling to my knees, I heaved beside the doomed, palms mixing with the dirt and bile. Most of my life I'd felt ungrounded. Now I knew where it came from—where I came from. The fallen Angel of Water. A stabbing sensation dug into my scars as if ripping them open, stripping me of my senses and the ability to latch on to anything but the pain. I dug my blunt nails into the ground until they bled, panting while the anguish gradually weakened to a prickle.

"I've seen enough here." It could have been my own proclamation, but it came from my mom's lips.

"Have you?" Akosua pressed. "You truly know what's at risk? To the Kingdom? To the Earth? To us?" Each syllable rocked me like an aftershock. There was so much more than love at stake, and my mom still sacrificed herself for it.

Was love worth risking everything for when it triggered the end of the world? That, I did not have the answer for.

No wonder the Voices—the Watchers—were so hard on me. I was a walking reminder of Mira's betrayal. Yet they never gave up on me, until recently, and my world felt more upside down *without* them. What had happened to change their course? There was no way our spat at Grad Night—

now, looking back, I realized it was Akosua's voice I'd gone head-to-head with—had been the final straw.

"I do know what's at risk," my mom affirmed. When her hands slipped between the part of her robe, I swore they rested on her belly for a second before clasping together.

Red flared as the Angel of Fire swished her cloak's sleeve, summoning an escape route with a simple flick of her wrist. "To your watchtowers then."

The others did the same, the sky twisting into funnels after their subtle gestures.

Akosua left first, followed by Fei and Gaia, disappearing as soon as they stepped into the swirling airflow, the vortices spinning faster until they folded in on themselves. Ash, mud, and floating specks were all that was left to mark their presence.

One angel remained, her aqueous robes flowing like a river against the dry landscape. On the brink of departure, she glanced behind her, removing her hood. Haloed by the hydro-powered rays, she drew in her wings, then extended them like colossal sails.

For ten rapid heartbeats I locked eyes with my mom. Not the version stitched together by dreams and washed-out photos, but her in her truest form: flushed with passion, fishtail braid flipped over her shoulder, with a close-lipped smile that didn't reach her blue—*flaming-blue*—eyes.

Even after she'd gone, the cerulean fire that flared behind her pupils burned in my mind.

I waited for the dust to settle, for land and sky to bend, for the portal she'd gone through to turn to vapor, but it continued to undulate without its maker.

Or maybe it was waiting for its new master: me.

I took a step closer, a salty drizzle kissing my cheeks as I reached its opening.

Slowly flipping my hands, I gazed at the lines in my palms and the veins running through them, down past my wrists. When my mom died, did that mean I…did that mean I inherited her Source? I'd seen no trace of any such abilities up until recently. Fei had mentioned a transfer of power was near complete around my eighteenth birthday. Was that what was happening here?

My hand inched forward, timid and slow, until it grazed the cool barrier of the swirling vortex. I twisted my wrist, moving it further in, and thicker droplets splashed my palm. When I drew back my skin was damp but still intact—a small part of me had worried it'd be acid rain or something equally gruesome to my half-mortal touch. Glancing around, I hoped for a sign of what to do, but aside from the cursed…I was alone.

There was only one path out, and it churned in front of me. Willing my pounding heart to calm, I took a shuddering breath, and stepped into the watery whirlwind.

CHAPTER 28

THIS VORTEX SEEMED TO BE THE GATEWAY TO WATER, and it led me to the deepest part of the ocean. Once I'd left the barren mesa, and stepped into the rippling whirlpool, everything went black. My eyes were open, but I couldn't see my hand even if it was in front of my face.

A familiar lilt rang off the darkness and echoed in all directions.

Was it my breath? The Voices? A manifestation of my Source? I didn't know. Whatever it was, it tugged at my heartstrings, begging me to let it in. Each time it sounded more dire, more desperate than the last.

Something in its timbre made my eyelids flutter, and its persistence quickened my pulse. Fervent pressure marked my cheeks, my nose, my forehead, my lips. So plush and warm and...*intoxicating*. Whether I was dead or alive or somewhere in between, it was enough to bring me out of the dark.

Awareness jolted through my body as my fingertips twitched and my eyelids slowly peeled open.

River, River, River. Was my mind playing tricks or was

someone calling me? I willed my blurry senses to resolve the shadows into shapes and the sounds into meaning.

"River, you're going to be okay." The person stressed it as if there was no other alternative. "Stay with me baby, stay with me."

A grogginess clung to me, so thick and heavy that it took everything for me to give an "mmph." My mouth full of spit, I coughed back gibberish. The motion made my chest cave in painfully.

Coastal humidity stuck to my skin and salted my lips. Rhythmic chirps reverberated off the coarse strands of grass that tickled my arms. The moonlight broke through the hazy layer of clouds and the summer night dawned around me. Pushing off my elbows I caught a glimpse of a Victorian before collapsing back down to the ground.

Oof. I squeezed my lids shut—my back was *killing* me.

Worn fingers slipped beneath the nape of my neck. "How's your head?"

My ragged inhales grew a little steadier, but it was the fresh scent of pine that coaxed me to open my eyes. A boy draped in twilight crouched beside me on this side of the reverie. Ryder. That's right. We were at Madame Myrian's.

Cringing, I mumbled, "Feels like it's been hurtled through space and time."

Ryder's relief left his lips in a soft exhale. He spotted my back as I tried to sit up again. "I'm worried you have a concussion."

"Yeah?" My hand dropped to my tailbone—*ouch.* "Why's that?"

He tucked a loose hair behind my ear, his thumb stroking a specific spot on my temple. "That piece of plywood just nailed you when the earthquake hit."

I froze, lungs seizing. "What?"

He pulled back and searched my expression, the gold churning in the green of his eyes. "Do you not remember?"

I remembered everything, including the shakes and rumbles as I unlocked Myrian's lair. But I'd made it inside… My forehead crinkled. Did Ryder mean it hit *his* head?

"Everything else on this block seems to have made it." A rare timidness shook his voice. "But Myrian's…" He broke off, letting the carnage speak for itself.

Eyes adjusting to dusk, I scanned the horizon, picket fences jutting out of the shadows, the pastels muted by the distant streetlamps, mosquitoes orbiting the bulbs like satellites. Three-tiered rooflines jutted into the sky, waiting to come alive in the moonlight. But one lot between the quintessential architecture stood empty except for the stars. The lot we were in.

"River, I'm…" He lowered his head and grasped my hand, the other still planted firmly on my middle back. "This is shit luck. I'm sorry." His words flew over my head into the graveyard of lumber and nails. The vaulted arches, the stained-glass accents…the gateway to my mom was a pile of debris.

With shaky legs I rose to my feet, then came tumbling down like the house. These walls didn't level due to natural causes. Something wanted me out. I sucked in a breath that burned my throat. Ryder joined me in the rubble, where I slumped next to a broken gargoyle's toes.

Parting his long legs, he settled behind me, my back

flush against his chest. "We'll find another way." He curled his arms around my waist and spoke into the crown of my head.

"I found the way. It was there." I stared at the wreckage. "Madame Myrian showed me."

"She didn't, though." He caressed my cheek, tilting my head towards him. "River, no one was home. You didn't make it in. The beam knocked you unconscious while you were on the doorstep, and I carried you out here, where we've been for only a few minutes." His gaze flickered to the home next door. "We should get going. You're hurt and we have an audience."

Shifting curtains in the neighboring window caught my glare. "No. I was there." A fever tore through me, drenching my body in sweat-lined panic. I turned and fisted his shirt, bringing his nose inches from mine. My eyes were wide and wild as I whispered, "I saw *them*, Ryder."

Concern dipped his brows. "Who?"

"The Voices, the Watchers. They're *real*, and I know where I came—" A piercing scream cut me off and seemed to echo in the night. A guttural shriek that could be felt as much as heard, one that raised my hairs to their ends and wrapped me in sorrow: the cries of the Fall.

Was I still there? Or did the fallen somehow follow me here?

My gaze swiveled to every side, landing on Ryder. I twisted in his lap, my knees digging into his thighs as I practically crawled up his chest. "Do you—" I gasped as another nebulous wail of torment corkscrewed into my ear like a wine opener. "Do you hear that?"

Ryder gently shook his head, wisps of hair curling behind his ears as he retreated from me to stand. He scooped me into his arms. I didn't fight it. "C'mon. We need to get you somewhere you can lie down properly."

"To our watchtowers, then," I mumbled into his chest, limbs immediately going slack.

"To our what?" He tightened his grasp.

"I..." The thought slipped away from me. Curled into his chest, my head nestled between his pecs, I dozed to memories I never knew I had.

CHAPTER 29

THIS TIME WHEN MY EYES PEELED OPEN, I STARED AT
the perfect wave. One I'd woken up to every morning since
I'd plastered it on my ceiling when I was nine—a flawless
curl of turquoise water on the precipice of breaking. Blinking away the eye crusties, I turned my head from the poster
and the rest of my bedroom filtered into view.

Sunlight trickled past the slits in the blinds. The air was
warming up but still had a crispness that tickled my throat.
It was morning. Aside from the hums that slipped beneath
the crack of the door, and the new memories rattling in my
skull, I was alone.

I grasped a clump of hair near my temple. Ugh, it was
too early to reminisce on the things that did or did not happen yesterday. At least...I reached over to the nightstand
and tapped my phone's screen to life. I blew out a sigh of
relief. Yes, yesterday.

So many things.

For starters, the Voices were freaking real. I could just
see the dark humor in Gaia, the sweet breeziness of Fei, the
cool indifference of Akosua, as I remembered all the times

they had hacked into the sounds of the world, just to speak to me.

And my mom wasn't just any old angel, but an *archangel*. The Angel of Water. Or at least she used to be, before forsaking Empyrea in the name of love. It didn't take a huge leap of logic to understand what had happened to her. She'd been sentenced to the Fall. I shuddered and swore a faint scream bristled my ears. There truly was a punishment worse than death.

My arms plopped to my sides atop the duvet, disturbing the comforter's feathers. A few slipped through the seams and drifted above me, stuck in the airstream from the overhead fan.

Not only that, but my mom's betrayal also threw humanity into the middle of a centuries-old battle between two paranormal realms. One where the Voices, the Watchers, were powerless to help because, well, Mira fell for a mortal. Seemed like a steep price to pay for love. An unfair one, really.

And where did that leave me?

I honestly had no clue. I was Nephilim and a descendant of an archangel, but what did that mean? Was I supposed to take her place or something? Laughable, really. I couldn't even control my senses, let alone my Source. How was I supposed to protect Mortal Earth?

I strained against a tide of pain that didn't affect my physical body.

Sometimes life really did feel like hell on earth.

Maybe Chthonia had already won.

Shifting to get comfortable despite my spiraling thoughts and the ache in my bones, I pulled the covers up over my eyes and attempted to go back to sleep. A throb ran from my elbow to my shoulder at the jerk of my arms. In the darkness beneath the blankets, I pressed a hand to my heart. A hot bolt of panic shot through me when I brushed against skin, not my necklace.

I threw aside the duvet, my back freaking killing me as I twisted to check under the bed, crammed my fingers between the mattress and the bedframe, tossed pillows aside— every place as empty as the pockets of my hard-washed lilac shorts I hadn't changed out of yet.

Maybe I'd taken it off? I jumped out of bed and bee-lined for my dresser, sorting through the tangled pieces of jewelry. Not there, either. Spinning on my heels, I moved to the door, but when my fingers wrapped around the cool metal handle, I stopped. My gaze traveled up the length of my arm, lingering on the dried blood and smears of dirt. Another jolt of panic zinged my core. How did I even get home? Obviously, Ryder must have brought me, but did he sneak past my dad? Had my dad been here? Oh my God, did they meet?!

I pressed my ear to the door. As the muffled sound of my dad's talking grew louder, I had to think it meant he *hadn't* been here for my homecoming—if he had witnessed me being carried in by a hot British guy in leather, knocked out, and covered in blood, I'd be in deeper shit than when the teratorn chased me. There's no way I could walk into the kitchen now, flushed and bruised, with matted hair, as if I'd been kissing death itself. I drew in a long breath, ballooning out my rib cage.

Okay. First, a shower.

Old pipes shrieked with each turn of the knobs, triggering my nerves, an echo of pain that'd been stoking my senses ever since I left the Fall.

I entered the narrow stall, where the steam rose above the tile and enveloped me like a warm cloud. While I stood beneath the faucet and let the water hit my shoulders, I could almost taste the blood and tears of the fallen. But it was the salt from my own eyes, the fresh scabs from my own skin that whirlpooled down the drain, injuries Ryder said were not from crossing realms but from the house collapsing on me during an earthquake.

I still didn't understand his take on the events. Like, how were our experiences so different? I'd assumed hours had passed by the time I came to, yet he declared it'd only been a matter of minutes—and that I'd never really *left* left; I'd just been struck unconscious.

As the water ran from red to clear, my confidence seemed to slip with it. I found myself wishing for patterns or signs or symbols in the vortex of shampoo and conditioner. But the water pressure didn't speak to me. The vapor didn't part for me. The bubbles didn't change their form. It was just a shower, and I was just a girl, trying to make sense of it all.

No closer to God or enlightenment, I shut off the valve and opened the curtain to grab my robe. Dripping wet, I froze, struck by the simple, watercolor portrait of a lighthouse that hung on the wall across from me.

Akosua's near-forgotten words danced on the tip of my tongue. "To your watchtowers," I whispered out loud.

The Watchers may have been citizens of Empyrea, but they were guardians of *this* realm. Having some sort of Earthbound base for them to warp to didn't seem too farfetched. If I could find their towers, it could lead me to them, and who knew—maybe they could help me hone my Source or explain why demons were chasing me. Fill in the pieces I was missing.

Letting the idea percolate, I threw on a marbled over-sized tee and some stretchy black biker shorts. After another unsuccessful check around the bed for my necklace, I headed down the hall, nothing but the cold pressed air to fill the bare space at the base of my neck.

As my nose suspected, charred pancakes and crispy pork were the items on the menu that morning. I faltered when my bare feet reached the kitchen's cool tile. Partially hidden behind an unfolded newspaper, his glasses slipping down his burnt nose, one crocs-with-socks-wearing foot bouncing on his knee, my dad looked every part mortal. An unwelcome pang of hurt rocked my heart. Did he know about my lineage or was he truly oblivious, as he seemed now?

Clearing my throat, I sat and reached for a plate.

"Hey, River," my dad said like he just realized I was there. "You slept well. I'd ask if you want breakfast, but"—he glanced at his watch—"it's almost noon. Brunch?"

I tried not to let that sting of sadness crawl up my chest into my throat, but I couldn't stop thinking about his connection to everything. Dismissing those thoughts with a scratchy swallow, I focused on the most pressing detail for now: the watchtowers and where to find them. I kicked my voice up and plastered on a too-wide grin. "Morning!"

"Bacon?" My dad picked up a platter, stopping mid-pass. "Holy…"

My lips began to twitch, but if this was a test, I wouldn't let my fake smile slip. His eyes widened and I couldn't stop mine from mimicking the movement. What? What was it?

"That is one hell of a bump you got there."

My hand shot to my temple; I winced as I tried to hide it from view. "I, uh…" I, uh, what, River? C'mon. "I got hit in the head with my surfboard." Or a piece of plywood. Or a crystal ball. It was debatable at this point. "I had a wipeout yesterday, and wham." I pretended to smack myself, sending a whoosh of air breezing by my forehead.

"Geez." He leaned in, and I swore it visibly throbbed. "That thing is huge."

This was worse than having a giant pimple between my eyes. I brought my damp hair out from behind my ears, trying to angle the shorter layers so they swept across my temple.

Rolling up his paper and setting it next to him, he asked, "You need ice or something?"

"No." I needed a subject change. I needed answers. Instead, I settled for stuffing my face with a blueberry pancake as if that was proof that I was totally fine. He returned to his own stack, and we ate in silence—until I asked what probably sounded like the world's most random question. But if anyone knew random facts, it was humanities professor Corbin Harlow. "Dad, what do you know about watchtowers?"

"Generally speaking?" He wiped his lenses on his navy-collared tee. "They're tiered freestanding structures that oversee a particular area. The Romans built epic ones throughout Europe, some that have survived since the early Middle Ages. In fact, I just did a lecture on them."

I twisted my fork in the syrup covering the strips of pancake in front of me. "What are they actually used for?"

"To aid those who are lost, to detect threats, to restrain demons." He winked, returning his glasses to his face, picking up the newspaper again. "Depends on the geography."

I tried not to let that last example sink its teeth into me. "So, a watchtower doesn't have to be part of a medieval fortress—it could be something simple? Like…a lighthouse?"

"Sure." He nodded as he gulped down his coffee, the bitter aroma wafting from the cup. "They're all essentially built for the same purpose: to protect the people."

That was good news, because the term *watchtower* itself sounded all sorts of medieval, and I wouldn't be dragging myself to Europe any time soon. But it also expanded my search criteria to limitless. "Do you think I could take a look at your lecture notes?"

He peered at me over the weekend headlines. "Seriously? River, it's Saturday. The waves are pumping, and you want to sit inside and look at my lecture notes? Are you sure you didn't hit your head too hard?"

"Yeah." I gulped. "I'm interested in…history?"

"You're weird, kid." He sighed and stood, slapping the paper onto the table.

A few minutes later he returned with a manila folder.

"Go wild." It left his smudged fingertips for my sticky hands. "I'll be surfing at The Hook when your eyes start to hurt."

"Thanks, Dad." I gathered up my hair, twisting and tucking the ends into a knot on the crown of my head. "I'll do the dishes. Now get out there."

He ruffled my top bun, buying into my sudden fascination with history without a second thought as he slipped on his sandals and grabbed his Ray-Bans. To be honest, it killed me to miss this window of swell, and I just about grabbed my wetsuit to join him.

But the only thing I was grabbing when he ducked out the side door and that salty draft came in were the papers that had scattered across the checkered tile. Two pages fell to a syrupy death; the rest were crinkled and dispersed.

Between the faded ink and the semi-legible scribble, I attempted to put them in order.

There were some common themes I picked up on: military, nonmilitary, modern. One page in particular stopped me mid-shuffle. I cast the stack of papers aside as I held the grayscale printout, studying the cylindric tower it depicted.

I'd never really thought about the history of the Santa Cruz Lighthouse—even if I'd spent thousands of days resting against its red brick, watching the surf until its lantern burned brighter than the stars. It was a pretty standard landmark. All coastal towns have them.

But according to the article in my hand…there was some local lore to it. A tendril of anticipation formed in my stomach and coiled around my heart.

The area surrounding the Santa Cruz Lighthouse plays an important part in the region's history. The first mention of it can be traced back twelve thousand years, to the indigenous peoples of this land, who noted massive, geometric markings perfectly cut through the tall grass, similar to a modern-day crop circle. They respected it from a distance, leaving what they referred to as her land in peace. Colonizers arrived in 1769, and although they eyed the unsown ground, they refrained from disturbing it until 1795.

I tucked my knees beneath me, too enthralled to get up. The pitterpatter against my ribs seemed to reverberate through my body, especially in my fingers, the article shaking in my grasp as I read on.

Questions arose amongst the colonists, such as who tended to the luscious patch of soil on the bluffs, and why hadn't they introduced themselves to the town. They waited for a sighting, but the owner would vanish, some claimed before their eyes, and there were murmurings that it was a woman. They marched at nightfall, armed with torches, and incinerated the grass to the roots. When the fire sputtered out, they saw the intricate designs had been etched deep into the earth.

Spooked by the incident, the townsfolk backed off and the land was once again left alone until 1852, when the newest generation forgot about the tales and construction of a lighthouse began. The build proved to be impossible: when steel hit stone, the tool ricocheted back.

Some workers lost limbs, another his life, and for seventeen years, the project was put on pause. Then, in 1869, construction of the lighthouse was finished, seemingly overnight. There are no records of who completed it.

Goosebumps raised along my arms as a shudder worked its way down my spine.

Myths of the watchtower grew more sinister. Stories circulated that the original owner of the land never died; that she was a witch, and she was its one, true Keeper; that she harnessed the winter white caps, and her power drew rip tides; that she worshipped the Eldritch and the fog bell would ring not for ships but to conjure evil. Over time, the whispers have ceased, and its history has become legend. City officials approved an expansion to accompany the structure in 1967. The lighthouse has persevered, its original frescos have faded, its filigree dulled by erosion. But the candle still burns, and the door to the tower remains locked, as if waiting for its Keeper.

I lowered the paper and slid my palm over the text, releasing a breath that'd been trapped.

Loosening my shoulders, I flipped the article over, ready to sort it, when every inch of me tensed. Hundreds of sketches littered the page. There wasn't a blank space left.

Circles, droplets, swirls, and flames. And four-pointed stars, clustered around them.

Jolting off the floor, I sprinted down the hall to my dad's den, the flimsy page crumpling in my death grip. As I flung open the door, shafts of tinted light from the stained-glass window cast the ordinarily brown room into a prism of color. I marched across the beige carpet, sharp prods of unease cauterizing my stomach. I'd stood in front of this window millions of times, as I did now, but somehow, this felt like my first. How severely misguided my brain must have been to think these were just simple knights, winged beings, and beasts cut into the glass.

They were the four horsemen of the apocalypse, clashing with their female equivalents: the four archangels guarding the earth. Gaia's keen stare, chiseled into chartreuse flames, ensnared me even though it was only a weak imitation of the real thing. Her lips were carved into a knowing smile, and I swore the image of her winked as my eyes trailed from her porcelain hands set atop her full hips to her platinum locks braided atop her head like a halo. Wisps of long, black threads of hair from the angel next to her flowed into her frame, as if caught in an immortal breeze. Fei's cunning amber gaze bored into me like two brilliant, violent suns, the freckles on her wide cheekbones and her ivory oval face illuminated by their permanent glow. Her outstretched slender arms brushed the angel beside her. Akosua's thick twists of brown hair tousled over her body, which seemed to be built for slaying monsters, as if her sable, steepled palms could birth a spark quicker than a match. Her smile was like smoke—it reached her crimson, kindled eyes, igniting a fire in me—one I didn't know if I wanted to put out or let burn.

My blood froze when I reached the Angel of Water. Because…it was me.

Me with cerulean flames for eyes. I blinked. Aside from

their hair and skin tones, all four angels became faceless, nameless, generic—as they'd always been to me. Was *this* what Ryder meant about truly seeing?

A glare from outside illuminated the glyphs in the center of their green, yellow, red, and blue robes—the symbols I'd seen drawn on the back of the article by my dad: earth, air, fire, and water.

My hand floated to the place where my necklace usually rested, the urge superseding the facts. Anger engulfed me. I curled my fingers and closed my eyes to try and contain the wrath—but those elemental symbols just burned into the darkness behind my lids.

My dad knew.

No matter how badly I wanted to unsee that repeated pattern, to chalk it up to doodles or coincidence. No matter my desire to pretend he hadn't kept me isolated from my own source of power and let me mistake magic for madness. No matter my utter desperation to think he hadn't *lied* to me my whole life—he knew.

He fucking knew.

My exhale dragged as I opened my eyes and ripped the article to shreds. Tears burned my eyes as I mentally sorted through truth and lies. I couldn't even think straight, the raw pain razing my insides and turning into white-hot fury.

A violent fire hose of energy thrashed beneath my skin, fighting for me to release it. My gaze swiveled from the wall-to-wall bookcases to the opened French doors that led to the living room. I'd wipe out this entire condo—every stupid photo, keepsake, surfboard, I didn't care.

I needed a conduit for my anger.

Remnants of the paper flittered to my sides, shining so bright in the rays funneling in through the windows that it looked like they had caught fire. A torn piece with a cluster of numbers landed on the crease between my knees, the scribble stealing my attention.

36.951696, -122.026677
63.568315, -19.608209 (near)
26.0 ??
34?

My blip in concentration diluted the brewing power within me, and a guttural, ragged gasp of agony escaped. The pain lodged itself in my veins like cracks in a vase. If I didn't do something, it'd spread and settle in the deepest parts of my soul and break me beyond repair.

Untucking my legs, I kneeled up to standing and went to grab my phone from the kitchen. I set the scrap of paper on the table, unlocked the screen, and input the first line of numbers into the browsers search bar. I reviewed the results without so much as blinking, without even a hint of surprise.

How could it be anything but the coordinates of the Santa Cruz Lighthouse?

As I stared at the map, the marker centered on the coastal point's green, the memories started to flood me. My wet hair cascading down my back as I rested my bare skin against the brick and listened to the drumbeats of the ocean. Lying on its slick grass, using the dandelions to point out faces and shapes in the clouds with Javi. Gripping the iron railing when my senses couldn't process the sounds of the world and the competing words of the Voices. A subtle flux of power tickling my skin anytime I drew near.

A faint trace of that power seemed to rush through my veins right now.

It wasn't just a lighthouse—just a watchtower. It was sacred, something that called to me like a pulse in my chest.

I shook my head, a gruff blow of air slipping past my lips. I was done believing any of this was coincidence. I was enraged, but more importantly, I was empowered.

Hands and breaths steady, I opened my messages to see an unread one from Javi.

The heavy chains of regret tightened around my heart. It was rare for us to go a couple hours without texting, but we hadn't spoken since boba. Days. It'd been days. How could I let that happen?

My thumb hovered over the screen, and for a moment, I imagined responding—spending the rest of the day in a makeshift fort made out of driftwood we'd found at the beach, perfectly safe, where everything made sense and magic only existed in stories. But this was no longer a story. This was my life.

And for once, I was going to claim it.

I clicked the name on the message below his.

"Ryder?" My voice was even, determined, as he picked up. "Can you meet me right now? We need to talk about what happened yesterday. I think I figured out what's going on with me."

CHAPTER 30

A FEW HOURS LATER, I PEERED THROUGH THE FISsures of a rusty iron door leaning off its hinges.

My nose wrinkled as I took a step back, getting a full view of its frame, and caught a whiff of the sulfuric air.

"Ryder?" My echo was the only thing that answered. I twisted my hair into a low bun to get it out of my face and pulled out my phone. Of course, there was no reception. I glanced at the defaced walls of concrete that towered on both sides of me. This was a far cry from a lighthouse. This wasn't even a *place*. It was just an alley between pee-stained buildings that, for some reason, he wanted to meet in, because there was no way he wanted me to actually step inside that wretched, rat-infested place.

My voice scattered the pigeons, and they drew my eyes up to a symbol engraved in the stone above the bronze trim: a circle containing an eight-pointed star, four of its arms twice the size of the others. Almost a dozen more spikes jutted out from behind the smaller ones, shorter in length and with a twist to their ends, like sunrays. It reminded of a figure I'd seen on a nautical chart. What was it called…? A compass rose. But I'd also seen it someplace else…I racked my brain until it came to me: it'd been carved into the moonrocks above the Wizard of Auto.

No more coincidences, I reminded myself, glass from the shattered windows crunching beneath my feet as I reapproached the entrance.

Bolts dotted the door's scrap metal like stray bullets had struck it. Slightly concerned it'd collapse on me when I touched it, I held my hand back, letting it linger inches from its surface.

My eyes played tricks on me as I stood there, and a pattern started to emerge as if I'd been staring at the passing clouds, not a door. I swore the bolts formed a shape—a coupe glass with a garnish that looked like a star on its rim. Then I blinked, and it was gone.

Swallowing against the acidic burn of uneasiness, I pressed the door open and gazed into a musty warehouse with bowed rafters and chipped cement. A cool draft rustled my hair, tickled my arms and legs, making me regret the distressed black shorts and high-neck tank I'd thrown on. More glass, rusted nails, and rodent droppings dotted the dusty ground between the dozen or so pillars. Grimacing, I stayed put in the alley and scanned what seemed to be an empty hall for Ryder.

The roar from a muffler passed in the distance, rattling the busted plumbing, and I nearly jumped out of my skin. A stray cat leapt from its trash can burrow, the aluminum crashing to the ground, its screechy roll across the pavement raising my shoulders and drawing up the hair on my arms. The *clang* when it hit the building might as well have been inside my skull.

I clutched my forehead, careful to massage around my temple. Breathing back the anxiety, I willed the sounds to stop building. I was still on edge, but they faded to a level I could manage.

So, inside it is, Ryder. I squared my shoulders and stepped through the doorway. As one foot rose and crossed over the threshold, something truly amazing happened. It landed on solid oak ground, sturdy wood replacing the broken foundation in a long, shimmering brushstroke of what I could only describe as magic.

When my body finally unfroze, I stepped inside the warehouse, the heavy door slamming shut behind me. The harsh *bang* didn't faze me: I was too busy watching the glossy finish run up the walls, washing over the cracks and the holes and correcting the sags in the vaulted ceiling. Unsteady beams straightened and twinkled as an invisible hand wrapped them in holiday lights.

The stale interior warmed with the glow of candles and the sun peeking through the stained-glass windows. A small gasp left me as I walked over to them, the glass no longer in shards beneath my high tops, but reset without a scratch. Medieval scenes in primary colors shimmered in the natural glow from outside. A similar style, but these were so much more lighthearted than the one in my dad's office, the figures laughing, dining, praying, sparring—was it a trick of the light or did I just see their swords clash?

"River!" a distinct, melodic voice called and made my pulse skyrocket.

I spotted Ryder sitting near the center of a bar that ran the entire west side of the space, his chair facing my direction, one boot planted on the floor, the other resting on the lower footrest. We locked eyes and he lowered his hand, bringing it to rest on the inside of his thigh. I shamelessly tracked the movement—my gaze dropping to his distressed black jeans, then up and over the tight curves of muscle beneath his V-neck. I glanced down at my own all-black outfit.

Oh my God, now we were dressing alike.

Biting back a smile, I snaked past the interspersed tables and went to him. It was still musty in here, but that was the beer.

I slid onto the stool next to him with such unnatural grace I couldn't fathom where it came from. But I didn't hate it. "What is this place?"

"Elsewhere Tavern." His wavy hair was primed to sweep across his face with one small motion. I curled my fingers around the lip of my seat, fighting the urge to push the dark strands back with my fingers. "What do you think?"

Tearing myself from his emerald gaze, I swiveled around, taking in the once-empty room. Now filled with barrels and laughter and patrons I had clearly overlooked on my arrival, because I might've dropped dead at the sight of the mini trolls with grass beards playing cards at a table next to us. I looked to the windows for confirmation, shapes and shades of the alley wavering behind the tinted glass. There was no denying that this was the warehouse, and I existed here, but also…elsewhere.

"How…?" My voice came out hoarse.

"Remember our conversation about the parallel dimension that allows the supernatural to exist alongside humans?

This is a living example of that—a parallel realm carved into the one you just came from that shares the coordinates and footprint of the warehouse, but inside…it's a whole 'nother world." He traced invisible shapes onto the solid wooden bar top with his finger as he talked. "That seal I'm sure you saw above the door allows Nephilim, among others, in, and is a barrier to keep mortals out. So, looks like you have an acceptable amount of Source in your blood." Ryder tipped his glass and took a swig. "But we knew that all along."

"So, the warehouse is the true mirage," I muttered. A million questions formed on my tongue, but one tugged at me more than the others. "What would have happened if you were wrong, and I was mortal?"

"You'd combust the second you walked in."

My eyes widened at the potential for how bad this could have gone. He didn't seem the slightest bit disturbed.

"Kidding," he added, lips twitching. "You'd see an empty warehouse. Like the junkyard we saw before we crossed the threshold into the Wizard of Auto. You look like you could use a drink."

I opened my mouth to fight him as he raised his hand but…I did need something to take the edge off. The adrenaline hadn't had time to wane, and I'd been stuck in a constant state of it. Over the course of a week my entire life had crashed and burned, and I was still choking on the ashes— one drink wouldn't kill me.

The round top of a bowler hat skimmed the bottom of the counter. Was the bartender crawling on hands and knees? Golden caps from a ladder hitched onto a groove in the bar right in front of us, and the felt brim drifted upwards, followed by flattened pointy ears and overgrown brows that fused with the tips of a wiry handlebar moustache. Beneath all the hair, there were so many human elements—deep folds in his rosy beige cheeks, a youthful gaze, a natural pout to his bottom lip. But there was a distinct air of *otherness*, one that made my heart flutter.

He presented us with two pints of golden liquid, tipped his hat, then shuffled his way back down. I wanted to smile in thanks, but I had trouble reeling in my jaw, which had fallen to the floor.

"Dwarf," I whispered, as if I needed to confirm it out loud to myself.

Ryder nudged me with his elbow. "Staring is quite rude."

"I-I'm sorry." I closed my mouth and focused on the bits of upturned skin on my cuticles, tearing off the dry pieces. Ryder grabbed my hand and tucked it under his, hiding it. "Sorry," I muttered, raising my head to meet his. "This is just wild—" The words caught in my throat as my attention snagged on the scene behind him. "Is that a centaur playing a fiddle in the corner?" My head hadn't stopped shaking, the disbelief stubborn and unwilling. "Sorry. I'm getting distracted again. Anyways, I wanted to thank you. For yesterday."

"They're a faun," he corrected me. "And stop apologizing. Maybe this is wild, but it's new and you're adjusting. It's pretty unheard of that a Nephilim doesn't know what they are, let alone to find out at your age. You've been conditioned to think none of this is real." He leaned closer, spearmint breath a pleasant burn that awakened my senses. "But let me tell you, there's nothing more real than this." He held up his glass with the hand not shielding mine. "Cheers for breaking through to reality."

I raised my drink. Our eyes and pints met. The bitter aroma tingled my nostrils. "To reality." I sipped the froth gingerly, and my insides flurried. "What is this witchcraft!?"

"It's a pilsner." I couldn't tell if he was laughing or choking. "So, what did you want to talk to me about?"

The bubbles tingled in my belly and instead of fizzing out, they rose to my chest. I took another big gulp, which quickly turned into me downing half the glass. We had just toasted to reality but suddenly…I needed to escape it. Suddenly, I didn't want to brood on my past and talk in circles about yesterday or discuss what I'd found out about my dad. I wanted to live in the moment, to get caught up in the present—and presently my hand slipped out from under Ryder's palm and lowered to his thigh. I trembled at the bold move but pushed past my nerves and lifted off the chair, coming to stand between his angled knees. Every inch of him stilled, waiting.

My fingers slid over the exposed part of his tatted upper chest and went around his neck, my gaze snagging on the vibrant blue peeking out from his shirt hem. I ran the back of my fingers over the ink in the lightest sweep. "You still haven't told me what this means." I picked up his hand, stamping the Celtic letters with my lips. "Or this." Although Leif had pretty much disclosed the N and S stood for some sort of secret Nephilim Society. But I wanted to hear it from him.

Goosebumps trailed in the wake of my touch. He

cleared his throat, dipping his chin to divert mine. "It's just a mark of the hunt. It's nothing."

"Fine." I let out a breathless laugh. "You want to do something else besides talking?"

He wet his lips. "Like…"

Something burned in me, a feeling that only warmed as the light changed in Ryder's eyes. As they flared greener, brighter. Someone strung a lute in the background, but all I could hear was him, the slight quickening of his breath. He clenched his jaw and shut his lids, and in that moment, I could see him trying so hard to keep his feelings locked down. It was cute, actually. But I knew my kiss would ignite him.

It incinerated both of us.

The warm pressure of our lips coming together made everything else fall away. Those rigid arms he'd kept at his sides wrapped around my waist, reeled me in closer so that nothing except the heat of our bodies existed between us. A second instrument laced the air, the music building with the pace of our kisses.

Another urge overtook me.

"You know what else I want to do?" My words were muffled against his lips. A sexy hum answered. The tips of our tongues met, and for a second, I almost forgot about where we were—and who might be watching. I slowly pulled back, taking his lower lip with me. When I released it, I told him, "Dance!"

Ryder stayed fastened to his seat, his earring dangling from our fluid motions, tousled hair finally toppled over his forehead. God, he looked so kissable—and stuck. Like I'd cast a spell that glued him to the spot.

"Come on!" Fingers intertwined, I led him to the stage I'd been eying ever since we sat down. A small crowd had formed around the mythical musicians—three of them now—turning this corner of Elsewhere into a dance floor.

The fiddle's strings rang quick and clear above the steady strum of the guitar and the lower plucks of the harp. I tugged on Ryder's hand and pulled him into me, putting my other arm around his waist, swaying to the upbeat music, smiling up at him as if I were drunk in love—and maybe I was. But I didn't care.

He squeezed my hand tighter, and in a move that totally surprised me, he twirled me. Again and again.

My hair unraveled from the hasty bun I'd put it in, the layered strands flowing down my upper back, tickling the scars that peeked out of the racerback cut of my tank. I became so lost in the moment I couldn't tell when Ryder let go of my hand or when I latched on to another's. All I knew was that to dance was to escape, and these bodies cocooned me, their hoofs and wings and outstretched arms protecting me from…

My hips froze. Protecting me from what? I thought I'd stopped running.

Cool sweat drenched the nape of my neck. My head tossed around, searching for Ryder. All I saw were strangers, their smiles twisted and no longer enchanting. As I snaked through the sea of unfamiliar faces, they pulled at my wrists and cursed me for leaving. I didn't want to stay, but for some reason my knees started bending, like the music had a hold on my soul, sucking me back in. And then I saw him watching from the bar.

A thousand secrets lay behind those furrowed brows. I didn't want to become another. I wanted to feel seen, and he made me feel like I'd never have to hide again. My hips swung like a pendulum as I strode over, ready to serve my heart on a platter. Maybe that was too much, but again, I didn't care. His gaze tracked every movement until I reached the edge of his shadow.

He took a ragged inhale as I stepped into the crook of space between his knees and where he rested his elbow on the bar. A shiver worked its way through me as his eyes left my face and slowly drifted to my neck, my chest, my ribs, like an invisible finger was dragging down the very front of me.

He dropped his stare to the counter. "What did you find out, River?"

Huh? Oh. I'd almost forgotten why I'd called him. It wasn't to make out in a magical bar. I slunk back onto my seat. Right. New developments. A sigh left my tingling lips.

How was I supposed to get deep when my cheeks still hurt from smiling?

By remembering how my dad betrayed me, that was how. I looked at the twinkling ceiling. The pain was an ice pick that chipped at my heart. The more I thought about it, the more it broke. My mouth curved into a snarl.

"He knew—my dad." My fingers curled into the wood. "He knew this whole damn time."

"That you're Nephilim?" Ryder guessed.

Teeth clenched, I nodded. "Ask me why he kept me in

the dark for eighteen years?" I gritted out, staring at the girl across from me. Translucent glass bottles framed her strained face, her nostrils fuming as a reddish hue bloomed in her cheeks. And her eyes were a cold, abyssal blue that could freeze hell itself over.

It was me. I was staring in a mirror.

Between the racks of liquor, I saw Ryder lift his gaze in the reflection. "Why…did he keep you in the dark for eighteen years?" he asked softly.

"I have no fucking clue." I whipped my head towards him. "But who does that!?"

He didn't flinch at my anger, even as I slammed my palm onto the counter.

"You know what's even more messed up?" A round of applause muffled my voice as the band ended one song and dove right into another. "He played a role in my mom's death. And I *know* he struggles with that guilt. We could have…" I bit back the tears. My dad didn't deserve them. "We could have bonded over that."

"What do you mean? I thought your mom died in a drowning accident."

Straightening my shoulders, I took a deep breath, but the words came out fast and harsh. "Angels can't have relationships with mortals, right? Well, my mom was an angel, and my dad was clearly a mortal and what do you know, she ended up dead—actually worse, she was sent to the Fall. Did you know that's where they take them?"

Ryder shook his head no, his eyes narrowing as he processed what I said.

"Yeah. She was sentenced to an eternity of *dropping* for

betraying Empyrea, where she gets to relive her agony again and again. I just don't understand why they waited so long to take her." I scowled, the memory of that fated day at the beach muddied by my mounting frustration. "Was it even a rip current that got her?"

I glanced at his hands, which stayed slack at his sides, waiting for one of them to inch forward and hold me. "I think it's the most realistic possibility," he said, "because we don't have enough evidence to say otherwise. I mean, she could have been in hiding all those years and that's when the Sainthood found her—that's what happened to my..." He stopped himself and clipped out a sigh. "You saw what you saw. It was a rip current...right?"

I tugged at the hair closest to my temples. Honestly... it could have been a storm or an angel or my mind playing tricks, and instead of being a big girl and addressing the trauma, I'd spent ten years hiding from it.

"I don't know what I fucking saw!" My outburst earned a glare from the bartender. I swallowed the fire building in my throat, my voice shaking with the effort it took to remain low when I spoke again. "What's gnawing at me is that I shrugged off the people who actually cared, the ones who've been trying to tell me everything. The Voices."

A subtle tension that only I would notice furrowed Ryder's full, dark brows.

"They're not just voices, Ry," I continued, my voice low. His back went rigid at the nickname, but I was in such a frantic train of thought it had honestly just rolled off my tongue. "They're the archangels tasked to guard Mortal Earth—the ones you said were legend. My mom didn't just leave Empyrea; she left her place among the Watchers. I saw how it all started when we were at Madame Myrian's. That's how I know what the cost was for her to leave." Tears burned against my squinched lids. I hated the sensation so fucking much, but I hated how Ryder just *sat* there even more.

Touch me, I begged him with my mind. Hug me. Comfort me.

"River." He made sure to annunciate every syllable. "You didn't make it inside Myrian's house. I told you this. A piece of plywood knocked you out when the earthquake hit."

My entire body stiffened. I blinked once. Twice. "*That's* what you took from what I just said?" I threw my hands up in the air. "Why are we arguing about this again? I did make it inside, I saw the past, I saw the Fall, I saw their wings, I saw my mom choose love. I saw *everything*."

Ryder turned his focus to his drink, like he was purposefully avoiding my glare.

"Oh, is our fighting make you uncomfy?" I snorted, matching the scowls of the dwarves who had posted up next to us. "I thought you got off on it."

He shifted in his seat. "Why would you think that?"

"Because you're always pissing me off."

He rolled his eyes, and that just provoked me even more. Digging into my front pocket, I pulled out a tiny scrap of paper and placed it on the counter. "Look." The crinkles from being shoved into my shorts distorted the writing. Whatever, it was still legible.

He peered at the numbers. "What am I looking at?"

"Coordinates," I said with no room for hesitation. "I

found them written on the back of an article about a light-house that shares the same coordinates as the first row of numbers."

He tilted his head. "Where's the rest of it?"

"Um…" A hot flash of embarrassment rushed me as I envisioned myself ripping the page to shreds earlier. "Doesn't matter. Anyways, there were also dozens of patterns scribbled on the back, but not just any patterns, the Empyrean symbols for the elements. Like the ones we traced onto Madame Myrian's door."

"What are you getting at, River?" he asked with an irritated ring in his voice.

"Okay…" Palms steepled beneath my chin, I continued, ignoring the bite of annoyance in his tone. "Hear me out. I think these are tied to specific places the Watchers used to access Earth. Kind of like wormholes, but they're actual structures. Watchtowers." I pulled out my phone. "I haven't researched what the other coordinates are, but I think if we go to them, we can find out where the Watchers are…"

"River." Ryder lowered the cellphone from my face. "This is a bunch of scribble."

"No." My eyes clung to the bright light of the screen. "My dad knew what my mom was. He must've known about the Watchers and their connection to these sites, that's why—"

Ryder's demeanor hardened. "We both know your dad isn't the most reliable…"

"What?"

"Listen." His hands hovered beside my arms, as if he were about to start rubbing them, then they dropped to his lap. "This sounds like a story your dad tells himself so he can live with the facts, that your mom died and there was nothing he could do to save her."

"How can you say that?" I clenched my jaw to keep it from quivering. "I'm telling you this is real."

He sighed dramatically, like this was the biggest waste of his time even though he *knew* how important this was to me. "Say the Watchers are real—hypothetically. Their job is to protect mortals, right? So…where are they now? The world's gone to shit."

I twirled the frays on my cutoffs, tugging at the loose threads. "When my mom left, it…broke their power."

He scoffed. "And let me guess, you think you're the one to save us?"

He might as well have thrown his drink in my face. What the hell was wrong with him? "Well, that did cross my mind, but now you're making me feel stupid for even considering it."

"Oh, River." Ryder doused my name in a bitterness that made his lips pucker. "There are no chosen ones in this life. You said your eyes were open now, so look around." He stretched his arms along the wooden curve of the bar top. "Earth isn't made for you to rule, it's made to make you suffer. You're not a savior. You're one of us. Forgotten."

My jaw dropped. "You're the one who pushed me to find out who I was. Now you don't accept it?" I had no words. Actually, I had two. "Fuck you."

Ryder shrugged and downed his glass. I didn't think it was possible, but my mouth fell open even wider.

"I have to go." His chair screeched across the hardwood

as he stood and threw down a twenty. "Leif and I are going hunting."

The conversation I overhead him having with his brother at their house resurfaced in my mind. "Oh, to find that person you're looking for."

A muscle around his jaw tightened. "We already found her."

Her.

Heat engulfed me as shame flooded my system. Maybe that's why he was suddenly being so standoffish.

I swiveled in my chair. "You planning on stringing her along, too?" The comeback burned in my throat, and I salivated with ire.

"Not if I can help it." The light from this angle made it look like a sheen coated his eyes—but there was no way Ryder cared. He'd wielded his words like throwing knives, and they'd found their target, right in my heart. With the little dignity I had left, I met his stare.

And immediately wished I hadn't.

Iciness radiated from his eyes, such a deep hunter green they bordered on black, and squelched the fire in my veins. His shadow fractured in the dim light, stretching out behind him in two elongated pieces, dousing me in a bitter coldness. At some point my nails had snuck between my teeth—he didn't reach to stop me.

He left without another word.

The scent of his jacket—aged leather and pine—lingered in the air. I stared, unmoving, any loving part of me emptier than his vacant seat. I don't know how long I sat there as the blood rushed to my head, and the shock settled over me. As my toes and fingers tingled, and every inch of me went numb. As the part of me that waited for him to return withered and died, and I chugged a second and third drink. I do know at some point autopilot kicked in, deciding it was time to go, and I mindlessly shuffled out the door.

Twilight steeped the alley in the hues of the dwindling sunset. Dragging my nails against the building, I stumbled towards the street, letting the bumpy stone scratch my fingertips. Tears stung my eyes, and my breath came in heaves, and I was cradling the wall before I could stop myself. Scream sobs echoed in the narrow space as I withdrew from the world, tasting, feeling, seeing, smelling, hearing *nothing* but the buildup of pain and humiliation as I whittled down to a shell of a human.

There were a lot of crappy outcomes in this hand I'd been dealt, but nothing compared to this—opening myself up just to be shut down. To be left with no sense of belonging.

I reached for my necklace, forgetting it was missing. A pulse of anguish lingered where my hand brushed bare skin. Fresh tears lined my lids.

A translucent tendril of energy reached out from my body, as if searching for a conduit. I watched, *felt*, the smoky wisp sweep across dumpsters, the windows, as if it were an extra limb that moved as inconspicuously as a shadow. Touching, prodding, weighing its resources—metal and glass—and stalling at the lack of…elements.

A ragged exhale left me as my Source petered out. What would I have done if it found something worthy to latch onto? Bring the whole place down? Bring myself down? I glanced at the door to Elsewhere and shuddered.

Caving into dusk, I dragged myself home, taking the long, windy route, wading through the ripples of loneliness until I reached my front yard. Feet planted on the flagstone pathway, I stared up at the second floor—a simple place where I'd spent my childhood dreaming, growing, living. Suffering.

It didn't feel like home anymore.

CHAPTER 31

WHERE THE HELL HAVE YOU BEEN!?"

Arms crossed, my dad yelled from his perch atop the stairs. He couldn't even wait until I closed the door. I'd anticipated this reaction when I lost service in Elsewhere for half the day and then turned my phone off because I couldn't deal.

His shadow stretched across the tiny foyer, blotting out the light. "No answer, no call, no text? If you're going to be out all day save me the wild-goose chase and tell me."

So that's what this was. He had finally decided to be a good parent. Too late, *Dad*.

Eyes bloodshot and bagged, my restless fists balling and straightening, I heaved myself up the steps, the knot in my stomach tightening with each drag of my breath. Resentment burned my throat as I reached the top.

"Is that alcohol I smell?" He must have caught a whiff.

"Isn't that how us Harlows deal with our feelings?" I bit out. When that didn't have the desired effect, I added, "Why, you want some?"

He staggered, as if my words had slapped the rosy circles onto his cheeks—but we both knew what that was from.

Pale red speckled the front of his white shirt, shifting and creasing with the frantic wave of his arms. "You're eighteen! You're not allowed to drink. Who gave it to you?"

"Careful, you're dadding so hard right now," I drawled. "Wouldn't want to overdo it."

He stilled, his wispy caramel-streaked hair falling over the metal hooks of his eyeglasses. "What'd you just say?" His voice was dead quiet. Usually this would've stopped me, but tonight I burned too hot.

A scratchy cackle left my lips. It honestly startled me, but it didn't slow me down. "I said you should be careful. Or I might think you actually care."

The vein popped in his temple. "Of course, I care," he said through gritted teeth.

"Don't be so angry." Stepping so close his chin could graze the top of my head, I patted his cheek. "It's the truth." I whisked past him, squinting against the bright ceiling lights. As I neared the threshold to the living area, I spun on my heels. "Isn't that why you lied to me for eighteen years?"

Anger streaked his tanned cheeks with red. "What are you talking about?"

"The term *Nephilim* ring a bell?" I held my chin high as he marched towards me, my voice rising and echoing through the narrow hallway. "How about Empyrea? Chthonia? The Watchers?"

The color drained from his face. "W-what?"

"She was cursed from the moment she met you." Tears seared my eyes, splashing my raw cheeks. "Did she even drown? Or did she get sucked up by some Angel of Death?"

"River—" His throat bobbed like he was stuck on the

words he couldn't speak. He raised his hands, as if his touch would comfort me. I dipped out of reach. The crumpled shred of paper burned a hole in my pocket. I pulled it out and thrust it against his chest.

He caught it before it drifted to the carpet. "What is this?"

"You tell me." I tilted my head and sucked on my teeth.

"This is…this is…" The air bloated his chest as he held it in and stared at the rows of coordinates. I waited for that exhale, for the one that'd release the truth. When it came, it was calm and steady, like in that moment he'd been able to get a hold on himself.

That made one of us.

"Wait a minute. I'm the parent here. I don't have to explain myself to you." He took a purposeful step forward, the floor creaking beneath his weight. "*You* should be telling *me* why you're out at all hours and ditching class."

WHAT. I could not believe he was deflecting. "Oh please, missing curfew was so last week." I retreated from his slow pursuit across the open living area.

"You think because you're eighteen the rules don't apply to you anymore? You still live under my roof." The evenness in his voice drew a shiver from me. It was far more unnerving than his rage. "Your therapist called me. She told me everything, and how combative you've been—"

Blood rushed to my head and flooded my eardrums as the vision of Dr. Finis, pinned against the bookcase, drowned out whatever else he said. How would she know any of this? I hadn't told her a damn thing. How was she still alive?

Hitting an invisible wall, I halted. "You can't honestly say you believe that demon?"

"Don't call her that." My dad stopped inches from me. "She's concerned. And so am I."

My mouth was too dry as I rasped, "Her concern isn't *real*, and yours isn't necessary—especially if you're going to continue lying to me."

His vivid slate eyes dimmed with shadows as his shoulders slouched. An emotion I knew all too well tugged his lids closed, and his wrath dissipated right in front of me. I stayed strong until he finally lifted his head and looked at me—*really* looked at me—with a reverence like he was standing before...an angel.

"I'm the one who raised you since Mom passed. The one who chauffeured you all over town, who packed every lunch, who rubbed your head and read you stories to help soothe your senses so you could actually fall asleep at night..." The slight shake in his hands made it to his words. "I have dozens of flaws. I know I do. But one thing I will never apologize for is what I've done to protect you."

A sob crept up my throat. I swallowed it back. The air stung my nostrils. "Dad, I'm not a little girl anymore. I understand you want to protect me, but the way you've gone about it..." I shook my head. "It hasn't been good for my mental health, but now it's affecting my safety."

When his lips parted and his shoulders unfurled, for a wild, desperate moment, I thought I'd finally gotten through to him. The truth was one heartbeat away. But I should've known the lies had been too ingrained in his mind for him to give in after one fight. Worse, maybe he even started believing them.

"I think you should go to your room." There was a flintiness to him, but it was forced. "For the remainder of summer, you are to stay in this house unless it's for an approved activity. Approved, River. No sneaking out to go surfing. Do you understand?"

No. No, I didn't understand. My spine buckled beneath the weight of disappointment. His touch was caustic as he brushed past me down the hall.

I stomped after him. "You can't hold me hostage!"

Features as stoic as his tone, he turned to me. "I can. You're still under my care. You don't like it? Move out."

Air whooshed into my lungs, angry words waiting to be spoken, and I let it loose in a hiss. "I just told you I was basically in *danger,* and this is your reaction!?"

"Then it sounds like staying here is the safest thing for you." He slipped into his room and closed the door so fast I didn't even have time to form a reaction.

Staggering back a few feet into my own bedroom, I slammed the door and whirled to lean against it, my back scraping against its indents as I slid down it. My knees provided a cushion as I laid my head onto them and let it come: all the tears, all the emotions, pouring out.

The skin below my eyes felt scalded now, bearing the brunt of so much pain. The only part of my body that endured a worse fate was my heart. *That* felt like it'd been ripped out at the bar—and my dad was the one who stomped on it until it was nothing but a splattering of muscle.

Hands gravitating to the empty spot above my chest, I pulled at my phantom necklace. As my eyes drifted shut, its symbol pierced the pitch-black behind my lids. A raindrop with two four-pointed stars. The Empyrean symbol for water, one of four. Four Watchers. Four elements. Four watchtowers. I still had the coordinates—the paper had fluttered to the floor, flattening under my dad's crocs as he'd stepped on it to follow me. I hadn't heard him leave his room to retrieve it, so it should still be there, crinkled on the carpet. Waiting.

I didn't need Ryder—I didn't need my dad to carry on with this quest. I was a descendent of a freaking archangel, the Angel of Water, a guardian of the mortal realm. It was time to follow Akosua's directive. I would no longer rely on anyone but myself.

"To your watchtowers," I whispered. Shooting to my feet, I changed out of my cutoffs, slipped on some leggings, and laced my high tops. I gathered some bobby pins and tossed them into the pockets of the black jacket I zipped up, in case I needed to pick a lock. Which probably wouldn't work on a popular landmark, but whatever. It was all I had. I cracked open the door.

After assessing the sounds—the steady hum of idle appliances, the sporadic knocks of the ice machine, the muffled voices from the TV in my dad's room—I snuck into the hallway, cringing at every ungodly loud creak that broke the silence.

Sure enough, the scrap of the article lay atop the brown-and-beige shag. It joined the rest of my arsenal in my windbreaker's pocket, up against my phone. A flutter, tiny but undeniable, stirred in my gut. I'd meant to text Javi back earlier, but I got sidetracked.

Fingers trembling, I pulled out my cell phone and tapped the screen. Two percent battery. There was no time to charge it. Tonight would either build me or destroy me, and I couldn't let our last words be the ugliness that spewed from my lips. On a soft inhale, I started typing, trying to stave off the worry that the words wouldn't be perfect.

ILY and I'm sorry.
I didn't mean to hurt you.
I promise I'll tell you everything.
Soon.

I should've ended it there, but my thumbs pecked with abandon.

Keep this JIC
36.951696, -122.026677

I didn't even care to take it with me or lock it. It'd be dead before I descended the stairs. I continued on my journey, tiptoeing across the hall, down the carpeted steps. With a quiet twist of the lock and a turn of the knob, I stepped into the moonlight.

CHAPTER 32

THE CHILL IN THE AIR CARVED ITS WAY TO MY BONES, carried by the onshore wind. Needles of brutal cold snuck past my jacket, teasing strands of hair out of my hood, turning my breaths into clouds. As the bright lights of a car crept past, my stomach dropped.

The goosebumps on my skin grew so sharp I thought they might pierce my windbreaker. I tightened the strings of my hood around my face and let my seething anger override the rush of panic. Reminding myself I had nothing to fear anymore.

If anything, the world should fear me.

I stuck to the shadows, where neither the moon nor the streetlamps shone.

When the ground began to slope, a barbed-wire fence seemed to pop out of nowhere in the dark. It shielded the entrance to the old truss that bridged the San Lorenzo River, connecting the east and west sides of town.

The surrounding eucalyptus hid a skyline of wood and steel, sporadically revealed by the wind parting their branches. Strips of moonlight and chips of bark floated to the pavement, the piles crackling beneath my feet as I drew near, and beams started to replace the tree trunks. In between them, an unobstructed view of the ocean and my favorite roller coaster greeted me.

I stepped onto the platform. My stomach dipped along with the soggy planks. The briny mist fell on my tongue and tickled my nostrils—the Santa Cruz version of snowflakes. I sneezed, and there was a snap—a decayed piece of wood fractured and collapsed, plummeting to the stagnant river below. My hand shot to my mouth, suppressing a gasp.

At this point even breathing seemed risky.

Filling my lungs with air, I braved the remaining panels, testing the durability of each with my toe. Breath slipped out of me with each creak and groan. I couldn't remember the last time I walked this so late. Oh, actually, it was Grad Night. The night I met *him*.

My feet stopped shuffling as my eyes started to betray me again. I wouldn't let him do this to me, wouldn't let him have this moment. No more letting things that did not serve me take hold of me.

Cool air calmed the burn when I opened my eyes and stole a glance at the shimmering whitecaps. The tide bellowed around me. Conversational, in a way. Not with words, but in the thundering beat as it crashed against sand and rock, and the sluggish burble as it retreated. After midnight, the surf was even more unruly, spraying the tops of the bluffs, drenching the stairs to the Boardwalk, stealing the warning flags that dotted the shoreline. The ocean rebelled against the limits the world had set for it, and right now, I couldn't have felt more connected to it.

I drifted to the end of the bridge, as if a riptide had swept me up and taken me to where the platform fused with the sidewalk.

Dodging an incoming headlight, I pressed myself against a muraled wall. I focused on counting the stains in the pavement, as if looking anywhere but the street would help keep me unseen.

Hoping the amusement park security guards were too sidetracked or bored to notice my presence, I hiked my upper body over the thick metal fence that barricaded the grounds.

I swung one foot around, and then the other, the blunt angles of the top bar digging into my chest as I teetered unsteadily at the top. Stifling a groan, I lost my grip and slipped off, my legs caving in and sending me to my knee-caps as I landed, the sharp pain radiating in a bullseye over the bone. I grasped a neon pillar and pushed off it to stand. Sticking to the shadows, I hobbled down the path.

A green-scaled dinosaur watched me with lifeless eyes from its fiberglass ledge above the tracks of the Cave Train. Its dead, red stare bored into me until I rounded a corner—and careened into a Neanderthal statue. My heart leapt out of my chest. Even in the day, they were creepy, but now, their permanent grins turned menacing in the darkness.

Both of us wobbled from the impact, but my body never stopped shaking, unlike his.

It was weird to see everything closed, no lines for the thrill rides, the amusement park barred and barren—like I was visiting the doppelgänger of the Beach Boardwalk, the macabre twin to its lively counterpart.

A draft whipped through the wide berth of the midway, evoking a distorted tune out of a claw machine—just the wind, I told myself. It set off a row of others, and I hurried past, their chipper melodies way too high-pitched and out of sync for my brain to detangle if I stayed and listened.

My wild-eyed expression stared back at me as I passed the carousel's mirrored windows. I froze, swearing at a flutter of movement between the antique horses. Pressing my nose against the glass, I peered at the golden support poles, the painted mounts, the giant mouth of the clown that ate the rings from ring toss. Nothing. No one. Not for long, though.

Certain at any moment I'd bump into a security guard, I spun on my heels and launched into a jog—and hit a wall of flesh. It knocked me to the ground, and I blinked against stars that seemed to have dropped from the sky. When they no longer speckled my vision, I took in the person who'd literally stopped me in my tracks.

Thick-soled boots. An all-black uniform. A blinding flash of silver-white.

"Ryder?" I lifted myself to my elbows, my gaze darting between his hardened stare and his arrows. "What are you doing here?"

In the shade of the building, he loomed above me, with a full quiver peeking out from behind his shoulder. His broad shadow draped me with an air of indifference as I lay there, breathless. He said nothing—no offer to help, no outstretched hand—he was a ghost of himself, of the Ryder who once held me in this theme park.

Wincing at the weight on my sore knees, I stood up. He

tracked me with a hunter's precision, the hollowness to his eyes almost sucking the life out of me. I took a step back, but he matched every movement, cornering me in the merry-go-round's alcove. Hands clenched at his sides, he left nothing but a breath between us.

He hadn't come to apologize, that much was clear. So, what then?

"Do you need something? I'm kind of busy." I shifted to go around him, but he blocked my way, and I noticed a thin braided thread of silver dangling from his fingers.

A shockwave of awareness jolted through me. My gaze followed the metal up to his fist, where a glimmer of blue snuck between his knuckles. There was no doubt in my mind—that was my necklace.

My hand drifted to the space surrounding my collarbone, as empty as my heart. "Why do you have that?"

He loosened his grip, letting the pendant peek out from between his fingers. "This old thing?"

In his care it gleamed dull, lifeless, its beauty muffled by his corrupted touch.

"Yes, that *old thing*. Last I wore it was…" My eyes grew wide, and the realization hit me so fast I almost reunited with the ground. Half Moon Bay, at the fortune teller's house. I'd had a concussion—or something like it. When I was cradled in his arms or wiped out on the grass, he must have slipped the jewelry off my neck.

"Looks like you're piecing things together."

My head snapped up at his voice. "I am. And not only are you an asshole; you're also a thief." The hopelessness was a sinking ship dragging me down so deep, it had me gasping for breath. "Why do you want it anyway? It's just an old family heirloom. It has no value to you."

He smirked, and it was all bitterness and scorn. "But it has immeasurable value to you."

I didn't meet his eyes—I couldn't. So I focused on the stone lying flat against his palm. "What does that matter?"

Ryder curled his fingers around the pendant, hiding it from sight. "Because it's a conduit for your powers. Without it, you can't channel your Source. Well, I guess you could if you knew what you were doing…but it's not like you do."

My feet stood on dry land, but I might as well have been underwater. His words weighed a thousand tons, pressing against my skull, the air suffocatingly thick with tension.

Memories replayed before my eyes as if I were literally drowning. Meeting on the bridge after Grad Night. Finding me after work in the alley. Showing up at school just in time to whisk me away from the teratorn—and taking care of me, after. Saving me from a gnarly walk home after running from werewolves. The Big Dipper. The Ferris wheel… Teaching me how to drive. Tears formed behind my lowered lids. Showing me a world with angels and magic and…I swallowed, fighting the knot forming in my throat…Elephant seals.

It hadn't been because he actually cared. It had all been for *this*.

"It's me," I whispered, the shock constricting my voice. "It's always been me. I'm the one you've been looking for. When did you know?"

Weariness pinched his eyes. It was so brief, it had me second-guessing if I even saw it. "I had a hunch it was you the night we met. That's why I sent the sprite for surveillance. This necklace was the smoking gun." His words chilled my blood, numbing my veins like frostbite. "An Empyrean water stone, crafted out of the element itself." He rubbed his thumb over the surface. "There're only three others like it. You can guess what those are."

Earth, wind, and fire. Did he actually think I was crazy at the pub when I told him about the Watchers, or was that just an act to humiliate me? Render me defenseless? Unfortunately for him, it did quite the opposite. I'd spent my entire life trying to dampen the pain. Now I let it fill me, fuel me, forge my path forward.

"You used my ignorance of this world against me." I lunged for the jewelry. In one fluid motion he loaded his bow and aimed an arrow at me faster than I could blink. I flapped my arms in frustration, striking the sides of my thighs. "Why?"

With his weapon locked, the déjà vu slammed into me. My dream, the dream from the night we met. It had predicted this exact scene. Deep down, I must have always known he'd betray me.

"My, my, my," a deep voice crooned from the darkness. I jumped and gasped, my palm smacking against my heart. Leif. What the hell was wrong with these guys, always sneaking up on people!? "Was worried you didn't have it in you, brother."

Using the distraction, I whirled out of the alcove, and out of Ryder's reach, onto the main pathway. His brother stepped into the moonlight from behind the tiled wall of the frozen dessert stand. Disdain draped his features as casually as the leather jacket over his shoulders.

I had no problem matching his snarled lips, meeting his wroth eyes. He'd shown nothing less since the moment we'd been introduced. "Why are you here?" I spat.

"I couldn't miss my little brother's initiation into the big leagues." He settled next to Ryder, wrapping a firm arm around his neck, shaking his shoulder.

"Initiation into what?" I emulated Leif's glare. "Your ridiculous Nephilim Society you were going to tell me *all about* at the body shop? Isn't he already branded for that—or is this the official test?"

"Make this easy on yourself, River." I *fumed* at the way Ryder drew out my name, and how it still managed to reach some wanting part of me. "Back down. You can't outrun them."

I finally looked at him, ignoring the flare of golden green trying to shatter the darkness that wrung his irises. My finger pointed at him. "You don't get to act like you care."

"Oh, don't take it out on Ryder," Leif drawled. "He's just following orders."

"That is the lamest excuse in the history of excuses." I swore smoke was going to blow out my nostrils, and any minute I'd start exhaling fire. "Can someone explain *what* orders? And who's 'them?'"

A heavy flapping whooshed from the rafters of the bordering bumper cars, rustling the cables. All three of us snapped towards the aerial wires sparking and popping from a focused gust of wind that blew nowhere else but inside the ride. Fallen leaves and trash funneled into mini cyclones, twisting over the floor. The tempest grew fiercer, stronger, cars crashing into each other, until the *clang* of metal against metal and a searing flash obliterated everything within the oval track.

Shielding my face with my hands, I dropped my chin to my chest, the ringing in my ears drilling into my nerves. I was stuck in a serrated bubble of blinding light and echoes from the blast, a putrid char burning my nostrils and souring my tastebuds.

My efforts to control my breathing were simply lost as the panic pulled me into myself. I wasn't sure how long had passed, but I knew the effects were dampening when I started to feel my body shaking and I was able to take a conscious inhale.

When the sounds became clearer, I dared a glance between my fingers.

Slowly, my eyeballs dragged over the brothers. They hadn't moved, aside from parting and getting into a still, wide-legged stance that reminded me of two predators staking out their prey. I flicked my gaze past them to the destroyed carnival ride, the shadows dispersing into smokey forms like phantoms of amusement park goers before they dissipated into the ashy air.

One splintered off towards us, intensifying in color, its translucent tendrils molding into limbs as it evolved into a familiar figure that made my mouth go dry and my hairs stand on end.

She looked hungry for blood. Of course, she did; the last time I saw her I tried to kill her. Or something like it.

Dr. Finis glided towards me, corvine feathers shedding from her shoulders, singeing as she emerged from the explosion—like she'd been born from it.

I glanced to my right. Ryder blocked the path to one of the main gates. My heels shifted to turn, then sand and gravel crunched a few paces away—a purposeful sound. Leif wanted me to know he had moved behind me. The urge to look over my shoulder left me.

"River. I told you we'd meet again." The demon's words tried to catch the breeze, but the element simply refused. In a motion that made the blood leave my face, she turned to each brother, the corners of her lips upturned as she nodded in acknowledgement. In *thanks*. "Night Stalkers."

The phrase set off an internal alarm even though I'd never heard it before. A persistent clawing in my gut told me to run or brace myself for the worst, but the confusion held me in place like a fishhook.

"River," she purred. "You look confused."

Not only was I racking my brain for some sort of indication as to what *Night Stalker* could mean, I was also trying to process the link between these three inhumans who clearly all wanted to end me. My eyebrows pushed together so hard it felt like they had fused together. "No shit."

A hoarse laugh left the demon, as if her windpipe hadn't been used in years. Tiny moths flew out of the black pit of her mouth. I recoiled a half step backwards, until I remembered Leif blocked my exit.

"Did the boys not fill you in on their end of the bargain?" Glancing their way, she tsked.

"W-what bargain?" My breaths were so shallow I could hardly form the words.

Onyx liquid pooled with her saliva and coated her lips. "To find you and deliver you to me," she said, spittle clinging to her chin. A pallid tongue darted out, licking it clean. So very reptilian. "Don't be sad, River; these aren't your friends. These are Night Stalkers, nothing more than hit men with no strings attached. With the way they parade it all over their skin and clothing, I'm surprised you didn't figure it out sooner."

Unfazed by Finis's praise, unfazed by my hurt, Ryder remained still as a statue, with an arrow nocked. At least he pointed his weapon at the ground. Though I'm sure if I so much as flinched, he'd aim it right at me. My eyes glossed over his hand holding the bow, the tattoos etched on his knuckles, the inverted abbreviation between his thumb and index finger. NS. I craned my neck, the eyes of a snake head wrapped around the S triggering a flurry of images.

This whole time, it'd been staring me dead in the face. Scribbled on building corners, patched onto moto vests, forever inked on his and his brother's skin. *It's more of a syndicate, really,* Leif had started to tell me. *You got peddlers, thieves, and…*assassins. I finally filled in the blank.

Finis was right: Ryder wasn't my friend. He was my enemy. I clenched my fists so hard to keep myself from biting my fingers that my jagged nails pierced my palms. I'd found his introversion to be different and charming…Was that even him? Was his fascination with me all just a ploy to get me to trust him? Did he even care about who I was? Did he ever even *see* me?

My eyes fluttered open and shut. That rare, dimpled smile; that feverish green stare; the way his calloused touch gently scraped my skin—it had all felt so *real*.

The writing had been there on every damn wall. It'd been inked onto his fucking hand. My gaze shot up his arm, recalling the only hint of color amongst a sea of black and gray art hidden behind his jacket: the blue streaks and white brushstrokes that flowed under his bicep.

A river tat, I realized then. The mark of his prey. How original.

Could I even call it betrayal though, if it was never anything more than a shady business transaction to him?

"Why?" I croaked out, unsure who I was directing it to.

Finis pirouetted closer, in an answering dance of sorrow and devastation. The rotten stench of eggs and burnt rubber polluted the air with each twirl. I clutched my stomach.

"When Mira deserted eternity, we figured we'd won—that the absence of the Daughter of Gabriel, the Wielder of Water, would destroy the power and protection of the Watchers, and Chthonia would be able to seize Mortal Earth." Her eyes were obsidian inkpots, incapable of reflection, so dark and bottomless they swallowed the light. "Imagine our shock when the western watchtower did not fall. That it still stood because she hid from the consequences for eight years, and when she was finally captured, a *child* took the place of the Angel of Water."

As if I wore a dozen soaking layers, I buckled to a force

that weighed on every fiber of my being. It wasn't just about my mom losing her immortality for my dad—she had sacrificed herself for *me*.

"Because of you, the Watchers get to keep their power. Faulty, but strong enough to hold up a ward. The only way to break them is to break you…" She broke off to grin at Ryder, revealing her nubby, ground-down teeth—stained by the black-tinged saliva that drizzled out the corners of her mouth. I knew she was evil, but right now, she didn't hold any part of that demon back. She clasped her hands, nails bruised and sharp as daggers. "Now, give me that Empyrean water stone so I can fulfill this sacred oath."

Ryder's grasp loosened around the handle of his weapon and an orange bracelet slid out from his cuff. The paper wristband was frayed, the numbers were faded, but the white text still legible said *Boardwalk*, printed in diagonal patterns behind the date of our first real hangout.

"You never took it off," I whispered. I hadn't meant for him to overhear it, but it traveled to his ears and ripped his moody stare from seeing through me, to me. A tremble rocked his grip, fracturing his hardened shell, and we locked eyes.

The prolonged creak of string being stretched against wood sounded behind me.

Uneasiness struck the top of my spine like a bullseye. I didn't need to turn and see to know Leif had nocked his own arrow at me. But his words were directed at Ryder.

"Don't forget who you are, little brother. Don't forget where we came from." His voice reverberated down the bow, tickling the hairs standing on the back of my neck.

"The Sainthood takes our wings because of people like her—people like her mother."

W-what did he say? I couldn't have heard him correctly, but then I remembered the way Ryder's entire demeanor had shifted when he'd spoken about the Saints. The scars prickled on my shoulder blades—perfect vertical slits, as if they were purposefully cut, too precise for a childhood accident. Could that be where…? Could I have had…?

Every muscle in me constricted. I was going to be sick.

"We are Night Stalkers." Leif sidestepped around me and into my peripheral. "Born of shadow and darkness. We do not fear judgement for vengeance…"

Ryder's muscles strained as he looked at me and also took in the words. For a split second I thought he might drop the weapon, as it slipped down his clammy grip. But something changed when he tightened his fingers. Setting his jaw, he brought tension back to the bowstring, the arrow once again aimed with deadly power. "For we have already fallen," he finished.

"Wait!" I ventured a shaky step towards him. "Ryder, please, you don't have to do this."

"Yes, he does, River. He's committed by blood." Finis's croaky, tuneless croon was the melody of a nightmare's lullaby. "That's a bond that can only be broken by completing the oath, or death. I don't think he wants to die today."

"Neither do I." I spun just in time to see wispy shadows curling over her cadaver fingers. Leif sneered as I recoiled. My eyes darted between them.

"You don't have to lie anymore. Not to us." The translucent black tracers of energy thickened and spun around her hands. "We both know this is what you've really wanted. To meet the empty, thoughtless void where you no longer feel. If anything, I'm relieving you of that task."

The grief and guilt and mental isolation had sunk their claws deep into me. So deep that at many points throughout my life I literally thought they might end me, those emotional scars just as tangible as the physical ones on my back. What I'd slowly come to realize was that I was honored to wear them. They were what made me…me.

Chin high, I stated, "Maybe I changed my mind."

"Too late now." Caught on the final syllable, the demon's pitch dropped to a growl and reverberated into the esplanade. At first, I just thought it was me that was shaking. But then the path folded and split, a crack growing between my feet, pulling my legs outwards into a standing split. Before it could rip me in two, I sprung off one crumbling piece of cement and onto another, my knees once again breaking my fall.

Each beat of my heart hit my ribs like a mallet. Light flickered in the corner of my eye. As I turned to see what it was, the thousands of neon carnival bulbs blazed on and off, strobing so many colors it was impossible for my brain to process them all. My hands shot to my brows—a temporary shield, because then the soda dispensers flooded the food huts with the force of a dam that had blown, and my fingers covered my ears—but not for long. The ground beneath me shuddered and furled, gathering into a wave of cement, and my arms left my head, flailing about just to keep me from rolling over.

I knew what she was doing, exploiting my senses until it

put them in overdrive, and I couldn't do anything but cave to the episode.

Black spots crept into my vision as the sounds funneled into my nerves. I gritted my teeth. I couldn't let her win; I *wouldn't* let her win. My palms slapped the torn pavement.

Willing my lungs to work past the shock, I gulped down an inhale before the darkness stole my ability to breathe, Dr. Fairmore's near-forgotten words coaxing me to focus on the expansion of my lungs. Redirecting every ounce of myself remaining, I exhaled and let the chaotic Source around me become something else entirely—the lawless momentum of the ocean that I craved and harnessed—and let its power wash over me.

The world came into focus as the blurry specks that shaded my vision started to retreat. Another wave of cement rolled beneath me. I faltered but made it to standing.

An unmistakable energy eddied in my gut and pulsated in my fingertips as an idea grew and took root around me: this undulation of rebar and rock was identical to a pumping morning at my favorite surf spot.

It gathered for another set: taller, faster, the blocks of stone bending beneath me. I whipped my head around, searching for something to use as an impromptu surfboard. A jagged steel sheet that must've been part of the top of a concession stand drifted by me.

Holding on to the vision of the ocean I'd mustered, I sprung after it. Using my core to steady me, I planted my feet between the corrugated grooves of metal and rode the fake swell like a sketchy reef break, headed straight for the demon.

Surfing the concrete, I whizzed past Leif. He attempted to mimic my footwork—and fell right on his ass. Even Ryder, someone so self-sufficient and strong, struggled to remain standing as a spray of rock fragments shattered atop his shoulders.

An unwelcome shock lacerated my heart as he yelped out in pain. My arms hesitated over whether to stay put at my sides or follow that twinge of emotion and reach out to him. But why would I try and save him after all he'd done to me? After finding out what and who he was?

Knowing full well he was willing to let *me* drown in the rubble…I still lurched forward and outstretched my hand as I rode the crest of the rocky wave past him. If I could get him next to me, I could hold him steady. Our fingertips brushed. In that half a second of contact, his eyes grew wide, shattering the darkness that had eclipsed their light. They flared a green so electric it stole my breath—I didn't even have time to realize my hand had closed around the lapis pendant, not his calloused palm.

The second I touched it, it exploded in color, blooming with the hues of the open ocean. The tiny specks of silver-white embedded into the stone glistened like bioluminescence under the starry night. The last glimpse I got of Ryder before I spun to face forward was of concrete pellets raining onto his head. I didn't have time to consider why he'd given me my necklace—why he didn't grab me when he had the chance—as the gray wave curled towards the demon.

There was no time to channel whatever Source was tied to the necklace. I bent my knees, shifting my weight forward to gain some extra momentum, and dipped my shoulder, slamming it up as I hurtled into Finis.

A screech like a thousand hungry bats had taken flight penetrated the soundwaves. The impact reverberated through my bones, into my clattering teeth. I fell face-first into the trough of the wave, the metal slipping out beneath my feet as the broken cement crashed over me.

Chipped pieces of stone snuck into every crevice as it washed me almost fifty yards from where I'd made impact with Finis. When the swell slowed to a ripple, I hopped up and took shelter within the Pirate Ship's exit, choking on the chalky dust. I peered between the railing's orange support poles into the heavy cloud of debris, crouching and shading my eyes.

Someone—something—lurked by the gates on the opposite side of the courtyard. Finis, I surmised. Or maybe it was Leif and his perfectly coiffed man bun. Or had Ryder come to grips with what he'd done and come to retrieve what I'd taken?

I braced myself, fingers tightening around the metal. Except…none of the above was the perpetrator darting through the open square.

Their silhouette didn't cast any evidence of extra limbs or pairs of horns. I sized them up, their wavy hair bouncing as they…tripped over their baggy cargo pants? As they tossed back the hood of their…Santa Cruz Skateboards sweatshirt?

This was no fiend at all.

"Psst! Javi!" I hissed from my hiding spot, flapping my hand to wave him over. The moon cast a glow over his half-open mouth and raised brows as he stepped through the destruction and made his way to me. "What are you doing here?"

"Heading to the coordinates you sent me." He coughed on the ashy plumes that wafted in the air. "What's going on? Are you okay?"

Oh my God, he wasn't supposed to actually come. I was going to grab him, no, scream at him, no, knock every bit of sense into him.

"I'm fine." I ignored his wide eyes that tracked the coating of dried dirt, blood, and dust caking my clothes and skin. "But what are you doing *here*?" I waved my hand and gestured to the Boardwalk, frantically scanning for the foes that seemed to have shrunk into the shadows. It wouldn't be long before they attacked again.

"I'm cutting through, so I don't get in trouble for wandering the streets at midnight. Same as you're doing, I think?" Javi's gaze roved over me once more, and then at the uprooted walkway. "It looks like a bomb went off in here. What happened? Where's security?"

Pulling myself to standing, I jumped over the railing. My knees locked, but Javi caught me by the waist before I could tumble to the ground. Without hesitation I wrapped my arms around him and brought him so close there was no space between us. The hug was brief, but so long overdue I almost didn't let go, even if he didn't squeeze back until the very last second.

Retreating to arm's length, I gripped his elbows as I spoke. "Listen to me, Jav. You need to get out of—" A tremor rumbled through the earth and stopped me short.

"What the deuce?!" Javi swiveled around. "What was that?"

"I—" The words got cut off as an invisible force clamped my jaw shut. My fingers shot to my mouth, nails scraping against my lips as I fought to pry them open. My nostrils flared and my breathing grew more frantic as I tried to *hum* what was happening to me.

"River? Are you okay?" He searched my wild stare. "What's going on?"

A figure came into view across the ravaged concourse, smoky shadows trailing it like wings. Finis stopped under a moonbeam and drew a finger so broken it bent the other way to her puckered lips. *Shhh.*

With a frenzied shake of my head, I rose my hands to point and try to warn Javi, but that same force compelled them to my sides, as if they'd been tied with invisible string. He pulled at me now, trying to untwist me, shouting for help I knew wouldn't come.

The darkness that followed the demon broke off into tendrils that coasted over the ground like a fog. Moving with unbelievable swiftness, they wrapped around my legs, my neck, my forehead…Tears splashed my cheeks as my frustration built and shadowy bands of pressure cut off my thoughts. Fresh laps of agony coursed through my body. I couldn't even open my mouth to cry. I couldn't hear past the brutal pounding in my ears, couldn't see past the sharp ache in my temples.

I was lost to the pain. I'd forgotten where and who I was—who was tugging at my hands, who was snapping their fingers, who was flapping their arms right in front me.

Their brown—or were they green?—eyes looked so familiar, creases pulled down by the heavy weight of sadness.

They said something—what? Intuition fluttered in my chest but…the shackles of shadow tightened. So, I didn't know. The world wasn't making sense, only the torment was.

I became the pain, and it became me.

Light flared so bright it was all I could see. I squinched my eyes shut to escape it. When the flash subsided, and the silhouettes stopped dancing behind my lids, I opened them and stared at the mess of the courtyard: the shattered glass, the flattened walls of a game stall, the mangled wood of a ride. Someone lay atop the wreckage, their body limp, limbs splayed with an almost…peaceful look on their face. They could have been mistaken as dreaming.

The fog lifted from my brain, and I suddenly understood everything that had happened when I went blank.

Javi.

"No!" Every single ounce of oxygen inside me rushed out in a bawling gasp. Whatever demonic spell bound my arms and legs released, and I dropped to the floor.

"That wasn't very nice of you to take the necklace." Finis's shadow fell over me, and it felt like I'd been trapped beneath the ice of a frozen lake. Goosebumps erupted and brought full-body shivers. "Where is it? Give it back. *Please.*"

Her guess was as good as mine. It'd somehow left my hand, and my leggings didn't have pockets, and my jacket felt far too light. In fact, I was pretty sure my phone had dropped out at some point and was another casualty of the concrete wave she had summoned.

I covertly folded my hair behind my ears to scan the ground for either, but it revealed nothing. Not wanting my unease to be obvious, I changed the subject. "Where are Ryder and Leif?"

"By the sound of it…" A guttural yell pierced the night that made my heart skip a beat. The demon cocked her head. "Your boyfriend is getting quite the beating." She sighed, sounding more annoyed than anything. "That's what he gets for not following orders. Which means I get you all to my-self." I ignored the flicker of hurt that sparked inside me. "The necklace." She stepped closer on exaggerated tiptoes, offering a smile, sharp teeth bared to the cool night air. "I asked nicely."

Tuning out another scream and the zap of distress it ignited in my chest, I focused on what was in front me: Javi was out cold, and I really didn't care how politely Finis asked—she wasn't getting my fucking necklace.

"That's the last thing I'll do," I ground out, rising to my feet. It didn't matter if I had it or not—she never would. I'd make sure of it.

Another low rumble shot through the theme park. Slobber dripped from her lips. "These aren't decisions your mother would be proud of."

I shrugged. "Yeah, well, you can't please everyone."

Her laugh screeched on the night, sharp enough to break glass. My shoulders shot to my ears. "At least we can agree on that." Honing and nurturing that wispy shadow magic, she shaped it into a sphere with her cracked, pallid claws. My breath caught at the black spit dripping off her elongat-ed fangs, combusting when it hit the sphere of dark matter like tiny fireworks. "Then at least do it for your friend?" She gestured to Javi. "He's not dead. Yet."

We both shifted towards Javi lying silent, inert, bleeding, and—by a miracle—still alive. My heart jumped into my throat with hope and then with fear. I'd never forgive myself for this. "Don't drag him into this. He's innocent. If you want the jewelry so bad, why not just kill me?"

"Trust me, I've had the impulse on more than one occasion, but alas, I'm to bring you to Chthonia." The skin over her jaw started to deteriorate—her human disguise was slipping, revealing something avian and serpentine all at once.

Dread like I had never known before washed over me. "W-why?"

"You mortals have this saying that everything happens for a reason, and you know…I think I'm beginning to believe it. If Mira hadn't betrayed Empyrea and given birth to you, then Akosua, Daughter of Michael and Wielder of Fire, might never have joined Chthonia." That name, smushed between the diabolic bullshit, perforated the thin layer of confidence I'd just rebuilt. "And then we would never know how rich the Watchers' Source is! Killing you *is* easier, but siphoning your powers is a far better strategy in the long run. Then not only can we infiltrate Mortal Earth—we can rule it."

My head shook at the memory of Akosua standing beside my mom as they overlooked the Fall. She'd been so adamant about the consequences for choosing love; it didn't make sense that she'd commit such a blatant form of treason herself. "Akosua swore to protect Earth. Not destroy it. Why would she be in on this? You're lying."

"You think your little meltdown at your Grad Night is what made the connection to the Watchers disappear?" Her lips curved into an evil smile. "You can thank Akosua for severing it."

I gasped for that impossible breath, sputtering for the oxygen that'd been ripped from my lungs.

"It's interesting…" Finis studied me intently, as if seeing me for the very first time. "You make it seem like Akosua is the problem, when your *mother* is the one who abandoned the Watchers and left Mortal Earth so vulnerable in the first place. Mira cared more about her own selfish needs than protecting humanity. I can see the family resemblance…"

Those words stilled the blood in my veins and lodged a ball of fear in my pipes. There was truth to them, truth that'd been warring against the lies I told myself.

"Did you ever stop to think maybe Akosua is just cleaning up her mess? That without the burden of Mira, she's able to see clearly now?"

Only because I wouldn't let myself think it, but the reality was those thoughts had already lodged themselves in the back of my mind since Madame Myrian's.

"And maybe Chthonia's mission speaks to her?"

See, *that* was the part I couldn't wrap my head around. It just didn't make sense. Steeling myself, I asked, "What exactly is Chthonia's mission?"

"We want to bridge the realms, so angel and demon and every species in between can be together," she hissed, now more creature than human. "You know what it's like to walk alone—isn't it cruel to keep us apart?" She cooed at the Source cradled in her arms like a newborn. "To keep you and your mother apart?"

The pit in my stomach could have swallowed me whole.

"You want this too, River."

I hated to admit it, I didn't even want to *acknowledge* it, but part of me did. What'd I'd do to see my mom again…I shook my head and pushed that tiny sliver of curiosity deep down inside, swearing to never be tempted by it again.

"You're telling me you just want everyone to live happily ever after?" I didn't buy that—I *couldn't* buy that. This was a demon.

"Sometimes happiness must be sacrificed for the greater cause. You wouldn't understand. Mira wasn't the best example of that…" The demon's shoulders jutted inward, a fresh batch of black feathers exploding from her back. She grimaced in pain, then released a sigh that sounded far too pleasurable for the circumstances. I felt myself moving backwards, but I was already up against the railing. "We'll need to rebuild, and not everyone will be *happy* about it. Those who join us will be offered positions within the Court of the Cursed. But those against us, those not…convinced of our cause, will be rounded up after we breach the wards."

How could any Nephilim—how could Ryder, how could Akosua—be okay with this? A flush of cool sweat coated the back of my neck. "And taken where, exactly? I'm sure you won't be escorting them to the nearest five star hotel."

"That's on a need-to-know basis, but I can assure you, the accommodations are more than appropriate for the circumstances."

"What kind of cause do you expect humans to support when you're unleashing demons and rounding up anyone who opposes you like cattle?"

"Humans," Finis spat, droplets of black spit sizzling on the sand-grouted floor. "They're as many as deer yet they're the *chosen ones*. The only thing they're chosen for is reestablishing the glory Chthonia has always deserved."

A tidal wave of guilt, of pain, of every emotion I liked to ignore swelled to life inside me. I wanted to hide, to feel nothing, but instead of shutting down, I let the final scene of that cursed, forgotten memory from when I was eight rise from the depths.

I hadn't been able take my eyes off the figure in the storm because it had been her—my mom. Her brilliant pearly white wings, a blue-tinted aura haloing the crown of her head, the bead of light on the tip of her extended pointer finger shining like the beacon of a lighthouse. By that time, her body had already been swallowed by the ocean and there was nothing I could do but watch as her soul drifted upwards, summoned by storms and shadows. Lightning flashed, illuminating a being at the top of the tempest, their skeletal arms and charred black wings outstretched. Watching. Waiting. Just as I had been then, I wasn't sure now if it was a demon, an angel, or the Creator themselves. Whatever it was, it took her, and as her screams blended with the bellows of the waves, so did the voices of three others: SWIM. FAR AWAY.

Taking a ragged inhale, I made myself a vow—in the presence of Finis, in the midst of this destruction—that this mental anguish would no longer control me.

I was more than my grief. I was more than my trauma.

Most importantly, I was stronger for it.

Releasing the breath, I could practically hear the Source roaring within me. It crawled beneath my skin, uncurled my fingers, and…stung my toes? My eyeballs darted to my feet. The tide had risen, abnormally high, the cold water lapping my thick white soles and seeping into my socks. An icy shock of realization ran up my nerves and jolted my heart, and I knew, with or without the necklace, the element was waiting for me to summon it.

My gaze flicked back to the demonic woman before me, and I slowly raised my hands. The ocean followed, churning and channeling around my feet into a small vortex, readying itself for my command.

"What are you doing?" Finis's question came out muffled between her viper fangs that continued to lengthen and sharpen. She coiled in on herself, and as her slithering body sprung forward, my outstretched arms shot out in front of me. The water rushed forward, crashing into the demon moments before her teeth sank into my neck. A deafening *crack* reverberated off the buildings as it smashed into her, solid as concrete. Liquid flooded her slitted nostrils, her mouth, her ears, every orifice it could slip in.

A heaviness settled over my wrists as pure, unfiltered power shot through my hands. But as long as the doctor still writhed, I wouldn't stop, no matter if the pressure split my brain in two. No matter if I could *feel* the Source weighing on my muscles, dragging down my elbows, and my body shuddered with the effort.

Clenching my jaw, I bit against enamel and skin. The

water sputtered just as surely as everything within me was tiring, flowing more like a kinked hose than a gushing river. Fever seared my skin, but I didn't dare relax long enough to draw a breath.

I released that final push of magic, my lips parting on a scream, and a wave barreled past. It curled and crested then broke over the demon, slamming her into the pavement, leaving the rest of the park untouched. The effort knocked me back into the railing. The pain of the metal digging into my spine didn't even faze me; every speck of attention was on the saltwater wrapping around her limbs, squeezing her chest, stealing her air and her shrieks.

A shadowy phantom dislodged from her body, what I could only assume was her soul. Plumes of darkness billowed out of its back as it hovered over what remained of her mortal vessel: a chimeric, flaccid, figure that spun around and around while the Source slurped her down like a drain.

When the last of her floppy limbs vanished, the ocean retreated, swirling past my calves and snaking through my fingers with a purr-like rumble, claiming me as its master.

Finis's faceless soul turned to me, the air around it splitting into a depthless, dark rift. A sulfuric smell stung my nostrils, and a draft of heat burned my skin.

Fear and sorrow pressed against my soul as Chthonia vacuumed up hers.

The demon let out a long, hopeless wail that shot past my ears and went straight to my nerves. It could have splintered bones and ruptured blood vessels it was so awful and *doomed*. But there was also something…beautiful within the darkness. Magnetic. Familiar. My hand drifted out, seeking the shelter of the pitch-black nothingness. But as it suctioned her up, the dimensional rip sewed itself back together, and the aching desire to join the darkness left me.

I blinked, thinking my eyelids must be bruised because of how much the movement made me wince. Nothing remained of the demon. No feathers, no fleshy charred stain, no particles whatsoever. It was just me, the moonlight, the wreckage, and…

Javi. I sprinted through the puddles, already sobbing before I reached him.

"Javi!" I dropped to his side, the debris harsh on my knees, checking for signs of life the way he did with me—squeezing his hand again and again. I'd do it until my fingers fell off.

Throwing my upper body over his, I pressed my cheek to his temple, and then laid it on his chest. A faint thrum reverberated against the side of my face. He lived.

Fresh tears erupted and I stroked his hair, matted with ash, dust, and blood. "We're getting the hell out of here," I promised.

Sliding my palms beneath him, I grunted at the pain shooting up and down my arms. With muscles bound to collapse at any moment, I lifted my best friend and shakily rose to my feet, shards of glass and metal raining from his clothes. Every step felt like it could kill me, but I carried him through the Boardwalk's destruction towards the exit.

CHAPTER 33

I'D BEEN STARING AT THE GRANITE GRAVE MARKER for so long my eyes had started to cross. Its ashen surface blurred into one long, illegible carving I wasn't ready to see clearly yet.

Glossing over the etchings for maybe the hundredth time, I peered at the rows and rows of graves instead, the sun reflecting off the various gray and black stones erected imperfectly across the hills. I took a deep inhale, the crisp air burning as I drew it in.

Goosebumps abraded my skin, and a ragged sigh left my lips. I was screaming in my sleep again, and the strain it put on my already raw throat made it impossible to even breathe without it feeling like it was on fire.

That was why I liked it here: nobody expected me to *say* anything. The dead didn't force me to speak until my vocal cords were in shreds or force me to relive that horrific night at the Boardwalk. And I bet the person I visited wouldn't have made me, either…if they were alive.

Which they weren't. Thanks to me.

A horn honked from the cemetery's parking lot. I jumped so high I swore my feet left my Vans for a sec. Glancing over my shoulder, I spotted my dad's small SUV idling in the loading zone. Catching my attention, he opened his door and stepped out, pointing at himself, speaking in some form of parental mime language: *Do you want me to join you?*

With a smile that soured my cheeks, I shook my head.

After the "incident" a few weeks ago, he was *always* there, hovering—which would have been way more bearable if he was down to acknowledge what really happened when he found me carrying my unconscious best friend, bawling and bleeding and shoeless—but anytime I said the word *demon* or *angel* or *Source* he clammed up and turned greener than an algae bloom.

I got it—he was scared. And I felt for him for that. But why continue to tiptoe around it?

Especially when we *both* knew what ignoring the truth had the capacity to turn me into—something uncontrollable. Something dark. Something fated for ruin.

I crossed my fingers, squeezing them tightly together, as if the pressure could wring out my annoyance, and willed my attention back to the headstone. My eyes meandered down the circular sides, counting every little fleck of granite, as I laid the bundle of daffodils I'd been clutching at its base.

The easy thing to do would be to drop the flowers and split. But I remained crouching, as if my knees were unwilling to bring me back up until I faced what was in front of me. My arms flailed at my sides and smacked into my thighs. Oh, this was ridiculous. *Come on, River. Just read it.*

Fighting this very persistent, very *annoying*, urge that told me to do otherwise, my gaze lifted to the feathered angel wings flanking the epitaph and drifted over the words in the center. With each hushed syllable that left my lips my heart beat faster, and then all the air rushed out of me.

Olivia Fairmore
A bringer of truth in a world all too absent of it.
May her light shine on those who seek it.

Tucking my fingers into my cropped long-sleeve, I buried my face in my palms. I breathed into the cotton, damp from my tears, until I was starved of oxygen. A blast of air cooled my skin as I lowered my hands. I wanted to keep hiding—but I saw her when I closed my eyes.

The glint of understanding behind her umber stare. The glossy ringlets that cascaded to her cheekbones when her fingers went to grip mine. The way her voice seemed to soothe me and challenge me at the same time—and I'd never hear it again. I thought back to the first session we'd had—did she get enough time with the goddaughter she'd mentioned?

I'd thought this would bring closure, but confusion scrambled my thoughts. Why did she have to die? Did the Night Stalkers take her out, or was it the demon posing as her replacement? The demon *the guy I would not name or ever think of again* was working with. A slow exhale hissed past my teeth. I mentally swatted at the images of *him* flooding my brain, especially the one from the Boardwalk when he seemed to willingly hand me my necklace.

Anger seared my veins, manifesting into something as vital as blood. It numbed my other senses, but it also nourished an animalistic part of me that wanted to scream and claw at the dirt. He'd snapped my heart in two as if it were a fawn's leg, and—

A faint command echoed across my mind. *Take a deep breath.* I stopped spiraling and let Dr. Fairmore's last words to me sink in, as the inhale filled my lungs. I held it and counted to ten. This wasn't even about him.

Massaging my temples, I released a slow, controlled exhale. The anger threatened to bury me deeper than the dead. But I needed there to be meaning. I *needed* to understand.

Was Akosua behind all this? Why? What did she see in Chthonia that made her denounce the Watchers, especially when she was so insistent about the potential fallout if one of them left? How could there be any good in Chthonia's vision if it meant innocent people hurting and dying? I couldn't deny the sting of responsibility that came with this line of thinking. If my mom hadn't followed her stupid, smitten heart, none of this would be happening. Dr. Fairmore wouldn't be in a grave. Javi wouldn't be in a coma. I wouldn't be nursing a broken heart. Demons wouldn't be trying to take over Mortal Earth. And I wouldn't be left here wondering how I could possibly rectify my mom's actions when I couldn't do something as simple as pass high school econ.

I couldn't even hold a job at this point—no-showing my shifts over these past few weeks gave Tom all the reason he'd been looking for to fire me.

Why was everything so fucked up?

A tepid gust wove through the gnarled oak trees that lined the pale gravel paths, shaking the leaves and acorns free. Orange flickered before my eyes. I held my hand over my brows to shield the glare and tracked the flash of color up into the sky. To my surprise, my lips twitched upwards as I watched the monarch butterfly coast on the breeze. I lifted a shaky finger as I rose, offering it a perch. It floated nearer, its toothpick-thin legs tickling my skin.

I actually smiled at the sun reflecting off its wings while it opened and quickly closed them.

My insides fluttered as the butterfly drifted to the rounded top of the headstone. And as my eyes narrowed in on its intricate pattern, my brain also picked up on all the other intricacies of the grounds I'd initially looked over—the white puffs dotting the air not dandelions at all, but winged spirits that seemed to be forged out of light. They hummed, bobbing between the dead and the mourning in blessing. And there was a reason some of the stones caught the glare more than the others, forcing my hand to my brows—tiny hobgoblins, so round and gray they could have been passed off as rocks, polished the markers until their little nubs blistered and bared their fangs at any that tried to breach their plots.

I blinked, and it was like a film rolled over my eyes, making the cemetery perfectly quiet and solitary again.

A fissure of hope cracked my hardened heart. I'd never be able to undo my mom's actions, but she'd made a sacrifice for love. For me. While I couldn't change the past, I did have a future, one I'd been all too willing to throw away. There was Chet's tribunal, which I still hadn't technically committed to, and even though it'd be hard, not showing up would be letting him win.

A shiver snaked its way up my spine at the thought of facing him on the stand. But I'd do it. Not just for me. For Shanley—my friend.

And there was Javi, who…my front teeth punctured my bottom lip as I imagined him lying in the hospital bed, hooked up to all those machines in a room so dull and colorless, the antithesis of him. I'd be by his side until he woke up—or until the nurses booted me, which was usually after only an hour. Today they'd let me stay for two.

And there was the scrap of paper with the other watchtower coordinates I'd shoved to the bottom of my hamper, in hopes it'd end up in the wash with my dirty clothes. Yet somehow, it always seemed to make it through laundry day unscathed. I didn't know where they led or what I might uncover; after the night at the Boardwalk I still hadn't mustered the courage to face the one in town, but it could be a starting point for finding Akosua. I knew she had the answers, even if Chthonia claimed her as one of theirs.

Of course, I couldn't forget, there was also school. Perhaps the least exciting thing, but I'd be damned if I let myself fail again.

Black-and-orange wings lifted off, capturing my attention. My neck craned, following the butterfly's invisible trail into the vista of blue until the light burned my eyes, and it became just another speck amongst the sunspots.

I glanced at the grave once more when something struck me. The epitaph—it had no dates. That seemed like critical information to forget. Strange…

A prickling sensation swept across my shoulder blades, igniting my scars. I awkwardly bent my arm to reach behind

me, the tips of my fingers brushing against the burning skin,
alight with intuition. I broke my gaze and walked to the car.

Maybe this wasn't my end.

Maybe this was my beginning.

ACKNOWLEDGMENTS

I WROTE AN ENTIRE BOOK, yet somehow *this* feels like the hardest thing I'll write, because words cannot adequately express how grateful I am for the following people:

My sweet Kaia, the little girl behind the dedication. When you were born, you ignited something in me—you made me want to be the best, most true version of myself.

My husband, Tyler, for giving me the time and encouragement to follow my wildest dreams.

My parents, for your unconditional love and support, and throwing an epic launch party for me.

My parents-in-law, for all the times you watched Kaia so I could finish my edits. To all my friends and family that have been cheering me on since day one. Thank you.

My amazing editors, Sara Schonfeld and Lynsey G. I literally could not have done this without you. Sara, you've been there since my first developmental edit, and have been such a guiding light. Lynsey, your encouragement meant everything.

My formatter and the book's interior designer, Emily Snyder, a tremendous thank you for bringing this book to life, and for being so patient with me.

My beta readers, who read an unpolished version of the manuscript with such enthusiasm and attention to detail. Your feedback helped shaped this book into what it is today.

My Writing with the Soul-mates, especially Group 4's Glitter Word Witches. You give me confidence, encouragement, and most importantly, a community. I couldn't ask for a better group of people to be on this writing journey with.

My Bookstagram friends, I am forever grateful for your friendship and support. You make our corner of the internet so bright and fun, and much less lonely.

And the biggest thanks to *you,* the reader, for loving these characters as much as I do, and for taking a chance on me.

TORY GUYON grew up dreaming about dragons, pretending to craft potions, and eagerly awaiting to be summoned by the realm of the fae. She lives with her family in Santa Cruz, CA and continues to actively seek out the magic of this world. Whether that's working with orangutans in the jungles of Borneo, summiting Mount Kilimanjaro's grueling 19,341 ft. peak, or looking for fairies in the redwoods with her daughter. Connect with her at www.toryguyon.com or on social media at @wri_tor.